THE C.I.

BOOKS BY LES ROBERTS

Milan Jacovich Mysteries
Pepper Pike
Full Cleveland
Deep Shakeer'
The Cleveland Connection
The Lake Effect
The Duke of Cleveland
Collision Bend
The Cleveland Local
A Shoot in Cleveland
The Best-Kept Secret
The Indian Sign
The Dutch
The Irish Sports Pages
King of the Holly Hop
The Cleveland Creep
Whiskey Island
Win, Place or Die
(with Dan S. Kennedy)
The Ashtabula Hat Trick
Speaking of Murder
(with Dan S. Kennedy)

Dominic Candiotti Novels
*The Strange Death of
Father Candy*
Wet Work

Saxon Mysteries
*An Infinite Number
of Monkeys*
Not Enough Horses
A Carrot for the Donkey
Snake Oil
Seeing the Elephant
The Lemon Chicken Jones

Stand-Alones
The Chinese Fire Drill
Sheehan's Dog
The C.I.

Novella
A Carol for Cleveland
(later made into a play by
Eric Coble for the Cleveland
Play House holiday season)

Short Stories
The Scent of Spiced Oranges

Non-Fiction Memoir
We'll Always Have Cleveland

LES ROBERTS

THE C.I.

DOWN & OUT BOOKS

Down & Out Books
3959 Van Dyke Road, Suite 265
Lutz, FL 33558
DownAndOutBooks.com

Cover design by JT Lindroos

ISBN: 1-64396-303-1
ISBN-13: 978-1-64396-303-7

For my BFF, my personal chauffeur and so-called manager,
my kind, generous next-door neighbor who drives me nuts,
an all-around amazing friend who keeps me going
when some days are tougher than others,
Amy Helene Schneiderman

CAPTIVE

It was the first time in his life he'd been inside a police station, and it was scaring the bejesus out of him. He'd seen those precincts in the movies and on television. "Law and Order SVU" had been on TV almost as long as he'd been alive. Their New York City headquarters were dingy and depressing. None of the chairs matched the others, and no cops had framed family photos on their desks. None of the fictional precincts looked like this particular police station, right in the middle of downtown Cleveland, and halfway up a high-rise building that also held the county sheriff's office and the municipal courts. Those phony-baloney Hollywood cop shops all seemed as though scenic designers created them after lazy three-martini lunches and thought about getting out of there to see a long line of producers running expensive offices in Beverly Hills, in which a hyper-sexy receptionist fixed them exotic Starbucks coffee drinks while their bosses were getting their nose hairs plucked and their pubic hair waxed.

Not this police station, though. Not the real one. This one looked like something out of a 1950s horror flick, and smelled like fear, sweat and ancient farts—a place where you check your dreams at the door. Odds were against ever seeing them again.

He'd majored in business at college, working post-grad as middle-management at a computer-software firm in the southeast suburb of Twinsburg, even though his apartment was just west of the Cuyahoga River in Cleveland-proper—a neighborhood known as Ohio City, approximately a half hour drive to where he'd grown up and where his mother still lived, across the river in Shaker Heights with her boyfriend—a guy the kid had very little use for—so he didn't see Mom as often as he'd like to.

No techie, he knew little about software, but that's where the economy seemed to be headed, so he was learning the business every day, and how to reach out to companies needing specialized software—at a salary lower than he'd hoped for when he accepted his diploma from Case Western Reserve University after a generous scholarship got him through four years as a marketing major.

But now he was officially under arrest, handcuffed behind his back. The plainclothes cop who pulled him in had roughly shoved him onto a hard wooden bench until someone was ready to pay any attention to him. It was the most humiliating hour-and-a-half of his existence—being on public display so anyone would think him a busted serial killer on his way to Death Row. The cuffs were too tight around the wrists, and he kept flexing his fingers to keep them from falling asleep and tingling.

Why the cuffs? Did they think he was going to escape—to "make a break" for it—run past ten other cops with guns at the hip, then push the elevator button and wait patiently to ride down nine flights so he could jog off into the night, screaming—as if there were anyone around to help him? Doubtful.

Barely past adolescence and his teeny-bop complexion, he had dark blond hair, blue eyes, and a baby face, and looked as if his only crime was changing lanes on the I-271 freeway at two o'clock in the morning without signaling, so he was certain he wouldn't get more than half a block away without getting caught again—or worse, being stopped by a downtown street gang, robbed, and had the snot beaten out of him just for the hell of it.

He'd scarfed down a Subway sandwich a few hours earlier, and now it was doing a hot merengue inside his stomach, and his throat was more than halfway closed. Stress does that to you.

It was November, when more pumpkins are purchased and eaten than at any other time of year. He knew whatever might happen to him in the next hour, he wouldn't have one damn thing to be thankful for when his mother cooked her annual holiday turkey and invited her single or divorced friends for dinner—people estranged from their own families or loved ones and had no overcooking feast-giver to beckon them to an annual food fest where everyone sits around the table and lies about all they were thankful for in the past year. His mother always called it the Thanksgiving for Orphans. That was how she met her current live-in boyfriend.

He hated going there for early dinner each year, as he was pretty close to being vegan, unwilling to eat anything she cooked besides the green beans with almonds, and the mashed potatoes minus the meat gravy. He rarely enjoyed a TV football game, either—watching football in the living room with young adult guys fighting over who gets the turkey legs, banging into each other from too much wine or beer, and topping off the dinner with pumpkin pie while watching big, tough men ram each other and then all fall down together in a heap.

For the past two years, he'd dragged his girlfriend, Jill Taggart, to that so-called banquet along with him. This time, though, she'd left town for three weeks to be with her own parents in Cincinnati.

She hadn't invited him to come with her.

Right there was the real reason he was stuck on that damn bench with his hands cuffed, as those of both genders walked by and gaped at him as if he were an obscure animal entrapped in some cheap roadside zoo.

Finally, more than ninety minutes later, a bulky man whose disappearing hairline was a red-blond Marine buzz cut, wearing an old cardigan over a plaid shirt and a bright red tie, stopped and studied him carefully as if he was to be a Master's thesis subject? More probably, he thought, he'd be tossed into a dog-

fight training facility as bait.

The bulky guy, a detective badge affixed to his belt, most resembled a paper sack filled to capacity, no room left for one more can of mushroom soup or the sack would burst, groceries winding up all over the floor. He might have swallowed a soccer ball. His stomach stretched the shirt so badly one could easily see his bare skin between the buttons.

At length he said, "So you're the drug kingpin, huh?" His contemptibly raspy voice might come from having Coke and Drano for lunch. It made the kid want to clear his own throat.

"I don't think I am," he said.

The cop's face turned from interested observer to werewolf horror. "Argue with me some more, boy! No one will hear you because your head'll be up your own ass. On your feet. You and I need a little talk."

He grabbed an elbow, yanking the prisoner off the bench, then turned him around and marched him down a long hallway and into a medium-sized room that was obviously somebody's office.

Then the cop locked the door for no apparent reason and glared at the cuffed young man as if looks could kill. It wasn't one of those interrogation rooms with a one-way mirror on the wall so other cops could sit behind it and watch and listen. More frightening, it was totally private—nobody could see what went on in there. The kid feared a hidden vidcam somewhere in the walls or in the overhead light fixture, but didn't have the balls to look for it. He wondered instead where his captor kept his rubber hose.

"I'm gonna take your cuffs off," the cop said. "But if you try to get away before I say so, I'll kill you with my bare hands. Just look at me, boy—you know I can do it." He took a deep breath, pushing out his chest as far as his belly, easily spun his visitor around as if he were a mannequin, and unlocked the cuffs, leaving sore red circles on either wrist. The kid rubbed them and shook his hands as if he'd just washed them and no towel was in sight, trying to get some life back into them.

"*Siddown, young warrior!*" *It wasn't much of a visitor's seat—more like a chair left over from a fifty-year-old kitchen set. The cop hung over the boy for a while, one eye half-closed—a real threat. Maybe he was fixing his suspect's face firmly in his mind so he could make a portrait later from memory. Then he flopped down behind the desk in a chair that looked a lot more comfortable.*

"*My name is Detective Keegan Mayo, Cleveland Police Department,*" *he announced, holding up sweaty, meaty hands.* "*Life and death are right here between my fingers, boy, so be goddamn careful what you say.*"

"*Yes, sir,*" *the boy answered, because he knew if he said anything different, he'd have to pay for it.*

Keegan Mayo took a yellow legal-sized pad from his desk drawer, and a ballpoint pen he'd commandeered from one of the branches of the Huntington Bank. "*What's your name, boy?*"

"*Jerry Paich,*" *the kid told him truthfully.*

"*Is Jerry what's on your birth certificate? Is it just plain old Jerry, like you call a four-year-old—or is it Jerome? Is it Jeremiah? Gerald? Or maybe it's short for Jerk-off.*"

"*It's Jericho, sir.*"

"*Jericho? Like the town in the bible where the walls fall down when some Jew blows a trumpet?*" *He snorted,* "*That's from the Old Testament. You a Jew?*"

Jericho wondered if he'd been arrested for a certain religion. "*Catholic, sir. But I don't much go to church anymore.*"

"*Too goddamn bad,*" *the cop said,* "*because you got a hell of a confession to recite to some pedophile priest.*" *He shook his massive head sorrowfully, as if every criminal he'd ever busted was fallen-away from his religion, and every Catholic priest was a sexual abuser of little boys. Then he said,* "*What's your last name again? Page? Like a page in a book?*"

"*No, it's Paich. P-A-I-C-H.*"

He wrote the name down on his pad. "*Polack, huh?*"

Jericho shook his head. "*Slovenian—on my father's side. My mother is Italian—well, she was born here, but...*"

"*Who gives a flying fuck where your mother was born? Lemme see your driver's license.*"

The prisoner dug his wallet out of his hip pocket and surrendered it to the cop. No one with even a modicum of sense, innocent until found guilty, would hand his wallet over to a cop behind closed doors, money and all. Mayo read everything on the driver's license, made some more notes so he could check Paich's driving record and see if he'd ever been arrested before, and ran his thumb over the paper bills to determine how much his captive was carrying. When he found less than twenty dollars, he was no longer interested, pushing the wallet back across the desk. "Twenty-three years old and you live in Shaker Heights, huh?"

"*That's where my mother lives,*" *he told him.* "*I have an apartment on the Near West side.*"

"*What's your Slovenian father gonna say when he has to come down here and bail you out?*"

Jerry flinched. "*He's dead, sir. Died four years ago. Cancer.*"

Mayo stack back in his chair. It squeaked. "*I got news for you, Jericho Paich. You have just stepped in shit.*"

CHAPTER ONE

Jerry Paich was not much of a toker in Catholic high school in the Saint Clair-Superior neighborhood. He was a good boy back then, never got into any trouble. He joined no clubs except the Political Science Club, which met once every two weeks. Not being a teen-age jock, he never went out for sports. He never stuck out his neck mouthing off wise to any teacher. As nearly every good old American kid alive did, he shared joints with his high school buddy-boys—"regs," they called them, really crappy, inexpensive cannabis full of seeds and stems they'd picked up from black guys hanging out on street corners. Jerry's main reaction to it was getting giggly and then getting sleepy.

He did smoke weed a little bit in his four-year stint at Case Western Reserve—just on weekends and never during the summer or whenever he visited his mother.

Jill Taggart—girlfriend during his senior year and eighteen months beyond that, was more into grass than he was, even cocaine at times, and he hadn't yet processed in his mind they never had sex unless she lit up a joint first. When she did, she turned into a wild woman—scratching, biting, hair-pulling, slapping, ball-sucking, fisting, rimming, all of which scared him silly. He loved the kinks of it, but was uncomfortably aware he couldn't really live up to it.

As the relationship slowly rattled along—hardly ripening of what might turn into something permanent—he worried she

7

had to get high first, all by herself, thinking he was a lousy lay and needed artificial stimulus to get through it. But he went along with it, relatively inexperienced in previous sexual adventures—a few one-night stands and short stints lasting six weeks or so—and he certainly enjoyed fucking her, whether he was stoned or not.

Mid-twenties straight guys didn't need much more stimulation than a young woman just showing up and taking her clothes off.

Then Jill surprised him by saying she quit her job at a public relations firm for a too-low salary and heading to Cincinnati, the far south "C" city as opposed to Cleveland on Lake Erie or Columbus in the middle of the state, for three weeks at her parents as her dad recuperated from a back injury—and just possibly looking for a better-paying job

Then she confessed to him she had more than half a pound of cocaine hidden in her underwear drawer, along with enough meth to make her stoned for a month.

"Methamphetamine?" he said, not realizing no one ever used the long ""version. "Are you kidding me? Getting caught with all that shit could send you to jail forever."

"I don't use meth, Jerry. I sell it. I started selling right after graduation."

"Why didn't you tell me?"

"Because you're a tight-ass," she said, holding up a clenched fist indicating what a tight-ass he was.

Annoyed, he sat on the dark tan sofa bought at a resale shop when he moved into his apartment. "I'm no tight-ass, Jill. I just outgrew drugs. I know you haven't, which doesn't bother me. But peddling it?"

"I sold while we were still in college—you didn't know that, did you? Well, now I do it full time, making triple the money I did working for some boring assholes, and that's why I can afford this long holiday trip. But I can't just leave the stash in my drawer for three weeks, so I want you to keep it for me."

"Me? I don't want it. Don't you know anyone else?"

She raised her shoulders. "Not that I could trust."

He gritted his teeth. "Well, I'm not going to use it, so don't worry."

"Yeah," Jill said, and was quiet for a moment. Then she said, "I've given several people your phone number in case they need to buy any."

"I'm goddamned if I'm going to sell it!" he said, his voice teetering on the edge of spasm.

"You've got to. You're my boyfriend, Jerry—we help each other out all the time."

"Not anything that's above the law!"

"Look—I'll be glad to give you a piece of it," she said. "Maybe fifty percent of my profits—besides which, I have to pay to get the stuff in the first place."

"Who are you paying?"

"The less you know, the better off we both are." She opened her large purse, took out a hollowed-out jewelry box full of ganja, some plastic sandwich bags, a large fabric freezer bag with enough meth in it to shock Jerry, and a small digital scale, putting all of it on the coffee table. "It's no big deal. Just answer the phone and whoever wants to buy, they'll have to come here. How hard could it be?"

Jill had no idea.

Jerry was to keep strict accounts of the sales, and return whatever was left, plus the money, when she came back from her trip. What the hell was he supposed to be, anyway? An accountant?

She confided she got weed, cocaine and meth through a wealthy, weird-looking man who'd never gotten a suntan, ever, who she met at her public relations job when he was there giving a speech—and he'd really be cheesed off if she didn't pay him a large chunk of whatever money she made—and that scared Jerry more than anything.

Still, he wasn't a guy who says "No" to anyone—not to his parents, and not to a regular girlfriend who got stoned and crazy in bed. So he agreed, which brought Jill such a smile she creatively fucked him goodbye before heading off to Cincinnati.

He stared at the accoutrements for more than an hour. What the hell was he going to do with all of it? He'd never used crack in his life and had only done cocaine a few times because it sent him through the roof and terrified him. Now the thought of selling it to people he'd never met grew weirder by the minute.

Three weeks of tiptoeing and keeping his head down when the doorbell rang, and then he'll want no more of it. What was three lousy weeks, anyway?

Jill had only been gone two days when Jerry got the first phone call from one of Jill's best friends who wanted to come by and make a purchase.

Jaimie Peck rang his doorbell just after dinnertime. An attractive young African American who had majored in art history and worked as a docent at the Cleveland Museum of Art, she wore her hair in a long, tight, springy weave intertwined with white strands. When she moved, those curls bounced and writhed around her head and face like giant earthworms impaled on fishhooks.

"Thank god Jill left her stash with you," Jaimie said, unzipping her jacket. "Otherwise, I wouldn't know where to go when I run out." She almost giggled. "I can't just buy from some strange dude on the street corner—you never know what you're getting. There might even be rat shit mixed in."

"Rat shit," he mumbled.

"Jill, though—she only handles the best."

"Good to know," he said without fervor. He hauled out his scale and measured out as much as Jaimie wanted, then sealed the freezer bag. When she left, he put the money in an envelope. Selling drugs was big-time felonious, and he'd had no idea Jill had suckered him into helping her sweeten her income this way.

He'd have to think hard about their future. As much as he loved sex—a serious educational experience for him—he had no desire to become a full-fledged drug pusher, nor to live with anyone who was. When she returned from Cincinnati, they'd have a serious talk about what was in store for both of them.

Since Jaimie Peck's call, he'd dealt with several of Jill's customers, usually male. A few he'd met before through her, as her friends, but most were complete strangers to him. Jeff Tate, Chuck Williamson, Richard Hunter, Jamal Robinson, Michael Greenwood, and many more. He began losing track of them, as he had to stay home each evening for the arrival of the cash-bearing shoppers. The days ticked by slowly as the stash grew smaller and the wad of cash grew thicker.

At first, Jerry acted nervous around his visitors, but after a while it just seemed ordinary, almost a habit, to weigh the products—but it took a lot out of him. It became hard for him to fall asleep, so he taped TV shows and watched them late at night until he dozed off on the sofa. Then his eyes were closing at his work desk at about three each afternoon.

Guilt hung over him like the sword of Damocles.

He couldn't wait until Jill got back.

Midway through the second week, he got a call from a man who introduced himself on the phone as Mark Brucco.

Immediately on the alert, Jerry asked him, "How did you get my number?"

"From Richard Hunter," came the reply. "He and I went to Akron U. together, and we've been buddies ever since."

Jerry checked his list of customers and found Richard Hunter. He remembered him—pleasant-enough guy, even joked a little bit about the Cleveland Browns while he waited for his merchandise—a rugged-looking black man somewhere in his thirties and built like a dedicated weightlifter. Brucco, though, was the first one who hadn't used Jill's name, which raised up the hairs of Jerry Paich's neck. He always felt like a major criminal; everything made him jump out of his skin. But Brucco, using Hunter's name for the connection, sounded legitimate, so they set an appointment for the following evening at eight o'clock.

Jerry left work early. A bachelor, he fussed to straighten up his apartment, making sure the appurtenances Jill left with him were out of sight but easy to reach. Since her customers had become his, even temporarily, he was often too much on edge to take time for dinner. As the clock ticked toward eight, he quickly slapped together a peanut butter and jelly sandwich on rye bread and ate it leaning over the kitchen sink. When the doorbell rang, the last thing he did was wipe off his mouth in case a speck of peanut butter remained.

When he opened the door, though, Jerry became startled and off-balance. Brucco wasn't what he'd expected. He was older than Richard Hunter. The rush of customers for both crack and meth were more and more middle-aged or even seniors, which drove Jerry Paich crazy, leaving him with only a vague memory of what Hunter had looked like or how old he was.

To Jerry, Brucco resembled a human Mack truck. A rugged build, thick wrists, and an oft-broken nose made him unlike most men in their twenties who purchased from Jill Taggart. He wore casual black slacks, a plaid sports shirt over a black T, and a faux suede sports jacket.

"I'm looking for Tina," Brucco said. "All you got."

Jerry hesitated. "Tina? There's no Tina here."

"Meth, for crysakes! Whadda you talk? Lithuanian?"

"Why would you need so much?"

Brucco seemed annoyed. "Look, pal—I'm from Toledo, okay? But I'm stuck here for two weeks more, and I didn't get enough from my guy before I came. Cleveland's not my territory. When I started running out, I called the only guy I knew in town, Rich Hunter. And he sent me to you. That's why I need enough to keep me going another week." He took a thick roll of bills from his pocket, held together by a rubber band. "I won't dicker price. Whatever's fair, I'll pay it. Can do?"

"I guess so," Jerry said. He went into his bedroom and dug out what meth he had left and took it back out to the small round table, which was designed for an outdoor patio but fit better into his tiny apartment.

"Your hand is shakin', kiddo," Brucco said as he watched.

"You're gonna drop that shit and probably step on it—and I'm not ingesting anything you have to scrape up off the floor. Calm down. Don't be scared. You did biz with Hunter, and he was okay—so I gotta be okay, too—right?"

"Not scared," Jerry said. "But to be honest—you're an imposing-looking guy. Big and tough."

"Not so big. Tough, maybe, in my college days. I played a little football."

That explained it, Jerry thought. Offensive lineman, the guy who protected the quarterback—and got hit the hardest. He managed to stop shaking enough to give Brucco what he'd asked for.

"Good job, kid." He removed the rubber band from his money and peeled off seven twenties and a ten. "Buck and a half do it for you?"

Jerry pocketed the money. "I won't be doing this for much longer. I'm just doing a friend a favor."

"You're doing me a favor, too," Brucco said. He reached into his pocket and flipped out a badge. "Cleveland Police," he said. "You're under arrest, Jericho Paich. You have the right to remain silent..."

CHAPTER TWO

Detective Keegan Mayo spread out across the table in front of his prisoner the hundred and a half dollars Marc Brucco had paid Jerry Paich. "Look in the bottom right-hand corner of these bills, where the small inked letters spell out *M.B.* For Mark Brucco. See 'em? That's where he marked the bills before he got there to prove you took his money for drugs. And thanks for showing him where you kept the rest of your shit money—in a shoebox in your closet—except we would've gotten a warrant and found it ourselves. You saved us the trouble—and saved a judge having to sign a warrant." He mused, "Nothing pisses off a judge more than having to sign a search warrant."

He sat down, leaning easily back in his chair, hands folded across his belly. "You're a bad boy—and no matter how good a shyster you get to defend you in court, you're going to jail because we got you dead to rights. No city jail or county jail. You're going to fucking prison for a hell of a long stretch."

Jerry wheezed an inhale and then dropped his head, embarrassed, and ridiculed too. How can you be embarrassed for gasping in shock in front of a cop telling you about the prison you're headed for?

"I don't know which one yet," Mayo said. "That's up to the judge, whoever he is—or she." He shook his head. "Damn, I hate girl judges. Half the time they sentence you to death because they're on the rag. Well, you'll probably wind up in Lima.

Dayton, maybe. Grafton, Ohio. I hear that's a rough fuckin' place." He took a deep breath and blew it out between his lips. "Or Conneaut." His mouth smiled; his eyes did not. "Pray to Jesus Christ Almighty that you don't get sent to Conneaut. Privately owned, ya know—and way up north right on the lake, colder than a witch's tit. You walk in the door and you're a fuckin' slave. You eat horse meat, and veggies past their due date. They rent you out for dirty labor for private companies and then they pocket the money, not you."

Jerry stammered, "Is that even legal?"

"Selling a buck and a half's worth of crack out of your bedroom *is* legal? Wake the fuck up!"

Jerry rubbed his forehead, expecting a headache.

"And that," Mayo said, "ain't even the half of it."

"What do you mean?"

"Look, son," Keegan Mayo said. *Son.* Jerry Paich had suddenly become *"Son."*

"Most guys in prisons—gang members, armed robbers, rapists, murderers killing women and kids with their stolen guns—they've been in there for years and years. Decades since they've ever seen or touched a woman. Talk about horny? And here you are. Cute. Young. Smooth. Clean. You'll be making tortillas on your first night inside."

"Making tortillas?"

"Grow up, for crysakes! Getting fucked by bigger, stronger inmates." He leveled a finger in Jerry's face. "Don't bother taking off your shoes to count your toes, or you'll lose track of how many different guys have used you as a cum receptacle."

The color fled from Jerry's face and neck. He was about to cry, but he was frightened Mayo would think of him with contempt—until he realized he didn't care *what* Mayo thought of him.

"Don't send me to prison," he finally said, his voice ragged and close to a whine. "Please."

Mayo shrugged. "You should've thought of that before you became a drug pusher."

"I'm not!" he protested. "I was just doing it for a friend."

The cop leaned forward, his chair slamming hard. "Give me his name!" he barked, pushing the yellow legal pad and a ball-point pen across the desk. "Write the name right here—and maybe a word from me to the judge will make things a little better for you—for your sentence. Otherwise—you go to prison and you're fresh fish! Get me?" He closed his mouth, his lips a slash across the lower part of his face, and regarded Jerry Paich with amused interest, as if he were a mouse who had just stepped into glue paper that will trap him there until he starved to death.

"I'm waiting, kiddo," Mayo said, drumming his pudgy fingers on the desktop.

He'd have to wait a long time, because Jerry was unable to speak at all.

After more than two minutes, Mayo rose quickly from his seat—so quickly Jerry flinched, afraid the cop was going to beat him to death. But Mayo didn't touch him. He said, "I gotta go drain my lily," he said, squeezing his dick through his pants. "Don't dream about getting your ass out of that chair—or you'll die before you got near the elevator. You lucked out—for now." He leaned his nineteen-inch neck close to his young prisoner. "Think hard, boy. Think hard."

Then he left.

Jerry was alone in a small room that made him think of solitary confinement while in prison—twenty-three hours a day in a cell away from other inmates in which you have nothing to do, nothing to read, no human being you can see or speak to. Just to nap or pace, hoping not to go slowly out of your mind. They call solitary confinement "The Hole."

He didn't want one single moment in prison. He just wanted to go home. But more fearsome would be scribbling on Mayo's legal pad the name of the person who supplied him with the drugs to sell.

Jill Taggart. No totally committed love there. He was too young for Love Forever. He'd hoped he'd learn something new to do with a new woman, something he'd never even read about. But they'd been a couple for a long time, sharing laughs, companionship, weekends at Bed-and-Breakfast mini-vacations, the winter flu, an old car breaking down and dying on the road—and wild sex whenever she was high. It was impossible to throw Jill under the bus and walk away with a wrist slap while she went to prison, a pretty young woman to be passed around like an oft-read magazine between tough, hardcore long-timers who decided during to become Diesel dikes just to survive. She'd look fifty before she reached thirty.

Jerry Paich's usual escape from problems was to fall asleep and hope when he eventually awoke from his nap, everything would be fine again—but drifting off to Dreamland at Keegan Mayo's desk would be a disaster, so he struggled to stay awake. Finally—*finally*—he realized his criminal trial and sentencing was not going to go away.

So he sat bent over with forearms on his thighs as though shot in the stomach, memories invading his brain, whirling around and making him dizzy.

Mayo returned to his office fifteen minutes later. He didn't sit down, but loomed over Jerry like an enormous movie monster. He said nothing, but glared volumes. Eventually, he exploded. "Where's that fucking name you were supposed to write down for me?"

Jerry tightened his bend-over, expecting a crippling blow across his back. Instead, Keenan's mouth was inches from his ear when he roared, "Answer me, you little prick!"

Jerry opened his mouth, but no sound came out. Mayo grabbed a fistful of his hair and pulled his head up so their eyes met. "Okay, kid. Your candy ass is now a prison pocket for the rest of the goddamn world!"

"I can't, sir. I just can't give you that name. That'd be betraying a trust. I'm sorry, but—"

"Sorry my ass! On your feet, boy, you're headin' for the tank!"

That just about did it. Jerry Paich began sobbing, tears running down his cheeks and bubbling mucus erupting from his nose. "Please," he said. "I'll do anything, sir. Anything. Don't make me go to prison. I'll—I'll die in prison!"

"When you get to prison, you'll wish you died."

More sobbing. Mayo waited for almost a minute before he let go of Jerry's hair. Then he went back around his desk and sat down. "Don't *cry!* If you start crying in the Joint—I can't *think* of what'll happen to you."

The kid tried to control his emotions, fighting for breath. Not carrying Kleenex, he wiped his nose on his sleeve.

"Gross," Mayo said, and opened a drawer—but he wasn't looking for tissues. He removed a small container of Tic Tacs, shook out a few in his palm, and popped them into his mouth. Slurping on them, he said, "So you don't wanna go inside, huh? Then what's in it for me?"

Jerry Paich stopped sniffling, and his eyes grew wide as saucers. He gulped. "Wh—what?"

"Quit being an asshole, okay?" Mayo chewed, and when he spoke, Jerry saw white Tic Tac crumbs on his tongue. "You want me to keep you outta prison but won't write down a name, which for you is a megamajor fuck-up! Who is it anyway?" He made a *pffft* sound with his lips. "Better come up with something, kiddo—I don't do nothing for nothing."

Jerry felt panic creeping up his spine again. He managed to stammer, "I don't have a lot of money. Maybe just four thousand or so in the bank, but I'd let you have it."

"I don't need your fucking money," Mayo said quietly, almost a rattlesnake's hiss. "I been a cop for twenty-two years, and Detective First Class for three—and I hate it. I hate bustin' stupid-ass dirtbags like you. So here's what it is. Time's comin' up to take the lieutenant test. I been studyin' for it. I want it. I want that louie's gold bar. That's more money—and more power, too. I want that power. I wanna tell these other Joe Schmoes around here what to do and when to do it. I wanna choose what cases I work on. I wanna get outta this division and into somethin' exciting." He leaned so close Jerry could smell tobacco smoke on his breath. "You wanna help me get it? Or spend ten bein' everyone's syph-drippin' fuck toy?"

"How can I help you get a police promotion, sir?"

"Button your lip," Keegan Mayo said, "and I'll tell you."

It was past five in the morning when two uniformed cops in a squad car drove Jericho Paich home—and he was expected to report for work in four hours after getting no sleep at all. He wondered if he'd ever sleep again.

No arrest record filed yet, and from what Mayo said, he'd been dubbed with a new title: a C.I.

Confidential Informant.

There were more C.I.'s on the street than Jerry realized. Cops called them "squealers" or "pigeons," paid out of police pockets for knowing about things even the cops didn't. Every Cleveland officer with a snitch under their thumb had a much better arrest record.

But Jerry wasn't getting paid one cent.

Jerry was screwed.

His "job" was to find people to buy illegal drugs from him, and then report directly back to Detective Mayo, who would then arrest them. As long as he did so, Mayo could rack up a ton of collars, and Jerry wouldn't be incarcerated for one large chunk of his young life.

He knew if he'd written Jill Taggart's name on Mayo's yellow tablet, he would have been treated better, at least from what the cop had told him. But he didn't have it in him to squeal on his girlfriend and send her to prison. For him, there were morals—-and then there were *morals*.

Even deliberately involving other people he hardly knew, tattling on them to cops and making them convicted felons, was something he'd have to get used to.

He had no other choice.

It was his task to find those buyers—whether he knew them or not. The first ones to tackle were those who'd bought from him before—all except Richard Hunter, who was an undercover cop himself and the one who'd given his name to Mayo.

He was promised no one he fingered would ever be told who did it—but he wasn't sure about that. Snitchers being found out had a tattered history of survival.

He wasn't sure about anything. Maybe it was not getting any sleep, but he was emotionally paralyzed, thrust into a new, scary world he'd never believed existed.

As he stumbled out of the back seat of the squad car and headed up the steps to the porch outside his own small apartment, he thought bitterly he should have kicked himself squarely in the ass for not requesting a lawyer.

Too late—C.I.'s don't have lawyers.

C.I.'s don't have squat!

CHAPTER THREE

Fourteen people were placed under arrest for purchasing meth-amphetamine or coke from Jerry Paich in the first few months of involuntary servitude as Confidential Informant to Detective Keegan Mayo. The first, of course, was Jaimie Peck, a good friend and customer of Jill Taggart's. Three were young men who worked at the same office as Paich—marketing tech apps to whoever might want them—and had little experience with drugs before Paich had suggested to them, off-hand, to try his brand. One was the obscenely wealthy son of a powerful real estate maven in Northeast Ohio, who would undoubtedly walk away free and clear with no police record on file, due to Daddy's deep pockets. The other ten adults had been selected by Mayo as targets, just as Jerry himself had been chosen when he filled in as Jill Taggart's substitute dealer.

None of them had a clue as to who fingered them; Jerry was untouchable and could continue wending his way through his customers with sacks of coke or meth in one hand and a direct phone line to Keegan Mayo in the other.

Did that make Jerry feel like something slimy and degenerate that crawled out from under a swamp rock? Damn right it did.

He had to present himself at Mayo's office every two weeks or so, contrite or not. Sometimes there were no orders at the moment. More often, he was given a name to approach, sell to, and then squeal on them to Mayo and wait to hear of their arrest.

A ratfink. Childish and archaic, something few people did anymore, but that's how Jerry felt every time he turned them over to Mayo. If he didn't, he'd be locked up for many years himself wearing baggy prison-orange jumpsuits and sharing a tiny cell with some off-beat degenerate who weighs four hundred pounds and would cuddle him to sleep after violent and brutal sex.

Autumn turned into a cold, slushy Cleveland winter. Jerry's life had become a stressful continuum of undercover spying and little else—except for one thing.

He was no longer seeing Jill Taggart.

She'd returned from Cincinnati expecting Jerry to turn over all the money he'd raised by selling *her* drugs, along with whatever he had left over. All that, however, was stored in the police evidence room—all that hadn't mysteriously disappeared into the pockets of Keegan Mayo and his cop buddies.

Jill's immediate problem was selling shit on consignment from *her* dope courier, a middle-aged hermit living in a sprawling eight-acre estate in Hunting Valley, an upscale east suburb of Cleveland, in which, ironically, hunting was illegal. His name was Marshall Ruttenberg, who had several other people on his payroll. Annoyed with Jill not turning over his advancements of cash and drugs was an understatement. He cut her off from anything—which caused her to angrily dump Jerry Paich.

Keegan Mayo expected results from his latest C.I. But when Jerry reported to his office in early November, things got more tense as the cop scrawled a name on his ever-present yellow pad and pushed it across to him. Jerry's next victim was a recent graduate from Ohio State, one John Malatesta, now living in Bedford Heights.

"Malatesta?" Jerry was shaken. "That's Italian, right?"

"What's the difference?" Mayo demanded.

"Uh—is his family—I mean—well, you know?"

"That's my business, punk. You mind your own—and get me what I want."

"Yeah, but—"

"I don't wanna hear buts, I don't wanna hear bullshit." Mayo ran his hand over one end of the desk, under which he kept the arrest report that could put Jerry Paich behind bars. "Don't forget where you'll be if you fuck up."

Finding it hard to breathe, as he always did when in this office, Jerry actually put a hand to his chest. "I've been doing this for more than five months, sir!"

"Five months?" Keegan Mayo sneered. "You'll spend ten years in prison if I send you there. And if you don't like bars and cells, that means for the next ten years, you'll be working for me."

Jerry's heart hammered.

Mayo's laugh was snarky, condescending. "Maybe time off for good behavior. Or maybe you'll die doing whatever I tell you. It's up to me, you little fuckwad! Get that through your pitiful brain!" He paused for a deep inhale. "Now get your ass out of my sight and don't come back without this Malatesta kid's head on a platter." He stood up, threatening. "Go!" he barked.

Jerry didn't start shaking all over until he found himself outside the main police department headquarters downtown. He stopped and leaned against the building, sure he would faint dead away. Will he be under the cruel thumb of Keegan Mayo into the future? Will he be ordered to do something else besides selling illegal drugs turning casual users into addicts? He was now what he'd always loathed ever since childhood: a tattletale.

He'd spent the better part of half a year worrying more about Mayo and his own illegal activities than about his job. His efficiency at the office had visibly slipped, and he feared if his drug business continued, he might be eliminated altogether. Jill had dumped him and disappeared. She no longer lived in their apartment, she had no available phone number, and Jerry hadn't heard from her for months.

In the meantime, pressure was on him to contact John Malatesta, and he had no idea as to how he could do that—sell him some meth, and then tell Mayo to arrest him. And if Malatesta was related to someone in the Italian mob—what would happen to Jerry then?

He needed advice—someone to talk to. But where could he reach out for help?

Being of Slovenian and Italian background, he was a fallen-away Catholic since his teens, so there was no priest to turn to. He couldn't afford a lawyer or a psychologist. The only real friend he had to whom he could truly open up was Jill Taggart, now long-gone—and she wouldn't discuss this topic anyway, since she was the one who sucked him into it in the first place.

His mom? Not hardly. Arielle Paich—formerly Arielle Pingi-tore—had lived a quiet and supportive life, first with her dicta-torial Italian father and then with her strong-willed Slovenian husband. When she'd become a widow three years earlier, she had enough of a bequest to live on comfortably as long as she kept her office manager job in Twinsville with a company that made bushings.

Jericho truly had no idea what bushings were, mainly because he never asked.

Growing lonely during off-job hours, she volunteered for various charities, meeting new people with whom she was com-fortable and at ease.

Then, at one of her legendary Thanksgiving dinners for orphans, Arielle discovered Laird Janiver. *Major* Laird Janiver, USMC, Retired.

That, as they used to say, was all she wrote.

It didn't take Jerry Paich long to dislike him; that Laird Janiver was coffee-with-cream black had little to do with it. Jerry grew up when interracial relationships were common, and that didn't bother him in the least. He thought it might have both-ered his mother at first, but apparently, she was currently ignor-ing it.

Laird Janiver, though, was Marine right down to his toes, at least the ones on his right foot, as he'd lost the left one from the ankle down when an ISIS mine had exploded under his truck on a dusty road in Baghdad. After eighteen months of VA Hospital therapy in Singapore, Germany, and finally in the United States, he returned to his hometown. He'd been born and raised on the east side, in the Cleveland Heights suburb just east of the city—bringing along with him an addiction begun at Walter Reed Veteran's Hospital. When one is looking for heroin to chase away the constant ache, it's no harder to find than asking the person next to you. The man in the bed to Janiver's left, an infantry grunt who'd lost both legs and the better part of one ear—had picked up his heroin habit in a German hospital, and passed on his local connection to the one-footed major lying next to him all day.

Shaker Heights, where Laird wound up when he returned to the Cleveland area, was named after a strictly religious cult. Much later, the Shakers were nearly forgotten, and the area had become an area known only to the rich, well-nigh impossible for the black population to even get into Shaker Heights past the cement blocks separating them from the wealthy and entitled. If somehow they did get in, the streets were laid out in such a haphazard fashion that anyone not a resident would get hopelessly lost.

But by Janiver's homecoming, things had changed in the country, especially at Shaker Square. He'd grown handsome and dashing during his military career. A shiny gold leaf cluster insignia glowed on his lapel, and his artificial foot worked almost as well as the real one, so hardly anyone could tell. He continued tae kwon do training he'd begun in the Marines, and except for doing some high kicks with his good foot and trying to balance on his artificial one, his skills made the black belt he'd earned deserved.

He was patriot enough to know the monkey on his back does nothing to aid him further. A phone call found a place similar to Alcoholics Anonymous—except this one dealt with getting free from heroin and other chemical habits. It took him a year and a half to get out of the street drug fixation, but he did. However, there were still moments when Laird felt the tingling, the stomach cramps, the rapid heart thumping, and pain in toes he no longer had, reminding him kicking H will always be with him.

After the beguiling meet with Arielle Paich, and some months later moving into her home in Shaker Heights, only about two miles from the home of his birth but still far, far away, he rarely went anywhere socially without her.

Italian, Arielle was highly emotional, and Jericho Paich resembled her in that way. Janiver, however, was stoic almost to the point of apathy, and hadn't a scintilla of melodrama, even in the deepest recesses of his own nervous system. Jerry didn't get that—and didn't like it. Even in a T-shirt, Laird looked as if he wore a formal dress uniform and carried himself ramrod straight as if he still displayed a chestful of colorful fruit salad— the Bronze Star, a Purple Heart and a dozen other medals. When Jerry visited his mom's house, he felt he should snap to attention and salute.

Janiver was used to being in charge. He had turned his Iraq battalion into a frighteningly effective war machine, and those under him respected him, though personally they had mixed feelings about him. His demanding military orders were to be obeyed quickly, efficiently, and without question.

Jericho couldn't understand how his mother could put up with Laird Janiver. She'd always been in the background, first to her father, then her husband, and finally this Marine. He felt her weak and spineless subjugation to her "fancy man" as he'd come to think of Laird, and resented him for it.

He now found himself mired in such a difficult situation that Janiver might be the only one he could turn to for help—and to do so ripped him up inside.

Mainly because Major Laird Janiver was fucking his mother.

CHAPTER FOUR

The house was a few blocks east of what used to be legendary Shaker Square, a setting in which there's a multiplex movie house, several good restaurants, a coffee shop, a Saturday Farmer's Market during decent weather months, a big and expensive spruce-up in progress, and lousy parking facilities. The home where Jericho Paich had grown up was a white two-story Colonial, with stately Grecian columns on the porch, a hilly front yard boasting perfect grass—a big deal to Shaker Heights residents—and a smaller back yard with a flagstone patio. Added recently was a barbecue oven as big as one in a mid-level restaurant. A flagpole on the front lawn proudly displayed the American flag floating in the breeze above one of the United States Marine Corps.

Jerry Paich told his mother he'd arrive at eight o'clock that evening to speak privately with her live-in lover. He'd prefer not to come for dinner and have to sit at the table, sweating and squirming, knowing he'd have to ask Laird Janiver for help as soon as the dishes had been cleared away.

Arielle Paich, like many Italian women who grew more lovely as they aged, hugged him at the door as usual, holding his face with both hands while she kissed him. He tried not to inhale her perfume, as she always wore too much of it. Her brand smelled to Jericho like the hand soap that restaurants put into public restrooms.

She stepped back, frowning. "Jerry," she said, "you look tired. Are they working you to death, baby? Come on in. I made pumpkin pie for you."

"I'm fine, Mom," he said, taking off his coat and hanging it in the entry closet, "and the job is okay. But I'll skip the pie tonight, thanks."

Her face fell. Had he disowned his entire family and heritage? "You always loved my pumpkin pies!" Arielle whined.

"I do love your pumpkin pies," he lied—they were often tasteless. "But I had a big dinner." He tried peering over her shoulder. "Is Laird around?"

Arielle looked around nervously. Jerry wanted Laird's attention that evening, though usually they barely tolerated each other. "Why do you want to talk to Laird?"

"Just a few business questions he can help me with."

"He's a Marine officer."

"Retired, Mom. But he's—smart." Jerry fought the urge to shove his hands into his pockets. "Where is he?"

Her shoulders slumped. The conflict between her lover and her son had been bristly from the start. Their meetings ran better when there were others present, as at her annual Thanksgiving Dinners. An agitated woman even at the best of times, fear of a one-on-one made her nerves jangle. "Come on," she said, and led Jerry into the comfortable living room.

Laird Janiver was in his easy chair—the one Jerry's father used to sit in to watch TV—studying that morning's *Washington Post*. Reading glasses—the drugstore non-prescription kind—rode well on his sculpted nose. He wore neatly pressed Dockers and a sports shirt that would have looked sharp and dignifying even if he'd worn a solid tie to go with it. He looked up, removed his glasses, and put down the paper. "Jerry," he said.

Jerry thought it silly to refer to an ex-Marine as "major" because he wasn't one anymore, and he loathed the idea of calling him "sir." His name, Laird, was strange to Jerry, almost insultingly casual, and he'd be double goddamned to call him "Dad."

So he tried not calling him anything at all. "Hi," he said.

"You told mom you had something to discuss with me. Is that right?"

Jerry looked nervously back at Arielle, standing in the doorway. "Uh—it's kind of a private matter."

Arielle clutched at her heart with both hands. "Oh *God*, Jerry—you've gotten someone pregnant?"

Blood rushed to Jerry's face—very humiliating in front of his mother. "It's nothing like that. Business, that's all."

Arielle retained her grief-stricken look as Laird Janiver rose, as if to take full command of a battalion again. "Arielle, it's all right, don't get upset." He stepped toward Jerry. "Shall we go into my study?"

It was a small room on the first floor, designed for a live-in servant, complete with a tiny bathroom and shower. When Jerry was a kid, it was a room no one used except to toss things into—dirty laundry, rarely used kitchen machines like a no longer-efficient Waring Blender, old magazines or unwanted *tchotchkes* to hide from sight when company was coming. When he moved in and took over mortgage payments, Janiver had cleaned it out and built sturdy bookshelves on an entire wall, filling them with nonfiction—history, politics, and material dealing with race. He had read them all, some twice or more, adding a computer desk for a MacBook Air and printer, and a boom box either tuned to National Public Radio or to the all-classical music station, WCLV.

He sat behind his desk—Jerry thought it should have a bronze plaque reading *Major Laird Janiver, USMC, Ret.* Laird gestured at one of the other chairs in the room. "Get comfortable."

Jerry sat.

"You have a business problem?"

"Uh—it's not exactly business."

"What is it, then?"

"It's—hard to explain."

Irritated, Laird glanced at his wristwatch. Jerry didn't know what kind it was, but was certain no one could afford such an elegant watch on military retirement pay. "I'll wait, then" Laird said. "For a while."

Jerry had trouble swallowing. He didn't know where to start, and as he thrashed around searching for a beginning, he watched Janiver's face grow taut with annoyance.

Maybe, he thought, the guy was hard-line, no-holds-barred, and violently opposed to bad-news drugs, especially since he had been a field officer, not a grunt. Janiver was not doing drugs now, but in earlier years, when ducking Taliban snipers and ISIS bombs until one of them blew off his foot, he turned himself on every night in Iraq just to refresh his brain and mellow out. After recovery and rehab, he might have done a one-eighty and is down on the alt-right side of getting high. Jerry thought if either were true, his mother's boyfriend might welcome him with open arms—*or* send him packing.

But he had nowhere else to turn.

He tightened his stomach muscles, about ready to cry. He couldn't do that, not in front of a Marine. Boys don't cry. *Men* don't cry. That's how he'd been raised.

"I'm embarrassed to tell you this," he finally said, "but I'm in trouble. Big—*big* trouble."

Laird Janiver listened quietly until Jericho Paich had talked himself out, hardly moving in his chair. Then he took a deep breath and shook his head sadly. "Jerry, Jerry—how dumb were you to get caught like this in the first place?"

"Dumb," Jerry hated to admit. "I didn't do it for me, though. I did it for Jill—my girlfriend back then—because she went on vacation and needed somebody to fill in for her."

"Fill in? She was pushing junk? Working for a big-time pusher?"

"I should have realized, but it'd never occurred to me."

"Now that *is* dumb!" Janiver nodded. "You shared a bed

with a drug dealer and you didn't even know it?"

"I didn't know how much drugs she was selling until she left all of it in my lap. I wasn't standing out on a corner, though. I only sold to people who knew her and called me—and of course people the cop suggested, too."

"So you got busted."

Jerry nodded.

"What about this cop whose paperwork on you tucked away in his office?"

"Keegan Mayo." Just saying the cop's name made Jerry's tongue swell and his mouth go dry. "Detective First Class Keegan Mayo."

"From downtown Cleveland? He arrested you?"

Jerry shook his head. "His partner—Mark Brucco. He was waiting outside my door. The guy_who gave me the money in the first place, his name was Richard Hunt, I think. They were all cops—but I guess Mayo is the boss cop."

"A Detective First is an underboss," Laird said, "kind of like a Master Sergeant in the Corps." His mouth tightened for a moment. "How many other cops in that precinct are in on it? You can't even go to a supervisor—a lieutenant or even higher—and complain. You never know who to trust anymore."

"Is it that way in the Corps?"

"Don't be an asshole!" There was a ballpoint pen on the desk. Laird Janiver picked it up and toyed with it, clicking the point in and out while he frowned, thinking. "Mayo said he wouldn't arrest you if you turned Confidential Informant?"

Jerry miserably studied his own knees. "That's what he threatened. Otherwise, I'd go to prison for ten years."

Janiver said, "That's a long stretch for a first-timer."

"What if it was just for two years! I don't want to go to prison at all!"

"Nobody wants to. That's why most of us don't break the law." His eyes locked with Jerry's. "Why didn't you tell them Jill's name? It might have got you off easy—or even completely."

"I couldn't do that. She was my girlfriend. Send her off to prison instead of me? Jesus!" He licked his parched lips. "I know what you Marine guys say—no soldier ever gets left behind."

"Don't quote Marines to me, you little wuss!" He leaned across the desk close to Jerry, his dinner still on his breath. It wasn't easy for anyone to directly meet his gaze, especially if they were afraid of him. "You know more about open heart surgery or moon rockets than you do about the Marines. In other words, you don't know shit." Then he leaned back in his chair again to calm down. "Now pay attention. How long did Mayo say you had to work as a C.I.?"

Jerry sniffled, close to tears. "As long as he wants me to. And he can change his mind any time and slam me into prison, anyway. I've never been so damn scared in my whole life."

"I don't blame you." Laird shook his head. "I don't get why you're here, telling me all this. What do you expect me to do about it?"

Jericho Paich felt tears coming. "Help me," he whimpered

CHAPTER FIVE

After Jerry left, Laird tried explaining as quietly as he could to Arielle Paich what her son was going through. Her first reaction was shock, moving quickly into paroxysm, followed by two hours of wailing and blubbering. Finally, she insisted Laird Janiver go somewhere right now—*anywhere*—to rescue what remained of her family.

Arielle's Italian beauty had sewed up the deal for Laird within five minutes of their meeting. He'd never married, never had a meaningful relationship. He was wed to the Corps—*Semper fi*—but he was now disabled and retired, unable to function in any more combat, and he'd thought about finding someone special and settling down.

Arielle was better in bed than he'd imagined—but she also cried too much, sulked too much, missed her late husband too much while Laird Janiver was sitting right in front of her. Her wimpy son had slowed Laird down—but Jericho was an adult, living on his own, and he only bothered Laird during end-of-year holidays. Arielle wasn't beautiful now when she was weeping and slobbering. The thought of sex with her sent Laird into the outer edges of depression. He tried holding and comforting his live-in lover after they'd retired to bed, but eventually he moved himself to the guest room, needing sleep more than a long night of crying and moaning.

Jerry's explanation was confused, but Janiver got the idea,

and it stumped him. His career had been Marine combat. What did he know about Confidential Informants?

The next morning, he was sitting on the edge of his bed in his boxers and T-shirt, deciding what to wear when he headed to downtown Cleveland's main police department. His military uniforms were in plastic bags in one corner of the guest room closet, but being retired, he wore them rarely, and would feel ridiculous to be in a room with plainclothes detectives, the only one in uniform. He thought about a dark gray sports jacket, black slacks, an off-white shirt and a favorite Jerry Garcia necktie—but too casual under the circumstances. He considered one of his suits—black, gray, blue or light brown, finally choosing black pinstripe, with shiny black dress shoes and black socks long enough to hide his faux foot. This felt too businesslike, but no other brilliant idea struck him as he stood before his closet.

He didn't want to seem arrogant or demanding, nor did he wish to appear beggarly and desperate. He just wanted a talk with Detective Mayo and perhaps straighten things out. Jerry Paich—the son of the woman he loved—was guilty. But for a first non-violent offense, perhaps probation and community service would do the trick. Instead, though, the young man was falling apart after performing stool pigeon tricks for Mayo for the past half year.

It was past time to destroy that so-called arrest report—and Janiver seemed the only man in Jerry's life to do it.

The main police department in downtown Cleveland was opposite an ancient garage right across the street. Janiver had to take a slow elevator to the top level before finding an empty parking space—and then a long wait for the elevator to come back.

After he had become accustomed to his prosthesis, Laird Janiver walked so easily that no one noticed he limped—but when he emerged onto the sidewalk across from the city police main headquarters, his stump was aching, and he tended to put most of his weight on his right foot—the good one—meaning the right knee and hip would ache by end of day. When pain pangs started, the wicked heroin twitches began too, deep down inside him. No one noticed, but he was resentfully aware it was still there.

When he walked into the building, several floors of which were the city jail, he ran into a problem he hadn't considered. Like in TSA security lines at all American airports, visitors had to file beneath a claustrophobic metal detector or X-ray machine which would blast a screeching warning of possible terrorist danger if anyone had so much as a spare nickel left in his or her pocket and not placed on the moving ramp in one of those plastic baskets. That loud siren cost him an additional five minutes, as his metallic leg had kicked off the alarm. Taken to a private room just off the lobby, he had to hike up his pants to show three armed cops his metal foot—but if they believed it was a bomb and ordered him to remove it, someone was going to get hurt. However, one cop shook his hand with both of his, saying "Sorry, pal," and touched his own heart, a quiet way many thank the military for their service.

It ground his guts when people did that who never got any closer to the Middle East than eating in an Aladdin's Lebanese restaurant all over Greater Cleveland and never had any brush with combat other than playing that Battleship board game.

Nobody ever told him "Thank you for your foot."

Fuck them.

On the seventh floor, he showed his business card to the desk sergeant, saying he hoped to see Detective Mayo, but was summarily brushed off because he hadn't made an appointment. When he announced he was there to discuss Jericho Paich, his voice resonated in such a severe and authoritative way that it was heard all the way down the corridor. He'd been a highly decorated major, after all, so the sergeant, nearing sixty and balding, fifty pounds too chunky and loving his secret glee of turning people away—simply nodded at Janiver's business card, made a quick whispering call, and said, "Just take a seat—

Major. Detective Mayo will be with you as soon as he can."

"*As soon as he can*" turned into more than forty-five minutes of Laird chewing on the quick beside his right thumb to make him forget the aching stump and the heroin reminders, but then the desk phone rang, and the sergeant pointed down the hallway to indicate which door belonged to Mayo.

Keegan Mayo didn't rise from his desk, nor did he offer a handshake—but then handshakes from police officers while on duty were rare, especially if they were right-handed and wanted to always be quick to draw a weapon. The cops did not carry their guns in the office, though, but still, Mayo was not pleased to see Laird Janiver. Always annoyed by any uninvited visitor not already in handcuffs, he was head cop in the Narcotics Division, and resented ordinary civilians who bothered him.

A private racist, he despised black civilians wearing thousand-dollar suits. When Janiver's business card identifying him as 'United States Marine Corps Major (ret.),' Mayo's face grew red. He was aggrieved over any officer who'd actually put himself in the line of enemy fire. He had never served in the military, thrilled that he'd managed to evade it. He wanted no goddamn Marine hotshot in his office, trying to squeeze him—about anything.

Janiver, though, was accustomed to police precincts, raised in an East Cleveland quasi-ghetto in which he saw very few Caucasians other than those who were driving through toward a better neighborhood.

Born too late for the LBJ civil rights laws, he was unfamiliar with being referred to as a "Negro," which became a no-no in the mid-sixties. His father said when *he* was a kid, folks with his complexion were called "colored people," making young Laird wonder what color he was? Purple? Green? Turquoise? As he grew older, even the N-Double-A-C-P name angered him each time he heard the "National Association for the Advancement of *Colored People*." He was black, of course, and pleased when it irritated honkies to spew out seven syllables, *African*

36

American, instead of just one—or *especially* two.

Even in the eighties and nineties of the waning twentieth century, he'd heard the N-word often. *Holy Christ!* he thought. *Why don't bigots just say the fucking word and be done with it?* The whole world knew what "N-word" stood for. But the few times Laird heard it from a white guy during his childhood and youth, his violence erupted along with his fists and his feet, and he'd found himself in too damn many police precincts.

He tried to tame his anger by taking *tae kwon do* lessons, but even in friendly practice he hurt too many of his fellow students without meaning to. His next step was to get out of East Cleveland and into the United States Marines. Hoping for an upward boost, he joined the Officer Candidate School to calm him down and send his anger into more proper environs. He turned into a gentleman, a black belter, a reader of military non-fiction, and intelligent novels without graphic sex scenes. Becoming an excellent military leader, it took him sixteen years to earn a full-fledged major cluster.

When he'd racked up twenty years, however, he decided enough was enough. The loss of a left foot relieved him from active duty and his creativity and adventuresome passion. He didn't have to worry about money anymore.

Mayo didn't know any of that shit about him and frankly didn't care. Double Irish and a west sider, black was not his favorite color—particularly when one waltzed into his office uninvited.

And what's with that "Laird" shit? What kind of name was that? He vaguely recalled reading somewhere that "Laird" was the Scots word for "Lord." Did this guy think he was some kind of *god*?

"So what's the big fucking deal with this Paich kid?" he demanded with annoyance. "I haven't even filed his arrest report and sent him to court. What is it your business?"

"Jericho Paich," Janiver said, "is a good boy—a good man. Never got into trouble, not in high school or college, and he has an up-and-coming middle-management job he does quite well."

"He sells dope quite well, too," Mayo fired back, "and got caught at it, red-handed—as *some* people say." He deliberately stared at Laird Janiver's hands, which were not red, but light brown, almost beige.

The bones at the corners of Janiver's jaws jumped as he clenched his teeth, not responding to the cop's look. "It's a first offense, detective," he said. "Paich didn't kill anybody. He was just peddling drugs temporarily—to help out a friend, that's all. As far as I'm concerned, since I met him, I doubt he used crack or meth at all."

"So what's your fucking problem, then, mister? He ain't locked up, and I haven't even submitted his arrest papers. He's not a convict yet—and I don't plan to make him one, either. In fact, I'm doing him a big favor."

"You're not making him a convict. You've turned him into a slave instead."

Mayo's eyes almost disappeared behind two malevolent slits. "I guess you know about slavery, then. Right?"

Janiver said nothing for thirty seconds as each held the other's eyes in a torrid stare down. Then he asked, "Are you sarcastic for the fun of it, detective, or just being a bigot asshole?"

Mayo's face grew purple. "Who the fuck do you think you are, walking in here and talking to me like that? I can slam you behind bars right now!"

"For rudeness? I gravely doubt it," Janiver said easily. "Calling a racist asshole a racist asshole isn't a crime—it's a pure definition of a police officer. And I arrived here—my own idea—to talk to you man to man. I still can, if you'll lay off the bigotry bullshit."

For almost a minute, the two men glared at each other again across the top of Mayo's cluttered desk. The cop looked away first. "What do you want from me? The kid committed a crime—and he wouldn't tell me who put him up to it, which is another crime right there. I catch bad guys. That's my job.

That's what I get paid for, Mister Major." He leveled a finger at Janiver's face. "That means you haul your ni—uh—your ass out of here and don't come back no more—or I *will* find a reason to arrest you for trying to fuck me around about some kid you hardly know."

"I know him very well. I'm—a part of his family."

Detective Sergeant Mayo half-closed a squinty eye, regarding the man sitting across from him. Then he said, "Funny, he doesn't look a bit like you."

Miserable sonofabitch! Janiver thought as he made his way back down in the crowded elevator, tightly hemmed in between lawyers coming from the courts, and likely relatives of small-time criminals standing trial. The attorneys smelled of after-shave cologne and cigar smoke, and others of unwashed armpits and unmistakable fear.

As he left the building and waited at the corner for the traffic light to change, Laird Janiver's stump still bothered him. He felt discomfort—phantom pain in the toes he no longer had. He limped across the street, bothered that the sock on his prosthetic left foot often wound up springing a hole in it more easily than the one on his right. He bought new socks at least three times per year.

What in hell was he doing here in the first place? He'd been in a chain-of-command for much of his military life, and he knew if he took his Keegan Mayo complaint to a higher power—the captain, the police chief, even Cleveland's Safety Direc-tor—they would all defend their Detective First Class, pull wag-ons into a protective circle, and hope everyone would eventually go away.

He was sticking his neck out—and for what? He lived in Arielle Paich's home, but he was not Jerry Paich's stepfather. Jerry was an adult with a good job, needing no one to "take care of" him. Besides, there was no love lost between them, es-pecially on Jerry's side. Janiver wondered if that was due to his race, his military background, or the sexual intimacy with his mother—or possibly all three.

But like or dislike didn't matter to Laird anymore, nor did a marriage license. He was Arielle Paich's committed partner. Therefore, if her son was in deep trouble, it was up to him to do his best to mitigate what might throw the family off-balance.

Mayo didn't operate Confidential Informant slave torment on his own recognizance. Higher-up cops would save his ass, no questions asked, probably running C.I. operations themselves—a great way to gin up the numbers of drug arrests.

Laird Janiver had no personal relationship with any judges, and thought it impossible to make an appointment and get them on his side. The only known crime lay at the feet of Jerry Paich himself.

By the time he got to at his parked car, the stump where his foot once was raised hell, intense pain shooting up his leg to his hip. He rummaged in the glove compartment for a bottle of Tylenol and gulped down three tablets—without water.

After Laird Janiver left his office, Keegan Mayo sat at his desk, simmering quietly, biting down hard on his own teeth. He loathed the guy at the start—and the relationship hurtled downhill from there.

Mayo never served in the military. He disliked rules, dangers, the total lack of control any soldier had whose rank was any-where below four-star general. He hated someone who once was a big-shot Marine major coon trying to fuck him around and tell him what he could and couldn't do. He'd worked and pushed long and hard for his rank. Any threat to his power and ambition was highly serious, if not lethal.

Part of Mayo wanted to pull the plug on Jerry Paich, file his arrest report, and watch the kid go to prison, just to spite who-ever the hell Laird Janiver was to him, but that would wind up in a courtroom in which Paich was likely to whistleblow on him, and the fainthearted Cleveland snowflakes would howl like banshees for his demotion, if not worse. No—he had to get Janiver instead.

He picked up his landline and punched a few buttons.

"Brucco!" he barked into the mouthpiece. "Get in my office. *Now!*"

Then he stood, took Laird Janiver's business card to the desktop printer, and ran off a copy, which he tossed at Mark Brucco as soon as he entered his office.

"Your new assignment," he said. "This baboon just forced his way in here. Find out everything about him—and I mean everything, including does he scratch his ass with his right hand or his left hand."

He hooked both thumbs over his belt the way John Wayne used to do, except his was just a belt to hold his pants up and not one attached to a holster and a Smith and Wesson .44. He always wore his department weapon in a shoulder holster, although never in the station house. A second gun, carried only as a throwaway, was strapped around his left ankle. "One more thing, Brucco. His bank account—all of them if there's more than one. I want to know every penny he owns. I need to know how powerful the cocksucker is."

"Bank accounts?" Brucco sounded surprised. "How can I get to his bank accounts without a warrant or a court order? I mean, like him or lump him, he still has a constitutional Fourth Amendment like everybody else."

"Don't be a complete putz," Mayo warned. "I been around. I got leverage at most of the banks. I'll write some bank manager names on paper for you. You memorize them and you'll eat the fucking paper. Then you'll make some calls and get busy. "

Mark Brucco put his elbows on the desk in front of him and managed to avoid putting his head in his hands. "When do you want all this shit? I get it, all right, but I'd really like you to tell me why."

Mayo's cheeks turned mauve, his eyes snapped with fury, and he breathed more loudly and heavily than normal. "He was all over me letting the Paich kid you busted take a walk instead of being my snitch—for which I pay him nothing. And if I don't?" he growled, "this black-ass Marine who dresses like a movie star and talks like he's some sort of goddamn genius college professor could blow me right out of the fucking water." He inhaled loudly through his nose. "And if he does, Brucco, I swear to Christ I'll take you right down along with me!"

CHAPTER SIX

Marshall Ruttenberg came out the side door of his mini-mansion in the suburb of Hunting Valley and down the long driveway to the larger of the other two on-site houses he used for his work. Despite the swimming pool, uncovered from May through Labor Day even though no one ever swims in it, he rarely went out in the sun, as his skin was unearthly white. His cold blue eyes were like two ice cubes set in white spaghetti sauce, and snow-white hair since his birth. Many of those involved with his so-called business referred to him as "The Albino," which was the truth, or even "Rabbit Eyes," which was close to the way his face always looked—but never where he could hear them.

His face, also white and flat, was like a mask, never showing any expressions. What moved him to anger, fury and revenge happened inside his head where no one else could see it.

Now, at fifty, he had acquired a subtle potbelly, and enough money to do anything he chose—thus the sprawling estate, with a resident chauffeur-bodyguard named Randy, a full-time gardener, and a young live-in maid/housekeeper who also attended John Carroll University a few miles away, majoring in English Literature. He occasionally fucked her if the notion struck him, as a too-high thousand-dollar a week paycheck for her had more requirements than just dusting the furniture and mopping the bathroom floor.

Strolling through his seven-acre seigneury, he inhaled the fresh, clean spring air, much cleaner than where he'd grown up in Cuyahoga Heights, just south of Cleveland proper and a few hundred yards from the giant steel mill spewing smoke, flame and air pollution into the sky each day from its towering chimneys. Both his grandfather and father had toiled on the furnace floor of that mill—each dying in their mid-forties. As kids find cruelty and exploit it whenever they can, Ruttenberg's childhood was a nightmare. His nicknames from vicious schoolmates ranged from "freak" to "bunny face" and all the way to "Casper the Friendly Ghost."

Reaching adulthood and swearing to never set foot in the mill in his lifetime, Marshall Ruttenberg kept his word. When he'd pocketed his first three million dollars after cleverly acquiring and re-selling cocaine supplied by a Mexican cartel, he purchased the suburban Hunting Valley estate, three houses in all, plus the unused swimming pool.

He also bought for his aging mother a condo down in Naples, Florida. His mother quietly thought he was a freak, too, and moving her to the deep South where she'd never have to look at him again made both of them happy. She thrived on the beach every day, played bridge four afternoons per week, and never confessed to her new friends that her son was an albino drug cartel all by himself, especially since nearly half the Florida Napolitanos retired there came from Cleveland—Italians with solid ties to the organized hometown Mafia.

After emerging from public high school, Marshall somehow found enough tuition money to spend two years at Cuyahoga Community College—"Tri-C" as it's called—and earn an associate degree. Two more years in an expensive university would be a waste of money and time, so through some of his classmates—college-age students not as inhumane as they were in elementary school—he managed to meet the local "kingpin" of illegal drug distribution and get a full-time job selling dope to the young junkies who commonly drifted around Public Square and on Prospect Avenue, or across the Lorain-Carnegie Bridge over the Cuyahoga River to West 25th Street where the West Side Market was an ancient and much-loved landmark in which to buy foodstuffs, and even further to West 65th Street, spruced up with clean gutters, but once the home of a sprawling and bloody slaughterhouse.

It took Ruttenberg only five years to figure out how to take over the business entirely, which he did very shortly after the so-called kingpin and his two top muscle guys mysteriously disappeared from Northeast Ohio and were never heard from again.

Coincidentally, those disappearances happened at the same time as the pouring of concrete for an enormous new shopping district market on the near west side.

Ruttenberg knew the people to talk to when he needed to get things done.

That happened more than twenty years earlier. When taking the reins, Ruttenberg figured he could recruit college-aged people could to fill the jobs he had performed when he first got his feet wet in this most illegal métier. His search was quite successful, and in the past two years, one of his special hawkers was a woman named Jill Taggart. She was allowed to keep a handsome percentage of the monies she collected—a generous offer considering each time she made a delivery she was likely to be busted by an undercover cop.

Then she went on a vacation to her parents in Cincinnati and gave the temporary job to her then-boyfriend, Jericho Paich, who got himself arrested for taking her place. Dumb-ass punk!

The problem was Jill Taggart had under her control approximately fifteen thousand bucks worth of crack and crystal meth Marshall Ruttenberg had to buy from his Mexican cartel guy in Ciudad Juarez, right across the Rio Grande from El Paso. If Jill stuck to her guns, Ruttenberg would have made a hell of a lot more money than he'd paid. Jill's money and all remaining drugs were taken by the cops who nailed Jerry Paich, and everyone else was totally fucked.

Give the Paich kid credit. He didn't rat on Jill, which got him into a hell of a lot more trouble than if he'd sung like Luciano Pavarotti, as now he was a C.I., a confidential informant for the police. He was selling illegal substances for those cops who supplied him with more than enough from what they'd already impounded in the evidence locker. Though he was identifying stupid buyers right and left who got arrested, Jerry Paich didn't earn one plugged nickel for his efforts. In that small area, Ruttenberg suffered an empty pocket, thanks to Jill and her dumber-than-shit boyfriend she'd brought into the well-oiled drug distribution business—along with a simmering rage at all concerned.

For revenge, and a slow payback of the money he'd lost, Ruttenberg forced Jill to quit her job, set her up in a cheap apartment on Clinton Boulevard and was pimping her out for three hundred bucks a trick after he sat back and watched two of his hired goons strip her naked and beat the shit out of her with their leather belts—not with the buckle ends to leave permanent scars—until she told him her boyfriend's name. No matter how long the beating lasted, she refused to reveal his name, address or workplace, knowing if she did so, she'd be signing his death warrant. Eventually, she was forced to identify him as Jericho Paich, or she would not survive much more punishment.

It took more than three weeks for the bruises to all but disappear before Ruttenberg demanded she take her clothes off for any heavily panting john who just happened to have three hundred bucks in his pocket.

As for the incredibly idiotic douchebag who caused all this crap in the first place, the aforementioned Jerry Paich—well, Marshall had plans for him, too—terminal plans. He chose to wait several months, so no police officer investigating the douchebag's accidental death would think of following the trail of bread crumbs back to the wealthy, chalk-white resident living in the Hunting Valley mansion.

Ruttenberg entered the smaller house where his office is located, and grunted a solemn good morning to his office manager, Bria Harstad, an attractive blond woman in her thirties, who was immensely efficient and thorough about everything in Ruttenberg's business, including answering any summons coming from the front gate; only she could push the button that would open those iron gates.

Shortly after starting the job, she ascertained what industry he really commanded, and ignored it, especially when her salary doubled after a few months. Like the young housekeeper, Ruttenberg had occasional sex with her, too, until she told him she was more important as his most valuable assistant than she was in his bed. Being an intelligent, observant man, he was also aware she found him physically revolting. He hated that—but throughout his life, most found him unpleasant to look at.

Ruttenberg glanced around at some of the other people working there, mostly young men of Latino descent. He didn't know who they were, their names, or what jobs they did. It didn't matter. Bria knew these things, hired all of them, and kept the office up and running. That's what brought the money rolling in.

"Bria. Write this name down," Marshall ordered her. "It's Paich. P-A-I-C-H. First name Jericho—like the city in the bible. This Paich kid—he's got an apartment somewhere in Ohio City."

Bria scribbled it on a memo pad. "What else do you need?"

"Everything. Anything about him you can find out. Where he goes to work, what car he drives, where he hangs out, whether he has a family of some sort—and most of all, where and to who does he peddle drugs for the Cleveland Police Department."

Bria Harstad had a master's degree in Politics from the University of South Dakota and a minor in English, so she was aware he'd erroneously said "who" instead of "whom," one of his many spoken transgressions. She knew better than to correct his grammar or vocabulary, so instead she said, "I'll get some-one on this right away."

"Not *someone*," he grumbled. "You. You do it."

She still had the ballpoint pen in her hand, thoughtfully roll-ing it between her fingers as she tried not to frown. "Can you tell me what this is all about?"

His tone sharpened. "If I wanted you to know all about this, I'd tell you! Just get it done!" He turned one hundred eighty degrees and stalked out of the building. She watched him, his rocking walk as if he weighed much more than he actually did, looking like a kid avoiding stepping on a crack which would break his mother's back.

Damn! she thought. He *is* albino—and he's creepy. The first time she saw him with his clothes off—pale white all over, hair-less and pencil-dicked, she tried not to hug her arms to her chest and take a shaky breath, keeping her eyes closed during the sex, as she might very well have barfed her lunch at an inopportune moment.

Now Marshall Ruttenberg was more involved with money stashed away in his numbered Cayman Islands bank account. What money and product hadn't been returned to him by Jill Taggart and Jerry Paich was chump change, not noticeable to anyone else, as if they lost a twenty-dollar bill through a hole in their pocket. But he had zero tolerance for mistakes by other people. Having punished Jill physically, he would continue to make her turn expensive tricks for as long as he chose to, and then sell her off to some mega-pimp in the Middle East or in Southeast Asia.

Jerry, whom he'd never laid eyes on, survived for the past several months because Marshall wouldn't want anything traced back to him. But now some time had passed; the kid needed elimination. Bria, he knew, would find out how and where—after which some people in his employ would execute their assignment with a minimum amount of trouble.

Bria went into her private office—what used to be the master bedroom when people actually lived there long before Ruttenberg bought the estate. Not much of a view from the window—only the back of the second, even smaller, house on the property in which well-guarded coke, crack, meth, and stolen European and Asian antiques were stored. At least, though, she had her own private bathroom into which she would sometimes disappear, usually when she wanted to sniff some coke when she was under the most stress—coke she bought elsewhere.

No stress this time, though, but the pressure was there.

She didn't wait. Using her personal cellphone instead of land lines provided throughout Marshall Ruttenberg's scattered estate, she made some calls.

The first one was to one of the three Cuyahoga County (Ohio) Commissioners—on *his* private line.

CHAPTER SEVEN

Laird Janiver stayed in bed for quite a while after he and Arielle made love that morning, staring up at the ceiling, thinking and remembering and trying to find the energy to get himself completely awake and ready for the day. The morning fuck was more to distract her from worrying about her son, so it wasn't satisfying for him. He preferred morning sex to nighttime sex, but Arielle's proclivity was in the opposite direction. Janiver found himself tiring early in the evening. Maybe it was the adjustment to living minus one foot—or perhaps he was just getting old.

He preferred to wait until she'd gone downstairs to put on the coffee and make breakfast before attempting to limp into the shower, using crutches, after which he strapped on his prosthetic foot. Over time, it had grown easier to put it on, but still humiliating if anyone watched him, especially the woman he loved. In pajamas and slippers, it didn't bother him the artificial foot was visible, but it was an awkward struggle to get it to fit properly that degraded him, even though he knew it shouldn't. It had also disturbed him in those months in a veteran's hospital, learning to walk again, falling on his ass almost every day in front of nurses and therapists. To him, it meant weakness and helplessness—a man who'd lived his first forty-five years proud and strong and nearly invincible.

When the aroma of coffee found its way up the stairs and into the bedroom, Laird knew it was time. He hauled himself upright, took up the crutches, and hobbled into the bathroom for a morning shower and shave.

After affixing his prosthesis and taking a careful stroll back and forth a few times to make sure he was comfortable, he opened his closet door and considered what to wear on his mission that day. He'd dressed in one of his high-priced business suits to speak to Detective Sergeant Keegan Mayo at main police headquarters on the previous day—and was ill-at-ease at the cop's contempt for his elegant choice, as Mayo's clothes looked as though they were purchased at a Salvation Army Resale Store.

Today, though, he aimed to visit an old friend in his home. A suit and a sixty-dollar necktie would not have cut it.

His final decision was khakis, a tan corduroy sports jacket with elbow patches, more often worn by middle-aged writers or obscure absent-minded professors than by retired U.S. Marine field officers—and a black turtleneck.

Arielle brightened when he came downstairs and walked into the kitchen. "You look pretty spiffy," she said, offering him a kitchen-type kiss. "Got a hot date?"

He smiled. "Yes, I do. After breakfast. I'm going to see Ayman Kader."

Her smile dimmed a bit. "Oh? How come?"

Laird shrugged. "I haven't contacted him for a few months. After all, he was my commanding officer in Iraq. He was there for me when I needed him. It's damn lucky we both live in the Cleveland area, so we can stay in touch."

She cracked open two eggs into the heated skillet. "Does this have something to do with Jerry?"

"Ayman has never seen Jerry, so you don't have to be worried about it. Meeting with him today is just—old friends drinking coffee together."

She waited about ninety seconds before scooping the two cooked eggs from the skillet onto a plate, added two pieces of rye toast, and served it to Laird sitting at the round kitchen table.

"You and I are drinking coffee together, Laird."

"Yeah—but Ayman and I talk guy talk sometimes. Let's face it, you don't know anything about football."

"Football," she murmured. Then: "Is that what you talk about? Football?"

"Sure, sometimes. Sports. Girls. Old buddies."

"Yes, Laird—but you were Marines. You killed people."

His fork had speared a piece of the sunny-side-up egg, but he stopped it halfway to his mouth. "Arielle, you know damn well in all my time in Iraq, I didn't even point a weapon in anyone's direction, never mind pulling the trigger."

"No," she said. "But you and Kader ordered a bunch of young American kids to do it for you—and lots of them got killed or hurt in the bargain."

"Must I remind you I had to leave my foot in Iraq?" He said it coldly. He was a Marine, born and bred, knowing exactly what he was getting into. He'd adapted as well as possible to the amputation and the prosthesis, and now it hardly slowed him down—but he couldn't get past the notion a missing part of his body would never be recovered, and that he'd never again command a battalion.

Arielle Paich had to catch her breath. "My God, Laird, I didn't mean anything by that. Your career was fighting wars. People got hurt. People got killed. I just think of you and your colonel sitting around talking about who died, and how, and where. It—bothers me. I'm sorry."

He put his fork down. "Years ago, when you and I first got together, did you think I was a Certified Public Accountant? You knew I'd spent my entire adult life in the Marines. I'm a civilian—but a Marine is a Marine forever. Ayman and I get together and talk because we care about each other, as friends. Brothers. And sure, we reminisce about combat experiences, but we talk about other things, too. It's not every weekend, or lunches twice a week. I don't begrudge your friendships with other women."

"I don't have many friends."

"That, honey, is not my fault."

She didn't comment further. She didn't have to.

When Laird and Arielle had begun dating, she had many friends from when she was married to her first husband. They assimilated to this new relationship, smiled and were sociable to both Arielle and her new man, but Laird understood quickly the interracial affair troubled most of them, especially those who were present at Arielle's first marriage, and beyond. No offense, no insults, no N-words were spoken, but he knew they were saying them in their heads.

Well, he'd thought, that happens when a mixed couple has to be in their midst, and he'd learned to let it bounce off him—but it stung Arielle found more often her longtime friends were drifting away. They still went to backyard parties, get-togethers and picnics, but the invitations to small, intimate dinners had just about disappeared.

For the moment, at least, he'd had just about enough thinking about his sex life. He gulped down the rest of his coffee and pushed himself away from the table, having eaten only one slice of toast and barely touching the eggs.

"I'll be back later," he said. "Do you want anything from the store while I'm out?"

As he slid into his car and started the engine, he was glad she'd answered in the negative. He was in no mood to stop at a Giant Eagle or a Heinen's and pick something up for dinner.

It took him a short drive from Arielle's house to that of Colonel Ayman Kader, USMC, ret. One of the nicest things about living in Greater Cleveland was no matter where you live or where you're going, the trip is hardly ever longer than forty-five minutes—unless there's a rush hour accident slowing everything down to a crawl.

The Kader home, three stories high with a sweeping front porch big enough to house a family of eight or more, was nearly a century old, located on Edgewater Drive in the suburb of

Lakewood, not far from the Cleveland city border.

Lakewood is a strange civic mishmash, as are twenty-eight different communities in Cuyahoga County. Each has its own mayor, city council, police, EMS, and fire departments, and always a city park complete with a gazebo for flag-waving holidays and concerts—and jealousies abound between two or more suburbs close to each other. Yet the residents really consider themselves Clevelanders, rooting for the same sports teams and boasting of the world-famed symphony orchestra, the large downtown theater district, a brilliant art museum, and the Rock and Roll Hall of Fame, despite their not having to pay taxes to support any of them.

Beth Kader came to the door, recognizing one of her husband's closest pals with a welcoming smile. She hugged Laird and pressed her cheek to his. "It's been too long, Laird," she said. "You look great, as always."

"You're the one who looks amazing, Beth," he replied. "You get younger every day—while Ayman and I turn into old farts."

It was almost true. From early days, marrying Ayman Kader when he was only a captain and not a bird colonel, Elizabeth Kennedy Kader had always been a trophy wife—almost twenty years younger than her husband, blond and shapely, blue eyes and turned-up nose, the complete opposite of her dark, handsome Lebanese husband. Laird Janiver had met her shortly thereafter, and now noticed except for a few extra pounds, Beth had changed little, though he quietly surmised some Botox had boosted a youthful look around her mouth and eyes.

"I'm flattered," she said, "but I don't believe you for a minute. How about breakfast?"

"I had breakfast," he lied, remembering a slice of toast and hardly touched eggs. "Maybe just coffee?"

"Ayman is out in back, exercising the dog. Join him. I'll bring coffee to you."

"You're terrific," he said, heading toward the glass door at the far end of the spacious living room overlooking the lake. He was sorry to be leaving her. He loved Arielle very much, and rarely even looked at another woman, but Beth Kader was an exception. He'd always felt the tiniest jealousy over Colonel Kader's lifetime partner pick—but Ayman Kader had the Midas touch whatever he came near—money, military power, fame, women. It was fortuitous Ayman's Lebanese given name translated into English as "lucky."

Kader was born in the United States—in Stow, Ohio, a few mini-cities north of Akron—and like his Beirut-born parents, a Muslim, though he wasn't so religious to perform all the rituals. It was difficult on the battlefield, rifle fire and cannons peppering them all day long as they lay flat on the dirt facing Mecca. Before those of the Muslim faith were falsely labeled as possible traitors by the American government itself, many fought bravely in the twin wars in Iraq and Afghanistan, and Kader rose as high as any Marine field officer who didn't wind up with a general's star or two.

Edgewater Drive was well-named, virtually hanging over the southern coast of Lake Erie on somewhat high ground, as was much of the beachless west side shore. Even in the teeth of the heavy Canadian wind rolling across the inland sea, from any home located on the north side of the street where the dramatic view of downtown Cleveland, especially at night when the sky-scrapers' lights glowed, made everyone's heart beat a little faster. If desired, one might stroll out into Kader's back yard and piss over the small cliff directly into the lake. But on this somewhat chilly day, the colonel was tossing a ball for his huge bronze-colored Doberman to chase. His Irish-knit white pullover sweater matched his bright white hair, still Marine-cut into a neat buzz. His dark cheeks were flushed red from the chill breeze blowing off the lake. He ceased the throw-and-retreat when he saw Laird Janiver.

They shook hands and then hugged, with mandatory back-slapping—retired military field officers first and friends second. The dog sniffed around them, cropped ears flat against his skull and paying extra attention to Laird's crotch, not sure whether or not he approved the new visitor until his master patting his neck and sides seemed to reassure him. He finally broke away, strolling to the doorway and stretching out in front of it, tongue lolling out of one corner of his mouth but on complete alert. Any stranger entering the house from the backyard would have to step over him—and no one would knowingly step over a Doberman they did not know personally.

"The lake looks great," Laird observed. "The view from here must knock your socks off every morning."

"I admit, it's better to look at than Parris Island after a week of war games. Trust me. I'm glad to see you, Laird. How's Arielle?"

"She's—good."

The colonel frowned. "Good? That's the best you can come up with? Good?"

"No, she's terrific," Laird reassured him. "It's just—her old friends are quietly and subtly throwing us under the bus. They haven't yet figured out it's well into the twenty-first century, and interracial couples are actually legal."

Kader said, "Being a Levantine, I'm no Great White Hope, either, and my wife has always looked like a 1940s blond film starlet." He walked over to the wrought-iron fence that kept him from falling off the cliff into the water. "It's easier now than when we got married and I was a captain—no gold leaf on the hat—but that shit never goes away. Live with it without going on a rampage and mowing down everyone with your AR-15."

"I've never owned a combat rifle," Laird said, coming up beside him, "and when I had one, it was issued to me by the USMC. Now I'm retired, and out of the war business."

Kader frowned. "You know better than that, Laird

"Marines are never out of the war business until they get so old they can't remember who their war enemies are."

Beth Kader came through the back door carrying two steaming mugs. She knew both men, like many other macho veterans, drank their coffee hot and black. The Doberman stood up and followed her closely to the edge of the yard as she handed out their coffee mugs, both of which were affixed with the USMC logo.

"If you guys need more coffee," she said, "just holler." She kissed Ayman's cheek before going back inside.

"She took good care of me even before I got the bird," Ayman said, referring to the silver full colonel's insignia. "When I was never offered that shiny silver star because my religion is the same as those we were fighting and killing, she took it well. No chance she was going to trade me in for a general. She's something else. Cheers." He clicked his mug against Laird's before sipping.

They leaned on the rail and looked out at the lake, the whitecaps skipping over the surface of the water, the wind ruffling the shirt collar that peered over the neck of Kader's sweater. He finally said, "You mentioned on the phone Arielle's son is in trouble."

"Jerry. Jericho Paich. He's in his mid-twenties. He made good grades in college and got a decent job—but he did something so stupid it blows my mind. So he asked me for help."

"What kind of help?"

"Right now, he's under the thumb of a totally corrupt cop."

"That's really shitty news," Kader said. "What does he expect you to do about it?"

"I don't know. I guess I'm the only person he could come to."

"From some of our previous conversations, I thought he wasn't all that crazy about you."

"He's not. But where else could he go?"

Kader gave it a moment of frowning thought. "Let's go into my office, okay?"

The two men went back into the house, the Doberman close behind. They passed through the living room with its wide windows looking out at the choppy blue-gray water, then into a second living room at the front of the home, and into a cozy office off to one side. When Kader slid into his chair behind the neat desk, clear on the surface other than a MacBook Pro, a telephone, and a large silver-framed photo of Beth Kader in an off-one-shoulder evening dress, posing like an old-time movie queen, Janiver noted the retired colonel was more at home in this small room than anywhere else. Bird colonels one step short of a general's star rarely ran around Iraq or Afghanistan carrying a combat rifle in the open.

"Is your coffee okay, or do you need a refill?"

The coffee was superb, much classier, and much more expensive than the good-to-the-last-drop Maxwell House coffee Arielle brewed every morning. Beth Kader confessed she bought most of her high-end coffee from Trader Joe's in the Crocker Park shopping area, as she had a critical taste for coffee rivaled only by an experienced wine drinker.

Laird answered, "Thanks, but I'm good."

"Then," Colonel Kader said, "What's the whole story? And don't pull any punches."

It took Laird Janiver twenty minutes to fill Kader in on the bizarre gyrations of Jericho Paich, from the time he filled in for Jill Taggart—as a "substitute pusher," the colonel thought but did not say—until the present.

The moments after the tale finished were silent. Then Kader said, "Why not just give the police his girlfriend's name? It would've gotten him clean off the hook."

"That was a red line for him. He felt turning over his girlfriend would've been immoral," Laird said. "He thought it was like tattling."

"Tattling?" Kader looked angry. "She's not his foxhole buddy, for crysakes. She was fucking him!"

"Everyone has their own set of values, Ayman."

"Then stay the hell out of drug-dealing!"

"Jericho understands that—with bells on. But he wants me to help him stop being a ratfink, and I don't know what to tell him. That's why I came to you."

"You think I know more about all this shit than you do?"

Laird shrugged. "I figured you might, since you were two grades higher than me."

Kader closed his eyes for a moment. "Brilliant," he said, opening them again. "This cop—Keegan, is that his name?"

"His first name. It's Keegan Mayo."

"Forget about him."

"Why?"

"He's a Detective First—more or less a cop shop big shot and not some dumb uniform busting people who don't use their turn signals. With that kind of rank, he must have a rabbi—a mentor—someone high up in the department who usually looks out for him. Cops protect themselves like doctors do, or the Mafia—a brotherhood of men wearing badges, including Safety Director, Chief of Police, detectives, traffic cops and meter maids. Even the women who come in nights to mop floors and empty the trash cans. They're a well-protected tribe. You won't get shit reporting him to a higher-up. It's like talking to a wall. Let it go."

"Why?"

Ayman Kader closed his eyes—he did that often when he was discussing something important, and leaned forward, elbows on the table. "If you poke Keegan Mayo's hornet's nest, he just might come after you, too—and if he finds out you have more cash in the bank than he's earned in his entire lifetime, the whole damn world is going to hear about it."

"You have way more money than I do, Ayman—and that didn't come from a colonel's monthly paycheck."

"You got a chunk of it, too. If you screw with this dirty cop enough, he'll start investigating, and if he digs long and deep enough, he'll find out you and I did business together in the international black market. He'll kick both of us to the curb. We'll get busted and wind up washing other inmates' laundry or feeding geese who live on the lawn just outside the federal lock-up!" Ayman sucked most of the air out of the room with a deep inhale, which made Janiver feel suffocated. "The Iraqis haven't invaded Cleveland yet, Laird, and they probably won't—so forget about it. We both have our little secrets; let's keep it that way."

"That means Jerry Paich either stays a snitch for the rest of his life, or he'll be the one feeding geese in prison. Christ, even the President of the United States called for all drug dealers to be put to death—believe it or not."

Kader closed his eyes for a moment and shook his head. "Did he really say that? I didn't get the memo."

"Either way, Jerry is Arielle's son—and I don't want to deal with an angry, sobbing woman for the next twenty years."

The colonel drummed his fingers on the desktop as though he were playing Chopin. Then he stood up. "Your call, Laird. But in case Detective Mayo decides you're his next victim of prey, forget you ever heard my name."

CHAPTER EIGHT

Jerry Paich was no longer as terrified as he was the first time he sat across the desk from Keegan Mayo several months earlier. He'd been there every three weeks since then, give or take a few days, but always by appointment. This time he got a gruff call from Mayo the previous evening, at least two weeks earlier than planned, telling him to get his ass downtown first thing in the morning. He had to call in "sick" to his day job, worried one of his superiors might phone his home when he wasn't where he should be—getting bed rest, keeping warm and downloading Vitamin C by the fistful.

That might cost him his position with the firm.

"I had a visitor here," Keegan told him when he arrived. The snarl in his voice and the red fury on his face made him resemble a ravenous wolf. "This is a police station, not some goddamn summer resort. I don't like visitors sashaying in here all the time just to have a fucking chat—but this one? Holy shit, he's the Creature from the Black Lagoon!"

Jerry managed to croak out, "Who?"

"Who? Your mommy's friend with benefits, that's who! Laird Janiver!"

Jerry closed his eyes, shook his head, and put his chin on his chest. Laird pushing right into Mayo's office was astonishing—and terrifying.

"Poking his nose around, asking all sorts of questions about *you,"* Mayo continued. "That ruffles my feathers, because you work for me, punk. You wouldn't be if you told me who got you peddling their shit. But you're too loyal for that, which is why you're my personal, private C.I., whether you like it or not. That's the deal, which keeps you from getting gang-fucked in prison every night for the next twenty years. But that means you don't go shooting off your mouth about me to some fuckin' coon!"

For a moment Jerry Paich was too petrified to breathe for fear Mayo would dig his arrest report out of his desk drawer and put him in a jail cell downstairs, awaiting trial for something he did months earlier that could imprison him for his entire active adult life. Then, from some place deep inside he'd never touched, never even known about before, he found some courage.

"I've busted my ass for you, Detective," he said, his voice quivering no matter how he tried to hide it, his shoulders lifting, pulling back, straightening his spine. "I've fingered so damn many junkies you've taken down and put in jail you should be grateful to me for jacking up your arrest numbers. But you'll never let me go, will you? You'll keep me doing what I do for you—for no damn pay—until I'm fifty years old. That's why I went to the only person I know who might help me, advise. I never thought he'd come right to you about it—but now I'm glad he did."

Keegan Mayo hardly blinked while Jerry was speaking, but his broiling spleen bubbled behind his eyeballs. Gritting his teeth, he remained quiet, though his glare could peel the skin off Jerry's face. Then he actually smiled. "Well, by god," he breathed, "you *do* have guts, don't you? And all this time, I thought you were nothing but a dumb cunt. Took a lot of balls to mouth off at me that way, eh? Good for you, kiddo."

He stood up and walked around the desk toward the door. Jerry stood up, too.

"Glad you came in to tell me what's on your mind," Keegan said. "I hope now everything is ironed out between us."

"Well—"

Kindly smile. "No, no, I get it. I know exactly where you're coming from."

Relief spread across Jericho Paich's face like a drunken blush. "Well, thanks. Very much. I'm—I'm really grateful for that, Detective Mayo."

Keegan affectionately threw his left arm across Jerry's shoulders. "Sure," he said. "It's important people understand one another. Makes life just that much easier."

Then he drove his right fist deep into the pit of Jerry's stomach, bending him over almost double. Jerry desperately gasped for one clean breath. The punch had caught him by surprise, buckling his knees. He reached out and supported himself against the wall, or he would have gone down on his face against the gritty linoleum floor.

Keegan Mayo waited patiently until Jerry no longer sounded like someone going underwater for the third and last time. Then he grasped a handful of Jerry's hair and yanked him upright, and put his face right into the younger man's. His stinky cigarette breath made Jerry want to vomit even more than he already did.

"Now listen to me good, you ugly little faggot twink!" The voice was barely above a whisper, as Mayo didn't want anyone on the other side of the door to know what was happening. "Mouth off to me one more fucking time and you'll spend the next twenty years in Grafton, washing out the underpants of your fellow inmates in the prison laundry. And tell your ma's nigger fuck buddy if he comes anywhere near me again, I'll rip his goddamn face off. Now get outta my sight!" He let go of Jerry's hair and jerked open his office door. "And don't yak all over the floor out there or I'll make you lick it up!"

A shove in the middle of his back sent Jericho Paich lurching into the corridor. The sound of the slamming door behind him went deep into his head, and his stomach ached fiercely from Mayo's sucker punch, harder than any blow in his entire life.

Some police officers in the corridor as he came spinning out the door looked at him with amused contempt. They knew for a fact that no one visiting Keegan Mayo behind a closed door was a welcome friend, though surprised a young, clean-cut white man would be in such trouble. Mayo usually invested his abuse time with men of color.

When he got to the elevator and punched the DOWN button, Jerry slumped against the wall, trying to breathe more normally, certain he'd be unable to swallow a bite of food for days.

The desk sergeant looked at him and frowned, leaning over his desk and raising his voice. "Hey! You okay, kid?"

Jerry waved him away, worrying if he spoke one word, he'd lose everything in his stomach. He wobbled into the elevator when the door opened, perspiration pouring down his pale face, his breath coming in forced gulps. The other passengers were unsure whether he was having an epilepsy attack or just gone batshit crazy. Either way, they wisely moved out of his barf range toward the back of the elevator car.

Finally crossing the street-level lobby, he hurled himself out of the revolving door onto the sidewalk, trying to straighten up as he tried sucking in some fresh, clean air—or whatever passes for fresh air in Cleveland. Once his head cleared and his nausea faded away, he made his way across the street to the garage, pulling himself up the steps to the fourth level where he'd left his car. When he got behind the wheel, he laid his head back on the seat. Transfixed by terror, all the fight and gumption drained from him as he realized he'd never be free from the clutches of Keegan Mayo. He'd be selling cop-owned drugs and fingering clients forever.

Eventually he drove home, crawled into bed, put the covers over his head, and went to sleep. Before drifting off into dreamland, his last thought was he didn't really care if he ever woke up.

Detective Mayo wasn't sleepy, though. He was furious with Jerry Paich for groveling to his mother's boyfriend for help. As for Laird Janiver—he was frightened this elegant, obviously well-off former Marine would bring him down just for the hell of it. That had to be stopped.

He poked out three numbers on his phone and waited for an answer.

"Brucco," he snapped. "How's that search for the coon coming along?"

CHAPTER NINE

Texas de Brazil is a steakhouse in the eastern suburb of Woodmere Village, only a few blocks long, and defined by high-end
shops and restaurants on Chagrin Boulevard. Local cops loved
writing speeding tickets when one drove three miles over the
speed limit and treated them as though they were on the FBI's
Ten Most Wanted list.

This particular steakhouse features Brazilian-style food and
all-you-can-eat meat dinners. And Marshall Ruttenberg was a
semi-regular customer. He sat alone as he always did, in a dark
corner, enjoying his exotically spiced ribeye steak and drinking
a gin martini with a lemon twist, always turned completely
away from the other diners. He didn't want them to notice
him—nor did he want to see them, either. They were mostly
rich, which made his guts roil in contempt. He didn't like rich
people. He liked poor ones even less.

Part of this shopping sprawl is the Eton Collection, an elegant shopping center anchored by the Barnes and Noble
Bookstore, and adjoins the only Trader Joe's market for miles
around. Ruttenberg sometimes ate at Paladar Latin Kitchen or
Mitchell's Fish Market, to remind himself the diners and shoppers in the neighborhood are comfortably rich, and he, whose
childhood background was two steps up from stark poverty,
had more money than any of them. It boosted his ego and self-
esteem, even if his stark white skin made some gape at him as

though he were a well-dressed zombie.

He mostly dined alone, usually at seven o'clock, and all his restaurants knew he preferred being seated toward the back where few other customers would notice him rather than at the window where many like to look out at the cars and pedestrians visiting the mall—and those outside liked to look in. Ruttenberg could not endure being stared at by strangers while he ate his dinner.

He never had "dates." He didn't need them; he already had sexual outlets. A dinner date was different from a fuck-and-forget. For those under the age of forty, even a first date suggested a second, a third, and possibly a forever. For Ruttenberg, though, other than his student housekeeper/whore, they were all one-time encounters with expensive call girls whose names he would not remember two days later.

This particular evening found him eating slowly and thought-fully, as he'd had a long conversation that afternoon with Bria Harstad. The relentless snipe hunts he ordered her to undertake always brought him satisfaction—and this time when he needed information and a small taste of political power, she'd called one of his old acquaintances—Francis Patrick Murgatroyd, a Cuyahoga County Commissioner, known to all as "Franny."

Murgatroyd had been entranced the first time he met Bria, because when Ruttenberg moved to take over the illegal drug business in Greater Cleveland, he had to choose which of the commissioners to befriend. He took each of them to an aesthetic gourmet feast at the upscale Giovanni's, right down the street in Beachwood, and decided Franny Murgatroyd was the guy to trust, mostly because he had consumed enough food and drink for three people that evening, laughed the loudest, ogled every woman in the room, and begged his new best buddy, Marshall to introduce him to some truly gorgeous and top-level expensive hookers.

Here was a guy with whom Ruttenberg could do business.

When they first met, Ruttenberg lied to Franny he was a

"private financial advisor." Franny didn't question it, nor was he suspicious as long as it wouldn't harm him—so they became friendly, even though Marshall worried he'd eventually run through all the high-priced Cleveland prostitutes he knew and would have to import them for Murgatroyd from Atlantic City or Chicago for replacements.

The vague and half-drunk Franny had no clue what Ruttenberg's real business was, even after he'd visited the office, probably because he became instantly and totally bewitched by Bria Harstad. That romance would never work out for him, though. She must be taken, though she wouldn't tell him by whom. She ran the office efficiently—all businesslike, and to Ruttenberg, irreplaceable. Also, she was in her late thirties—too mature for Franny Murgatroyd, who was more intrigued by high school and college girls. Franny felt any woman over twenty-three, whom he often referred to as "recently retired critters," should quit their jobs, marry, and bear one child per year for the next seven. Franny, an Irish Catholic, fervently believed in large families, even though he was a confirmed bachelor.

Still, he was delighted Bria called him this time. When he found what Marshall needed to know about Jerry Paich, he dropped whatever he was doing for Cuyahoga County, which, by all accounts, was not much, and started calling important people who knew a lot more about what was happening in the county than he did—and doing something about it.

After three days, he called Bria Harstad back.

He was cheery with her on the phone that afternoon, though curious—a bit *too* curious.

"Why does Marshall want all this info on Jerry Paich, Breena?" He never got her name right. "The kid is such small potatoes, you couldn't even see him in the dark unless he shined a flashlight into his own face."

"I can't get into it, Commissioner," Bria replied. "As far as I know, it's personal for Mr. Ruttenberg."

"Damn! Listen, this boy's real name is Jericho. What the hell kinda name is that?"

"It's biblical," Bria said. "What've you got on him?"

She heard him shuffling papers on his desk. "I don't got much. Graduated from Case Western three years ago. He works for a tech company in Solon—in marketing, from what I found out."

Too close to Ruttenberg's business, she thought—too close to his home. Too close to *her*. Hurriedly she said, "Where does he live? That's where people spend most of their time when they're not working."

Franny gave her an address in Ohio City, just west of the Cuyahoga River, which for more than a century is now no longer a city but just a neighborhood. In case anything bad might happen, it was far enough away from her and Ruttenberg she wouldn't have to deal with it.

"So Breena, what's going on? Is Marshall thinking about hiring this Jerry Paich guy or what?"

She clenched her teeth to keep the anger from rushing out at his mispronunciation of her name. She'd corrected him at least twenty times in the past before she just gave up. "I don't know. He didn't tell me."

Now Franny's voice oozed misplaced jealousy. "Please don't say it's you who's got a thing for him! That'll break my heart."

"Don't be silly," Bria snapped. "He's too young for me."

"And I'm too old for you? Is that what you mean? You're too picky, lady."

"That's what they say. Anything else, Franny?"

"I'm not sure I want to tell you anymore." He sounded like a thirteen-year-old boy whose feelings were hurt.

"Get over it," she said. "I'm calling for my boss. He's your good buddy, remember? He takes you out to expensive dinners, makes people do repairs and additions to your house and pays for it himself—and hires gorgeous young hookers for you who are too dumb to talk. Don't fuck around with us, Franny—you won't like it."

She heard him gasp, thinking she was too much of a lady to

use four-letter words. Finally, he whispered, "Jesus."

"Jesus has nothing to do with it. Be nice with us—and we'll be nice with you, just like we always have. I wouldn't have called if it wasn't important."

Slumping in his downtown office in rolled-up shirt sleeves, stockinged feet on the desk, Franny Murgatroyd felt as if his head had just been run over by a tractor. Nobody talked to him that way—especially not women. His longtime lust for Bria Harstad disappeared completely. He knew she operated Ruttenberg's office for him, but he'd never dreamed she would be that tough.

"What else have you got?" Bria demanded.

"Uhh—" He crinkled some more papers. "All I know is he was born in Shaker Heights, and his mother—she's a widow—still lives in the old house. With a boyfriend."

"Address?"

Franny gave it to her, then added, "Here's a hot piece of news for you. Paich's mother is shacked up with a colored guy. A Marine—retired now. He used to be a major. Shit, go figure something like that."

Colored guy, she thought. In this day and age? "What's his name, Franny?"

"Janiver. Lord Janiver."

"His first name is Lord?"

"That's what the guy told me, I think."

"You think?"

"Well—yeah."

"Nobody names their kid Lord, Franny," Bria said. "Who's this guy who told you?"

Franny Murgatroyd cleared his throat. "Aw, come on! I can't tell you his name."

"Why not?"

"Cuz then you'll call him instead of me in the first place. I don't wanna get aced out, Breena."

"Aced out?" Her voice was flat and menacing. "You have no

idea what aced out means. And for the twentieth time, my name isn't Breena. It's Bria. B-R-I-A. If you're so goddamn hot for me, learn my name—and if you call me Breena again, I'll cut off your balls with a butter knife and pull out your guts to make a necklace. Are we clear, Franny?"

He didn't answer her, but she actually heard him gulp.

After she printed out Murgatroyd's comments, Bria walked from her office to the main house, found Ruttenberg in his study, and put the information on his desk.

He read it over carefully, then put it face down in his inbox. "Not much here I didn't know already. This is shit."

She shrugged. "Franny is like a child in the dark—but this Paich kid doesn't have much going for him."

"He's taking money out of my pocket."

"Not much money."

"If it was one lousy nickel, that's too much." He leaned back in his chair, folding his hands over his potbelly. "I've had just about enough from him, the little prick." He was quiet for a bit, breathing through his mouth. Then he said, "Well, I'm going to do something about it." He picked up his cell phone and started trolling for a number.

Bria Harstad's body grew cold all over. She said, "What are you going to do, Marshall?"

He grew angry. "What do you care? Keeping a journal now, are you?"

"No," she said quickly. "Just wondering."

"Well, don't wonder! It's none of your business."

She shrugged. "I thought it *was* my business."

"Well, it's not, so keep your nose out of it."

"You're not going to hurt this kid, are you?"

"You just keep the books, Bria—and keep this place running ship-shape. That's your job. That's what I pay you for." He waved the phone at her. "Now, I've got to make an important call—so haul your ass outta here."

She hesitated for a long moment. "Whatever you want."

"Wait!"

She stopped and turned to look at him.

"Whatever I want, huh?" His smile, using only the left corner of his mouth, turned into a toxic sneer. "I want a blow job before you run out of here. That's what I want." He pushed his chair away from the desk, reaching for his zipper.

Her mouth grew so dry she could barely get out the words. "Not today," she said. "I have a headache." She left quickly, hoping she'd not slammed his door as hard as she wanted to.

CHAPTER TEN

Laird Janiver finished his second drink of the evening—bourbon and water, just because almost everyone else in the room was drinking bourbon and water, too. Where he was on this particular evening carried no single-malt Scotch. Bored silly, he tried to look as if he were paying attention to what was on the TV set behind the bar, a monster truck rally in which he had no interest. Most members of the American Legion post in South Euclid, Ohio—some in their seventies and wearing various Vietnam or Korea Veteran caps for their monthly get-together—watched with little enthusiasm, not giving a damn about monster truck rallies, either. But it was better than sitting home and watching TV alone.

Several younger men were quietly present who had served in Afghanistan and Iraq. Some had been wounded and disabled, too, but they'd wanted to make the military a career and were frustrated at no longer having a war to fight. After returning home, they still jumped, cringed, or held their ears when they heard a fireworks display on the Fourth of July or a car backfiring.

The meeting had started earlier. Called to order, everyone stood and recited the Pledge of Allegiance with hands on hearts, with a few of them, secret atheists, quietly not saying "...under God" aloud, as those two words began appearing in the Pledge in the 1950s by order of the Republican congress. One combat survivor of the short-time Desert Storm conflict during the

George H.W. Bush era spoke at length about the problems of waiting weeks—months—before getting medical assistance from the local VA hospital. A few of the guys actually wept as they hugged each other, and the clock on the wall ticked late— almost ten o'clock. The old-time vets don't stay up past eleven—or hardly sleep at all.

The younger men still longed for the fighting, even though nearly two decades of battle in the Middle East was different, impersonal compared to the LBJ-Nixon boots-on-the-ground killing machine of the 1960s and 1970s.

Many had been in battle-ravaged Asia back when there were two countries—North Vietnam and South Vietnam. The capital city was called Saigon before the communist victors changed it to Ho Chi Minh City, and unlike the current wars perking in the Islam world, Vietnam was often hand-to-hand combat— knives, bayonets and personal handguns.

Looking at these old-timers, Janiver halfway wished he could have fought in that war too, when he had two feet and could easily murder a Charlie with one well-trained *tae kwan do* move that would break a face or shatter a throat. He remembered his long-ago youth just off Woodland Avenue, fighting and badly hurting members of a rival gang, or racist white guys who never knew when to keep their mouths shut. His adolescent injuries were minor—bloody lips, bloody noses, and even a gash in the scalp where no one could see the scar.

He hoped he wasn't too obtrusive to his fellow American Legion bar-sitters when he flexed the kill-fingers of his hands, thinking of the old violent times, feeling sad his combat days were over.

Laird was uncertain why he attended these veteran colloquiums on the third Monday of every month. Few members were close to his own age, and most were former enlisted men, whereas he had been a field officer. With a few exceptions, they were all Caucasian. Some of them seemed sincerely glad to see him whenever he arrived. Those who served under fire considered an American comrade-in-arms as their brother, no matter the race, creed or color. A few, though, were born-and-raised Southerners who never got the 1964 memo racial enmity was a thing of the past, and voted repeatedly for bigots. None knew Laird had more money in his pocket than they had in the bank, nor did they know how he'd made it.

It's not that he didn't function brilliantly as a commander of daring skirmishes during which shots were fired back and forth, and four times more Iraqis and Afghans perished than did his Marines. He'd earned the colorful medals worn on his uniform. His own money, however, was a different story.

In Afghanistan, where he'd spent most of his overseas service, Laird Janiver and his immediate supervisor, Colonel Ayman Kader, watched in horror as the marauding ISIS or Al Kaeda forces deliberately destroyed and ruined hundreds of centuries-old temples, statuary, and sacred objects—just for the hell of it. It had been Kader who first realized the best way to save these valuable pieces was for American Marines to knock down the temples themselves so he could black-market the antiquities to other Western countries like the Netherlands, Switzerland, Sweden, the Czech Republic, and even France and Germany. He brought in Laird Janiver, a great political asset—handsome, charming, elegantly serious, dazzlingly intelligent—to oversee the highly illegal sales and shipping.

Obtaining a vast amount of control in Afghanistan's heroin industry came next. During their tenures, Kader had managed to pocket twenty-seven million dollars—besides, of course, his full colonel's pay—banking about three-quarters of it in a Swiss Bank account that carried only a number. Janiver earned just sixteen million because when an explosion took off his foot and put him in a long-term hospital recuperation, he could no longer perform as the second-in-command guy in one of America's most vibrant black markets.

Arielle Paich had no idea about his side jobs. She knew he was financially comfortable—he paid her monthly mortgage, bought most of her groceries, and always made sure her car had plenty of gas—but she'd always thought his money came from stock market investments and his monthly military checks for retirement and disability.

He'd been physically attracted to her from the beginning, but nervous to even pursue a mixed-race relationship until she encouraged him. After moving into her home, he realized she was in an endless depression over the loss of her husband and the sadness of the empty-nest syndrome caused by her son's graduation from college and moving out into the world to be his own man.

After a few cohabiting years, Laird Janiver grew restless, and considered ending their relationship. Then along came Jericho, who didn't like him anyway, begging him for help getting out from under the thumb of a mean, twisted Cleveland cop.

He didn't know what to do about that, either.

Not in the mood for a third drink and tired of ignoring the TV, he announced it was late, and he was leaving. Everyone came over to shake his hand and wish him a good drive home. Several hugged him, even though he didn't remember their names. Two actually saluted and snapped, "Goodnight, Major," mortifying him as he wasn't in uniform, but wearing a black windbreaker. Still, he held the highest military rank of anyone else at the American Legion post.

A grizzled forty-one-year-old named George Wharf, a Marine who'd risen to the rank of Master Sergeant during four trips to Iraq and had lost three fingers on his right hand and part of his hip from an explosive device hidden in the sand, threw one arm across Laird's shoulders during the goodbyes. "I swear to god, Major," he said softly, "I'm proud as hell to be a part of this post and rub shoulders with everybody once a month and watch crappy TV and swill down discount booze— but a part of me wishes I was still over there, running my platoon, eating a ton of sand every day, taking out bad guys." He made a pistol from his thumb and the one finger he had left and squeezed it as if shooting an Al-Qaeda back there, making a *pew-pew* sound in the back of his throat like a handgun. "I'd bet you do, too."

"Sometimes," Laird said. "I don't miss the hundred-plus degree heat, or the sixty pounds of shit strapped to my back."

Wharf grinned. "I didn't think field-grade officers had to carry around all that weight like grunts did."

"The snipers never asked your rank before they blew your head off."

Wharf's arm around Laird's shoulder became a hug. "I'd be proud to have served under you, sir."

"Don't even say that, or one day they might call us back in, even though parts of our bodies are still over there. Drive home carefully, Master Sergeant."

The two exchanged salutes and went out into the parking lot for their own vehicles.

Janiver headed home, driving on Van Aken Boulevard, a broad, busy road cutting through the middle of Shaker Heights. He had the radio on. After two hours of monster truck crashes, he was in the mood for whatever music he found when he saw police lights flashing behind him.

Quickly checking his speedometer and realizing he was only a few miles over the speed limit, he pulled over to the curb, shut off the engine, and waited as two uniformed officers left their own car, marked Cleveland Police Department, and stomped toward him. He placed both hands on the steering wheel in the ten and two o'clock positions; in this day and age, every black male driver knew what to do with his hands when his car was stopped by the fuzz.

The officers were white, wide, angry-looking. The one on Laird's side of the car was middle-aged, his face lumpy, one hand resting on his holstered gun. The other one, not much more than a kid, was on the passenger's side, peering in, shining his flashlight all over both the front and back seats—looking for drugs, looking for a weapon, looking for any reason to turn this traffic stop into something brutal or violent.

"How you doin' there, fella?" the lumpy-faced cop said.

"I'm fine, officer—and how are you?"

"Driver's license and proof of insurance."

Laird said quietly, "My license is in my rear pants pocket. Can I reach back and get it?"

"Goddamn slow," Lumpy Face said. "And keep your other hand where I can see it."

Laird Janiver leaned forward and pulled his wallet from his pants pocket. "I need to open this to get my license."

"Slow!"

Using both hands, he removed his license and handed it out the window. Lumpy Face examined it as though it were a scrap of the Dead Sea Scrolls. Then he tucked it into a pocket of his leather folder. "Insurance!"

"It's in the glove compartment," he said, nodding his head toward the driver's side of the car.

"Get it—using just your left hand. You understand me?"

The younger cop put his hand on his weapon. Laird reached across his own body and fished out the insurance paper. Lumpy Face snatched it from him, once again studied it.

"May I ask why I was stopped, officer?"

"Because you were weaving!" Lumpy Face stuck his head clear into the car. "And I smell booze on your breath. You're a goddamn drunk!" Then he moved backward a few paces. "Step out of the vehicle—both hands out in front of you."

Laird opened the door and swung his legs out. When he tried to stand, he grasped the side of the door to lever himself up, as he always did when exiting a car. Immediately Lumpy Face drew his pistol to shake in Laird's face, and actually shrieked: "I told you to keep your fucking hands in front of you, goddammit!"

"My foot..."

"Shut up! Shut your fucking mouth! You wanna die? You want me to shoot you? Don't say a fucking word until you're told to! Now exit the vehicle."

Not easy with a prosthetic foot, but Janiver managed to get himself out to stand on the ground. Lumpy Face removed a Breathalyzer from his thick belt and handed it to Laird. "I'll check your alcohol consumption. Put this in your mouth and breathe out."

"I've had two drinks. My first one was three hours ago. My second was just before I left the American Legion post."

"Don't make up any goddamn lies, boy! Just breathe!" Lumpy Face ordered.

The older cop seemed disappointed when he checked the reading on the breathalyzer. His pursed mouth, wrinkled into an angry kiss face, expressed his annoyance. He said, "Get back in your car and take the test again. There's wind out here blowing away the alcohol reading."

Laird Janiver got back into the driver's seat and repeated the test twice more. The innocent results upset the older cop, who mumbled obscenities under his breath.

Laird was certain he passed the test. He cocked his head quietly. "What's the reading, sir?"

Lumpy Face's lips almost disappeared as he squinted at the numbers. "Point zero six three."

"The minimum number that gets one arrested for drinking and driving in Ohio is point zero eight. True?"

That antagonized both cops. The older one grabbed Laird's elbow with an iron fist and yanked him back out the door and spun him around to face his car. "I'll decide the fucking number, boy!"

Boy, Laird thought. In this day and age in the twenty-first century, even racists in Mississippi no longer called black men *boy*. Missing his own foot and carrying no weapon at all, he could still rip out Lumpy Face's throat—except then the younger cop would empty his weapon into Laird's back.

"Put your hands flat on the roof and assume the position!"

Laird did as he was ordered. After all his years of combat, after a truck blowing up beneath him and taking his foot, he was more likely to die in the next two minutes on a street in secure, serene Shaker Heights, shot by a Cleveland traffic cop who seemed outraged about his very existence.

"Check him out," Lumpy Face ordered, and the kid cop started frisking him. When he got down to Laird's feet, he screamed, "He's got a weapon strapped to his ankle."

Now Lumpy Face's firearm was pushed into Laird's cheek, hard. "Don't even blink or you're dead, motherfucker!" he hissed. He actually hissed. Cobra snakes hiss before they strike. Laird knew that; he'd spent so much time in Asia, and though he never got near India, he'd heard all the tales about cobras—and he could spot a snake whenever he saw one, even the snakes on two feet.

The Kid pulled up the left cuff of Laird's pants and sucked his breath in loudly. "Holy shit!" he whispered. "This guy's got an artificial foot."

Lumpy Face's breathing pattern changed. His partner asked more quietly, "Where'd you lose your foot?"

"I was filing my toenails," Laird said, "and the time got away from me."

"Don't be a smart ass."

Laird considered straightening his back and standing up straight, but thought better of it and remained leaning on the roof of the car, his feet about eighteen inches apart. "Look, officers. If I broke the driving laws, write me a citation. If you think I'm dangerous, take me in and put me in the drunk tank. But let's not stand out here all night in the middle of traffic, because frankly I have to pee."

"Put your hands behind your back!" The Kid ordered, and when Laird did, he snapped a pair of handcuffs on—tight. Then he got into Laird's car; the keys were still in the ignition. He went into gear and drove to a side street where he parked it, then walked back to Van Aken Boulevard. "Are we taking him in?" he said.

Lumpy Face nodded. "The nearest Heights station is just a

few blocks from here. We'll run him in there and leave him."

They pushed Laird into the back seat of their cruiser—not brutally, but nowhere near gently, either. He sat with The Kid beside him. His stump sent electric-feeling shocks clear up his leg past his knee. His cuffed hands behind him were knotted into fists.

Mad as hell fists.

They marched him into the Shaker Heights police station just off Lee Road. The cop in charge was also African American with a well-muscled body beneath the shirt. He was ten years younger than Laird, with three sergeant stripes on his shoulder.

"What have we got here?" the Shaker cop said.

"One of your guys," Lumpy Face offered. "He was weaving."

"One of my guys? Seriously?" He thought about throwing a punch, but since everyone was armed, it could turn into a very bad situation—and cops simply do not kill other cops, no matter what. "Where was this?" he said instead.

The Kid had to think about it for a while. "On Van Aken, near—uh—what's the name of that street again?" he asked his partner.

"And you busted him for weaving?" He stood up. "What was his breathalyzer test?"

Lumpy Face looked uncomfortable. "Around point-zero-six something."

"That's a safety number."

The Kid shrugged. "Well—"

"Uncuff him, for Christ's sake, he doesn't look like a serial killer." The cop turned to Janiver. "You live in this area, sir?"

"Seven blocks from where I was stopped, coming home from an American Legion meeting. I had two drinks earlier this evening there, but I'm more sober than these two guys." He stuck out his chin at the Cleveland police. "And not weaving."

"What's your name?"

Laird shook his now-freed hands hard, trying to get some circulation back into his fingers. Then he stood as straight as he could. "Major Laird Janiver, United States Marines, retired."

Startled but pleased, the Shaker Heights cop snapped to attention and saluted smartly. "Master Sergeant Baker Smithton—also a retired Marine. An honor to meet you, sir. *Semper Fi!*" and he shook Laird's hand. "In the desert?"

"Sure. You?"

"Iraq, mostly."

"Me, too, mostly Afghanistan. I'm still shaking sand out of my shoes, Sergeant."

"When did you get home?"

"Most of me got home a few years back," Laird said. "All except my left foot, which didn't make the journey."

"God damn! Sorry for that, sir."

Laird shrugged. "I'm glad you came home in one piece. That's the important part."

"Still doing the PTSD shit, though."

"That's how us *Semper Fi* guys tough it out. The non-Marines all talk to themselves and go into combat mode whenever the garbage collectors make a noise banging a metal can." He turned to the Cleveland police officers. "Either of you guys been in the military?"

They both shook their heads.

Janiver just looked at the Shaker Heights cop and raised one eyebrow.

Baker Smithton turned on the Cleveland cops. "What the hell are you Cleveland guys doing in my town, anyway? Picking up black Marine officers and pretend they were weaving? Stay on your side of the border, gentlemen. Pop in here again with another bullshit arrest, and your asses are *mine*. Am I clear?"

He moved over so he was almost towering over Lumpy Face. "Now drive the major back to his car—politely, without the fucking cuffs—and remember, he's an American hero and you two are wimpy assholes. And stay out of Shaker Heights!"

He turned, sat down at his desk, opened a file and said "Out!" without even looking up.

The ride back to Van Aken and Ingleside was completed without a word—Laird Janiver in the back seat, the Shaker cops up front. The Kid was driving, and he pulled up beside where he'd parked Laird's car before giving Laird back the keys.

"Sorry, major," he mumbled.

Lumpy Face was nowhere near done, though. He got out of the car when Laird did, getting into his face one more time, though this time quietly. "We'll let you go with a warning, pal."

"A warning?" Laird replied. "I'm shivering in my boots."

"Yeah? Well, don't go sticking your nose into things that got nothin' to do with you, understand? Quit bothering cops with your fake bullshit."

"Bothering cops?"

"Don't fuck with me, or you *will* get arrested."

Laird's eyes opened wider. "Ahh," he breathed. "Now I'm beginning to understand. You're Cleveland city cops who stopped me for no apparent fucking reason other than the color of my skin, in a different city than yours, with a different police department—just a few blocks from where I live. Why is that?"

Lumpy Face's cheeks reddened. "You figure it out, asshole," he said, and pushed the license and insurance papers into Laird's face, just below his nose, by way of returning them.

Laird's fist knotted up, and Lumpy Face couldn't miss it. "Take your best swing, boy. Give me the least excuse to blow your fucking heart out! And stay away from Keegan Mayo and out of our downtown precinct!"

Both officers clambered back inside their cruiser and roared off, leaving rubber marks on the asphalt.

Laird slid in behind the wheel and slumped down, chin on his chest, but didn't turn on the engine. Orchestrating this bizarre stop was due to the bubbling hatred from Detective First Class Mayo, he now knew. Who else would send a patrol car from Cleveland into Shaker Heights to harass him for no reason and scare him away from further inquiry into Jerry Paich's problem?

And why?
He would have to think about that.

CHAPTER ELEVEN

Jericho Paich stared at the little digital clock, the only thing on the desk in his cubicle at work other than his MacBook Pro, which was open to display his desktop. Five minutes past six. Most other middle management workers had left already. A few still wandered around the building, probably the single ones who hoped to find someone else unconnected and unmoored who'd join them for a drink somewhere which might extend into dinner and more drinks afterward, thus chasing away one more by-yourself evening watching bad TV in a lonely living room.

Paich, though, struggled to keep his eyes open. Not that he was exhausted, but devastatingly unhappy with the Cleveland Police and his own personal slavedriver, Keegan Mayo. It was screwing up everything else in his life.

Like every other kid with a recent diploma, he'd eagerly looked forward to post-college twenties, but was crestfallen as he stepped bravely into the real world and became involved with Jill Taggart, who peddled illegal methamphetamine and crack on the side. He learned new graduates in the business industry were treated as uninformed teens who should wisely keep their mouths shut until they turned forty. For Jericho, still being in his twenties was a real lulu.

He felt empty. He once enjoyed his nascent career. Now it was dull and lifeless, awakening each morning not thinking about his job but fretting that he'd hear from Mayo. Then he'd have to identify a new target to fuck up and get arrested, so Mayo can chalk up another star in his crown to push him closer to a lieutenant's badge.

Jerry didn't want to go home right now—there might be a Mayo message waiting for him on his voice mail. Yet he didn't want to party, either. He was in no mood for festivities.

He felt someone behind him, and whirled around to see one of his other middle-management guys, Ira Erskine, hovering in the entrance to his cubicle. Dorky-looking, squinting through his glasses, forehead already too high and moving northward fast, his ears too big for his head. Erskine was a decent person, and Jerry had a certain appreciation for him.

"Hey, Jerry. You hangin' around pretty late, huh?"

"Just finishing up some stuff." It was a lie, and Jerry knew it. So did Ira Erskine, who could see the desk was almost empty, but chose not to mention it.

"I feel like getting a pop or two. Wanna join me for a drink, maybe over at the Burntwood Tavern?"

"Not tonight, Ira. Thanks."

"Got a date?"

"Hardly."

Erskine leaned against the wall of the cubicle, arms crossed. "You're not seeing that girl anymore, are you? What was her name? Jill?"

Jerry nodded. It was hard to even say her name aloud.

"What happened to her, Jerry?"

He breathed through his mouth to capture some of the saliva that had suddenly disappeared. "We—split up. I don't even know where she is."

"That's tough."

"Yeah."

"She's not dead or anything, is she?"

"I hope not—but for whatever reason, I'm not in her circle of acquaintances anymore."

"Right. Okay, let's go out and socialize tonight," Erskine said. "Maybe some terrific gal is hanging out at Burntwood, just waiting for you to show up."

"Maybe she's waiting for you, Ira."

Erskine blushed, turning his head away. "I'm not the hottest guy on the block," he said. "But you're bound to meet someone—and who knows, Jer, it might turn out fantastic."

Fantastic, Jerry thought. At the beginning, Jill Taggart had indeed been fantastic, especially in bed. But when he'd learned she was dealing drugs and then disappeared without even a so-long-I'll-be-seeing-you, leaving him to save her ass and take the rap for all of it, he found himself frightened to let any female near him—at least not now. Maybe if Laird Janiver could help free him from the tight harness of Keenan Mayo, get him off the C.I. hook, then he could start living normally again.

Ira Erskine finally realized going to Burntwood Tavern all by himself would be a total bummer, so he simply went home, thoroughly depressed, to watch a rerun of "NCIS." His twenty-something years were punishing to him, too.

Jerry stayed at his desk another ten minutes until he was left alone in the office—not counting the two cleaning women. He was terrified to go home, afraid of Mayo's threatening phone calls, afraid of what Laird Janiver might do next.

Had he always been afraid? He couldn't recall, but thought he might have been raised with fear—subtle fear he could never recognize. Like every other kid, he fantasized about monsters under the bed or in the closet when lights went off. He'd always tried to be a "good boy" and not upset his parents, though he'd never been afraid of them. Or had he been? Did he ever take a risk for anything? He'd been a good student but not great, not a sociable guy, not a sports performer or even a sports watcher. He'd never had a real girlfriend in college, then picked one whose adventurous sexuality mortified him even as it drove him crazy with desire, and eventually wound up getting him in life-long trouble.

He couldn't fathom being a C.I. for too much longer. He didn't want to live that way.

But he was afraid of killing himself, too—so what was left?

Finally, he put everything away and headed for the exit, saying goodnight to the cleaning women. One was older and very overweight. The other one, thirtyish, looked Latina. Neither said goodnight back to him, although the older one did nod. Perhaps neither spoke English anyway.

Outside, the parking lot was nearly empty. There were only two cars left other than Jericho Paich's. One was old and beaten-up, the back seat stuffed with housecleaning utensils— belonging to the two cleaning women, he guessed. The other, parked only two spaces away from Jerry's, was a late-year black Chevy Malibu. Two men stood beside it, watching Jericho's approach. One was big, wide, long hair, with one faux-diamond earring, looking very much like a wrestler—not the collegiate Greco-Roman wrestler but one of the showbiz WWE TV stars Dwayne "The Rock" Johnson used to kick hell out of every week before he became a major film star.

This one wore khakis, hiking boots, and a North Face jacket. The other was tall, thin, balding a bit, in a black suit and dead-gray tie.

The skinny one moved so he was between Jerry and his own car. "Mr. Paich?" he said pleasantly.

Sweat beads sprung up on Jerry's forehead and upper lip, and he grasped his car keys more tightly than he would a rescue rope dangling above him from a helicopter. Before this very moment, he'd had no knowledge of what was really meant by "fear."

"Yeah, I'm Jerry Paich," he managed to croak.

"Let's take a ride. Someone wants to talk to you."

"I—don't want to take a ride with you."

"That's disappointing," Skinny said softly, "but it's your decision. You can ride with us in the car, or you can ride by yourself in the trunk."

Jerry Paich didn't say anything. He couldn't. He was too busy trying not to faint.

They didn't force him into the trunk, but allowed him to ride in the back seat with The Wrestler, while Skinny drove. They had handcuffed and tethered Jerry again, but this time his hands were in front and not twisted up behind him, so he knew instinctively these were not cops. Cops hadn't handcuffed people in the front for decades.

Whoever they were, they blindfolded him tightly, making it impossible for him to see where they were going. Nothing felt so helpless as losing one's sight, even for only minutes.

For a moment, Jerry thought these might be his final moments on earth, followed by an execution. He had no idea who was this angry with him—maybe Keegan Mayo, who obviously hated his guts. The men who'd kidnapped him looked as deadly as the worst movie bad guys in history, so he figured they would kill him. He desperately hoped death would be quick and painless.

Dumb as he was for letting Jill turn him into a criminal— even dumber for sacrificing himself to Mayo in order to save her—he wasn't so stupid not to realize this actual kidnapping had something to do with his current situation.

If they were going to kill him, he wondered, why bother blindfolding him? If he were dead, he couldn't tell anyone where they were taking him. He breathed a deep sigh of relief, thinking for whatever reason, they would spare him permanent termination.

At least on this particular day.

He couldn't tell in which direction they drove, but less than fifteen minutes later he felt the car leave the road and turn down a driveway—gravel, as the stones bounced off each other under the tires and rattling under the wheel wells.

Finally, the car stopped, the engine was cut off. Jerry heard the driver's side door open, then close, and footsteps moving around the car to the back seat. The door opened, and both The Wrestler and Skinny hauled him out, none too gently, and made sure he was standing up straight. He gulped fresh air into his lungs, which made him feel a little better.

He was outside; he knew that. A light breeze, ruffling his hair, felt chilly. Though he was standing on gravel, he could smell grass all around him, a fresh, clean scent as if it had been well-mowed that day instead of being abandoned in November by a landscaper who had little to do in his winter months.

Birds chirped nearby. As a kid, he could identify some of the local birds by their unique chatters and whistles, but no more. There were not many trees and birds near where he lived.

The short drive made him think he was somewhere in an eastern Cleveland suburb rather than out of Cuyahoga County or across the river to the west side. Otherwise, he had no clue where he was.

Being gripped on one side by Skinny and on the other by The Wrestler, he was guided to what felt like a tarmac. They walked several feet and stopped. Skinny let go of him, though The Wrestler tightened his large meaty hands around his upper arm. The next sound he heard was a shave-and-a-haircut knock, and after a few moments, a door opened and he was pushed inside. He was guided through that room and into a new, different environment. The temperature was about eight degrees warmer—still chilly for being this close to winter—and he felt he was in some sort of warehouse.

An unfamiliar voice said, "Is this the Paich kid?"

"Yes, sir," Skinny said.

"Take that thing off. I want to see his face."

The blindfold came off, making Jerry squint as soon as he opened his eyes. He was indeed in a large room, one that might have been created by knocking down walls to make it a very special place, but most of it was draped in darkness, as there was only one overhead light, a fluorescent light on the ceiling just above him. The man in front of him was creepy-looking, even more so than the two who'd fetched him here and were standing off to one side. This one was fish-belly white, whose eyes with such little color in the pupils besides pink made Jerry think he must be legally blind. Almost as skinny as Skinny, but with a startling pot belly, he was wearing a white dress shirt open at the collar and sleeves rolled up almost to the elbows. He strolled up too close to Jerry.

"So you're the famous Jeremiah Paich, eh?"

"It's *Jericho* Paich, sir."

Marshall Ruttenberg backhanded him across the mouth and his head snapped back. He stumbled over his own feet, almost falling. The Wrestler caught him and stood him upright again.

"If I say your name is Jeremiah Paich, it's Jeremiah Paich! If I say it's Cunt-face Paich, then *that's* your name! Do you understand?"

Jerry tasted blood; the backhand slap had driven one of his eyeeth into the inside of his lower lip, drawing blood. The right side of his face burned. He shook his head, hoping the torment would go away.

"Now," Ruttenberg said, his tone almost cordial, as if discussing a friendly business deal, "let's talk about how much money you owe me, shall we?"

"Owe you money?" Jerry said, aware his mouth full of blood made him sound odd.

"Five, six months ago, you took over a business from Jill Taggart—which, by the way, she had no fucking right to give you without my knowledge, even on a temporary basis. She had taken about fifteen thousand dollars of my merchandise—and whatever dough she collected, she was to keep one quarter of it for herself and deliver the remainder to me. She didn't. You didn't. You gave all of it to the police. Don't bother denying, I know all about everything. The money, crack, meth—all belonged to me in the first place—is now in police custody. Therefore, you owe me fifteen thousand dollars."

"I don't even know who you are, sir."

"Sir?" Marshall said. "Very polite, young man. I like being shown respect. Therefore, I am not going to kill you today. Isn't that exciting?"

Jerry's breath grew heavier and deeper, and he wavered to keep from falling over. "I don't want to die."

Marshall Ruttenberg was amused. "Nobody wants to die, unless you have stage five cancer and every fucking step you take is a million agonies. So, you're a lucky man, because I won't kill you today. I will kill you one week from today—or you'll put fifteen thousand dollars right into my hot little hand, plus six months vig, amounting to another six grand."

Jerry frowned. "Vig? What's that?"

"It's vigorish, Dumb-shit. Interest—on a loan. Dincha ever watch *The Sopranos* TV show?" He wanted no answer; the question was rhetorical. "Well, I'll show you what a nice guy I am, and round it off to twenty grand, even—and then, one week from tomorrow, I'll be twenty thou richer and you'll still be walking around. That sounds like a win-win."

"I—I don't have twenty thousand dollars, sir. Not even close."

Ruttenberg cocked his head, examining Jerry. "Then they'll find you floating down the Cuyahoga River with your dick in your mouth. But I'd rather have my money back."

"I'll raise the money, I swear to god. But a week—?"

The older man raised his voice. "You think I'm gonna stand here and dicker with you? One week. One week from now, my two associates here—" and he gestured to Skinny and The Wrestler, "—will pick you up from your work at about the same time and bring you here. No trying to hide out, because we know where you live. If you sneak away to Costa Rica or something, we know where your mommy lives, too—so don't fuck around. We'll find you." His shoulders lifted and fell. "I prefer the money, but—" Then his pleasant expression disappeared, his pale eyes bulging. "Borrow it, Paich. Steal it. Rob a bank. Rob a Seven-11—or rob twenty of 'em. Sell your ass—or somebody else's, I don't care. But bring the money. Don't be a Dumb-shit."

He turned to walk further into the large storage room, then turned, pointing at The Wrestler. "Give him a little something, Chooch—so he'll remember. But don't break anything—or hit where it'll show. I want him healthy so he can cough up the twenty large." Then he turned and almost smiled at Jerry Paich. "Don't worry, Jeremiah. By the time the week is up and you've found the dough, you'll just about be finished hurting."

As Marshall Ruttenberg disappeared into the darkness, The Wrestler stepped behind Jerry, put one arm across his neck, and choked him so hard he felt himself about to faint. But the Wrestler wouldn't allow that. He loosened the choke hold and with his other hand, punched Jerry so hard in the kidney he wet the front of his pants—just before he lost consciousness.

CHAPTER TWELVE

From the big front window at Johnny's Downtown, a view of the Terminal Tower and the front of the Renaissance Hotel on Public Square is almost as inspiring as the gourmet food served there. In a city where restaurants come and go with dizzying regularity, Johnny's Bar—still on Fulton Street on the west side of the river and later when Johnny's Downtown opened—have been true icons for longer than one generation, legendary for their amazing kitchen creations. Many regular customers are Cleveland lions—well-known politicians, athletes who aren't playing that evening, topflight journalists who may or may not have won Pulitzers, local TV celebrities. Others occupying those tables no one has ever heard of are sometimes richer and more powerful.

Bria Harstad sat close to the window, watching the sky turn from blue to orange, gray to black. She'd dined at Johnny's Downtown before—rarely with a date, more often on her own. Not too many women would eat dinner at Johnny's Downtown by themselves unless they had enough juice not to give a damn. She earned more at Marshall Ruttenberg's outfit than most legitimate company managers did, and could easily afford eating wherever she wanted to. On this evening she waited for her dinner partner to arrive—Francis P. Murgatroyd, county commissioner, hale fellow well-met, and a too-loud drunk. She hoped to keep him sober enough to glean whatever information from him she needed.

She watched him come in, waving, stopping to visit with almost everyone at other tables, air-kissing their wives, patting their backs, wringing their hands as though they hadn't seen each other for decades and were suddenly back from the dead. He looked out of place in such a classy establishment, wearing a plain red knit tie over his white shirt, slightly crooked at the knot, and a dark blue suit looking as if he had it dry-cleaned only when he spilled spaghetti sauce on it—all covered by a Lieutenant Columbo trench coat desperately in need of replacement. When he leaned down to kiss her, she turned her face away, so he only got her cheek and not her mouth. His breath tattled that he'd already been drinking.

"Ahh, my cupcake," he breathed as he sat down, looking at her lustily. "Breena, baby, you look good enough to eat."

"*I* invited you here tonight, Commissioner Murgatroyd," she said, quietly enough so no one else in the restaurant could hear. "Not Marshall Ruttenberg. This is my party and I'm paying for it. The least you can do is call me by my rightful name, and you know goddamn well what it is. It's not Breena, and it's not Baby, and it fucking sure isn't Cupcake. So let's get that straight, or you can go buy your own dinner at Burger King."

That calmed Murgatroyd down a bit. "Jeez, when did you get so tough?"

"I've always been tough—you just never noticed it. When I work for Ruttenberg, I'm polite to his friends—like you. I'm not working for him right this minute, so be aware of that." She looked around for a waiter and waved him over. "I'm sure you want a drink, right?"

He ordered a Jim Beam on the rocks, which she thought was middle-class tacky—but she considered everything about Murgatroyd tacky. She chose a Bombay Sapphire Blue martini, straight up with a lemon twist. When the drinks arrived, so did dinner menus, but she made no effort to open one.

"'*Slainte,*'" she said as they clinked glasses. Her first sip was delicate and ladylike, making her smile inwardly. A great marti-ni—the bartenders at Johnny's Downtown always iced the glass and kept the gin in the freezer. Franny gulped half his Jim Beam down in one swallow, and she knew her tab at the end of the evening would be higher than she'd hoped.

"You were asked to find out all you could about a man named Jericho Paich. You remember, right?"

Murgatroyd's nose wrinkled as he strove mightily to recall anything he'd done prior to arriving for dinner. Finally he said, "Yeah. Jericho. I learned all I could for you. There wasn't really that much to find out. Boring fucking kid."

"Lower your voice, commissioner, and watch your mouth."

His "Sorry" came out in a raspy whisper.

"He's not living at his apartment right now."

"How do you know that?"

"None of your business," she said. "He hasn't showed up to work for three days, either."

"Maybe he's sick."

Bria's heart quickened and breathing grew more difficult, but she decided not to think about it. "I checked his office. He called in sick—but he's not at home."

"Maybe he's staying with his mother in Shaker Heights," Franny said. "With her fancy man boogie."

Her eyes almost disappeared into slits. "You're some racist, aren't you?"

He shook his head almost violently. "No way. But hey, I grew up with a lotta Irish people on the west side. I like Irish people. I prefer them, that's all. Nothing against the boogies, though."

Bria thought of several insulting things to say to him, but discarded all of them. Too much trouble talking to a brick wall. She pushed a menu toward him. "Shut up and order dinner, Commissioner."

Bria ordered "light," as she was too tightly wound up to fin-ish a big meal. Franny Murgatroyd, however, wanted the largest and most expensive steak—a huge porterhouse which would have fed three, with double baked potatoes. He also went through two baskets of fresh rolls, which he dipped in olive oil rather than slathering them with butter. When they were both done eating, the dishes cleared away, and Murgatroyd working on his fourth bourbon, Bria Harstad said, "You have quite a staff working in your office, don't you?"

"Three law students part-time. A PR man who helps me write speeches when I need them. An executive secretary—not nearly as hot as you are, but she's pretty cute."

Bria ignored it. "No bodyguard?"

"Why would I need a bodyguard?"

"It'd take all night to list the reasons. Don't you have some tough-looking guy hanging around to keep the people who never voted for you at arm's length when you're out in public?"

"Well, yeah—one big motherfucker, around three hundred pounds or so. But he doesn't work for me full-time. Look around—I'm in public right now—and I didn't bring him with me tonight."

"You're not in public. You're in a dark restaurant using obscene words to a pretty woman you hope everyone thinks is your one and only—and that will never happen, Franny." She took her napkin out of her lap, folded it neatly, and placed it on the table. "What if I want to borrow your—big motherfucker some night, just to be on the safe side?"

"What for?"

"Need to know, Commissioner—and you don't need." From her purse she took two crisp new fifty-dollar bills. "Will this take care of him, assuming I'd only want him for an hour or so."

Murgatroyd took the bills, examining them as though they were counterfeit. "That's not much money. Even hookers earn more than that for ninety minutes."

"I'm not surprised you know how much hookers earn." She took a small spiral notebook from her purse and scribbled something on it. "What's his name, anyway?"

He had to think for a moment. "Demetri something. I can't remember offhand—I got it written down somewhere."

"What kind of name is Demetri?"

He shrugged. "I dunno. He's Indian, ya know—from India, not Arizona." Fear flickered across his face like a passing comet. "You're not gonna have him kill somebody, are you?"

Bria laughed, "Not for a hundred bucks, Franny. But here's the rest of the deal."

"Deal?"

"You sober enough to hear what I'm saying?"

Franny Murgatroyd looked offended. "I'm just buzzed. I'm always buzzed, and I get my work done pretty damn well." Then his look turned sneaky. "So, what do I get out of all of this?"

Bria considered it. Then she said, "Dessert."

"Dessert, huh?" Murgatroyd decided to become insulted. "That's cheap! That's sleazy!"

"Sleazy it may be, but that's it. Except for one more thing— and this is a biggie. Not one word to Marshall Ruttenberg about this dinner, about the things I asked you, about hiring this Demetri. Not one word. It never happened. I never called you. Nothing."

He started to argue further, but she put up a hand in his face to shut him up. "Because if you do," she said, her voice softer than a romantic murmur and five times more dangerous than if she'd screamed at him, "I'll make your life a living, breathing twenty-four-hour nightmare. You'll be wishing you were flat on your face on the floor of the Harp Saloon where you hang out—dead and gone. You said you think I'm tough, Commissioner." She shook her head. "You have no idea."

Murgatroyd, stunned and foolish, was close to crying. It was obvious to Bria he was a ridiculous choice to be a Cuyahoga County Commissioner, elected because the rich and powerful knew he was stupid enough to follow outside orders.

After more than two minutes of thorny silence, Murgatroyd

knew he was going to lose, anyway. His body relaxed in his chair and he raised his head for a terrified smile.

"Bria," he said, leaning hard on the right way to pronounce her name, and feeling good about himself for doing so. "So, how about it? Where's my dessert?"

She drove home in her previous year's Toyota Camry—all black, inside and out, which she secretly thought was sexy—and thought about the reasons she'd called this dinner meeting with Francis Murgatroyd.

When Marshall Ruttenberg had ordered Bria to discover all she could about Jerry Paich, she immediately contacted Franny. He was a doofus and a drunk, but a Cuyahoga County Commissioner. Not only was he Marshall's buddy—Marshall spent too much time sending Franny beautiful young hookers and not enough on doubling his impressive fortune—but he was in a political position to know everything about everyone in Greater Cleveland. If not, he knew how to find out.

Ruttenberg was menacing at best—and one of these days Bria would learn more about his business he'd want her to know. Thus, she carried Murgatroyd's on-again-off-again bodyguard's name and number in her purse.

Bria thought she'd learned enough for Marshall, at least for the time being—but then one day changed her mind completely, and she didn't know what to do about it.

One evening a few days back, she stayed late, taking care of some odds and ends in office chores, besides which Marshall had left an hour earlier. She walked over to the smallest of the three houses, the one he used as a warehouse. The more he was out of her sight, the better she liked it.

She really despised him, but few available jobs would pay her anywhere near what she earned—not for the sex-on-demand, which early on had gone the way of the dodo bird and the carrier pigeon because she was fiercely efficient and demanding.

She ran his business with no ripples in the water. She knew he was a smuggler—drugs and stolen antiquities—but she was far from stupid.

He'd only fucked her several times when she first started working for him, stopped when he realized she was the best manager he'd ever find, anywhere—and he was rich enough to get laid any time he wanted to. He knew she found him disgusting, ugly, and creepy whenever he took his clothes off. Probably all the hookers agreed, too, but they were paid for doing revolting things anyway, so he didn't give a damn.

She went into the bathroom to pee before she left, as she'd planned to grocery shop before going home. The opaque bathroom window was almost always left open unless it was cold out, as there was no fan in any residential building constructed in the nineteen forties or earlier, and as they often do, bathrooms get stinky after a while and need to be aired out.

When finished, she moved to the window to shut it, glanced out, and was shocked to see two of the men who sometimes worked for Ruttenberg—the tall, gaunt one with the pocked face and the one who looked like the front end of a Sherman tank—leaving the warehouse building, half-walking and half-dragging a man between them who could barely stand up. He was blindfolded, his hands cuffed in front of him, and from the front of his pants, he'd obviously wet himself.

She could only see half of his face because of the black blindfold, but he seemed young and she could see no blood anywhere. She figured he'd been badly beaten all over his body where it wouldn't show. She shuddered, turned away from the window without shutting it, put her face in her hands.

No proof—but in her gut she knew it was Jericho Paich—and she had made the phone call helping Ruttenberg find him.

She worked in a totally illegal operation. Most men employed here or even visited were working criminals or else undocumented aliens. But this kind of violence was new to her.

She hated violence. Shortly after college, she had involved

herself with a charming, handsome young guy who'd majored in business, landed a big job with a twelve million dollar per year firm, and had a habit of beating her up whenever he drank too much or when he had a bad day at the office.

She'd eschewed relationships ever since. She approached sex the way most men do—if she were horny, and saw someone she wanted, she fucked him. No promises, no I-love-yous. If a guy hung around her for more than six weeks, he teetered on the edge of destruction—and she made sure he knew it.

So her job with Marshall Ruttenberg had worked out just fine—for the moment, anyway. Now she was taking a chance of notably losing her job, but possibly chancing more violence.

To herself.

Sticking her neck out.

CHAPTER THIRTEEN

After four days of agony and four nights of not being able to sleep, Jerry Paich was still damaged, still rocky. It felt as if every bone in his body below the neck was bruised, every inch of skin purpled. He tried not remembering the beating, the punches and kicks to his belly, his back, his thighs, his groin and his shoulders, all carefully avoiding his face or drawing any blood. He couldn't banish it from his head—at least not yet. It was a nightmare hung on like a summer cold, a reminder every time he tried standing up, sitting down or walking—and only some merciful god could help him if he were to cough. He'd been more terrified of The Wrestler than of Skinny—he still didn't know their names—but Skinny was the one who hit harder, and obviously enjoyed it.

He was too physically devastated and emotionally shattered to stay home and take care of himself. He avoided seeing his nude body in the mirror—Technicolor bruises bloomed wherever he'd been hit or kicked—and that meant nearly everywhere. On the morning after the beating, he had called his mother and begged to stay at her house for a few days, which sent her into another long burst of sobbing and wailing—so draining to him he almost wished he'd stayed home. He refused to tell her exactly what happened, but later he did share it with Laird Janiver, to whom he'd gone for help in the first place.

Laird, uncomfortable in a stepfather-type relationship, couldn't believe Jerry had been kidnapped and beaten, and he had no idea of the name of the perpetrator, nor in what neighborhood it happened. Now Jerry would have to produce a huge amount of money to save himself from another beating—or worse.

Arielle's son knew Janiver could do enough. A retired Marine had limited power as a civilian in Greater Cleveland. Jericho had to help himself. It took him three days to realize where he might find unexpected assistance. It was a chance he had to take.

That evening he lurched down the driveway to his car—in great pain—and headed from Shaker Heights to the eastern edge of downtown Cleveland, to Murray Hill.

Little Italy.

It was a small, warm Italian village in the midst of a bustling city, a five-minute walk to University Circle, which includes Case Western Reserve University, the Cleveland Art Museum, the Museum of Natural History, and the home of the classic Cleveland Orchestra, Severance Hall. Little Italy was all art galleries, gift shops, Italian restaurants, and a famous bakery supplying amazing cakes, pastries, and the best donuts in the whole world, especially at two o'clock in the morning when the donuts were still piping hot.

Jericho Paich hadn't visited Little Italy often; when he did, on some sort of date or to one of the Italian religious festivals that packed the streets, he'd gone to La Dolce Vita, which his Italian mother recommended—always a happening place with great rustic food and a charming owner/chef, Terry Tarantino. But on this particular night he made his way up Murray Hill Avenue to a place few out-of-town visitors knew about—an Italian restaurant named for its longtime owner: *Rustica Malatesta*.

When Franco Malatesta had been younger, he was often found at his own booth in the far corner of the restaurant, facing the door, listening to the Italian opera music he had piped in all the time, or even better, when tenor opera singers appeared live with their own pianist to offer mostly Verdi and Puccini. Many people who knew him—mostly Italians—would find their way back to him to greet him, kiss his hand, and tell him how much they loved him.

They'd better—because Frank Malatesta—*Don Franco,* called "Frankie Ziti" by his friends because of his excellent place to eat—was not only a restaurateur, but for thirty years the *capo di tutti capi* of the Greater Cleveland mob.

Older now, he only arrived in the morning for breakfast, or for dinner on weekends or holidays like Columbus Day. American Italians considered Christopher Columbus their Number One Hero and choose not to think of his rapaciousness, greed and cruelty when landing in San Salvador.

The don's only son, John, managed the place. Almost thirty and devilishly handsome, John ("Johnny Pockets") Malatesta was happy running the restaurant as he wandered from table to table greeting diners who'd been eating there for decades—and he loved the first-time customers too. He popped into the kitchen every night and tasted what looked good, sweating it off five days a week at a nearby gym. He had naught to do with illegal businesses in which his family made their money, but he was the Malatesta heir-apparent—whether he liked it or not—and was treated with the same respect.

Parking in Little Italy always sucked, and Jerry Paich had to leave his car a block and a half away and gimp all the way to the crowded restaurant, pain attacking him with every step. He'd never met Johnny Pockets before and had no idea what he looked like. After scanning the dinnertime revelers, he tottered to the bar and lowered himself painfully onto one of the few empty stools. The bar top was genuine granite, feeling nice to the touch and never stained by someone spilling a glass of red wine on it. On many of the walls were paintings of seaside towns in Italy.

The pretty bartender with a lot of hair, make-up more suited to a chorus girl, and wearing a badge over her ample left breast, identifying her as Angela. When she asked what he wanted, it occurred to Jerry he was in no condition to drink, and told her so. "I'm—not feeling the greatest tonight."

She held her hands out, palms up. "Sorry to hear that. I'll bring you some water if you want, but I can recommend a much better medicine for you."

"Are you a doctor?" he croaked.

"Better than that, I'm a magician. I'll make you a stinger. It'll cure just about anything—except E.D."

"E.D.?"

She laughed. "Erectile dysfunction, sweetie. If you don't know what that means, you probably don't need it—especially at your age."

She swished away, and he watched her go. She had the thinnest possible silver ring band puncturing her left nostril, so delicate Jerry hadn't noticed it at first. Efficient as hell, she quickly constructed a stinger in a martini glass and brought it to him. "Are you eating dinner, hon? Shall I bring you a menu?"

He shook his head and sipped on his drink. It was his first stinger, ever, and the sweet taste almost made him forget he was a walking bruise. He said, "No dinner. I'm looking for Mr. Malatesta."

"The old one or the young one?"

"Uh—John Malatesta."

She nodded, glanced around, and pointed to a man standing and chatting with two couples at a table against the wall. "That's him," she said.

Uncomfortable with any quick move, Jerry turned to look. John Malatesta was having a much better evening than he was—laughing, smiling, toying with the better-looking of the two women. Somehow, her date didn't look annoyed.

"I shouldn't bother him."

Angela tossed her head back, so the hair got out of her eyes. "Go ahead," she said. "He loves meeting new customers."

Jerry sighed. "If you say so."

"Finish your stinger first, hon. And that's eight dollars."

Jerry left her a ten and hoisted himself up from the stool,

leaning on the bar to keep his footing. He moved through the restaurant carefully, because the tables were too close together and he twisted and turned, saying excuse me at least ten times as diners had to scoot their chairs out of the way. Finally, he reached the man he'd come to see, and stood there at length, waiting for him to finish his flirting.

"Mr. Malatesta," he said. "I'm wondering if I could have a word with you. My name is Jericho Paich."

"Hey, how ya doin'?" John Malatesta shook his hand warmly. "Jericho? Your name sounds familiar. Have we met before?"

"I don't think so. I'm a friend of Jill Taggart."

"Wow, Jill Taggart! I haven't seen her in—gotta be around six months." He smiled, breathing deeply. "Jill was a pretty girl. She used to show up here maybe once or twice a month. Hey, did you eat yet?"

"Thanks, maybe another time. Tonight, I need to talk to you in private."

That made John Malatesta twitch, and his smile faded at least sixty percent. "In private?"

The foursome he'd been talking to were looking at Jerry querulously. Malatesta pulled Jerry several steps away and said, *sotto voce*, "Are you a cop? Tell me, I don't mind. I know lotsa cops. I like them—so tell me we won't have any crap in here tonight, cuz I run a decent place."

"I'm no cop—not even close. I wanted to warn you about something."

"Warn me?" His chuckle had no humor behind it. "You know who you're talking to?"

Jerry nodded. "That's why I want to warn you."

John thought about it. Then he said, "We'll go back into my office. It's smaller than a shit stall in a men's room, but we can be private if that's what you want."

They made their way to the rear of the restaurant, to a tiny room next to the kitchen. When John Malatesta shut the door, the noise from outside was dim.

He sat behind his desk—there was no room for another chair—and removed a Glock from his top drawer and set it right beside his hand. "Just so you're not warning me about *you*, pal." He patted the weapon like he would a small dog. "I'm licensed, by the way, so don't freak out."

Jerry said, "I'm not freaking out—and I'm not armed. I wanted to tell you—Jill Taggart used to be my girlfriend."

"Used to? You broke up?" His shoulders lifted, then dropped. "I never had nothing going on with her, if you're here for revenge."

"No, no revenge. She just—disappeared."

"Jesus, how does somebody just disappear?"

Jerry said, "It's a long story." And he began to tell it.

Depending on a definition of "long," it took Jerry Paich twenty minutes. He knew he was talking too much, seeing Johnny Malatesta grow impatient, checking his wristwatch and shifting uncomfortably in his chair—the only chair in the room, forcing Jerry to spin his tale while painfully standing, not having much room to move around.

When he finally finished, falling silent, the young Malatesta stared at him. "Let me get this straight. You were a drug pusher instead for Jill Taggart, and now you're selling it for the police?"

"I'm what they call a C.I.—a confidential informer. I sell drugs and then point out the buyers to the cops, especially for a Detective Keegan Mayo. Know him?"

Malatesta's eyes rolled ceilingward. "Keegan Mayo is a fucking asshole—he comes marching in here with different ugly broads like he's the commander of an invading army—and he expects not to have to pay for his food and booze."

Jerry said, "He's been making me do this for the last six months. But now he specifically asked me to finger you, Mr. Malatesta."

"Finger me?"

"As a drug user. I don't know why, but he did."

John Malatesta chewed that information, his lips almost disappearing into the rest of his face. Then he said, "Jericho—you know who my father is?"

Jerry hesitated, then nodded.

"Then why me? Why not Papa?" He pushed a few stacks of paper away from him on the desktop. "Ah, I get it. One night Keegan came in here with a pretty hot chick—way too hot for a *strunz* like him—and I took her away from him."

Jerry thought John Malatesta was much better looking than Mayo, but he didn't voice it. Instead, he warned, "He'll put you in jail for ten years over that?"

"Believe it—if he can set up a crime for me to commit. Why do you take the chance and tell me about it?"

Jerry's eyes bugged and his cheeks turned red. "I'm just warning you that you're on top of Mayo's list. I don't want to insult you—"

"Don't be walking on eggshells. Mayo is a drug cop; he can't touch my father for anything, so he picks on me instead, setting me up to get busted for buying meth—just so he can get himself a lieutenant's bar." He rubbed his hands together as if he'd just washed them in a men's room and half-dried them on the hot air blower. "We'll just see about that."

"What are you gonna do, Mr. Malatesta?"

"John. Call me John—or Johnny, or Johnny Pockets— whatever you like better, okay? And you're Jericho. You did me a huge favor, Jericho, and I won't forget that. Swear to God. We're gonna be friends now—as long as you keep your mouth shut." He took out his wallet and extracted one of his business cards. "Call me if you need anything." He scribbled his home phone number on the back. "Bring a date next time. Whatever you order is on the house. *Anything.* I've got your back."

Jerry Paich did not know what to say. He was relieved at Malatesta calling him a friend instead of growing enraged and hanging him out to dry.

He halted out to his parked car, a hell of a long Little Italy walk ached even more with each step. When he slid behind the wheel, he had to catch his breath. Real pain can suck the energy out of everyone.

Another worry hammered at his head as he found his way back to Shaker Heights from *Rustica Malatesta* on Murray Hill. Franco is the Godfather of the Cleveland Mafia—and now he knows Keegan Mayo was making him and his family a target.

Jerry despised Mayo—for good reason. But will the mob make the detective the kill of the week?

CHAPTER FOURTEEN

Bria Harstad brooded for days, unsure about what she had accidentally seen. She feared if she did anything at all, it would cost her a high-paying job—or perhaps something much worse. Marshall Ruttenberg ran a big drug distribution ring in Greater Cleveland, but as long as what she did was legal and aboveboard, she didn't give a damn what was happening as long as she didn't have to see it.

She'd been working late four nights earlier, and when she was ready to go home in the early evening, she'd stopped in the bathroom before she left. The house in which she worked had been built so early in the twentieth century there was no outtake fan in the ceiling of the john—which was against the law—so the window was always slightly open, facing the other small house containing a dinky back door and no windows. Anyone peeping in was unlikely. But washing her hands, she glanced out into the twilight, and what she saw shook her to her very core.

Ruttenberg's two full-time bodyguards were marching out the door, holding up someone who looked as if he were young, though it was hard for Bria to tell. The person was blindfolded, handcuffed, and practically doubled over, groaning aloud while being supported on each side, barely able to walk.

My god, Bria thought, what the hell happened over there in the small house? Who was that poor, damaged man, and how had he been hurt? Then she recalled all the questions Ruttenberg told her to ask Cuyahoga Commissioner Murgatroyd about a name Ruttenberg had given her—Jericho Paich.

She'd tried to shake it off, forget it, but couldn't—the image of the badly injured man haunted her. She had to find out if the so-called victim was indeed Mr. Paich—and if so, why?

Her sense of rightness and order got the better of her. Looking at Murgatroyd's skimpy notes, she made several calls to the company at which Jericho Paich worked, only to be told he'd been calling in sick. Rather than going directly to her nearby apartment in Beachwood, she checked the home address Franny gave her, and headed to the west side and the run-down apartment house where he lived.

It was older than hell, Bria thought, possibly built a century earlier and now home to mostly elderly widowed persons who are marking time through their golden years. In the entryway downstairs, she pushed the button to Jericho Paich's flat several times, but got no answer. Frustrated, she summoned the manager of the building and was buzzed in.

The house manager, Dorothy Melgrim, opened the door of her first-floor apartment and came out into the hallway. Fiftyish, with long straight brown hair going gray, wearing a loose-fitting long-sleeved pink blouse and black slacks, she looked annoyed. Bria could see over her shoulder a rerun of vintage *Grey's Anatomy* was playing on the TV set in the landlady's apartment—Dr. McDreamy in all his pre-superstar glory—and she was irritated at missing the middle of it.

After the introductions, Dorothy said, "I don't know where he is. I haven't seen him for a few days, but I don't keep track of where my tenants go. If they show up on the first of the month with a rent check, I don't give a good goddamn where they are or what they're doing—except I hope if they do drop dead, it won't be here in my building. That'd be a real mess." She cocked her head and squinted at Bria. "Who are you? A cop or something?"

"No. I'm just—"

"You're a debt collector!" she crowed in triumph. "I get it! I can spot 'em a mile away." She cackled. "Debt collectors are bullies. Well, you're not gonna bully *me*, sister!"

"I'm not collecting money or a police officer. I'm just looking for Mr. Paich."

"Humph!" That's usually only a sound someone makes, but Dorothy Melgrim turned it into an actual word. "I haven't seen you around here before. Matter of fact, there've been no women coming to see him since he broke up with his girlfriend about six months ago."

"I'm not his girlfriend, either."

"I'd think not." Melgrim made her lips an irritating kiss. "I see men—different men all the time, coming to visit him at night, sometimes late. What is he, a fag?"

Bria reached for a business card in her purse, but thought better of it. Instead, she took out a small paper pad and a ballpoint pen. "I want to leave him a note. Which apartment does he live in so I can slip this under his door?"

Dorothy pointed at a door right across from her own, then flounced back into her living room, hoping to catch up on the medical show plot. Bria Harstad, not expecting an answer, knocked twice, and then scrawled on one small sheet of paper, "You don't know me, but I worry about you. Please call me. Bria." She carefully printed out her cell phone number and pushed the note under his door.

She sat in her car, motor running. Results had been zero, so she was hard-pressed to process her personal mission further.

She remembered Franny Murgatroyd had given her nothing in answer to Ruttenberg's demands—but he'd mentioned Jerry Paich's mother lived in Shaker Heights.

She took her iPad out and clicked on a file she'd named "Franny," flipped through it until she found "Paich, Arielle" and an address on Chalfont Drive, close to Van Aken Boulevard, and a phone number.

Should she call? If Jerry was hiding out, his mother would

undoubtably lie—whether grizzly bear, lion or buffalo, mothers protect their babies no matter what—but if she visited in person, perhaps she'd get lucky.

It won't hurt to ask.

She parked at the curb to check out the house on Chalfont Drive. Nothing spectacular, solid middle class, Bria thought, traversing the cobblestone walkway and hoping one of her high heels didn't catch on something and trip her so she'd wind up flat on her butt, legs flying, skirt up around her waist, right in front of Arielle Paich's home.

She got to the door, straightened her clothing and touched her hair to make sure the evening breeze hadn't mussed it too badly, and pushed the doorbell, hearing pleasant bing-bong chimes. She rehearsed what she might say, whether Jerry opened the door or his mother did.

She was taken aback, however, when she saw a handsome middle-aged black man in Dockers and a blue dress shirt with the sleeves rolled up, standing straight and tall in the doorway.

He looked surprised when he saw her. And pleased. "Hi," he said, smiling, his voice soft and low. "May I help you?"

"Oh," she said, then stopped, as that was all she could think of to say at the moment.

His smile widened; he had nice, straight teeth. "If you're looking for Arielle, I'm afraid you picked a bad time. She's not here—this is her book club night."

Bria said "Oh," again.

Very pretty woman, Laird Janiver thought. *Very classy-looking.* He said, "Shall I tell her you visited?"

"N-no—actually I was wondering—is Jerry Paich here."

His smile went away. "He doesn't live here anymore."

"I know—but I've looked for him everywhere else I could, so I thought I might try here."

"Why would a grown man, a college graduate with a good

job and a nice apartment, be living with his mother?"

Why are you *living with his mother?* she wanted to say but did not.

"Are you his girlfriend, Miss—uh—"

"Harstad. Bria Harstad. I'm not—"

"That's a pretty name—Bria. Scandinavian, I'll bet. I'm Laird Janiver. It's nice to meet you." He put out his hand for her to shake.

Scandinavian, she thought, was an excellent guess. She took his hand—surprisingly smooth and soft, but strong and warm. She asked, "Do you know where Jerry is?"

"He's been laid up here for the past four days. His mom was taking care of him, but he went out tonight. I don't know where, but I don't think it's a social thing, because he's still pretty rocky, physically."

"Was he sick?"

Laird hesitated. "Not exactly. If you're not his girlfriend, where do you know him from?"

Now it was her turn to pause. Then she said, "I don't know him personally. I never even met him."

Her shoulders slumped. "It's a long story."

"I love long stories," he said, "and I've nowhere to go. Please come in."

Her hesitation lasted microseconds, then allowed him to lead her to the living room. She studied it, as she always does when she visits a place for the first time. Neat and tidy, but not warm and cozy. Someone labored under an OCD, as everything was surgery-clean. The chair Laird hovered over was next to a small table with a reading lamp, a hardback book having something to do with the Marine Corps, a bookmark somewhere in the middle. A half-empty beer bottle was on the table—John Courage beer from the United Kingdom that had been retired years before. That told Bria a lot about a person, not knowing Laird had bought several cases of it in Chicago years ago, drinking it on rare occasions, hoping it wouldn't disappear too quickly—

and he drank it out of a glass, not straight from the bottle.

He waited until she was seated, thinking from her elegant appearance she was not a beer drinker. The smell of her cologne—flowery, but with a spicy—made him blink more than once.

She said, "I'm afraid this isn't a social call."

"I'm wondering, then, what kind of call it is."

"I'll try to explain it to you, Mr. Janiver—but there are conditions."

He smiled again. "Conditions? You mean rules, like a game?"

She held her hand out straight in front of her, palm down, and tilted it back and forth. "Whatever you want to call them. You don't ask me where I work, you don't ask me what I do, and you don't ask me for anyone else's name. Deal?"

"I don't know," Laird said, "what's in it for me?"

"Nothing. It's for your son."

"Jericho is not my son!" he said, a bit too forcefully. "He is Arielle's son."

One of Bria's eyebrows climbed. "And you just live here?"

"Something like that."

"Maybe I should just wait and talk to her."

"Not a good idea."

"Why?"

"Because she'll cry. She's a big cryer."

"She cries a lot?"

"Every day. And if she's not crying about her son, she'd be crying because you're here and she's not. Talk to me instead. I won't cry, I assure you."

"I'm not sure it'll help."

"Jerry already came to me," Laird said, "naturally wanting help. I did what I could—but I had no room to move." He leaned forward in his chair, inhaling her cologne too deeply. "You know stuff I don't. I never heard of you before ten minutes ago—so be straight with me instead. Otherwise, it'll just get worse for Jerry—and for me."

"The trouble is—I don't know whether I'm talking about Jerry or somebody else."

"Start," he said. "Just start. If it doesn't sound like Jerry, I'll stop you and we can say goodnight."

Bria closed her eyes and rubbed them with her index finger and her thumb. "I could lose my job for this, Mr. Janiver."

He nodded, serious.

"Or worse." She quivered. "You don't want to hear it."

"It's your choice, then. Open up with whatever you have to tell me—or take your bat and ball and go home."

She was staring at her own lap, her eyes not meeting his, and Laird found himself feeling sorry for her—and sympathetic, which are two different things. She was an exquisite woman, and this close to her he felt her fear, her danger for even coming here. He wanted to put his arms around her and hold her, make her feel safe—but he couldn't. Not here, not now.

"Let me begin, Ms. Harstad. Do you know what a C.I. is? Confidential Informant to the police? Or as the FBI calls it, a Confidential Human Resource."

She nodded, finding it difficult to breathe.

"Jerry is no snitch. The police caught him selling hard drugs to his girlfriend's regular customers while she was out of town."

"That's dumb," Bria said.

"True. But this one cop—Detective Mayo—is bucking for lieutenant, so he put Jerry to work. He sells people the drugs and then turns them in to the police, and the detective gets credit for the arrest. Jerry's been at it six months now, and it's getting worse. I tried talking Mayo into letting him go, but it didn't work. I even went to an old combat friend—a Marine colonel I worked for in Iraq. He didn't have any suggestions, either." He sat back in his chair. "I think it's your turn now."

She interlaced her fingers, then laid her hands in her lap. She said, "Recently my employer—no names, remember? My employer asked me to find out all I could about Jericho Paich, so I contacted somebody kind of important. All I found out about

Mr. Paich was his college experience, job, address and phone number. And his mother's. That's why I'm here."

"Okay."

"But a few days ago, I happened to see a man being ushered out of where I worked. He limped, bent over, being supported by two big tough guys, and he was blindfolded, so I never got a good look at his face. I knew he was hurt, but couldn't tell how badly. It bothered me a lot, because afterwards I spent some time researching Jerry Paich. I decided, on my own, to check on him, see if he was really okay. He hasn't been at work or home, so I figured this would be his next stop."

Laird Janiver's legs were flat on the floor in front of him, and he crossed his left leg over his right. Bria couldn't help noticing he actually lifted his own leg with a hand under his knee to cross it, which made her wonder.

"Now I'm troubled," Janiver said. "Yes, Jericho was beaten up pretty badly, but he couldn't tell me where or who. Or why. He moved in here after he got hurt so his mother could take care of him." He rolled his eyes. "Arielle never got out of the habit of taking care of her little boy. Anyway, this evening was the first time he left the house. He didn't tell me where he was going."

"Will he come back?"

"He left clothes here, so I imagine he will."

Bria took out her Spiral notebook again and scrawled her name and number on it, then tore out the page, leaning forward to hand it to him. "Have him call me," she said, "in the evening. Tonight, maybe, no matter how late he comes home."

Laird fondled the piece of paper as if trying to absorb its message into his skin so he'd not forget it. "I don't understand. You don't know Jerry, you never met him, and yet you're desperate to reach him."

"I don't understand why he came to you in the first place, either, Mr. Janiver. You're not his father."

"No, I'm—" He stopped, all at once baffled by what he

should answer. Eventually he said, "I just—live here."

Bria slightly pursed her lips as she rose. "Got it," she said, moving toward the door.

Laird almost trotted after her. "Thank you for coming."

She nodded.

"It was—nice meeting you."

Oh, for crysakes! she thought as she opened the front door and stepped out into the chill evening breeze. People always strain themselves saying something polite when they don't even mean it.

While she went down the walkway of Arielle Paich's home, Laird stood at the front window, watching her go. Her visit was a surprise, mysterious, inexplicable. She was overly concerned about Jerry. She thought she'd seen him after he'd been hurt, but had declined to indicate where she worked or what her job was. The phone number she left with him was her personal home contact.

That she was startlingly beautiful did not escape his notice, either.

He finished drinking his John Courage and poured another—unusual because once it's gone, it's gone and he'd have to choose another favorite beer. Once more he settled down with his book, but couldn't concentrate on it, eventually putting it down and turning on the TV. Still, his mind wandered.

He stared grimly at the sofa where he knew he'd spend the night—and it wasn't the first night he'd been banished from the bedroom. His left stump was throbbing. How does a neurotic pain reach down to a foot that wasn't there anymore?

He ran a hand over his face. Arielle would be left to sleep alone *again* this evening? Her late husband hadn't left her, either. He just died.

He took Bria's phone number from his pocket, deciding to wait until Jerry came home so he could give it to him. But he made another copy, putting it into his own wallet.

When he curled up on the sofa to sleep, he had to wonder why.

CHAPTER FIFTEEN

Don Franco Malatesta sat in his own restaurant on a snappy autumn morning in Little Italy. It didn't open its doors for business until eleven thirty, some two and a half hours later, but when the don wants a big breakfast, the head chef comes in at whatever time he's called.

The don was seventy-seven years old. His hands and his right knee were arthritic, and he preferred wearing thick glasses instead of submitting himself to optical cataract surgery scared the crap out of him. Listening to recorded Verdi or Rossini operas on the sound system, and sipping an espresso so loaded with sugar it might have been a dessert treat served at an old-fashioned drugstore soda counter, he nibbled on his favorite breakfast dish—a zucchini crepe with flour, eggs, green peppers, mushrooms, tomatoes and chopped cheddar, sitting amongst his chosen "family" that made him feel secure.

On this morning, he paid strict attention to his son John telling him Jerry Paich had warned he himself was targeted for trouble by a Cleveland cop.

Afterwards, the don stared out the window. The rush hour traffic coming down from Cleveland Heights had slowed to a trickle, and the street was quieter. During this stretch between rush hour and lunchtime, most who walked the Little Italy streets were really Italian—older, fatter, and feeling at home away from home on the other side of the Atlantic Ocean.

The old man moved along these same streets when he was a ten-year-old, recently emigrated from Sicily. After he became a "made man" and then the Cleveland don, he still walked, though he had plenty of company surrounding him, armed tough guys wearing dark suits and sunglasses loosely surrounding him, making sure no strangers could get near.

Several years earlier the son of one of the don's best non-mob friends had hustled up a ridiculous amount of investment to finance a movie he was making, and decided to film one of the scenes in the *Malatesta Rustica*, early, before it really got busy. The don, who agreed to be an "extra" in the film while sitting at his own breakfast table, paid no attention to the actors. Between scenes, he talked to one of his neighborhood friends about something important when the assistant director called out, "Quiet, please! Quiet on the set!" Don Franco's face turned deadly white as he rose from his chair, and croaked, "Did somebody just tell me to shut the fuck up?"

The assistant director, certain he'd be murdered on the spot, decided he had to go somewhere else that day and would report again when there would be no more scenes shot in the restaurant.

Since then, times had changed. Much of the Italian mob's power had been watered down as the criminal celebrities moved into other neighborhoods, other ethnicities. The nationalities in Cleveland numbered more than one hundred. Once, Malatesta wondered how many locals were actually from Bulgaria—as if he were aware of even a single Bulgarian living in town. Not many—and if perhaps five more showed up, there would be a Bulgarian mob in town, too.

Now, though, confronted by his son who, for all intents and purposes, was a legal restaurant manager, the don was quietly troubled. He mopped at the crepe with half an Orlando Bakery roll, chewed and swallowed it, then said, "So how did you get into this shit, Giovanni? Stoned outta your mind all the time? You a dope junkie now?"

John cringed. He was nowhere near an addict, but in the past his father had scorned the use of recreational drugs, and he didn't want to getting into trouble. "I do coke sometimes, Papa. Just sometimes. It's no big deal—like the way you love those caramel sundaes with sea salt. You don't eat one every day, like I don't snort coke every day. Everyone snorts coke."

"Everyone snorts coke? Pope Francis snorts coke? The President of the United States shoves coke up his nose? How about me, Giovanni? Am I a cokehead too? I should smack your goddamn face!"

The hair on the back of Johnny Pocket's neck bristled. It's not that his aged father could punch him that hard, but there were the hit guys, the bodyguards sitting all over the restaurant, and a whack in the face might end up a hospital sleepover. "Aw, come on, Papa—I'm twenty-eight years old!"

"Your mama spins in her grave with you being a dope addict!" The don waved his hand to make John be quiet. "So—these pushers are after you? For what? Who's this guy, anyhow? This Jerry whatsisname?"

"Paich. Jerry Paich. Actually, his name is Jericho Paich."

"He's a dope mule?"

"Not really. His girlfriend used to sell drugs. I heard she went away for a while, and he took over for her temporarily. Then the cops nailed him and turned him into a C.I."

"What's a C.I.?"

"Confidential Informant. That means the cops make him find dopers and sell to them, and then the cops come by and lock the poor bastard up."

Fretful, the don shook his head. "That's a shitty thing for cops to do. Is this particular cop looking for a promotion?"

John shrugged, not answering. He was sure his father would understand that.

"This Jericho guy, he tries to sell you and then drops a dime on you?"

"Paich, Papa—Jericho Paich. No, he did the right thing. He

came to warn me the cops gave him my name. They wanted him to nail me."

"You never done nothing bad."

"Yeah," John sighed, "but putting a Malatesta under arrest instead of some dumb schmuck who lives in a second-floor walk-up down the street would make headlines."

Don Franco put his hands together and interlaced his fingers, as if he were reciting "Now I lay me down to sleep," with one index finger extended, touching his lips while he thought. Then he said, "Forget this Jericho person. He's nothing—a lightweight. What's the name of the cop who set him loose on you?"

"Keegan Mayo. Detective First Class Keegan Mayo," John said carefully. "From downtown."

"Mayo, eh? An Irish stink pig." Franco Malatesta chewed on that for a while, then waved down his personal waiter. "Get Brigandi," he said, pointing to a table toward the rear of the restaurant occupied by four men drinking coffee and munching on Italian biscuits.

The waiter scurried off to that table and whispered to one of them, who immediately rose and made his way forward to the main table. He bent and kissed the hand of the older man, ignoring the tomato sauce on Malatesta's fingers. "My don," he whispered.

Don Franco half smiled his acceptance. "You know of a cop downtown, name of Keegan?"

"That's his first name, Papa," John interrupted. "His last name is Mayo."

The old man grimaced. "Sounds like what you put on a Protestant Baptist turkey sandwich. So okay, Keegan Mayo."

Nico Brigandi didn't have to give it a second thought. "I know him. I've seen him around. He's a narc cop, Don Franco. He's also—forgive me—an asshole."

"Thought so. Well, he's making Giovanni here his special project."

Nico looked surprised, giving John a quick glance. "Johnny

Pockets? No kidding."

"We have to do something about him," Don Franco said.

John Malatesta lowered his voice to a raspy whisper. "He's bad news, Papa. You don't ice a law enforcement officer, that's for sure. Icing one is crazy. We'll have every badge in Ohio up our asses if we ice a cop."

The don almost snarled at his son. "Giovanni, what kind of moron you take me for? Nobody's gonna kill him. Right, Nico?"

Brigandi nodded eagerly. "Definitely not, Don."

"Definitely not." The elder Malatesta gulped down the last of his espresso. "But we're gonna fuck him up good."

"How?" asked his son.

The Don reached up and pinched Brigandi's cheek hard, then slapped it gently. "That's why I got Nico. He's a smart guy. He'll figure a way. Won't you, Nico?"

"I'd do anything for you, Don Franco," Brigandi said as sincerely as he could. "Give me a day or two to come up with something."

"I'm pleased. Siddown here, siddown. You have your breakfast yet? Lemme treat you to a zucchini creche, huh?" He waved at the waiter again. "A breakfast here for Nico—and whatever he wants to drink, too."

"Just coffee, Don Franco, please."

"Bullshit with the black coffee. You should drink espresso, like me. Stronger—keeps you thinking sharp! Keeps your brain working. Like mine." He showed his yellowing, crooked teeth in a smile. "Nico Brigandi—you're my smart boy."

Which, to John Malatesta, sounded a lot like he was *not* the don's smart boy

CHAPTER SIXTEEN

When Bria Harstad left Arielle Paich's home, Janiver stood at
the window and watched her go. Her visit was inexplicable.
She'd never known Jerry Paich, but was concerned about him.
She thought she'd seen him at her own work after he'd been
hurt, but never saw his face and declined to indicate where she
worked or what her job was. The phone number she gave him
was her personal cellphone contact.

He once more settled down, book open on his lap, but
couldn't concentrate, eventually putting it down and turning on
the TV to a dark, moody action show resembling all the others.
Where were the good old days when a television program was
photographed with enough light illuminating it so one could see
what was going on?

His mind wandered.

Less than an hour later, Arielle Paich came home from her
book club meeting, calling a hello as she walked in the front
door. When she came into the living room, she said, "You're
watching TV? That's a new one."

"I was in the mood, I guess. How was your book club?"

"It's all right. The girls argue sometimes, but at least we all
read the same book and get to discuss it every month." She sat
down where Bria had sat and leaned back on the sofa. "I wish
sometime we'd read something besides a sappy romance novel."

"Who decides on the book each month?"

"We vote—and I always lose." Then she frowned, moving her head from side to side, tilting it ceilingward, sniffing the air as a dog entering a new territory. "I smell something funny."

The backs of Janiver's hands tingled as if they had fallen asleep. "What's funny?"

Another deep sniff. "Perfume. Not my perfume either. You know I have a great sense of smell, Laird." She sniffed again, and then her face grew stern and angry. "Some other woman was here this evening. Did you have a woman in here when I was gone?"

"*Have some woman?* Seriously? Don't be ridiculous. Yes, there was a woman in this room about an hour ago. I never met her before. She came here looking for Jerry."

Arielle got to her feet, her eyes turned to slits, her voice frosty. "You told her Jerry wasn't home and then invited her in? How cute!"

"She doesn't even know Jerry, Arielle. She saw someone leaving her place of business who looked as though he was badly hurt, thought it might be Jerry, and looked for him for the past several days."

"What place of business is that?"

Laird felt his mouth get cottony. "It was a short meeting, less than ten minutes. I wasn't going to make her stand in the doorway. She didn't tell me what business she's in."

"All right then—what's her name?"

The folded-up paper in his pocket with Bria's name and phone number on it was burning a hole in his thigh. He said, "She didn't tell me that, either."

"She was some damn hooker, wasn't she?"

"You think I'd be with a prostitute? Jesus Christ, Arielle!"

Arielle gasped, and when she let her breath out, the tears came with it. "Damn you, Laird, you cheat on me in my own house."

"If you think I cheated on you and lied about it—I hesitate to point out I pay the mortgage on your house, Arielle, and the phone, the utilities, and the Internet. I also buy most of your clothes. I buy the groceries. I could be by myself in an apartment. I chose to live here with you because I care about you. If you think I'm fucking a hooker right here in the living room the minute you leave the house? Well, I can move out tomorrow."

"Oh, shit!" she howled. "I'm going to be left alone *again!*" Her sobs turned into wails as she covered her face with her hands, rushed from the room, and pounded up the stairs. He counted to four before he heard the bedroom door slam.

The apartment Jill Taggart lived in for the past six months was smaller and crappier than the one she'd inhabited before. She'd been hustled into this one by Marshall Ruttenberg because she made a mistake. Now she's forced to share it with a big, tough female enforcer on Ruttenberg's staff, Barbara Hogan, who made sure she never left the building alone. That apparently was Barbara's only job,

On Jill's three-week vacation visit to Cincinnati, she'd turned over her drug sales to her boyfriend, Jericho Paich. When Paich was busted by the Cleveland cops, he refused to give up her name—pretty heroic of him, at the time—so they made him into a ratfink, selling dope to other people and then turning them over for jail time.

That left Jill with about fifteen grand owed to Ruttenberg, plus his loss of her sales in the future—and the big-time drug supplier got even—and worse.

Jill was moved to her lousy apartment, forced to quit her day job, and against her will was now a fairly expensive hooker, sent to visiting dignitaries or good local friends when Marshall Ruttenberg chose to. She never saw trick money, either, except whatever Ruttenberg decided to give her with which to buy food and to keep up her classy prostitute wardrobe.

He wouldn't even spring for anything but the lowest-priced cable TV.

Jill Taggart was just a slave—and she knew it.

On the same night Bria Harstad visited the Arielle Paich home, Jill let herself into her apartment, feeling dirty, exhausted, and aching all over. Her trick that night was a visiting alderman from the north side of Chicago who tilted the scales at three hundred pounds. His weight had squished her, his piss-tasting dick nauseated her, and since before she left for Cincinnati six months earlier, the last man she had sex with who was less than fifty-five years old was Jericho Paich.

She removed her shoes, peeled off her thigh-high nylons and tossed them into the middle of the living room, and sprawled onto the cheap sofa. How did she ever wind up being a professional whore, sleeping with anyone she's ordered to? Why do strange men pay large amounts to fuck her, yet she has nothing in her pocket or in the bank?

She couldn't run away, even if Barbara Hogan looked away long enough. She had no place to go in Cleveland; she didn't have enough money to buy an airline ticket to her parents in Cincinnati, and most dangerously, Marshall Ruttenberg was a far-reaching drug power, and could track her down damn near anywhere she could reach on the money she had in her purse. If that happened, the chances of her remaining alive were slim. She didn't want to be a hooker—but she didn't want to be dead, either.

Ruttenberg was physically hideous, especially naked, and mean as a snake. While peddling his merchandise, he sometimes asked her to service him sexually, too, even while she was living with Jerry Paich—but ever since he'd turned her into a whore, he was no longer carnally interested in her. Thank God, she thought, for small favors.

Now under his control, she was forbidden to contact anyone she knew—not even Jaimie Peck, her girlfriend—the first one to whom Jerry had sold meth, then fingered her for arrest. But Jaimie had no way of reaching her or even looking for her. She had no land line phone in this sleazy apartment, and her cellphone was new, and checked twice a day by Barbara or one of Ruttenberg's other hoodlums. They had been confiscated and thrown away her old phone.

Eventually, after downing three shots of cold vodka straight, no ice, she removed the rest of her clothes and took the hottest possible shower, scrubbing herself hard all over to eliminate the smell and feel of the man who'd just fucked her, until the water cooled off and made her shiver. Putting on pajama pants and a T-shirt—hardly what a high-class call girl wears to bed—she lay down on the sofa, clicking on the TV. Ruttenberg paid for the cheapest cable package, so she had little more than the four major networks to keep her attention—and she dozed off as she did every night, waking only when news shows no one ever watched at 3 a.m. loudly announced some "breaking political story," which happened several times per day.

Her sleep was, fortunately, dreamless. Her turned tricks a hundred times in the past six months were depressing memories. The rough ones, the hitters, were the worst. They wanted her to be submissive, slapping her face hard while she sucked them, pulling her hair, choking her and hitting her breasts, demanding she beg. There were the opposites, too—the masochists who liked to be tied up and hurt, whipping them, kicking them in the balls with her high heels, insult them, humiliate them. One of them demanded she throw oranges at him while she cursed him. That was more gross.

Most were stomach-churning, even ones just wanting to get laid and fantasizing. She wanted them as much as they wanted her. They never realized how they repelled her.

After work, getting home, she tried to forget, drank too much and created her own fantasies—the good ones to help her forget what strange men did to her. But getting drunk before closing her eyes made nighttime fantasies difficult, if not impossible.

Instead, she cried herself to sleep at the thought of the enormously obese old fart, his fat belly drooping down so low she couldn't see his dick when he was standing up, his wobbly man-tits, his wide hairy ass and massive cottage-cheese thighs squishing her into the mattress in his hotel room.

Jericho was in terrible trouble with the police, as he refused to tell them she was the drug dealer, not him. Honorable—but maybe if he had turned her in, she'd be in jail now and not doing what she did.

Her last thought before she fell asleep was probably jail would have been better.

CHAPTER SEVENTEEN

Jerry Paich went back to work in the morning, still limping, unable to eat much more than cooked oatmeal or chicken broth, still doubled over due to his cracked ribs grinding against each other. He told his boss after the attack he'd fallen down the stairs in his apartment building. "No stairs carpeted," he said, "so I really got banged up." His boss didn't know he lived on the first floor.

In a way, he was lucky the two guys smacking him around—for too damn long, he thought—had made a point not to touch his face, or he wouldn't have been able to leave the house for another two weeks. The rest of his body was red and blue and purple from the bruising. The hell of it was, he'd never laid eyes on Marshall Ruttenberg before, and he struggled to think doing Jill Taggart a favor had thrown him into a four-way nightmare. The mean cop, Keegan Mayo, jerked his puppet strings and watched him dance. Ruttenberg would kill him if he couldn't raise the money he didn't owe, anyway. He'd poked the wasp's nest at the Italian crime mob—and his mother's live-in black boyfriend was now pissed off at him.

Co-workers secretly thought falling downstairs was the biggest event in Jerry Paich's entire life to date. He was a quiet guy who didn't hang out with them for drinks after work, but went right home. None knew what he did on his own time, not realizing he survived at the end of Keegan Mayo's very short chain, nor Ruttenberg's demand to return the money given to the police would end up with a worse punishment than a beating.

He was drowning in water too dark and too deep. How could he get out of this mess and keep himself from going to prison? How can he survive when Ruttenberg found out he couldn't repay him?

And what happened to Jill Taggart in the first place? Had she come back from visiting her parents in Cincinnati? She'd not contacted him, and her phone had been turned off. He'd called her friends, those she had known in college, but not one had the foggiest idea of what happened to her.

Had he done right approaching John Malatesta? Did John ask his father for help? Is he, Jerry, in good favor of the Malatesta family, or in danger?

When he returned to his mother's house the night before, Laird told him about a strange woman who showed up looking for him. Now, on a coffee break, he studied for the fiftieth time the note she'd asked Laird Janiver to pass on to him, along with her home phone number.

Who the hell was she? And what kind of name is Bria?

Cuyahoga County Commissioner Francis P. Murgatroyd had not eaten in the historic Karl's Inn of the Barristers in years, though the restaurant had been around for many decades. It was on West Third Street, across from the hulking edifice that housed the main Police Headquarters, the City Jail, the Sheriff's Office, and most Cleveland courts. From the Inn, it was only a short stroll from Lake Erie. Many lawyers and judges lunched there on a regular basis, though Franny worked in his county office several blocks away. The Inn of the Barristers was one of those downtown places where most diners were involved in the law.

It was past noon, and Franny was enjoying his pre-lunch cocktail—Jim Beam and soda—waiting for his invited guest. But Bria Harstad, inquiring for Marshall Ruttenberg about the background and lifestyle of Jericho Paich had awakened Franny's curiosity. Since he always forced his assistants at county headquarters to do what little work he was supposed to be paid for, he had all the time in the world to call around and ask his own questions until Jerry Paich's name had rung a bell somewhere.

Thus, his luncheon guest.

Detective Keegan Mayo stormed in as though a strong wind blew him through the door—but that was how he entered every room. Posing in the entranceway, he looked around as if the place might be full of bad guys and he'd have to begin a shoot-out. Finally spying Franny in a corner booth, he waved, opening his jacket so his shoulder holster and police weapon showed to all what a big tough guy he was, he hitched up his pants as though his belly was twice as round and protuberant as it actually was, and walked over.

This was his first meeting with Murgatroyd, but a county commissioner—one of only three—gets his photograph in the papers and often appears on local TV news, so Mayo recognized him at once.

Their handshake was brutal—two chunky middle-aged Irishmen, each trying to prove who had the strongest grip. Arm wrestling might well have been the next contest. Evidently ending in a draw, the men broke contact and sat down.

"What do you drink, Detective?" Franny asked.

Mayo shook his massive head. "Don't you watch TV cop shows? I'm on duty."

The commissioner cackled. "I'm on duty, too, but no one ever stops me. That's what's so nice about being your own boss, like I am." He waved his empty glass at the waiter. "I suggest the corned beef. Best in town, y' know."

Mayo wrinkled up his nose as if he'd just smelled something toxic. He'd heard of "the best corned beef in town" about several Cleveland-area deli restaurants, such as Jack's, Slyman's, or Corky and Lennie's, and frankly he wasn't that crazy about the Irish dish anyway, other than the corned beef and cabbage dinner his mother used to make every Saint Patrick's Day. "If I go to a sit-down place for lunch, I like a white meat chicken sandwich," he said. "*White*—unless they use turkey in that shit and swears it's chicken."

"You work right across the street," Murgatroyd said. "Don't you ever have lunch here?"

"No. If I'm hungry, I grab a couple a sausage sandwich or a Polish boy from one of the stands on the street. I'm too busy arresting dope pushers and putting them in jail."

"Right. Well, I want to talk to you about one of those dope pushers, if that's okay."

Mayo squinted his right eye half-shut as he glared at his lunch partner. "Your boss is Cuyahoga County. Mine is the City of Cleveland. That's head-butting time."

"True," Murgatroyd said, "but from how I look at it, you and I are both good guys."

"Except I have no idea what you want, or why you invited me to lunch in the first place. You got some secret letch for cops?"

"I got a request from a friend to research a drug dealer you're very familiar with."

"Very familiar with?" His tone was insulting, mocking. Murgatroyd's manner of speaking bespoke a college degree, and that ground Mayo's guts, as he'd barely finished high school.

"His name is Jericho Paich."

At the mention of the name, Keegan Mayo's face lost all expression, as if someone had made a death mask of him.

"So?"

"I hear he's your C.I.—a confidential informant."

"And you hear that where?"

Franny shrugged. "Around."

"And who wants to know?"

Again, "Around."

"I *ask* questions, commissioner—and I always get damn good answers."

"Me, too, Detective—and I'm a commissioner.

The waiter brought Murgatroyd's drink and asked if they had decided on food.

"Corned beef on rye for me," Franny said, "and a chicken sandwich for the officer here." Then he added, "On white bread."

"On rye bread!" Mayo snapped. "Not white bread, rye bread—the kind with seeds. White bread sucks! Throw in French fries, too—I like 'em well-done, nice and crispy. And make goddamn sure it's chicken and not turkey, or I'll send it back to the kitchen."

Franny tried not to cringe. Mayo's reputation was being a mean, tough cop, which in some circles is admired. Meeting him made Franny consider him a major asshole. He said, "I got all I could with my phone calls—including Jerry Paich's late father was a big donor to the local Republican Party."

Mayo's laugh was staccato. "Republicans in Cleveland? There's no such thing. But this Jericho is a C.I., thanks to me. Check my arrest record. It's jumped thirty percent in the last six months, and most of that is because of him. He does a good job for me, and it's gonna stay that way."

"For how long?"

"For as long as I say."

"You don't sound like a cop. You sound like an emperor."

Mayo growled, "If I could, I'd take an AR-15 and blow every goddamn drug pusher straight to hell—but that's not legal." He lowered his head, his jaw jammed out as far as he could. "Not yet."

"Look, we're on the same side here."

"I'm on *my* side, Murgatroyd."

Franny sucked his drink, his heartburn attacking him even though he'd not yet had his corned beef. Then he nodded—sagely, he hoped. "I'm getting you, Detective. What's in it for you?"

Mayo slumped back in his chair, a smile playing across his

lips and looking much more like a sneer. He folded his hands over his stomach like a crewcut Irish Buddha. "I'd have to think about that a minute."

The commissioner glanced at his watch. "You *have* one minute. Then I'm out of here."

"You're the one who set up this meeting—not me." His tone grew supercilious. "You're a political hack, pal, but don't get bent out of shape about it. I know it and everybody else knows it, but you get votes because you're a jolly Irish alkie, making sure all the potholes get fixed in Irish neighborhoods. Negotiating is everything in politics. So—you want help, I'll give you help. For a price."

Francis Murgatroyd's heart raced. "Political hack" was an insult, but he had to reluctantly agree it fit perfectly. He'd served on the county commission for nine years, had power and connections to get things done when the right people asked him to, and in all that time, he'd never greased the skids for anyone without receiving something in return.

Quietly he asked, "What *is* the price, Mayo?"

"Listen carefully. Jerry Paich is none of your goddamn business! You think I treat him bad? Tough titty! I'm a cop and he's a lawbreaker, and I'll treat him any way I want!" He sniggered, pleased with himself so far. "You get your nose out of it—and while we're at it, forget you ever heard my name. It has nothing to do with your job or the county."

Murgatroyd breathed loudly through his nose. "Are you finished?"

"Not even close. You've nosed around getting information on this Paich punk. Why? Who asked you in the first place?"

"I promised I'd reveal no names."

"Then fuck you!" the cop growled. "I don't care about your promises. If you want something from me, you make promises to me and nobody else."

"You're asking a lot."

"I need a lot—at least a lot more than a crappy chicken

sandwich—and by the way, I asked for rye bread with *seeds*! There's no seeds in this shitty bread." Mayo lurched forward, taking Murgatroyd's forearm too tightly. "Listen! Paich's mother lives with a nigger who talks like a white man. He had the balls to come to my office and beg me to let his whore's bastard son walk free—and that'll cost me money and arrests. He doesn't live in Cleveland proper, which means I can only fuck with him so much. I work for the city, and he lives in Shaker Heights. You're the commissioner, whatever the hell that means. So whatever you got to do, keep him outta my face!"

Francis P. Murgatroyd was nearly paralyzed into silence. He pulled his arm from Mayo's grasp and drank down the last of his drink, realizing he'd had too many. He took a few moments to get his thoughts in order. Then he said, "Is that all?"

"Somebody set you up to find out about Jericho Paich—and somehow, that brought you to me. I want to know who it is."

"I've already said I can't reveal that."

"You can't, huh?" Keegan Mayo took a cop notebook from his inside jacket pocket and thumbed through it. "Well, I did a little research, too. That's what police detectives do." He flipped a few pages. "Research on you, Murgatroyd. Ah, here we go. First off, your social evening history sounds exciting. You eat dinners in places like Johnny's Downtown, Lola, Giovanni's, Morton's—and you never pick up the tab. Your rich business buddies ask you for favors—the ones you know how to grant. A construction company built you a poolside bath house next to your swimming pool about four years ago that probably cost eighty thousand bucks. But you paid them five thousand, didn't you? How is it they've gotten all the county's construction deals from then on? Four or five times a year you go to Las Vegas, and someone pays for your plane tickets and hotel rooms—to say nothing of sexy adolescent hookers running in and out of your room all day and night, high-class, gorgeous broads getting three or four thousand bucks per trick. You never pay for them, either."

Detective Sergeant Mayo closed his notebook and slipped it back into his pocket and grinned broadly, because Franny Murgatroyd's face had gone from flushed red to pallid white. "There's more here, but I don't want either of us getting bored."

Franny's drink glass was empty. Desperately, he waved it in the air for the waiter's attention.

"You oughta cut down on that a little," Mayo said. "It's still lunchtime, y' know."

"Jesus, Mary and Joseph," Franny mumbled.

"Don't worry. The notebook stays in my pocket—maybe. Or it might end up on the desk of some city reporter at the *Plain Dealer,* and at all the local news stations in town. It's up to you."

The waiter arrived with Franny's drink, and both men stopped talking until he went away again. Then Mayo said, "I'm being unfair, right? You invite me to lunch and now I make all the demands. So it's your turn. What did you want to know about Jerry Paich?"

Francis P. Murgatroyd half-emptied his glass in two long gulps. Then, gasping, he said, "When you arrested Paich, he must have been working for someone here in town."

Mayo nodded. "I didn't figure the little putz was a drug kingpin, now, did I?"

"But he wouldn't tell you who it was."

"No."

"He wouldn't even give you the name of who got him to fill in," Francis Murgatroyd said. "That's why you hang onto him, making him inform on young people he sells to."

"Recreational drugs are illegal, Commissioner—and my job puts away people who do illegal things."

"But you have an idea."

Mayo nodded. "Of course. I'm a drug cop."

"All I want is for you to tell me who he worked for before he started working for you."

"Sorry, pal, I can't just guess. I play strictly by the book. So you bought me lunch for nothing." He bit into his sandwich and chewed thoughtfully. "Not bad. It's really chicken. I gotta start eating here more often."

"Are you aware of someone around town named Marshall Ruttenberg?"

The chewing slowed down as Mayo's forehead wrinkled. He said, "I've heard the name. Why?"

"Just wondering, that's all."

"You're a county big shot and I'm a dumb cop, so you know more about this Ruttenberg than I do."

"He's a businessman. Imports."

"Great," Mayo said. "If I want a Persian rug, I'll give him a jingle." He held up his hand, his thumb close to his ear and his index finger pointing at his mouth as if pantomiming talking on the telephone.

"He imports lots of things," Murgatroyd admitted. "Even Persian rugs."

"I don't need a rug." Mayo swung his legs outside the booth. "I gotta get back to work. Thanks for lunch. This is a memorable day. You're picking up a meal check all by yourself." He stood up, waved to the waiter, and marched across the room to the door. Then he stopped, turned back to Murgatroyd, and loudly said, *"Ciao!"*

Then he was gone, leaving Franny alone, humiliated and steaming.

Keegan Mayo almost danced across the busy street toward police headquarters, trying not to let one of the cars bump into him—although everyone was driving so slowly he would survive a hit with no worse than a bruise.

The commissioner wanted to hear about Marshall Ruttenberg. Why? Mayo would hate if the county commission decided to go after Ruttenberg and shut him down, interfering with his long-running goal to nail Ruttenberg and lock him up forever. He'd not been able to do that so far. If he could become a saboteur—if he could throw a shoe into the slick solid work of the biggest dope pusher between New York and Chicago and wreck it forever—it might mean even more than a lieutenant's gold badge to Keegan Mayo.

It might even mean becoming a captain.

CHAPTER EIGHTEEN

The affectionate relationship between Laird Janiver and Arielle Paich had cooled off more than thirty degrees in less than twelve hours, with no global warming in sight. She couldn't forgive him having a female visitor in the house while she wasn't there—no matter they were doing nothing more than talking about Arielle's son—and he was resenting her insane jealousy and long-held habit of crying at the drop of a hat. Their comings and goings during the next few days were, at best, icy, not even saying good morning or goodnight to each other.

He'd been sleeping on the sofa, which was more his choice than hers. It was awkward for him because he had to remove his prosthetic foot every night and strap it back on in the morning before going upstairs for a shower and having to take it off and put it on once again.

As usual, on Tuesday, Arielle was attending her bridge game at a friend's home. Laird wasn't a bridge zealot, didn't care for the game. Early in their cohabitation, after he'd moved from his downtown apartment to Shaker Heights, he met another couple at a party whose first question was whether he played bridge. At his negative response, the man responded, "Well—we'll just have to list you as one of those nice couples who don't play bridge," another way of saying, "I have no desire ever to see you again."

Laird wanted to answer they preferred to stay home and fuck, but his inbred class and good sense got the better of him. Arielle admitted she liked bridge and shortly became a regular at the Tuesday card parties. There were occasions she held it at her house, and on those nights Laird went out to a movie or sat in a bar watching a sports game.

While she was upstairs primping in front of her mirror, he wandered out into the backyard. It had rained during lunch, and the grass smelled clean—almost rural, despite their home being just ten minutes from busy University Circle, in which there is precious little grass at all.

It was twenty minutes past six, already closed to twilight. He wandered around, occasionally bending down to remove a weed from the lawn, wrestling with a decision that chewed a hole in his gut. He finally drifted into the small wood behind the house where it grew quieter than the busy traffic on nearby Van Aken Boulevard, stopping between two beautiful thick black walnut trees, looking up into the blanket of branches in the hope of seeing a black squirrel or a family of birds. A snowy white barn owl hung out there a lot, but at the moment there was no sign of him. When he could dither no longer, he glanced back to make sure Arielle was nowhere near, then took from his pocket the wrinkled notebook page on which Bria Harstad had scrawled her home number for him.

He considered it a while longer, then took out his cell phone and tapped out the digits.

"This is Laird Janiver," he said quietly when she answered.

Pause, then: "Hello."

"I—need to see you."

Bria Harstad was silent for a bit, her index finger at her lips, but of course Laird couldn't see that. Thoughts jumbled around in her head like gym socks in an electric dryer until she made up her mind. "All right," she said.

Her apartment complex was in the upscale suburb of Beachwood, just off Cedar Road and east of the I-271 freeway ramp. Obviously, the landlords took good care of the property—it was clean and neat, the greenery well pruned and mowed, and many perennial flowering plants, now hiding their colors in this late fall season, slumbered peacefully. Laird Janiver followed signs and arrows indicating Visitor Parking. He wore a blue windbreaker over a patterned sport shirt and Dockers, as it would have been odd for him to put on a suit.

The light of day had nearly disappeared, leaving pink and purple stripes in the western sky, and he slowed to look at the sunset. The colors evoked in him the memory of a two-day-old bruise.

He found Bria Harstad's two-story apartment. Since being discharged from the veteran's hospital minus his left foot, he wasn't crazy about homes with second floors. He could do damn near anything wearing the prosthesis, even running a bit, but when he had to climb a flight of stairs—he did in Arielle's home several times a day—he remembered painfully he was no longer "all there."

His fingertip lingered over the door buzzer, not touching it, afraid of getting a shock that had nothing to do with electricity. He wound up knocking gently instead—four times.

"Good evening, Ms. Harstad."

"Good evening, Mr. Janiver. Come in." She was wearing slim black jeans and a white-and-black-striped pullover shirt with half-sleeves, making her look like a French high school girl in an old movie. When she had visited his home several nights earlier, she'd been dressed for business, her blond hair pulled back. Tonight, though, it was loose, almost to her shoulders. The formal office make-up had been replaced with perfunctory eye-liner and light lipstick. He could smell the shampoo she used—casual but subtle, almost the scent of a Mai Tai—which made his heart flutter. Everyone has different tastes when it comes to a person of the opposite sex; for Laird Janiver, the

Norway-blond Bria Harstad was the woman of his dreams.

Her living room wasn't elegant, but spacious, painted off-white on three sides and a light blue on the fourth wall. Several oils and watercolors hung on every available space, mostly land-scapes, and a close-up of a tiger's head and shoulders behind the sage-colored sofa, signed in pencil by the famous wildlife artist Guy Coheleach. The apartment was neat, unlike most male bachelor pads, but then Laird Janiver's two decades as a Marine field officer had taught him to be tidy and uncluttered, so he felt a bit more at home here.

They stood for a while near the door, not speaking. The silence was deafening. Eventually, Bria said "Won't you sit down?" and indicated the sofa.

He sat at one end, carefully putting his left leg under the cof-fee table in case she happened to notice his artificial foot. She sat at the other end, her legs tucked under her, and halfway turned toward her guest.

"What's up?" she said.

"I appreciate your letting me come by."

She waved the thank-you away. "You have a problem?"

"I think so. The Cleveland Police Department has a target on my back."

"Why?"

"I went to them about Jerry Paich and apparently pissed them off, because I got nailed by Cleveland cops in Shaker Heights for—'weaving while driving.' It was two blocks from where I live. There aren't many Cleveland cruise cars hanging around in the middle of Shaker Heights."

"Well, Bria wondered, "*were* you weaving?"

"Don't be silly," Laird said.

She inhaled loudly through her nose. "I'm sorry to say this, but all over this country, the police stop black drivers five times more often than white people."

"That's not what this was about—not the main reason—but they were careful to explain to me I should quit bothering police,

143

and to stay out of their downtown precinct." His lips tightened angrily around his teeth. "I've never bothered a police officer in my life."

"Did you go to their downtown precinct?"

He told her how he confronted Detective Sergeant Mayo in his office about Jerry Paich—and how Mayo had all but physically thrown him out the door.

She listened quietly, nodding on occasion, frowning along the way—but her eyes never left his face. When he finished, she finally looked away from him, down at her own knees. "Wow."

"Wow indeed," Laird said.

"Did you want a drink or something?"

He wanted a drink desperately. "No, thanks," he said. "I'm good."

She scooted her legs out from under her and crossed one leg over the other knee. "I'm wondering why you're here, Mr. Janiver."

"I—wanted to tell you that story."

"It was nice, but it has nothing to do with me."

Laird's beating heart was somewhere under his chin. "I—I suppose that's true—to some extent."

"To some extent," she repeated, trying not to smile.

"Look, Ms. Harstad, you came to my house the other night with your own questions—your own story. Before that, I'd never laid eyes on you."

"That was because I thought I'd seen your—stepson, I guess—just after he was hurt."

"He's not my stepson," Laird corrected her. "Someone had ordered you to look up all about him—where he lived, where I live. I came here tonight to find out who that was—who wanted to know his story up to the minute."

"I told you, I can't reveal that source. I still can't. And if you recall, I came to your house that night to speak with his mother."

"Oh."

"And she wasn't home."

"I remember."

"I'm guessing," Bria said, "she's not home tonight either."

"Why do you think that?"

"The same reason you wanted to come over here tonight. You wanted to see me again."

His pigment was light enough Bria could see the blush on his cheeks. He finally said, "Yes. I wanted to see you again."

"When you called an hour ago and asked to come over, did you notice how quickly I said yes?"

"I guess I didn't."

"You should start paying closer attention, Mr. Janiver."

Silence, for almost a minute. Then he said, "Am I supposed to leave?"

"Nobody's asking you to leave—or forcing you to stay."

He had difficulty swallowing. "What do we do now?"

Laughing, she said, "We should have made plans ahead of time, I guess." She stood up. "I think we should probably kiss first."

He arose, too, and moved toward her until their faces were very close. Laird had kissed close to two hundred different women over his adulthood, but now, for the first time, he had forgotten how to do it.

She leaned her head back to look up at him, her mouth slightly open. He put his lips to hers, neither touching each other on any other parts of their bodies. Finally, as their tongues flicked, danced, teased, he put his arms around her and pulled her close. Her hand went to the back of his neck, pulling him even closer. Against her breasts, his heart pounded in his chest.

The kiss lasted longer than ever seen in a Hollywood film.

They broke apart. Bria's eyes were still closed as both of them struggled to regulate their breathing. Finally, she looked at him. "My bedroom is on the second floor," she said, taking his hand.

"Wait."

"What?"

"You need to know this—I was a field officer in the Marine

Corps. I was in a truck that set off a bomb and lost my left foot. I wear a prosthesis."

"So?"

"It wouldn't be fair not to tell you before we..." He cleared his throat. "It might bother you—turn you off."

For half a minute, no one spoke. Then she turned and tugged his hand, moving toward the staircase. "I don't plan on fucking your prosthetic foot," she said.

CHAPTER NINETEEN

Nico is a shortcut from the Italian "Nicolai," which came from the Greek name "Nike," who was the mythological goddess of Victory. Nico Brandini long ago got over being stuck with the name of a Greek goddess or an athletic shoe. But he liked the "victory" part.

He'd worked for Don Franco Malatesta since his nineteenth birthday. Before he'd turned twenty-one, the Don had paid for his first two years at Cleveland State University, and he'd earned a partial basketball scholarship for his final two years. He never dreamed of going to college before. He majored in Computer Programming. His work in the cafeteria and the bookstore gave him enough money to pay for half the rent on at least four apartments he shared with the pretty women he'd met in class or just hanging around the college campus.

He loved Franco Malatesta like a father.

He got the job because of his own papa being a mechanic who took exclusive care of the Malatesta's family cars before his heart attack death; they found him sprawled across the engine of the Don's black Lincoln Town Car while he was changing the oil. Nico's full-time job with the family began by working in the garage or at the place where the mob guys hung out—a small house turned into a private club few in town knew about, just across the parking lot from the old man's restaurant.

Six months later, he became the Don's personal driver, and

wound up going to college on Malatesta's dime because one night at Giovanni's Restaurant, an elegant high-class eatery in Beachwood, one of the customers got drunk and began berating the man who was the godfather of the Italian mob in his city, trying to enjoy dinner with two council members. Nico, who sat in the other room at the bar—not old enough to legally drink alcohol except he was one of Malatesta's men and he lived by different rules—rushed in and, twisting the loud customer's arm so far up behind him it nearly broke, marched him out of the restaurant.

He never mentioned what happened between him and the loudmouth in the parking lot, but the fact is there was a fight. The loud customer, a guy in his forties who once played on the Miami of Ohio football team as nose guard, wound up with a sprained shoulder, a flattened cheekbone, two broken ribs, one eye swollen completely shut, and three missing teeth—two on the top and one on the bottom, right in front. Brigandi, on the other hand, suffered gashes on his knuckles from contact with the now-missing teeth. His college major had been techie computer stuff, but he'd studied Korean martial arts since he was twelve years old.

The former nose guard went to the police and swore out an arrest warrant for him, and Nico had spent about seven hours in jail until Don Franco learned of it. The arrest had been quietly quashed by a few phone calls from the family *consiglieri*. Nico didn't even spend ten minutes in court, and all his records at the department quietly disappeared.

There are places in the United States of America where you better pay attention after watching too many gangster movies before openly insulting any Italian citizen, especially if they happened to belong to certain "families." New York City was one of those cities, as were Chicago, Pittsburgh, Las Vegas, and several places in New Jersey.

So were Cleveland and Youngstown in the great State of Ohio.

Don Franco Malatesta's chain of command was altered after Nico Brandini beat up a loudmouthed Italian-hater just outside Giovanni's Restaurant. Nico rose to the inner circle that surrounded the godfather. A muscle guy—his job description—but he was too smart for punches and thumb-breakings. Forcing people into doing what he wanted them to was not only easier, but a lot more fun.

But Nico had a problem with his current assignment.

Detective Keegan Mayo wasn't a guy with whom you could joke or haggle; he'd maneuvered Johnny Pockets into being his target.

And Nico couldn't beat him up badly enough to get him to stop. One does not beat up high-level cops.

One doesn't kill them, either.

More skilled than ninety percent of ordinary people who owned computers, Nico one night looked up all he possibly could on Keegan Mayo.

Now forty-seven years old, Mayo was born in Lakewood, Ohio, just west of Cleveland proper. His late father was a native of Ireland's County Mayo from whence he got his surname. His mother had filled a non-medical job at the sprawling Metro Health hospital until cancer killed her. Two younger sisters and a brother all moved from Cleveland and had gone elsewhere in the country.

Keegan Mayo had been in the Cleveland Police Department for twenty-four years. Nico figured he was ambitious, aiming for the big Three-O, and wanted to retire as a full lieutenant. Five feet eleven inches tall, weighing approximately two hundred forty-five pounds, he'd lived in his late parents' home on East 107th Street until the house grew too lonely for him. For the past eight years he'd rented an apartment in a building converted from a one-family household in Tremont, close to downtown, and he probably couldn't afford the rent on a cop's salary, meaning he was on the take from somewhere, or probably from a lot of somewheres.

He had never married.

How could Nico catch Keegan Mayo "in the act?" Doing the act of *what*, he wasn't certain. Cops like Mayo took bribes, but who on the force would accept the report? They probably all took schmooze in one way or another—either cash money, a bottle of superb whiskey, some expensive sports shirts, a dinner out at a great restaurant, maybe even a pair of tickets to a Browns game close to midfield? Par for the course, especially when one rises above the rank of foot soldier pounding the streets.

Outright theft? Possibly. If a police squad raided the home of a crack dealer and ten thousand dollars in tens and twenties were lying around from the most recent delivery, cops getting rich quick was possible, as the street warriors split the pot and the bad guys wouldn't be believed.

Nico Brigandi regretfully closed the computer. He must give the problem more thought tomorrow when he was fresh and eager. He checked his watch. Almost seven o'clock. He planned to visit his girlfriend, and he'd run his problem by her. Courtney Holloway was thirty-two, a few years older than he. Divorced and a well-paid electrical engineer, she was pretty, more sparkly than any other engineer alive, and very bright, very sharp. Her hobby on the weekend was trudging through the Emerald Necklace, the string of green Metroparks encircling Greater Cleveland, taking her expensive camera with her to shoot photos of birds and flowers. Nico had gone with her twice before they both accepted he wasn't an outdoors kind of guy. Her Bedford Heights home was thirty minutes away from where Nico lived, just off Murray Hill in Little Italy. Maybe she'd get an idea.

He knocked on her door. They'd been lovers for over a year, and he slept over at her house at least four nights a week, but still had not exchanged house keys.

Courtney's nine-year-old son, Ian, opened the door. "Hey, Nico," he said, and they shared a fist bump. Behind him in the living room, *Wheel of Fortune* was the entertainment of the moment. Each time he caught a bit of it on early evening TV, Nico marveled the show's glamorous hostess, Vanna White, still looked drop-dead gorgeous after being on the program for thirty-nine years, never wearing an outfit more than once. When she began taping that show, neither he nor Courtney had been born yet.

"How's it going, kiddo?" Nico said. "Are you watching that crap and not doing homework?"

"I did it already."

"You sure?"

Ian regarded him with nine-year-old amusement. "You want to check it over for mistakes?"

"I'm too tired to correct your school papers. Where's your mom?"

"I think she's taking a shower."

"Great," Nico said, going to the refrigerator. "Want a beer?"

"I tasted some once." Making a monster face. "Gross!"

Nico took out a Dos Equis. Courtney didn't like beer, but bought Dos Equis for him. He twisted off the top. "What's for dinner?"

"Spaghetti and meatballs."

He grinned. "You know why that is, kiddo? It's because I'm Italian."

"Gimme a break," Ian said. "And quit calling me kiddo. You know my name, right?"

"I know your name, sure. I just can't pronounce it. Ee-yan? Eye-yan? Ain?"

"That's also because you're Italian. Hey, guess what?"

"How many guesses do I get? Three? Or is it only one? Come on, we have to negotiate before I guess."

"You're such a dumb-dumb!" Ian scoffed. "Our class is putting on a Nativity Play for Christmas—you know, like in the manger? Guess what part they gave me."

Nico said, "The second donkey from the left?"

Ian growled and hurled himself on Nico, windmill arms landing belly punches.

"Okay, okay!" Nico said, chuckling and holding him at arm's length. "All right, you're not playing a donkey. I bet they gave you a big part. I bet you're playing Baby Jesus—although how you're gonna fit in that little tiny cradle, I have no idea."

Frustrated but having a great time, Ian shouted, "I'm gonna be Joseph!"

"Jesus's father?"

Ian nodded proudly.

"That's a hell of a part to play," Nico said, not mentioning Joseph rarely had any lines to say—not did he remind Ian that Joseph was not really the father of Jesus. Also, though Ian was too young to understand it, some day in the distant future Nico would explain to him that during his life, Joseph never got laid.

"I always wanted to be an actor, Nico." Now the boy was more serious. "I watch lots of television and go the movies when I can—and I know I could play any part."

"You want to be the next Spiderman? You've got a great imagination, I'll say that for you." Nico pulled the boy toward him and gave him a quick, rough hug. "So, twenty years from now, when you win an Oscar, will you save a ticket for me? I'll even sit way up in the back to watch you."

"Come on!" the boy said, but his face glowed.

They were still laughing when Courtney Holloway came downstairs, her face without make-up, her medium-long, slightly damp hair pulled back in a high ponytail. Her Cavaliers T-shirt looked great on her. The tight jeans looked even better.

"Hey, Court." Nico came over to kiss her, his beer in one hand, but she turned her mouth away and gave him her cheek to kiss. "Lips that touch Dos Equis shall never touch mine," she grinned.

"How about lips that touch spaghetti and meatballs?"

"That's different. Let's eat."

After dinner, Ian was put to bed, and Nico and Courtney

cuddled up on the sofa with cognacs, listening to creative jazz music—the iconic Bill Evans on piano—that wouldn't keep the kid awake.

"Ian is bright as hell," Nico said. "Quick, sharp and funny. He'd make a hell of a stand-up comic. Or an actor. He wants to be an actor—for serious."

"All his good genes," Courtney said, "he got from his mother. He hasn't even seen his father in more than three years. Just birthday cards from Chicago, sometimes with a twenty-five dollar check—but not always."

"That means his dad is a bigger fuck-up than ever. Why he ever left you, I have no idea." He pulled her a bit closer. "Are you aware you have the best ass of any electrical engineer in the world?"

"Electrical engineers in my office are so damn busy reading tech stuff and diddling around with calculus and trigonometry that none of them bother looking at my ass."

"That's why I never become an engineer," Nico said, kissing her hair. "How was your day?"

"Ninety percent dull, as usual." She elbowed him lovingly. "My only excitement is hanging out with a hot-looking movie-star type who actually works for the Mafia."

"Court," he snapped, "I keep telling you, it's not the Mafia. There's no Mafia anymore. I work for Mr. Malatesta since I was a teenager. I do what he asks me, driving him wherever he wants to go. Everything else I do is mostly legal. The Italian group hasn't killed anybody for forty years. Besides, even in old Cleveland days, the mob murdered each other, not anyone else."

"I know about old Cleveland," Courtney said. "Italians are famous—but Danny Green was Irish and Shondor Birns was a Hungarian Jew. They blew into a million pieces when their cars got bombed."

"They were both criminals, too."

She said, "Are you after some criminal today?"

"Not hardly. But Don Franco asked me to keep an eagle eye out on a miserable cop."

Courtney stiffened. She sat up and pulled away from him. "Don Franco? *Don* Franco. Jesus, Nico,"

He just shrugged. "That's just what we call him."

"I don't care what you call him—but going after a police officer? That's bad shit."

"I won't touch him. But he's got it in for the Malatesta family—for John Malatesta."

She smiled in spite of herself. "What do you guys call John again? Johnny Pockets?"

Nico nodded a yes. "Johnny never did anything wrong. That's why he runs the restaurant—he's not sharp enough or mean enough to do anything else."

"Then why's this cop out to get him?"

"Maybe he just hates the whole family—or he's just scared shitless of Don Franco."

"So, if you can't kill this asshole or beat him half to death, what exactly *is* your job?"

"That," Nico Brigandi said, "is what I'm trying to figure out."

CHAPTER TWENTY

Laird Janiver left Bria Harstad's apartment a few minutes after ten—had to get home to the "little lady," Bria supposed. She'd put on a flowing white robe after their sex to walk him downstairs to the door, and the breathtaking memory of her in that robe would stay with him forever. After he was gone, she meandered around the living room, pouring herself a double brandy in a balloon glass, and slumped down on one end of the couch.

If nothing else, for her this had been an evening of firsts. The first time she'd slept with an African American man. Her first erotic encounter with an ex- United States Marine. The first time she'd had sex with anyone missing an appendage. She thought of her time in his living room the night before—asking him questions, plus the time the two of them sat in her living room. It added up to forty-five minutes—so fucking a perfect stranger was a first for her, too.

Also, the first time she'd experienced two major orgasms within one hour.

It hadn't been love at first sight for her, nor for him, either. Love at first sight was a made-up fable—like Hemingway's "the earth moved" or Snow White's "Someday my Prince will Come."

Lust at first sight, though, was something else altogether. Both Bria Harstad and Laird Janiver were struck by the same lightning bolt.

Laird was handsome. So were a lot of other men. But from

the beginning, there was a grace surrounding him. Classy, digni-
fied, thoughtful. How many would invite an unknown woman
into their home when the significant other was not around, and
then do nothing in the way of a come-on?

The sleazeballs she'd known in her twenties bored her. When
she outgrew them, she found somewhat older men more interesting and attractive, although she'd never had a romantic relationship that lasted more than six months—closer to six weeks
was more accurate.

That was not counting Marshall Ruttenberg. When he offered
her the managerial position with his company at a salary higher
than she'd ever earned before, she understood an occasional fuck
was part of her job. But in the sack, he disgusted her. His snow-
white body, pink eyes, pregnant-looking stomach and teensy-
weensy dick were not nearly as bad as his gross behavior and
obscene mutterings while he was inside her. After six sessions—
spread out over a few months, thankfully—she told him while
her salary was more than generous, she did a good enough job
in his firm to earn it without balling him, too, and if the sex
demands continued, she would leave. Ruttenberg, who on his
best day was a major asshole, was too wise to lose a great office
manager and all-around fixer just for his occasional use of her
body, beautiful as she was. There were a gazillion women all
over the place for a man with that much money to take to bed.

He still sometimes suggested a blow-job, just to see if she
might change her mind, but the thought of doing that with him
made her gorge rise. She always refused, and for nearly two
years, sexual enjoyment came only from two expensive dildos,
and on a very few occasions a set of ben-wa balls she'd purchased at a sex shop on the far west side of Cleveland where no
one would know her.

As for Laird Janiver, he was the strong, silent type who took
upon himself the problems of his girlfriend's son, which made him
a pretty decent guy. Bria always had problems getting involved
with men who had wives at home. In her twenties, two married

men had been "six-weekers," both ending badly. Laird wasn't actually married, but he was cohabiting with Arielle Paich, and that placed him solidly into her no-no category—or she thought he did, anyway.

To Bria, however, there was more to him than just a great lay, and it drove her crazy trying to figure out what it must be. Possibly her concern for the abused young man she thought was Jericho Paich had driven her to seek Laird out in the first place, which meant her high-paying job with the Ruttenberg troll was in the home stretch, nearing its end.

If Laird calls her again, will she see him? Should she call him instead? She wrestled with that decision in her mind while she finished the double cognac, and wound up falling asleep on the sofa and not waking up, stiff neck and a full bladder, until four o'clock in the morning.

She went upstairs to finish her night, crawling into the bed she and Janiver had torn apart earlier that evening. His scent remained on the tangled-up sheets and rumpled pillows.

She slept fitfully, and when she finally awoke at seven in the morning, she barely remembered the dreams she'd had—but most of them featured Laird Janiver.

It was shortly after two in the afternoon. Even though the senseless beating had taken place several days earlier, Jerry Paich still ached in almost every joint. It was difficult for him to be at his desk for any length of time, even harder to stand or sit without the help of sidearms on a chair. He assumed he'd be pissing blood for a month.

Until that brutal day, Jerry had never heard of the albino drug king who ordered his punishment. Now he was certain unless he came up with a large chunk of money, they would kill him. It sounded like a diagnosis for incurable cancer, that he should go home and get his financial assets in order. Fatal diseases give the sufferer time, but Jerry was certain he would not survive more than a week.

Twitchy, unfocused, worried crazy, he needed to get up from his desk and go outside for a few minutes, breathe in some fresh air, and try to come up with a solution.

Leaving his suit jacket on the hanger in his small space, he walked in rolled-up shirtsleeves toward the reception office, telling the young woman who sat at the front desk he'd only be gone for two minutes.

He never got outside. About to open the glass door to the front of the building, he glimpsed two men sitting in a parked car, waiting for him to come out. He actually felt his knees knock together. The overcast day offered no window glare to obscure the identifiable faces of the men who had attacked and beaten him under orders from Marshall Ruttenberg.

Skinny and the Wrestler.

He backed away in terror. The receptionist looked up at him, concerned.

"Is there a problem, Jerry?" she asked.

He looked around frantically, as if sadists would bust through the glass door at any moment. He battled to get himself together enough to say, "No—just taking a short walk—but I have too much work to do." He turned and walked back toward his office.

Instead, he ducked into the men's room, bolted himself into a stall, and stood there, vibrating all over, terrified while he was hiding in the john, those guys might walk into the building to get him.

He vacated the stall, splashed his face with cold water, and headed to his office. He didn't stay long, but put on his suit jacket and trench coat, and made his way toward the rear door, used only for deliveries and for maintenance people who come to clean up at night to take out trash to put in the Dumpster.

Careful no one watched him, he scooted out the heavy steel door and found himself at the rear of the building. The street on which his company was located had small plants and offices of many other smallish businesses, so there were Dumpsters up and down the area.

Behind all the buildings was a stretch of well-barbered lawns about fifty feet deep before the grass turned into a thick stand of tall wild trees, including a few weeping willows, all halfway to losing their leaves. Jerry figured he'd be safer in the woods where no one would see him.

What happens when someone noticed he had disappeared? What would his boss think, seeing his car still parked in front of the building? He'd explain later—if he had to.

Looking over his shoulder to confirm he wasn't observed, he half-trotted toward the tree line. As scared as he was, he had no idea what he'd do when he got there. Lots of vegetation was available behind which he could hide—pin oaks, mostly, and slippery elms, shagbark hickory—and there are few places in Ohio where one does not find buckeye trees and its yield gave The Ohio State football team its nickname.

Hiding, though, was not an option. He had to get out of there, go somewhere safe, and being a city boy all at once adrift in a mini-forest, he was truly nervous about the animals who left their dens and lairs after the sun went down—groundhogs, tree rats, predatory owls—even foxes or coyotes. He didn't want to be murdered, but was also frightened of being bitten.

It had rained hard during the night. What was not covered by thick, untended grass was pure mud. His mind worked overtime. What was on the other side of this stretch of heavily wooded acres? To his right, at least half a mile away, was a spread-out shopping plaza, with a restaurant, bar, health food market, several small shops, and a large parking lot crowded with cars of rich suburbanites willing to pay upscale prices on salubrious items they swore made them feel better.

To his left, not as far away, was a Cleveland Clinic building—one-fifteenth the size of those on the clinic's main campus on the east end of downtown. However, it was on a well-trafficked road off the OH 422 freeway and across the street from a Stauffer's factory and Nestle's water distribution plant.

Jerry feared he might be seen while trying to get there.

He kept his cell phone in his coat pocket, so he knew he could call for help—but who could assist him? Laird popped into his head, but to phone him or anyone else from the middle of a timberland, who would park in his company's lot where two tough guys awaited him, was unthinkable.

He couldn't stay in the woods forever. Besides, his anxiety had enhanced his need to pee, too momentarily flummoxed to realize he could urinate against a tree with no one watching.

He checked his watch—still mid-afternoon. There were no messages so far on his cell phone. His hands trembled badly.

One destination was closer than the other made him think he'd be safer in a hospital environment. He turned to his left toward the Clinic, ascertaining he was virtually out of sight amongst the lush greenery.

The birds chirping and squawking overhead jangled his nerves, and the leaves rustling all around him made him believe little animals watched him—some not so little. He knew well coyotes lived just out of sight of humans all over Ohio.

Moving as quickly as he could, low-hanging branches scratched at his face and made tiny tears in his coat, and the mud and other gook on the ground ruined his shoes. His heart tympani crashes inside his chest.

Eventually, after a twelve-minute trip could be finished in five if on a sidewalk or the paved curb of a well-driven road, he emerged from the trees onto the street. Early evening rush hour was beginning, cars heading toward the freeway on-ramp, but he cocked his head away from the moving traffic so no one could recognize him, and pointed his muddy feet toward the Cleveland Clinic.

He carefully glanced at passing vehicles, trying to recall what kind of car Skinny and The Wrestler had, waiting for him to emerge. After everything else, will he be the surprise victim of a drive-by shooting?

November daylight hid behind grayish white clouds, and car

exhaustion weighed heavy on Jericho. Though he walked faster now he was out in the open, it took him five more minutes to reach The Clinic.

He staggered into the lobby, looking shabby, but no one paid him the least attention. People don't get all dressed up to visit a hospital. A woman stood near the elevator with a beautiful white Golden Retriever wearing a coat that said "Companion Dog," and patients coming in or out would stop, pet him, and chat with his owner. The Clinic always accepts volunteers with friendly companion dogs to make visitors feel better.

Jerry didn't care about the dog. He just leaned against the wall, his breaths deep and shaky. Then he took out his iPhone and called a taxi to come get him.

CHAPTER TWENTY-ONE

It grew cooler as the afternoon wore on, and Downtown Cleveland and Public Square, just a stone's throw to the choppy and unforgiving Lake Erie, was crowded with locals—business workers, visitors and daily downtown loafers who'd unearthed their medium weight jackets and sweaters to protect them from the chill wind blowing down from western Canada.

Nico Brigandi wore his overcoat, the only knee-length coat he owned. When winter arrived, he'd zip in the wooly lining to stay warmer. Despite his well-paying job with Don Franco Malatesta, he owned no fancy coat like those worn by the upper-echelon family members milling about him. Don Franco himself was rarely out of his overcoat, except on those ninety-degree days in July and August.

Nico stood across the street from the Justice Center Police Department, studying the revolving door for the appearance of Detective Keegan Mayo, number two man in the drug division. He'd Googled a photograph of Mayo on his MacBook Pro at home and printed it out to carry it in his pocket, making the cop easy to recognize on the street.

He didn't want to appear loitering. Police officers came in and out of the building constantly, along with lawyers, judges, and accused or convicted prisoners and their worried families. He kept sauntering northward to the corner, then coming back. After almost two hours, his feet were hurting, as was his brain—he couldn't decide what to do about Mayo once he recognized him. The Don had given him no advice, thinking Nico smart enough to work it out for himself.

Finally, at a few minutes before five, Keegan Mayo walked out through the revolving door.

No Cleveland blue, he wore an untucked plaid sports shirt and a hideously ugly tie, a lightweight jacket, and blue trousers shiny with age. His brown shoes were slip-ons, perhaps because he was too chunky to bend down and tie his shoelaces. On his head was a Pittsburgh Steelers cap that made him one of the bad guys in a solid Cleveland Browns town.

He jaywalked across the street, passing very close to Nico but never looking at him, and went into the five-level garage in which he parked his car every day. He found his own car on the second level, a four-year-old red Ford Taurus. Being bright red, it was easy for Nico to follow, driving his own 2017 tan Honda Accord.

It didn't take Mayo long to arrive back home in Ohio City, the near west side of the Cuyahoga River, an old neighborhood run down until about twenty-five years earlier when yuppies descended, made costly house repairs, and turned it into a gentrified and fairly expensive community. Mayo lived on the first floor of an ancient house turned into a duplex no one had gotten around to upgrading. The occupants chose it for its relatively low rent, although as a Detective First Class, Keegan Mayo was hardly living on the dole.

The red Taurus parked on the street in front of the building, and Nico pulled to the curb half a block away. Apparently, Mayo had missed the tail behind him all the way from downtown. He had no idea anyone was following him. Still, Nico slumped down behind the wheel, pulling the sun blinder in front of him to help hide his face.

Mayo hauled himself out of the car, straightening his jacket and shirt and wriggling his shoulders to ease the tension. On the sidewalk between the curb and his house, three young boys ten years of age or so were tossing a football around between them. Mayo watched for a while, then stepped forward and intercepted a pass. Since he was at least two feet taller than the kids, his catch made no one think of legendary Forty-Niner Jerry Rice.

The boys whined while Keegan Mayo chuckled, tossed the ball back underhand, and rumpled the hair of the kid nearest him, then walked up the steps and used his key to let himself into the building.

Nico tapped the street address into his iPad and started the engine again, though he didn't move for at least two minutes. He was figuring how he could toss a figurative monkey wrench into Mayo's well-oiled machine and ruin it forever without violence.

He drove around the corner, parked once more, and called Franco Malatesta on his cellphone.

"I followed this Mayo cop home, Don Franco, so I know where he lives. I'm now wracking my brain how we can get to him without turning the whole city into a cop-killer hunt."

"You'll figure it out, Nico," the Don said. "You're smart. I believe in you." A startling observation from a septuagenarian Italian who believed in little other than the Virgin Mary, the Archangel Gabriel, and the first *Godfather* movie with Marlon Brando—not the second one and definitely not the third.

Nico pocketed his phone, leaned back, and closed his eyes. Not expected to create miracles every minute, he'd planned a quiet, loving evening—dinner and a Courtney sleepover.

Long divorced from a man she referred to only as "the bum," Courtney Holloway made a handsome living on her own. She was tall, black hair and blue eyes—a killer combination—and smart enough to figure from the start of the relationship just who Nico Brigandi worked for and what he did.

It didn't seem to bother her. Meeting Don Franco several times, she was charmed by his politeness, his twinkling eyes, and his unfailing admiration for her boyfriend. Besides, she was Italian on her mother's side—her birth name was Maria, changed when she began her profession, because "Courtney" sounded more modern and upscale, so she'd had it for more than twelve years.

On the way to her house, Brigandi had stopped to buy her one long-stemmed rose. After all, she was cooking him dinner.

When she opened the door, she beamed as she took the rose and gave him a deep romantic kiss right there in the doorway. Her son Ian was almost underfoot, on the floor engrossed in TV cartoons, but he'd grown used to watching these two adults kiss, even when he thought it was yucky and gross. When his dad had been around—"the bum" he barely remembered—there was little affection on display.

On this evening, though, he was jazzed at the arrival of his mom's special fella, and leaping to his feet and running to the doorway, he yanked on Nico's arm as he jumped up and down, his excitement overflowing.

"Nico! Nico! Nico! Guess what!"

"You got married?" Nico said. "Or are you going to jail?"

"Naw! We start rehearsals for the Nativity Play next week."

Courtney said, "His class starts rehearsing right away, just so nobody forgets their lines by Christmastime, or where they're supposed to stand."

"Hey, man, that's great! Congrats!" Nico said, and he and Ian high-punched. He really liked the kid—a lot. It was great to have a child to talk to, roughhouse and play with, without all the responsibilities of being a real father. At the moment, though, he forced his enthusiasm, still thinking of Keegan Mayo as his Number One Problem.

Courtney said, "I love the rose, Nicky. I'll put it in water." She disappeared into the kitchen.

The child said, "Will you come see the play, Nico?"

"You know I will, kiddo. Hey, how about the girl playing Mary? Is she cute?"

Ian was shocked and appalled. "That's Jesus's mother!" he said with solemn wonder.

"On the stage, she's Jesus's mother. In real life, she's just some ten-year-old girl in your class."

"Aw. Well, I guess she's sorta cute."

"That's a beginning," Nico said, moving into the middle of the living room and sinking onto the sofa. After standing on the sidewalk for several hours, he just wanted to kick off his shoes—but his mother had always warned him it was gross to take his shoes off while everyone was eating.

Courtney returned with the rose in a slim vase and set it on the dining table, then lit two candles with a Zippo lighter. "The teacher said he was so good at his reading she didn't even bother auditioning anybody else to play Joseph."

"Good for him," Nico said.

"My best friend gets to play one of the Three Wise Men," Ian said.

"Which one?"

"Lindsay."

Nico cocked his head. "One of the Three Wise Men is named Lindsay?"

"No, silly! Lindsay is my friend. He's not my best friend—well, kind of he is—"

"So which one of the Three Wise Men is Lindsay gonna be?"

Ian frowned. "Uh—the one whose name is hard to say."

"Balthazar?"

The kid nodded solemnly. "That's the guy."

"Sit yourselves down, gentlemen. Soup's on," Courtney headed back to the kitchen, saying over her shoulder. "Tell Nico what Mrs. Jonas said to you after you read the part of Joseph." She looked at Nico and winked.

Ian and Nico sat opposite each other. Nico said, "Is Mrs. Jonas your teacher who's directing the play?"

Ian nodded. "You know what she said?" He sat up very straight and inhaled, his chest thrust out proudly. "She said I was a really good actor."

Nico gasped, his eyes widening, as the pieces of a plan suddenly fell into his brain like a just-completed jigsaw puzzle. He was suddenly glad Ian's mom was in the other room and couldn't hear him, because what would come out of his mouth would earn him a bawling-out for cursing in front of the kid.

"Holy shit!" he breathed.

"Where the hell are you?" Laird Janiver was in his home office, reading a book—as he often did—when Jerry Paich phoned him.

Jerry whispered, "I'm home. When I saw those two guys lurking outside my office waiting for me, I sneaked out the back way and called a cab."

"Jerry, if they found you at work, they'll find you at home. Pack up some stuff, quick, and move back here for a while."

"I can't do that. What if they find me there, too? They might hurt mom."

Laird thought, but did not say, they might hurt *him* as well. "Where can you go, Jerry?"

"I don't know. If I did, I wouldn't be calling you."

Laird thought for a moment. His ex-commanding officer, Ayman Kader, was the first name that popped into his mind, but the colonel wouldn't like the uninvited guest. After all, Jericho couldn't just march into the Kader house, bag and baggage, when two possible guns-for-hire were looking for him. And all Laird's so-called buddies down at the American Legion weren't going to cooperate, either.

"Call the police. Tell them the same guys who beat you up so badly are after you again."

"I don't know who the bad guys are, except they work for the freakoid who ordered them to do it. What the hell could I say to the police, especially the one who keeps me a fucking slave selling dope?"

That troubled Laird. He'd already been to see Keegan, who turned out to be one kick-ass mean son of a bitch. "Pick a motel, then, far away from your neighborhood."

"I can't afford staying in a motel for a week or two. It cost me sixty bucks to get here in a cab, because I had to leave my car at the office. I have nowhere to go."

"I'll cover your motel costs for a few weeks, Jerry."

"I can't accept money from you."

"Then you're dumb. I have plenty."

"How did you get so fucking rich?"

"I went for two whole weeks without my lunch."

Jericho sighed. "Don't tell me, then."

"We're not discussing my money, Jerry. We're discussing saving your stupid ass."

"I'll—I'll just try some of my friends, I guess." The lie weighed like an anvil on his shoulders—because he had no real friends.

Hanging up, he sat there, stewing. He'd always been the studious type, so even when in high school and college, he never really made a friend he could count on when the chips were down. He didn't join his co-workers for a brewski during Happy Hour, rushing home to be with Jill Taggart—and when she disappeared without a trace, a note, a goodbye or even a mercy fuck, he lost interest in finding another girlfriend.

Jill's phones had been disconnected, but the thought of her gave him a tiny idea—and he sure as hell needed one instead of sitting in his apartment with the two-man hunting party expected at any moment. He doubted it would work, but he didn't want to be as dumb as Laird Janiver thought he was and stay where anyone can find him. So he poked his phone a few times until he found the number he was looking for.

"Hello? Hey, is this Jaimie Peck? I hope you still remember me, Jaimie. I'm Jill Taggart's ex-boyfriend? I'm Jerry Paich."

CHAPTER TWENTY-TWO

Laird stared at the phone, thinking what he could do to help Arielle Paich's only son—and whether it would earn him a few points at home, since she was hardly speaking to him—blaming him for inviting a strange woman into her home while she was elsewhere.

Arielle was overly emotional about everything. If Laird didn't absolutely rave over every single meal she'd fixed for him, for instance, she'd burst into tears, run from the room, and it would take several days for feelings to be smoothed over.

Bria Harstad had actually arrived there to talk to Arielle in the first place. What Laird did after that, he figured—seeing Bria at her home and going to bed with her—Arielle *would* deserve it. A kind of payback.

It was more than revenge. Bria had come to inquire whether the man she'd seen beaten half to death might be Jerry, but the chemical combination that happened between them was instantaneous and quite real. After his long career as a Marine when he felt he was married only to the Corps, he'd never had a genuine relationship with a woman until Arielle Paich—which became more rocky each day.

Bria Harstad was certainly beautiful—but in the crazy, now-shrinking world, every woman, despite her looks, appeared beautiful to *some* man, the magical reason so many unattractive people get married, sometimes to those more beautiful than they. Love has no rules and no user's manual. Bria and Laird were drawn together sexually, as if by some spiritual wizardry. To him, Bria was the most exquisite woman he'd seen in his lifetime.

Would they wind up in her bedroom again? Laird thought she was pretty good in bed. Not the best, not even as good as Arielle, whose Italian heritage allowed her unique carnal moves that surprised him. Bria, he felt, was much more than a crazy-good lay. His feelings were not exclusively in his groin. Whatever it was had overtaken both of them.

Bria was not only receptive, but thoughtful. When the ardor was immediate, he didn't really have time to disengage himself from his artificial foot, and when they rolled over and she was atop him, her foot brushed his metallic prosthesis and she asked if he was okay about it. Thoughtfulness existed side-by-side with sensuality, and he was touched by that. Arielle, of course, had never shared her bed with him while he wore the appendage, and actually preferred that he was in bed, under the covers so she wouldn't have to look at the abbreviated leg, or that he removed the artificial foot in the bathroom, entering her boudoir on crutches—which he loathed to use.

He tried to banish all erotic thoughts from his mind, but he needed Bria to open up to him, as she knew more about two men she'd seen with the beaten Jericho between them than she was willing to discuss.

He dialed her without realizing he'd already memorized her phone number.

Bria had been expecting a call from Laird Janiver, but not so soon. Smiling, she answered without so much as a hello. "Horny already, Laird?" she said. Amusement tinged her voice, along with a soupçon of annoyance. "I thought you'd take a few days to figure it out."

"It took me thirty seconds, starting when you rang my doorbell. I'm calling for another reason, though, I don't want to discuss over the phone."

"That sounds serious—and not very sensual."

"Everything sensual is serious with you—but this is more serious than that. May I come over?"

"Tonight? Are you leaving your resident sex partner alone again so soon?"

"She's not here. I don't know where she is, nor do I care."

She laughed softly. "I don't think I've ever known another man who actually says 'nor.' Come ahead, then—and think up more fancy words sounding like a visiting philosophy professor from Harvard. It's a turn-on."

"Give me forty-five minutes," Laird said. He went upstairs and put on a fresh shirt, topped with a black London Fog windbreaker. Then he scrawled a quick note to Ariel and propped it up on the small table near the front door where she always left her keys. "Gone out. Back later. L."

On his drive toward Bria's home, he began wondering where Arielle had gone that evening, anyway. She spent a few nights out and about every week—and all those nights could not possibly be a meeting of her book club. Is she having an affair as well?

As for Bria, he was pulled in two different directions, and was aware of it. It would be hard for him to walk into that condo and not take her directly to bed. He not only lusted after her, but he had already crossed the red line of falling deeply in love.

Still, she wouldn't reveal where she'd witnessed the end of incredible brutality Jerry Paich suffered. Where does she work, and for whom? Laird motored toward Beachwood—a ten-minute drive from where he lived, hoping to cajole, convince, actually beg, or in the end even frighten her into telling him the rest of it.

She opened the door as soon as he rang the buzzer. Denim blue jeans and a T-shirt this time, and knee-high lace-up boots—awkward to take off quickly in order to have sex. Little make-up besides a subtle lip color. Not glamorous at all. Maybe he'd sounded *too* serious on the phone.

"Sit down, Laird," she said, pointing to the sofa. "Want a drink."

"No thanks." He eased himself into one of the easy chairs on the other side of the coffee table.

"Better have one. When you go home tonight, she'll smell booze on your breath and think you were sitting in a bar with your old buddies."

"Whatever." She filled two brandy snifters and gave him one, keeping the other for herself, and sat on the sofa. "Here's looking up your ancestors," she said, and took a sip. "I can't seem to find a handle on why you're here, Laird. If you want to break up with me, if that's what anyone could call it—well, hell, it was only one night. You could have called and left a message—or else just lost my phone number and forgot all about it."

"The last thing I want is breaking up with you, Bria."

She shook her head sadly. "You already have a mistress, Laird. I don't like being a sloppy second."

He swallowed half the cognac in one gulp. It took his breath away momentarily and made his eyes sparkle. "Tonight, this isn't about *us*."

"Then it's about Jericho Paich."

He didn't answer. His nod, though, was subtle.

"This is the third time we're meeting," Bria said. "All have been over your not-really-a-stepson."

"He's a weak-kneed nerd," Laird observed, "but I don't want anything bad happening to him. You don't either, because you contacted me."

"I was trying to reach his mother, but got you instead—and until you opened your door, I had no idea you even existed. So?"

"Jerry called me. Today at his office, he saw the two guys who beat him up waiting for him to walk out the door again."

"I don't imagine he's recuperated from the last beating."

Laird said, "Jerry got the idea they're going to kill him."

Bria carefully touched the top of her chest with her hand.

"Wow!" she breathed. She took a cognac gulp. "Another beating could kill him, anyway."

He jerked his head up and down once.

"So what is it you want from me?"

"The last attack happened in the place where you work."

"I didn't see or hear it, or know anything about it. There are several buildings on the property owned by our company. I've only been inside two of them."

Laird shifted in his chair. His left stump was twitching. "*Your* company," he said. "Exactly what *is* your company?"

"It's not mine. I'm just an employee."

"And who signs your checks, Bria?"

She stiffened her back so she was sitting up straight. Her right hand was on the arm of the sofa, her fingers digging into the upholstery so hard her knuckles were turning white. "I understand you don't want Jerry killed. I don't think you want me to be killed, either—so don't ask."

Laird half-closed his eyes, his forehead lined. "Is it that bad?"

"I manage the office and take care of business correspondence. I send out bills to suppliers, distributors. I make phone calls for the—for my employer. I make sure the office staff works hard. And that's all."

"Do you make sure those two thugs who beat up Jerry work hard, too?"

"I don't know who they are," Bria huffed. "I've seen them wandering around, but we've never talked. They're not there every day unless they've been summoned."

"You mean they're hit men. Hired killers."

"I don't know what they are! Why don't you just call the police like everyone else?"

"Because," Laird said, "I've already been to the police, and they practically threw me out the door."

"Then," she said in frustration, "what the hell do you want from me?"

"I want you to *not* spend the rest of your life knowing Jerry Paich was murdered, and you did nothing to stop it!"

That got Bria Harstad off the sofa in a hurry. She turned and walked to the living room window, but the drapes were closed and there was no need to stand there, except she didn't want to look at Janiver anymore. She hugged herself, shivering. "Damn you for this!" she murmured.

He stood up, moved behind her, putting his hands on her shoulders. "Bria..."

"What?"

"You're the last hope. You know that."

She sighed. "I suppose."

"They're going to kill Jerry."

"He's not your son."

"He's a human being."

"So am I!" She pulled away from him. "Do you really think if I gave away the name of my boss and my company, I'll still be walking around breathing next week?"

"You can be protected, Bria."

"Really?" she said. "And who's going to protect me? You? A middle-aged retired one-legged black Marine who lives with and fucks somebody else?"

He weighed an answer, then decided not to offer it. "I have—contacts."

"The Marines have professional hit men, too."

"Nowhere near. They don't go around killing people—at least not in this country."

"What *do* they do, then?"

"I have to think about that, Bria. I can only say they are on your side because they're on *my* side."

"Knights on white horses running to save me, and all you have to do is wave your magic wand!"

"I don't have a magic wand handy," Laird Janiver said. "But I know somebody who has one."

Her usually full lips almost disappeared, her frown deep and thoughtful. "Do you trust me, Laird?"

He considered that. His feelings about those he'd lived amongst for too many months colored his every thought. "When I was in Iraq, I wouldn't trust any of *them* even if they wore American flag pins, loved our president, and stood at attention all god-damn day long to sing 'God Bless America.'"

"I'm not an Iraqi," Bria said.

"I noticed."

"Does that mean you do trust me?"

"I have to, because—" He stopped. It was too early to say "because I love you." Too damned early. He finally sat back down on the sofa. "Because I just do," he said. "Tell me, okay, Bria? Tell me all of it."

CHAPTER TWENTY-THREE

Jaimie Peck lived in a newer apartment building on the near west side of Cleveland, not too far from Lake Erie but, in Jaimie's opinion, too damn close to the I-90 freeway, as the noisy rumble of passing traffic never really went away, not even in the middle of the night. Still, it was a nice apartment, pleasant view, especially on her small balcony, of a park and trees that at the moment wore their late autumn colors. A spacious bedroom, roomy kitchen, and a pull-out sofa sleeper in the living room made Jaimie feel at home.

A lucky break for Jericho Paich.

When he'd phoned her, all he said was he was in dangerous trouble and needed a place in which to hang out for a few days until things cooled off.

Jaimie was surprised. She hadn't known him well when he was with Jill Taggart. No foursomes with her and her boyfriend joining Jill and Jerry for dinner or a party together. No summer vacations away some place romantic and sexy. The two women met for lunch at least twice a month, and sometimes had a "girls' night" to which males were not invited. At other times, Jaimie and Jerry had pleasant conversations in a happy hour bar or even a hello-or-goodbye hug, but no more. He was simply the guy Jill had hooked up with.

Now, however, after six months of no contact whatsoever, Jerry called Jaimie and asked to sleep on the sofa for a few days because he was in danger. That was strange, since Jerry's own apartment was only twelve blocks away.

He was now sitting on the sofa on which he'd probably sleep, his overnight bag at his feet. She wore sweatpants and a T-shirt in her recliner opposite her TV set, drinking coffee. At a few minutes past nine o'clock in the evening, she was proving to be a twenty-four/seven coffeeholic.

"What in hell happened to you, Jerry?" she asked. "You're moving like you came in second place in a fight."

"I was—mugged," he admitted. "Two guys—hard guys. Tough guys. But they made a point of not touching my face or anywhere it might show." He grimaced, his ribs and shoulders thumping. "I'll get over it, eventually."

"I hope so."

"They couldn't know you and I were even acquainted."

"Well," she said without much enthusiasm, "you can sleep on the sofa until everything gets smoothed over. I hope."

"I hope so, too. I appreciate it. You and Jill were good friends."

Jaimie nodded. "Until she left town to visit her parents and then fell off the face of the earth." Too curious, she cocked her head. "It's none of my business—but why did you and Jill bust up in the first place? She never told me. She just left for Cincinnati and then I never heard from her again."

"I—can't tell you why, Jaimie."

"Why not?"

"Because I don't want to implicate you in anything."

She raised her shoulders, rolling her eyes. "I'm implicated up to my ass, Jerry."

"In what?"

She brought her recliner to the straight-up position. "When Jill was in Cincinnati, you sold me some of her coke? I mean, I used to buy from her whenever I needed it. Remember?"

Jerry's neck hairs stood up straight, and the backs of his hands tingled as though they were falling asleep. He managed to croak, "I remember."

"Well—shortly after that, I got arrested."

Jerry tried to swallow, but couldn't. It was as if he'd just tried to gulp down a tennis ball and it got stuck in his throat.

"The bastard who's a maven in the police drug department told me I'd go to prison for twenty years," Jaimie said, "or else, to save my ass, become a confidential informant—to sell drugs to people and then turn them in to the cops. That's what they call a C.I." She shivered a bit. "What I call it is stool pigeon,"

Jericho Paich grabbed onto the arm of the sofa as if he were in danger of pitching off onto the floor. He was beyond shock. He'd turned Jaimie Peck in and the cops made her a C.I., too.

Of what is he now guilty? he thought.

Treachery.

"I hate this," Jaimie said, "I'm throwing my friends into prison—and in this country, they punish drug users worse than rapists and murderers." She ran both hands through her corn-row hair. "I'm like a fucking slave for the rest of my life!"

Jericho wanted to say, "Me, too," but certainly couldn't confess that, at least not at the moment. He was unable to say anything. He moved to sit next to Jaimie on the couch and put his arms around her for a hug. "I feel so bad for you, Jaimie."

"Don't make me cry," she said haltingly, pulling away from him. "Goddamn it, don't make me cry."

Laird Janiver donned his black microsuede jacket before going out shortly after noon on the following day. Each time the sun went down, the temperature went down as well, and never rose much after that during November. He didn't like to be cold any more than he enjoyed Cleveland's summer heat, but he could deal with winter weather as long as there was no biting wind. He'd read somewhere the best weather in the United States was in San Diego, California. He'd never yearned to live in California, mostly because they got their up-to-the-minute news three hours later than did Cleveland. They say California will one day suffer the worst earthquake in U.S. history, and coastal cities like San Diego and Los Angeles might break off from the mainland and go floating off into the Pacific.

They say. Who were *they*, anyway? Why don't people put their names to their imaginings and fantasies?

Laird called Ayman Kader early that morning to say he'd like to drop by agai—and this time, it was damn important.

Beth Kader wasn't home, but out shopping, or whatever it was most women do during the day when they aren't working. Ayman met him at the door, his alert Doberman at his side. He was dressed in a light blue Calvin Klein sweater over a darker blue shirt and blue slacks. In these days, if not at a formal job like a lawyer, doctor, insurance agent, minister or rabbi, men wore khakis if they were sophisticated and classy, and denim jeans if they were not. However, Kader had been a Marine for thirty years, and much of the time, if he were not in the midst of combat, he wore a summer khaki uniform. Now as a civilian, he preferred almost any other color pants.

"Coffee's on for you," the colonel said.

"I need it." The two men sauntered through the house into the spacious kitchen. "Ayman, did you ever know a Marine who didn't swill down coffee as if life depended on it?"

"That's what makes Marines tough." They sat at a breakfast bar in the kitchen, the Doberman at Kader's feet as he poured Janiver a steaming cup. "It didn't teach them to brew coffee, though, so Beth made a pot before she left." He sipped from his own cup, embalmed with his name, bird colonel rank, and the Marine symbol *Semper Fi.* "So *que pasa*, Laird?"

Janiver hesitated a moment. "You know everybody in town, right?"

"Generals know everybody in town, including the street sweepers. Bird colonels like me only know the important street sweepers. What do you have in mind?"

Laird rubbed his chin. Prickly. He'd forgotten to shave that morning. "I'm thinking the FBI."

Kader's eyes opened a tad wider. "Whoa Nelly! FBI—that's serious, my friend—unless you know somebody who's spying for the Russians."

"Not quite. But I found out who made Arielle's son Jerry into an indentured servant. And besides that, Jerry got horribly beaten up by somebody I think he was working for."

"You didn't tell me that the other day."

"It's happened since then. They never touched Jerry's face, but they beat the hell out of every other place on his body."

Kader scratched his chin. "That sounds like a professional job, not just two guys who got mad at him. Who's this cop who nailed Arielle's son for a confidential informant?"

"Keegan. Keegan something. Big-time drug cop." Laird Janiver screwed up his face, trying to remember. "Keegan Mayo. Like mayonnaise."

"The FBI doesn't mess with cops with confidential informants at their fingertips. Face it, that's how a lot of criminals get caught—by a C.I. turning on him. At the moment," Kader said, "the bureau is more interested in other things."

"Like the man who distributes coke and crack and meth all over the Greater Cleveland area? Summit County, Geauga County, Lake County? A man who has a big professional office and warehouse on his own property?" Laird leaned forward, one hand wrapped around the coffee cup, feeling the warmth. "You think he grows all that shit in his basement without anyone knowing about it? He ships it in, for crysakes! From Mexico, Columbia, from god knows where—even from Afghanistan. I'm talking big time, Ayman—big bucks. I'd think the FBI would be interested."

"Maybe so." Kader pushed his mug away from him. "There are several people who are into that. What's this big distributor's name?"

"Ruttenberg. Marshall Ruttenberg. The name is familiar?"

Kader shook his head. "I don't think I ever heard it before."

Janiver pulled a folded piece of paper from his left pants pocket. "This is where he lives—address and phone number."

With a frown on his face, Kader studied the name and address on the paper. At length he said, "Where did you get this information, Laird?"

Laird thought of Bria Harstad. For the last few days, his thoughts were always of Bria Harstad. He swore not to repeat to anyone the information she'd vouchsafed to him about Ruttenberg and his local drug empire. He said, "Ask me no questions and I'll tell you no lies."

"That's pretty fucking kindergarten!" Kader bit off the words.

"It was a promise."

"What happens if you break that promise, Laird? Does your nose start to grow like Pinocchio's?"

"I won't break a promise, no matter what. You can waterboard me, but this is as far as I go."

"As far as you go for the FBI?"

"As far as I go for giving up the name of the person who offered me the information. If it got out, it would mean—uh—his or her death."

Ayman Kader's lips pursed. "His or her death, eh? His or her."

"Forget it, Ayman."

"What if I forget about the whole thing?"

"Then Jerry Paich dies, Ruttenberg keeps feeding drugs to the population, and you'll feel like an asshole."

"I see." Kader put his hands together in front of him, as if he were praying. "More coffee?"

"I didn't come for coffee," Janiver said angrily. "I came for help."

Ayman Kader looked around nervously, as if there were someone else in the house, even knowing there was not. He lowered his voice to say, "I know plenty of FBI guys, including the local SAC. But when you and I were in uniform, we both made nice little fortunes smuggling sacred Iraqi items illegally."

"We didn't kill anybody while we did it."

"Oh, bullshit, Major Janiver!" Kader's brown eyes flashed with anger. "We were over there in the first place to kill Iraqis. That's what Marines do, what they get paid for—and they never ask why. When they get stuck in stateside duty in some sleepy southern town, it makes them twitch! They want to get a weapon back in their hands."

"Smuggling sacred objects on the black market like we did was not fatal to anybody!" Laird was getting furious, too. "But if someone doesn't do something about Marshall Ruttenberg and his full-blown drug distribution, Jerry will die. The cops are screwing him right and left, and so are Ruttenberg's bully boys!"

He stood up quickly, his stump throbbing, sending phantom pain all the way up to his hip, and leaned forward menacingly over the still-seated Colonel Kader. "So, Ayman—are you going to get the FBI working on this—or not?"

CHAPTER TWENTY-FOUR

Jaimie Peck emerged from her bedroom shortly after eight o'clock in the morning, already dressed for work. Jerry Paich, in a T-shirt and the wrinkled slacks in which he arrived the night before, sat on the pull-out sleeper sofa on which he'd spent wide-awake hours, though sheets and blanket had been neatly folded and put to one side. When he saw Jaimie, he lifted the mug of coffee he'd been drinking in a kind of salute and said, "I brewed some already. Hope that's okay."

"Fine," she said, not meaning it. She moved into the kitchen. "Sleep all right?"

"No," he said, cheeks flushing, "but that has nothing to do with your sofa."

"Want some toast or something? Maybe eggs?"

"Not hungry—but thanks."

She poured herself a mug and walked back into the living room. "Aren't you going to work?"

"I don't have my car here. Besides—"

She took a steaming sip. "Besides—?"

"There was—trouble where I work."

She laughed nervously. "That's what you told me last night. It sounds like a bad movie."

"There were two guys waiting out in the parking lot. They'd already beaten me half dead." He ran a palm over his opposite arm, the bruises having transmogrified from black-and-blue in the last few days to a faded yellow and purple. They still hurt; most of the rest of his body did, too. "Maybe they wanted to do it again—or something even much worse. I had to get out of there."

"Who were they, anyway, to get so mad at you?"

"I don't know their names. I'm not even sure who they work for."

"At least," she said, "you're not in trouble with the police the way I am."

He set his mug down so she wouldn't notice his hands shaking. "Yeah," he murmured.

"I had to break up with my boyfriend, too."

"Aw. Why was that?"

"He got hired by a white-collar law firm downtown as a tax attorney. He'll have to bust his ass for ten years in order to get on the partnership track. If they hear his girlfriend had a drug arrest record, he'd never make it. If I try wriggling out from under the thumb of this particular cop, he might get into trouble, too, just for hanging out with me. I couldn't risk that. He's too good a guy."

"You were going to get married?"

She inhaled deeply and blew it out between her lips, sinking into the nearest chair. "We hadn't gotten there yet, even to talk about it. I considered it, though. Instead, I dumped him without telling him the real reason." Her next deep swallow of coffee— too hot—made her gasp for air, fanning her hand in front of her mouth. Then she said, "Fucking cops!"

Jerry looked nervously around the apartment as if he were trapped. Lurching onto the slippery edge of truth, he wanted to confess it to Jaimie and get the hell out of there. But he had nowhere safe to go.

His voice softer than usual, he asked, "Are you familiar with a detective cop named Keegan Mayo?"

Immediately he was sorry he asked. He hoped beyond hope Jaimie's answer would be, "No, I never heard of him. Why?"

Then he could say, "No reason, I was just wondering."

Instead, Jaimie's eyes went hard and narrow, her full lips became a slash across the lower half of her face, and her spine grew stiff and rigid. It took her at least twenty seconds before she answered, "Keegan Mayo is the sonofabitch who threatened me. I'd either go to prison, or else turn into a squealer for *him*."

Jerry batted his eyes, forcing back guilty tears tormenting the inside of his eyelids. "Oh," was all he could say.

"Why do you ask?"

He put a hand up to his forehead, as if soothing a headache, hiding his eyes to disguise the hurt in his soul. He was ripped apart inside, and one more word would turn Jaimie against him, that the shameful story would get out, that everyone else on earth would despise him, and more than likely Keegan Mayo would pull him off his C.I. task and sign that arrest report, sending him to prison for a long time.

"I understand, Jaimie," he said, the words harder to expel than kidney stones. "Because—I'm a C.I., too. For Mayo."

Jaimie Pack put her hand to her mouth. "Oh my god, Jerry. Oh my god."

"You remember Jill was peddling dope to everybody she knew, don't you? I mean, you were her customer, too."

She nodded. "I've never been that heavy into it, but—hell, it was fun sometimes."

"Yes, well, when she went to visit her parents in Cincinnati, she got me to take over her customer list for three weeks. And I got caught."

"How?"

"I dunno," he said. He started realizing he was beginning to whine, but couldn't do anything about it. "One of the plainclothes cops I sold to pulled his badge on me and hauled me to Mayo."

"Jesus Christ! Why didn't you turn Jill in to save yourself, Jerry? That would've been easy peasy."

"I couldn't. She was my girlfriend. I couldn't turn yellow, point a finger at her and send her to prison."

"Tell me about it!"

"I couldn't help it, Jaimie. You know that—you and I are in the same rancid club."

She set her mug down on the nearest table and put her face in both her hands. Her deep but muffled breathing turned into some deep sobs, her whole body shaking. Then she raised her head and looked at him. "I know. It's a sacrifice for you, Jerry. You let yourself get sucked into a horrible situation by saving her ass." She forced a smile. "You're a very brave man."

"Not brave, Jaimie. Not brave at all."

"Why not?"

He could no longer meet her gaze. "You're going to hate me."

She rubbed her face with her hand, careful not to destroy her make-up. "Other than your sleeping on my couch all night, Jerry, I hardly know you. So why would I hate you?"

Again, he took too long to answer. But he'd gone this far already—he couldn't stop now, even though it was like jumping into a frozen lake in mid-January, just for the fun of it.

When he finally spoke, the words came out fast, taking a roller coaster plunge. "Because I sold you coke and then turned you in to Keegan Mayo."

Neither moved, staring at each other, although Jaimie Peck's eyelids batted. She wasn't crying anymore—she'd do it later, she knew. There was complete silence otherwise, except for the steady tumult of cars rushing by on the nearby freeway, trying to beat the morning rush hour.

Jerry expected she would attack him, or throw something heavy at his head—at least he hoped she would, just to move forward the awesome hush of the moment. Finally, though, her head tilted forward, her chin on her chest, and she sniffled back the tears that were there but simply would not fall.

"Jerry Paich," she almost whispered. "You poor, pathetic son of a bitch!"

County Commissioner Frances P. Murgatroyd was discombobulated. Why did Bria Harstad make him dig up all the bad stuff he about an unknown punk named Jericho Paich? Marshall Ruttenberg—an international fence who imported or smuggled everything that could eventually turn an extra buck for him—suddenly was showing a rabid interest in some kid so fresh out of college that he never heard of Kung Foo Fighters and still whacked off every night reading *Hustler*. And why was Detective Mayo involved all of a sudden? He was a cop. Was he on Ruttenberg's team or on that of Jerry Paich—on the off-chance Paich *had* a team?

Franny didn't really do much work. The three Cuyahoga County commissioners had to run around attending meetings, weddings and funerals, and every so often get together and sign orders to fill up the tire-busting potholes on a residential street, or something else that cost the taxpayers money. Now, things were different, and he didn't know why—but his gut was telling him to find out more about Mayo and about Jericho Paich. Going over Detective Mayo's head to someone higher up in the CPD might not be a good idea—but he was, after all, a commissioner with a much bigger venue than the city of Cleveland, and he had lots of buddies to deal with every day.

His next call was to Cuyahoga County Sheriff Murray Janssen.

The fact is, Francis Murgatroyd had no idea what a sheriff did for a living, either. He knew they were elected by the public who often had no idea for whom they voted. He'd grown up thinking all sheriffs shoot down outlaws who refused to take their guns off when they rode into town, especially if they were portrayed by Henry Fonda.

Almost every county in the United States had a sheriff, and most of them enforced the law, ran a jail of their own, served warrants and court-ordered subpoenas, and hung out with mob guys, as did Murray Janssen. No one remembers the last time Janssen actually busted someone from Murray Hill.

The sheriff was behind his desk in shirtsleeves, wearing a very muted tie and sporting bifocals on the end of his nose. He didn't look like a sheriff in a Randolph Scott western, but more like the guy who ran the local general store and probably got killed when the outlaws ride into town. He wasn't allowed to smoke cigarettes in the building, so he chewed on a toothpick—also a gross habit but, unlike smoking, didn't cause cancer.

"Franny Murgatroyd!" Janssen tried to sound happy as hell, but he made no effort to shake hands. "What brings you over here? You're usually busy driving everyone in the county nuts—and all I do here is catch bad guys and lock 'em up."

"I was hoping to chat with you." Murgatroyd sat down in one of the visitor chairs. "Murray," he said carefully, "I wonder whether you know all the bad guys in Cuyahoga County."

Janssen shifted his toothpick from the left corner of his mouth to his right. "If I knew all the county's bad guys, they'd be in my jail and none of 'em would be out on the streets."

"Sorry, guess that was a dumb question."

"Yep."

Franny flushed at the insult, but labored not to look irritated. "I'm speaking about one particular guy. His name is Marshall Ruttenberg—has an estate in Shaker Heights."

No answer. Just a nod, then an off-center turn of the head, accompanied by a skittish frown.

"I'm in touch with him sometimes," Murgatroyd said, "but more often with his office manager—a woman named Bria Harstad."

"Don't know her from a hole in the ground."

"But you know him?"

"You mean Rabbit Eyes? We've met."

"Rabbit Eyes?"

"Ever take a good look at him?" Janssen said. "He's albino. Snow-white skin and pink eyes like a rabbit."

Franny realized he never took a good look at Ruttenberg. He was pale, and Franny figured he had an eye infection like conjunctivitis, but it never crossed his mind Ruttenberg was one of the world's odd ones. He said, "Tell me about him."

"You know him, Franny, so you tell me."

"I know he's an importer. That's all."

"Really? No shit." The sheriff leaned back in his swivel chair. "What does he import, d'you suppose?"

Franny looked blank. "I'm not sure. I never asked him."

"Never asked him, huh?"

"Not really. He's taken me out to dinner a couple of times—with his—with Bria Harstad."

"She's his pass-around whore?"

Murgatroyd's back went rigid. "No such thing. She's a classy woman—smart and beautiful. I've had a woody for her since the first day I met her—but no way in hell is she a whore."

"Lovely, Franny. But you have no idea what he imports?"

"I—guess not."

"You let him buy you dinner, though." The sheriff took the toothpick out of his mouth, examined the frayed end, and tossed it into the wastebasket under his desk. Taking a new one from his shirt pocket to replace the old one, he got busy chewing again. "If the King of the Zombies stepped off *The Walking Dead* TV show and invited you to dinner at some too-damn-expensive restaurant downtown, you'd damn well go so you could stuff your face on his nickel, even if you ate what he ate—the flesh of some recently departed creature."

Franny gulped. Was Sheriff Janssen a vegan? He chose to ignore it. "That's not fair, Murray—"

"Save it, commissioner." Janssen's face looked tired and bored. "Ruttenberg imports antiquities from Europe—mostly European antiquities. Sometimes the ones belonging to the European country one of his associates stole them from. Some of that stuff is worth millions."

Murgatroyd's eyes opened wide. "That's illegal!"

"No joking." The sheriff leaned forward suddenly, resting his elbows on the top of his desk, his head down like a bull about to charge the matador. "You know what else he imports, Franny? Cocaine—that gets turned into crack—from Mexico and Colombia. That's illegal, too."

"Oh my god!"

"And meth, wherever that comes from—or maybe he cooks it in his own kitchen. But here's the big shocker. He also imports young teen girls from Honduras and Colombia. As soon as they cross the border, the coyotes send them up here, or to Toledo or Miami or a dozen other places in America and sell them off to sex traffickers like Ruttenberg. From there, Christ knows where they ship them off to. Those twenty-year-old girls look like they're fifty—if they hadn't already caught the syph. They've had all life and spirit fucked right out of them. Sex traffickers either kick them out on the streets or get rid of them some other way. Now you know all about Marshall Ruttenberg. Is that what you came for? Or did you want to know if he votes Republican, too?"

Words failed the county commissioner, as all he could do was sputter and stammer. Finally, he managed to say, "Why don't you arrest him?"

"We're not the Interpol to march in here with a small army." Janssen held up one hand, palm outward. "Ruttenberg lives in Hunting Valley. You think the Hunting Valley police are going to swoop down on him and make international headlines? Get real, commissioner."

Francis Murgatroyd's ulcer, which never really went away but sometimes cooled down, burned at his guts like fire, possibly due to the three drinks he'd imbibed at lunch. But it was more likely his rage, which was unusual for him. He endeavored to be a happy imbiber who rarely lifted his ass from his office chair, coasting on his easy job for more years than he could remember. Now he was furious Marshall Ruttenberg, who coddled him whenever he wanted something, was a major criminal allowed to walk around Greater Cleveland free as a bird. "If you won't do something about it, Murray, I will!"

"What's your mission, then? Fill up all the potholes on *his* street?"

"When I do," Murgatroyd said, standing tall and feeling courageous for the first time in his life and heading for the door, "you'll be the first to know."

CHAPTER TWENTY-FIVE

"I can't tell you where I'm staying right now." Jaimie Peck had left for her job, and Jericho Paich was still on her sofa, telling his mother's live-in boyfriend on Jaimie's phone he was okay. "My cell phone might be bugged."

Laird Janiver sat at his desk in Arielle's home, a second morning coffee mug steaming on his desk-top cup warmer. Nothing else was in sight but a book he was reading, a book-mark peeking out from between the pages. It was still too early in the day, prior to his second mug of coffee, for him to speak with an always irksome Jericho, so he was quite annoyed. "Did you do something treasonous to the United States of America?"

Jerry was shocked. "Of course not!"

"Then who the hell would bug your cell phone?"

"Maybe the cops, maybe whoever sent those two guys after me. I don't know."

"You've had your phone in your pocket all this time. Who could bug it?"

"They can do it electronically."

Laird looked toward the ceiling and mouthed "Oh shit." Aloud, he said, "If you believe that, fine. I'm glad you called, anyway. You want to talk to your mother?"

"No!" That was a one-note snap. Jerry was used to her usual tearful outbursts, as he'd known her longer and better than Laird Janiver. He wasn't ready for another mother-like outburst, so he just softened his tone. "She'll just be upset, and cry."

"She'll cry when I tell her you called." Laird gritted his teeth. Jerry could always hang up on his mother's hysteria, but poor Laird was only one flight of stairs away from hysterical fury. "Shall I talk to Keegan Mayo again?"

"Mayo has nothing to do with two guys hunting me like I was a feral dog in the middle of Cleveland—the ones who beat me up the first time. They knew where I work—but I haven't gone to the office for several days, and I'll bet now they're hanging around outside where I live. I can't go home."

"Then I don't know what I can do for you, Jerry."

"Just pray they don't find me."

Pray. That ground Laird's guts, as it always did. He'd not prayed since he was twelve years old. Prior to that, his mother dragged him to the Mount Zion Baptist Church every week, and flicked him on the side of the head when his attention to the preacher's sermon wandered or he tried catching a few extra winks on a Sunday morning.

He doubted Jericho was religious, either. People say they'll pray for you, and promptly forget about it. Besides, if there was a god, which he fervently doubted, prayers never get answered anyway, and if they do, it's a matter of luck. That's why the world is such a mess. "I haven't been to church in forty years, Jerry. What do you want besides prayer?"

"Be—gentle with Mom, okay?"

That wasn't so easy. The evening Laird asked an uninvited Bria Harstad into the home just to talk about Jerry, Arielle went berserk thinking he'd had sex with her, making him think getting blamed for something he didn't do made it perfectly acceptable to do it thereafter. While, Arielle didn't know that yet, the air between them had turned to glacial silence.

"I'll do my best, Jerry," he said wearily.

"As for those two guys—"

"You don't know who they are," Laird said brusquely, "so how the hell am I supposed to?"

"A big wide bear of a guy and a mean, skinny little shit."

Sure, Laird thought bitterly, *I'll look for the two guys wherever I go, and when I find them, I'll just speak very sharply to them. Christ, Jerry, grow up!*

He said aloud, "I'll talk to your mom—but she won't be happy."

He was correct. Arielle came downstairs fifteen minutes later in dressy slacks, an orange pullover sweater and two-inch heel spangled sandals, ready to go out somewhere. Too early in the day for her book club or playing bridge or mahjong with her so-called girlfriends, but probably headed to the elegant and too-expensive Legacy Village and the upscale shopping centers to buy something else. He took a deep breath and announced her son had just called.

"Where is he, then?" she demanded.

"He's staying with a friend for a while."

"What friend?"

"He didn't say, Arielle."

"Do I know this friend?"

Laird rubbed his eyes with his middle finger and his thumb. "I repeat: he didn't say."

"Why didn't he say?"

"He was afraid his phone was bugged, and he didn't want anyone finding out where he is."

Arielle put her hand up to her face for a still, statue-like moment, then started pulling at her own cheek. "Why did he call you and not me?"

"I don't know."

"That's damn insulting, Laird!"

"I didn't insult you. My phone rang, I answered it."

"You could have let me know he was on the phone." Her voice was whisper-quiet, as if she needed to take too many breaths to finish one complete sentence. Her face was pink from pinching it, and Laird steeled himself for what he knew would come next.

Fuck it, he thought. "He has your phone number, too, Arielle. He could have called you if he wanted to."

"He called *you.*" Her voice grew louder and shakier. "He chose you over me."

"I'm not his goddamned mother. *You* are!"

"You're taking him away from me," she said, leveling an accusing finger at him as though she were Dickens' Madame DeFarge choosing who next goes to the guillotine. "Everyone bails out on me—just like that woman, that slut! She's taking you away from me, too."

"Arielle—"

"Tell me, Laird," she said, louder, more fiercely. "Did you fuck her on the sofa? Or was it here on the floor in front of the fireplace?" She gasped as a thought was destroying her from within. "Oh, Jesus God—did you fuck her in our bed?"

"Arielle, I never laid eyes on her before. She came to ask *you* questions about Jerry, but as usual, you were at your book club, so she asked me instead. I really had no answers, so she said thank you and left after no more than fifteen minutes."

"My whole family is deserting me!" she wailed, and then the subcutaneous rage exploded and everything that bothered her came boiling out all over the living room.

It continued for more than two hours—crying, screaming, moaning, switching from total apostasy of everyone to Jerry in hiding to Laird's supposed dislike for her son to his infidelity which, while true, came directly from Arielle's fury and not of any smattering of knowledge.

It ended with "Leave my home! Get your shit and move out of here forever! I'd vomit if you ever touched me again!"

Surprisingly, Laird was not in traumatized in the least, but actually relieved. He went up to the bedroom, stump aching at the stair climb. Like a battalion commander setting up for a raid, he packed a suitcase and a barracks bag, assured Arielle he would return for the rest of his things when she was not present, and headed out, not even sure where he was going.

After driving around for a while and realizing there were damn few hotels or motels in the eastern suburbs, he headed downtown, finally checking in at the Hilton Garden Inn, catty-corner from Progressive Field where the Cleveland Guardians played ball, even though he knew 'catty-corner' had nothing to do with cats or kittens. Looking out his third-floor window at the field, he remembered two decades earlier when the shiny new ballpark opened and was referred to as Jacobs Field, named after the family that owned the team, popularly known as the Jake. The Jacobs family eventually sold the team, and it saddened Laird nobody called it the Jake anymore.

He almost felt sad about breaking up with Arielle Paich, too. Almost.

Their romance lasted more than three years, but like many relationships, early eroticism and passion gave way to friendship and trust, then drifted off to indifference and regret—eventually to dislike, resentment, and a very uncomfortable split.

Before this afternoon, Laird harbored no bad feelings about Arielle. Her weeping and howling were part of the package. His guilt, naturally, came from his sudden and overwhelming attraction to Bria, whose current life and past history were complete mysteries to him. Yet Arielle had blamed him for it before he even did it.

Life happens. Love at first sight? Sometimes hard to tell. Lust often leads the parade, as it did when he opened the door and Bria Harstad was on the other side of it. When he saw her the next time, the feeling was obviously mutual, despite his showing up only hoping to protect Jerry Paich.

He ran that through his mind. Well, he went there for *more* reasons than Jerry's difficulty, and he was forced to admit that to himself.

Why did he care about Jerry? The love connection with Arielle was gone—and gone doesn't come back. As far as Jerry was concerned, they hadn't given a damn about each other from the beginning. Part of it might be Jerry's thin-skinned racism, as in almost all human beings, even the kind, gracious ones. In the currently divided America, there was incipient fear and distrust of those of a different color. More probably, a dark-skinned intruder into Jerry's adolescent home and his mother's bed wouldn't be welcomed, no matter who it might be.

Yet Bria had to move left of center at the moment because Laird was now most concerned with the safety of Jerry, which might be life-threatening. In normal times, Laird would not get into such a perilous situation regarding someone he didn't like very much.

But Jericho was a human being. When his situation reached major danger, it was to Marine Major Janiver he turned to for help.

That's what put Laird over the edge. The law of combat, especially among the U.S. marines, was one doesn't leave a brother behind in battle.

He dialed Jerry's cellphone again.

"Jerry, are you eating?" he demanded. "Are you going out to buy groceries, or are you starving to death?"

"The person I'm temporarily staying with is doing the food shopping for me."

"Good. Don't even stick your nose out the door until I tell you to. It's not only perilous for you, but whoever you're staying with might get into trouble as well. If these two hard guys find you again, they'll harm your roommate, too. Strangers mean less than nothing to them."

Jerry made a whiny noise in the back of his throat. "I'd never do anything to put her in danger, Laird."

Put *her* in danger. *Her?* Laird would remember that in case it was important. "That's—good, Jerry. Keep her—uh—out of my way."

"Out of your way? Jesus, what're you going to do?"

"I'll tell you," Laird Janiver said, "as soon as I've done it."

After the call, Laird felt the urge for a stiff drink.

He'd grabbed a bottle of cognac before he left Arielle's home, knowing he was going to need it. Now he opened it and almost poured some into one of the paper cups supplied by the hotel, but eventually guzzled a deep swallow right out of the bottle.

From his rucksack, he removed the handgun he'd carried for most of the time in the Middle East and stuck it in his waistband at the right hip. It didn't weigh that much, but it felt strange to him, messing up the balance on his prosthetic foot. Then he donned a jacket long enough to cover it. Ransoming his car from the hotel parking lot, he drove over the Lorain-Carnegie Bridge, just forty-five seconds away from the hotel, heading toward Jericho Paich's apartment in Ohio City.

CHAPTER TWENTY-SIX

To anyone who saw him for the first time, Merrill Braithwaite seemed to be obsessed with OCD—obsessive-compulsive disorder, really resembling a department store mannequin. He was never known to have a five o'clock shadow, as if he shaved twice a day and had his hair cut twice a week. Always dressed to the nines in a blindingly white shirt and conservative tie, never taking off the suit jacket—today a dark gray with faint white pinstripes—where anyone might see him. One might swear he ironed his pajamas every night before going to bed. Despite his relatively good looks, no one ever thought another human being happened to be in the bedroom with him.

He was, however, the Deputy Special Agent in Charge of the FBI Division in Cleveland. He occupied the second-largest office in the building, right on the shore of Lake Erie. Broad windows looked out on the vast water's varied appearances throughout the year. However, his desk chair faced away from the window so if the sun shone in brightly, it was on his visitor's face to squint, and not his. No one ever teased him or dissed him regarding his overly-neat appearance—at least not to his face.

As Deputy SAC, he was more an administrator than a field officer—a paper-shuffler—long past running around on the street or making arrests, though he always wore the standard governmental handgun in a shoulder holster, even in his office.

He was good at his job, and serious about every moment of

his life, as a Fibbie should be. Born and raised in nearby Massillon, famous as the childhood home of silent stars Dorothy and Lillian Gish and not for much else—like so many others, he attended The Ohio State University, then to law school at Brown University in Rhode Island. He was glad to see a longtime friend—Colonel Ayman Kader, USMC Retired—with whom he broke bread at lunch five or six times per year, often at the elegant Johnny's Downtown on West Sixth Street, though he was far more addicted to middle-class ethnic foods, especially *klobasa*—Slovenian sausage—which he devoured at home at least three times a week, slathered with the locally made Stadium Mustard.

He was disappointed Kader didn't wear his dress uniform more often, but the colonel preferred civilian cable knit sweaters. On this occasion, he'd chosen a muted forest green. It was unusual for Kader to visit Braithwaite at his office unless it was not just casual but something more important.

The Deputy SAC waved Kader into a chair. "Keeping busy these days, Merrill?" Kader asked him.

"Mostly trying to forget half our fellow Americans hate the FBI and think we're part of a dark state. Otherwise, we look for Russian spies who live next door to you, barbecue hot dogs on the Fourth of July and buy American cars while some government hacks report directly to the Kremlin. Want coffee?"

"Too late in the day for coffee," Kader said.

"I know what you mean. How is Beth? Still beautiful, I'm sure."

"She says to say hello." Kader sat forward in his visitor's chair. "I'm here because a good friend approached me about something that has absolutely nothing to do with me."

"Oh boy!" the SAC groaned.

"He said I should contact the FBI. Luckily, since I've known you for a hell of a long time, I figured I'd come right to the top."

Merrill Braithwaite smiled with one corner of his mouth. Anything more than showing mild amusement would indicate he was laughing hysterically. "The top, as you say, is right next door in an even bigger office," he said, jerking a thumb toward his left. "I'm only the *deputy* top. Tell me this friend's story, though, and we'll see if it goes anywhere."

"Okay. Does the name Marshall Ruttenberg mean anything to you?"

The Deputy SAC's expression did not change at all, but his eyes halfclosed. "How'd you hear about Marshall Ruttenberg?"

"From a friend."

"*Your* friend?"

"A Marine friend."

"What does this friend have to do with Ruttenberg?"

Kader said, "His girlfriend's son might just get murdered by Ruttenberg's people."

"Murdered?"

"It's a long story."

"I'm not sure I need to hear it," Braithwaite told him. "The Bureau doesn't investigate most murders—especially ones that haven't happened yet."

"Merrill, this has nothing to do with me. I'm just repeating a story."

"Does this story start with 'Once upon a time?' If so, I'm not interested in bringing down the Wicked Witch of the West."

Braithwaite drummed his fingers atop his otherwise empty desk, which looked as though it were dusted and waxed every night. At length, he stopped drumming. "I'm listening."

It took Kader fifteen minutes to complete the tale of all he knew about Ruttenberg, including the aftermath of Jericho Paich's beating that took place on the estate.

When he finished, there was quiet in the room except for the howling noise of the wind through the closed windows as it kicked up waves on the water before they broke on the beach. Braithwaite swiveled his chair around to look at Lake Erie for a while. Then he turned back to Ayman Kader. He was vaguely aware of Kader's secret black market business when they were in Afghanistan together, but he was damned if he'd mention it.

It wasn't his business, and it was all over, anyway.

Kader hoped the FBI Deputy SAC would speak before he did. Then he gave in. "Do you believe me, Merrill?"

"I believe most of it. All of it, actually. I'm well aware Ruttenberg is Cleveland's biggest meth and crack king, but I didn't realize he churns out stool pigeons for the police. We've never had enough proof to hang his ass. As for sex trafficking—I don't know anything about this girl who used to be a mule for him, a C.I., who suddenly disappeared six months ago."

"So now?"

"So now," Braithwaite said, "we might be able to shake Ruttenberg up a little."

"Great."

"But thanks to you, I don't quite know enough."

"Why not?"

"Because this is a second-hand story, or maybe even third-hand. Before I pick up this telephone, or lift my ass out of this very comfortable throne of a chair I sit in, I have to know who is your Marine friend. I also have to know from whom he got all this information." He leaned forward slightly, head held high so the double chin didn't show. "Names, Ayman Kader. I need names."

Laird Janiver drove by the building in which Jerry Paich lived. He'd only seen it once before, and that was right after Jerry had graduated and moved out. He didn't react to it then—it was just a little sight-seeing trip so Arielle could lay eyes upon where her baby boy rented an apartment. She didn't like it—not fancy enough for Jerry to move into from his mother's nice neat home. It was a cheesy, run-down fourplex begging for gentrification, or more aptly, demolition.

More important was Laird saw two men who looked very much as Jerry Paich described them, sitting in the front seat of a four-year-old Dodge across the street from the apartment building.

The skinny one, sucking on a can of Coors, hunched low in the passenger seat. The heavyset one at the wheel was staring hard at the front door of Jerry's building, mouth slightly open as if he couldn't breathe freely and needed to blow his nose.

Laird drove around the corner and stopped. His throat was closing, and his stump throbbed angrily, sending pain all the way up to his waist. There they were, patiently waiting, as Jerry had predicted. Now what the hell could he do about it?

He thought for ten minutes with his head down, rubbing his forehead with his fingers, heavily aware of the pistol in his waistband, irritating his hip. He didn't intend driving up next to their car and executing two people he'd never seen before, then speeding away as fast as possible. Like every other soldier who'd had boots on the ground in Iraq or Afghanistan, he chose not to count the number of people he'd had to watch die. That was war, and it was best not to relive it every day.

This, though, was no war, at least not the definition most Americans live with. Now Janiver was tormented by the prospect of killing two people he'd never seen before.

He checked his wristwatch. Three-twenty p.m. Chances were good none of Jerry's neighbors were home from work, so he could get away with whatever he might do inside that tawdry building. A plan was forming inside his head—misty, uncertain, but slowly coming together.

Another ten minutes, and he was ready, hoping against hope the bad guys were still outside. He started the car, pulled around the corner again and parked behind the Dodge, in which two assailants still lurked. Giving them a slight nod, he crossed the street, walked up the steps to the porch, and into the house. Jerry's apartment was on the first floor, just to the right of the entrance. Knowing he was visible from outside through the main glass entrance, Laird banged loudly on Jerry's door, shouting, "Mr. Paich! I know you're in there! It's North Coast Financial, Mr. Paich. Open this damn door!"

Naturally, he knew Jerry Paich was not home, and there was

no organization called North Coast Financial, but now, for the first time, he was becoming someone else for the benefit of the two who waited. It flickered across his mind that his acting wasn't on the same planet as Morgan Freeman or Denzel Washington in all the action films they made—but he hoped like hell it would work.

"You can't hide forever, Mr. Paich," he bellowed, loud enough to be heard from across the street. "You better open this door in one hell of a hurry!"

The two men in the car looked at each other and then leaned closer to the open window, the better to hear him.

Hammering on Jerry's apartment door once more, Janiver let his shoulders slump, then turned dejectedly and shuffled out onto the porch, down the steps, and across the street to his car, allowing his face to brighten up when he saw the guns-for-hire studying him.

He walked over to their open window and spoke directly to the chunky driver, smiling sheepishly. "The little sonofabitch is in there, all right—but he won't open the door." His lie came easily.

"Why not?" the one Jerry thought of as The Wrestler asked. "You gonna kill him or something?"

"From your lips to god's ear. No, I won't hurt him physically. I'm a debt collector. This guy owed about two hundred forty bucks for the last nine months—and his unpaid interest is mounting every day."

The skinny one leaned forward. "So kick the door in."

"I would," Laird said. "But I'm a Marine. I'm walking around with a metallic foot." He stepped backwards and lifted his left pant leg so both could see the prosthesis. "Get what I mean? If I tried to kick his door in, I'd lose my balance and fall right on my ass. I'm in no condition."

"Oooh!" The Wrestler wrinkled up his nose. "Tough shit, man. Where'd you get that?"

"In Baghdad. I stepped where some fucking towel-head

thought I shouldn't, and he buried a bomb under the sand, just for me."

Skinny, sympathetic as hell, put his hand over his heart. "Wow! Thank you for your service, man."

Laird Janiver had to keep from biting his tongue. *Thank you for your service.* He hated that expression, especially when coming from someone who never wore a military uniform and never went anywhere near Iraq, Vietnam, or even Korea, having traveled no further from Cleveland than Columbus or Toledo. What about *their* goddamn service, anyway? Draft dodgers, probably—guys with money who bought off doctors to record in their medical reports they suffered bone spurs in their heel, or irritable bowel syndrome.

He said, "Yeah. But this Jericho Paich—I know he's in there. Frustrates the hell out of me I'm not strong enough—not tough enough anymore—to kick that door down. Now I'll have to hang around here all day tomorrow, too—screwing up my other assignments, which means I don't get a taste of this particular pickup." He looked right at The Wrestler, throwing in a humiliated smile. "I wish I was a big, strong guy like you."

The Wrestler didn't quite get it—but Skinny did, damning a black guy who talked like a white man. He said, "We can help you out—but what if anyone else is home in that building? We'd scare the crap out of them."

Laird shook his head. "I checked. All single people in their twenties and thirties, and they're at their own jobs. They probably don't have money, either. Who else would live in a craphole like this? Paich is the only one home." Then he crouched down, looking past The Wrestler to Skinny. Skinny was the smart one—obviously. "Jeez, if you guys could really help me out—"

"Well—"

"Look, I'll give you fifteen bucks each. It'd really save my ass, guys. I'll be your best friend forever."

Quiet for a moment. Skinny was thinking it over. The Wrestler was staring at him, hoping he'd say yes. "I'll tell you what, mister," Skinny finally said. "Make it twenty bucks each and your got yourself a deal."

They got out of the car and the three men fist-pumped each other, then proceeded across the street and up the porch steps. Now that they were all standing, Laird actually had to look down on both of them. Two short guys. Skinny was close to one hundred fifty pounds soaking wet, while The Wrestler, a few inches taller, was nearer to two hundred eighty, wide as a Patton tank.

The two men were breathing faster. They believed Jericho Paich was somewhere else, and would eventually visit his own apartment to collect some things, like socks and underwear and probably a warmer jacket, as Thanksgiving was right around the corner. Now they were thrilled to death he was home, and they'd see him within seconds and spirit him away to "take care of him," as per instructions. What would they do about this debt collector? They hadn't thought it all the way through.

Yet.

In their excitement at being steps away from fulfilling their important orders, they didn't look closely enough to realize Laird Janiver was broad in the shoulders, his jacket disguising hard, toned muscles in his arms and chest, and his eyes so dark brown at the moment they were almost black. They didn't know his name, nor did they care. The Wrestler looked forward to an extra twenty-dollar bill. Skinny was already thinking of Laird as either "the cripple with the make-believe foot," or just "the colored guy."

At Jerry Paich's door, Laird once more hammered on it with his fist. "Open up, Jerry. This is your last chance!"

No answer—naturally.

Laird stepped back, gesturing to The Wrestler to take his best shot.

Backing up as far as he could, the heavyset man took a run at the door, ramming it with his shoulder. The wood groaned but did not break. On his third try, though, the door flew open, and Laird stepped inside.

"Jerry Paich," he called. "Show yourself."

But no one was there. Laird indicated the two other men should come in, which they did almost gleefully.

"He's hiding somewhere," Laird said, then spoke to Skinny. "Will you take a look in the bedroom, please? And don't forget the bathroom—look behind the shower curtain."

Skinny giggled. "Got it, pal." He disappeared into the other room.

As soon as he disappeared, Laird turned to The Wrestler and slashed the edge of his hand across the big man's neck, just below his chin. The Wrestler's Eyes bugged, and he clutched at his throat, teetering around the room, gasping, trying to breathe. Laird followed him, this time swinging a fist at the side of his face, the spot where the upper jaw meets the lower. The jaw shattered. Wrestler's head jacked backwards, hard, as if it might simply fly off. Dizzy, he backed up and fell on the ratty sofa, still trying to breathe. Laird removed the Glock 26 9mm from his waistband and smashed the side of it into the big tough guy's head as hard as he could, cutting the scalp and bringing a steady trickle of blood. The Wrestler collapsed, comatose.

At the very least, Laird would have to replace the sofa for Jericho Paich. That much blood won't come out of the fabric. He worried for a nanosecond, thinking he might have killed The Wrestler, until he remembered these two men had beaten Jerry half to death and now were likely on a mission to finish the job.

When Skinny reappeared in the bedroom doorway, the first thing he saw was The Wrestler, sprawled out and bleeding all over the furniture, and Laird Janiver using both hands to point a weapon steadily at the middle of his chest. His first instinct was to reach for his own gun. Bad idea.

"Uh-uh-uh-uh! Just sit down, punk," Laird ordered. "Very slowly."

"What the fuck—"

"Sit." He gestured toward an easy chair. "Sit—or die."

Skinny sat.

"Sit on your hands."

Skinny slipped his hands under his thighs, palms down.

Laird approached him, patted him all over his body until he found the gun in the side pocket of his zip-on jacket and relieved him of it, quickly glancing over at The Wrestler, hoping he'd stay insensate for a while, because if he had a gun, too, it was somewhere in one of his pockets.

"What's the deal here?" Skinny said, half tough and half scared.

"The deal is I ask questions and you answer them."

"Are you threatening me?"

"I don't threaten," Laird Janiver said. "I just *do*."

"You're so goddamn tough with that phony foot of yours."

"Are you kidding? I've been walking on it for years, pal. I could dance Swan Lake for you if I had to. I could also ram it clear up your ass and then wash it off afterwards."

Skinny was losing confidence quickly. "I don't know who you are, man."

"I don't know who you are, either—but I know *what* you are, and I know this," Laird said. "I know you and your girlfriend over there beat the crap out of Jerry Paich a few days back—and now you're after him again."

Skinny didn't want to look at the Glock pointed at his chest. At such a short distance, it could have been a cannon. It would not miss. "I don't know what you're talking about."

"Sure you do. You both beat him up. You were seen."

"By who?"

"By someone who can point a finger at you."

"Well," Skinny said defensively, "it's none a your business."

"No? Why do you think I'm here? I was a combat Marine, shithead. I've killed more men than you ever dreamed of, and it didn't bother me. So let's cut to the chase. I'll ask you questions. If you lie to me, I'll start shooting off little pieces of you, one by one until you tell me the truth." He moved the gun down so it pointed at Skinny's crotch. "I'm not going to waste time, kiddo. The first thing to go will be your left testicle."

Skinny's eyes opened as wide as a silver dollar. He tried pressing his knees together, but since he was sitting on his hands, that made it impossible.

"Okay, here's the first question. Who are you and the fat guy there working for? Who paid you to beat up Jerry Paich?"

"I—I don't know the guy's name."

"Wrong answer." Laird jammed the muzzle of the Glock hard into Skinny's balls. "Goodbye, Lefty..."

"No, wait! *Wait!*" he screamed, less from the pain than the terror that might come next, and he helplessly pissed his pants. "I'll talk, I'll talk!"

Janiver was disappointed. He really wanted to shoot this murderous punk in the nuts and hear him wail his torment, but his two-decades-plus career in the Marine Corps stayed his trigger finger. He pressed the muzzle harder into Skinny's groin. "You've got five seconds. Who ordered the beating, punk? One. Two. Three—"

"Ruttenberg!"

He let up on the pressure a bit. "Ruttenberg? What is that, a Latvian word?"

Skinny shook his head so hard he almost looked like a wet dog trying to get dry. "His name is Marshall Ruttenberg," he blurted.

And that made Laird Janiver smile.

CHAPTER TWENTY-SEVEN

Marshall Ruttenberg's chauffeur and all-around handyman, Randy, dropped him off at the foot of the steps toward the entrance of the Federal Bureau of Investigation Headquarters in downtown Cleveland and then went to find a parking place. Ruttenberg appreciated being close to the door because he hated being outside in daytime, especially on a day like this one when the sun struggled to fight its way through a thin layer of clouds.

Driving a car himself was painful because of his eyes, so he only got behind the wheel at night to have a restaurant dinner close to his home. While outside, he always wore expensive sunglasses. His dark gray suit was chosen for a color people might admire other than his chalk-white skin, and hand-tailored to avoid undue attention to his little round tummy. He climbed steps with his head down, one hand shading his eyes, the other holding tight to the handrail.

He'd had little or no contact with the FBI, and never visited them before, so the call from Merrill Braithwaite made what little hair he had on his body stand up at attention. Braithwaite had been distant but polite when he suggested a meeting—and thoughtful Ruttenberg should come down to headquarters rather than a whole squad of Fibbies invading his estate out in Hunting Valley.

However, the FBI made Marshall Ruttenberg feel uncomfortable. Of course, the Bureau makes everyone squirm, even

Chinese women operating the dry cleaners and knew few words of English, or someone in a small factory who makes pieces of machinery nobody ever heard of.

Like everyone else, Ruttenberg had to go through an arch would beep at whatever metal he carried with him, so beforehand he had to dump his coins into a plastic tub, along with his ballpoint pen, his leather belt with the metal buckle, and even his sunglasses, the frames of which were metallic. It was humiliating the guards could see him squinting. It made him appear weak. If he were ever to become Emperor of the World, he thought, he'd outlaw those goddamned metal detectors—and the fucking FBI, too.

Getting himself back together and putting on his dark glasses as quickly as possible, he had to go through three other people—youngish men, impeccably groomed and speaking in respectful half-whispers—interns, if there was such a thing in the FBI. The last of the three, a thin, light-skinned young black man whose speech smacked of four years plus a master's degree at some Ivy League icon like Harvard or Princeton, guided him to the office of the Deputy SAC on the top floor, knocked trepidatiously on the door, and opened it so Ruttenberg could walk through.

Merrill Braithwaite rose to welcome him, but was taken by surprise at Ruttenberg's appearance. Damn! he thought. Ayman Kader never bothered mentioning this guy was a fucking albino. Even the handshake didn't feel human, but more like that of a first grader's doll made out of two grocery sacks.

"I appreciate your coming in, Mr. Ruttenberg. I'll try not to take too long." The Deputy SAC gestured at the visitor's chair on the other side of his desk, but Ruttenberg regarded it with contempt.

"I'm sorry, I can't possibly sit there, because I have extremely sensitive eyes—thus the dark glasses. Sitting facing the bright sky would be agony for me."

Braithwaite said, "Then let's sit on the other side of the room with the two easy chairs facing each other. I'll tilt one of them for you so the light will hardly be a difficulty."

"That's most kind."

When they finally settled down away from the window, Ruttenberg still wearing the sunglasses and declining coffee, tea, water, or something else, Braithwaite cleared his throat.

"The Bureau has been aware of you for some time, Mr. Ruttenberg. Unfortunately, we've never met before—but I recently heard things about you around town that, if true, might be very interesting.

Ruttenberg went on offense immediately. "If you've heard I'm an albino, Special Agent, you can see that for yourself. It's no secret—and last time I checked, being an albino is totally legal in the United States of America."

"Totally legal, sir—but that's not why I suggested we get together."

"Really? Well, I'm here—"

Braithwaite removed a small electronic recorder from his top drawer and set in on the desk. "Would you object if I record this conversation?"

"Yes, I would—unless I'm under arrest."

"Nothing of the kind, Mr. Ruttenberg. I'm just looking for some information, that's all."

"*Innocent* information?"

Braithwaite's smile was with only his lips. "Everything is innocent, sir—until it's not." He replaced the recorder in the drawer. "What is it, exactly, that you do for a living?"

"I am an importer and distributor, Special Agent—mostly, but not exclusively, from Europe."

"Importing what?"

"Antiques—not the kind you see in so-called antique stores in rural Ohio, where they sell old cans of Dutch Boy Cleanser from the 1940s, or posters of Joe Di Maggio saying how great Camel cigarettes are. I collect and re-sell the real stuff, mostly from Europe—some over two hundred years old."

"Re-sell to whom?"

Ruttenberg gestured helplessly with his hands. "Depends. I sell to museums—if they have the money. I sell to top antiques dealers, to galleries that hold lotteries, to private persons if they so choose. For instance, I have several paintings from Germany during the Second World War—paintings stolen from the Jews by the Nazis and squirreled away for when Germany won the war. Wealthy Jews in this country will pay a pretty penny to own those paintings once more."

His pronouncement of the word *Jews* was toxic. Braithwaite frowned, but let it go. "You obtained these art works—these stolen paintings—*how?*"

A sigh. "I don't know if they were stolen from Germany— and I don't know if they weren't. I run a business, Special Agent. That's how I make my money."

"A lot of money?"

"Sometimes."

Merrill Braithwaite thought Ruttenberg might have *winked,* but it was hard to be sure because he could barely see his eyes through the dark glasses. "What do you import besides stolen art?"

"A vast and diverse array. For instance—I have a genuine sword and scabbard used by one of the British forces in the Bo-er War. Do you know about the Boer War, Mr. Braithwaite?"

"I do, indeed. The British colonials fighting the Afrikaners— or Boers—at the turn of the twentieth century."

"Very good."

"We FBI guys all actually graduated from high school, Mr. Ruttenberg, so we know a few things. What else?"

"At the moment, I have a real prize item. You won't believe this because I didn't—but I have genuine papers, so it's actually true." Ruttenberg whispered, as if in a super-secret meeting. "It's an actual chamber pot from the Palace of Versailles." He chuckled. "I have no way of knowing if it were the chamber pot into which King Louis XVI actually took a dump—but maybe he did, at that."

"And how much are you asking for it?"

"I'll start the bidding at—" He stopped, thought about it, then extended his hand, palms down, and wiggled it back and forth. "Give and take, two hundred and fifty thousand dollars. It might get up to twice that amount."

"For a shit pot."

Ruttenberg raised both hands, palms upward. "If I could get a million dollars for clipping my toenails and putting them into a fancy glass box, I'd do that."

"So whoever got you this chamber pot—does he get a piece of the profit?"

"Sometimes. Other times, I buy things outright. It depends." He smiled a wolfish smile. "Business is about making a profit, Special Agent. That's the way our country runs—and has always run."

"Uh-huh." Merrill Braithwaite glanced over his shoulder at the window. "Are you okay sitting where you are? I don't want the sun bothering your vision."

"No, this is fine. Thank you."

"Good. You have a nice estate out in Hunting Valley."

"I'm comfortable, yes."

"You have three houses on the property, don't you? Of course, you live in the large one. What do you do with the other two?"

"In one," he said, "the bigger of the two—there's an office. I have an office manager there—excellent young woman, and I pay her a small fortune to keep things running smoothly. She has a secretary. Ah, I guess we can't call them secretaries anymore—that's not politically correct. She has an office assistant. That takes up one-third of the building. The rest of it, and all of the smaller one, is warehouse." The corner of his lips twitched—Braithwaite wasn't sure it was a smile. "I have a housekeeper, too, attending Kent State University, who works in my house for me, keeping things neat and orderly." His voice was factual, as if reading

Monday morning's football scores. "I also fuck her on occasion, if that fits in with your questioning."

Braithwaite said, "Your sex life doesn't interest me in the slightest," and tried not to shudder at the picture in his mind he'll never could unsee. "You have a warehouse. Naturally, you have warehouse workers?"

Ruttenberg thought for a moment. "Somewhere around forty or forty-five, yes. I can't really keep track."

"All American citizens or foreigners with green cards?"

Ruttenberg's back grew stiff. He grasped both arms of the chair and leaned forward angrily. "Christ on a crutch! Is that why you called me down here? Is the Cleveland FBI trying to catch and deport illegals now? Why don't you spend your time doing something more useful for your country—like arresting people who spit on the sidewalk?"

"I'm not ICE, Mr. Ruttenberg. I don't give a damn who works for you and who doesn't." Now Braithwaite's tone also grew cool. "The rumor is you're the Number One distributor of illegally imported crack and meth in Northeast Ohio."

The Drug King of Hunting Valley sat back in his chair. "Do you have proof of that, Special Agent?"

"If I had proof, you'd have been in federal lock-up for years. Since I have no proof, I'm inviting you to sit with me and have a civilized conversation." Braithwaite half-laughed. "I didn't expect you to confess and throw yourself on my mercy."

"Then you've wasted my time. And yours."

"Not necessarily." Braithwaite's next question would have to be phrased carefully. "Besides the warehouse people working for you, don't you have a few muscle guys hanging around, just in case things get rough?"

"Muscle guys? For an antique warehouse? Get serious."

"A few days back, some guy got the piss knocked out of him, apparently at your facility."

Ruttenberg's mouth went dry, and he licked his lips—to no avail. "Where did you hear bullshit like that?"

"I'm not sure about the attack, but this young man was beaten up badly on your so-called estate."

Marshall Ruttenberg licked his lips and tried clearing his throat, wish he'd accepted Braithwaite's offer of coffee or a soft drink. "By whom?"

"That's not important. I've got enough info under my belt right now to send a whole crew of my agents out to your place to take a much better look around."

Licking his lips, Ruttenberg asked, "Tomorrow?"

"Who knows, Mr. Ruttenberg?" the Deputy SAC Agent in Charge said. "Tomorrow? Next Tuesday in the middle of the night? On the weekend? How about this afternoon? Who knows?" His eyes actually twinkled. "Just think of it as a big surprise."

CHAPTER TWENTY-EIGHT

At the beginning of their romance, more than a year earlier, Nico Brigandi falling into the sack with Courtney Holloway startled him. He had not brought pajamas with him on their fourth date. He took her to a special celebratory dinner at high-ticket Giovanni's in Beachwood—this time in the main dining room and paying for the privilege—along with a personal greeting from owner Carl Quagliata and a complimentary bottle of fine champagne. Later, when they'd arrived home and dismissed the babysitter, they finally made it from Courtney's living room sofa to her bedroom. Shortly thereafter, the once-in-a-while sex then magically turned into several nights per week. Nico grew accustomed to sleeping in the raw, and Courtney got into the habit as well.

Fortunately, Ian Holloway, Courtney's ten-year-old son, had learned early not to burst into his mother's bedroom without knocking, although even at his tender age, he had a fair idea of what went on in there, though ignorant of specifics.

On this particular morning, when the wake-up alarm jangled at 6 a.m., Nico and Courtney shared a long, sweet good morning kiss, but not a reprise of the previous evening. Then he watched with his usual pleasure as Courtney got out of bed and moved naked across the room and into the bathroom. From the start, her body had driven him crazy, even when clothed. He wished another mad moment that would once more leave the sheets and blankets tangled on the floor, or even better, a sensual romp with her in the shower, but this was a weekday and she had to drive her son to school and then continue to her job.

Soon, he ruminated, he'd propose marriage to her. That would be no easy decision, as every other married man in the Malatesta group had chosen an Italian, either from Little Italy or from the further-out West 185th Street area. Nico was not ready to walk away from his adopted "family" and Don Franco, away from his friends and compadres—but he wouldn't give up Courtney, either. She was his dream girl, his soul mate.

Courtney was aware of where and how Nico Brigandi made a living. It didn't trouble her much. The Soprano-Goodfellas-Don Corleone days were movie memories long gone; no one wakes up with the head of a horse in his bed, and now there were no Italian Clevelanders who even remember the Sugar Wars during the Prohibition 1920s when rival liquor gangs used to mow each other down almost weekly in the clubs, barber shops, and on the sidewalks near the intersection of Woodland Avenue and East 110th Street—the "Bloody Corners."

Courtney knew Nico never killed anyone, never dreamed of it, despite his close association with the Italian mob. Being a gentle guy, he rarely hit anyone in anger—only if they owed his boss money and wouldn't pay up. She loved him for that, and adored going with him to the fancy ballroom get-togethers where all the Italian food was terrific, top-tier singers and comics were flown to town from New York and Los Angeles to be the party entertainment, the women—frequently in their twenties and carefully selected arm candy for the much older mob guys—were all beautiful. Everyone seemed to have a great time, including Don Franco himself, always especially charming to her because she was *not* some Italian girl who'd grown up looking to capture one of the handsome tough guys and live an exciting, dangerous but luxurious life from then on.

Now, however, Nico had asked her to help him with his latest undertaking. Weird, she thought. She had nothing to do with the mob, crime, or violence, and he'd promised her there would be no bullets flying around.

What shook her up was this time her son Ian would be centrally involved. Nico had proposed this adventure a few nights earlier, and while she'd earnestly refused, especially when Ian was supposed to be part of the misadventure, he joked and cajoled her into it, adding, in the end, a decent guy will be rescued and a bad guy would stop coming hell-bent-for-leather against the mildly innocent Johnny Pockets.

Eventually, Nico wore her down, and she gave in. For several reasons.

She was crazy about the guy.

The assignment, if pulled off correctly, was a good thing—helping a nice young man needing to be rescued, giving a little boy dying to be an actor something to talk about, and in the process totally screwing a bastard.

As for Ian—acting was in his blood, wherever it came from, and if Nico insisted it would be safer for him to be the leading player in this bizarre, possibly dangerous reality show than to feed pigeons in the park who do little besides fly over people and dive-bomb poop all over them—well, why not, anyway?

The three of them had breakfast together—Count Chocula cereal and a glass of orange juice for Ian, Scottish-cut oatmeal for Courtney, cream cheese and bagels for Nico, with jet black strong coffee. The two adults seemed more tense than usual. For Ian? Just another school morning.

"Hey," Nico said to him. "You're sure you're up and ready for this after school today?"

"Sure." Ian was busy checking out his cereal, but like any actor, child or adult, he was a bit nervous about his upcoming "debut" performance. Rehearsing to become Joseph in the Nativity Play was one thing—but Nico had been honest with him. Later this afternoon, there was a small but real hint of danger.

"It's just like being in another play," his mother said.

"Yeah," Nico Brandini agreed, schmearing half of his second bagel with cream cheese. "This time you're the star."

"I wish I was on TV instead," the boy said. "People get more money on TV these days."

"I can't pay you money," Nico said. "That's like bribery. It's illegal. But I promise if this works, I'll buy you the most expensive racing bike in Cleveland."

"If it works," Courtney said, not smiling until her lover winked at her across the table.

Ian stirred his Count Chocula around, scratching his head with his other hand. "If I bike around Cleveland, some gangs'll steal my bike right out from under me and I'll gonna get killed."

"You can be sure if you ride your bicycle around where I work, in Little Italy, you'll be as safe as if you carried a million dollars in your pocket."

"If I had a million dollars, I wouldn't be riding my bike," Ian said. "But I bet this is gonna be fun today." He played with his cereal, scooping it up in his spoon and then letting it trickle down into the bowl again. "Weird," he said. "But fun."

Courtney looked dismayed as her eyes sought the ceiling. "Men!" she said to the gods above.

She and Ian drove off to the boy's fifth-grade class in school, and Nico Brigandi headed toward Little Italy, as he did every morning, looking forward to black coffee and pastry with his friends at *Rustica Malatesta*. At times he was given assignments for the Malatesta family thought were important—and sometimes dangerous. For all his handsome Florentine good looks and his affable personality, Nico was not someone to be messed with.

Don Franco had not yet arrived for breakfast, but his son John was already on duty, normally logging in sixteen hours a day at work as the manager of such a popular place, known as much for its innovative Italian cooking as for the connection to the well-known mob.

Some days earlier, Jericho Paich had approached Johnny Pockets and confessed he was being forced to frame him by a drug cop named Keegan Mayo—so Nico felt it his responsibility to let the young man know someone was actually working to save

his ass. When Nico walked into Johnny's tiny office on this particular morning, mug of coffee in hand, the godfather's son felt
two things—a rush of relief, along with an icy stab of fear up
and down his spine. His powerful, much-feared father would
support him in any way possible, and Nico Brigandi was the
favorite guy in the group to do what the Don told him—but uncomfortably aware every *capo* walked around wearing a bull-
seye on his back. If any family sideline wannabes decided to
move in and take over, they probably will be washed over the
side as well.

"I can't be completely honest with you, Johnny," Nico said
cheerfully. "The best of plans sometimes get fucked up. But if it
works—and ninety-nine percent says it will—that guy who
came to see you the other day, that Jerry Paich, will be out of
your life. Same with that cop trying to nail you because he can't
get to the Don—he's gonna be flat-ass outta business."

Johnny looked more confused than anything else. "What are
you gonna do?"

"Like I said, I can't tell you."

"Why not?" Worried—no, more like scared to death. "Are
you gonna kill both of them?"

Nico frowned, rubbed his wrinkled brow with his hand as
though suffering a sudden headache. "Johnny—we're not the Al
Capone gang. Nobody gets killed. There are ways of convincing
people to do things without blowing their brains out."

Johnny patted perspiration from his upper lip, his nerves doing triple back turns. "You talking about torture, Nico?"

"Christ, you've seen too many shitty movies. I'm just gonna
convince him."

Nico Brigandi had given this plan a great deal of thought. It
might work—but it might backfire, too. Good people might get
arrested or hurt. Keegan Mayo, like every other cop in America,
always carried a gun.

That had to be dealt with—more importantly than anything
that can or might happen. Therefore, Nico will be heeled, too.

He sipped from his mug and went back into the main room of the restaurant. Don Franco had arrived and was just digging into his Italian breakfast, and Nico approached him carefully.

"Good morning, Godfather," he said quietly.

"Nico!" The old man smiled around a mouthful of breakfast. "Sit, sit—drink your coffee."

"Thank you." He pulled out a chair opposite the Don and sat facing him—smarter than being next to him for breakfast, because the Don tended to splash his food around too much. "You remember, sir, we talked about this cop who has Johnny in his crosshairs? Well, I have a great idea to slam the lid on this whole thing."

"What's your idea?"

Nico paused. Several other men who worked for the Don were already having breakfast with him. To expose his idea too early could cause all sorts of trouble. He didn't distrust any godfather underlings sitting all around him—but just in case, he'd keep quiet until he had a full report.

"I can't share it right now. If it works, though, I promise you'll never have to worry about it again."

Franco Malatesta stopped smiling. He put down his fork and mopped his mouth with his napkin. "You got some big idea, but you can't even share it?" He raised his voice so everyone in the room could hear him. "What the fuck is that, Nico? Don't give me no *agita*."

Nico Brigandi found it difficult to swallow before he could speak again, but if any of the other guys having breakfast heard what he'd planned, they'd want to muscle their way into it and then everything would be ruined. "Don Franco," he almost pled, "if dif I share it with anybody—anybody at all—it might not work."

"And what if it don't work?"

Silence. Nico had never imagined it wouldn't work. He found the breath to say, "It will."

"A good thing. But in case it don't," the Don said, munching on his breakfast, but his tone was sharp as a fine-honed razor, "don't come back."

CHAPTER TWENTY-NINE

Marshall Ruttenberg slumped low in the back seat of his car, seething with rage as Randy, his chauffeur, drove him home from his FBI visit. His dark glasses protected his eyes, even though his car was heading east, with the sun at his back. He was breathing hard, clenched fists, knuckles so tight they would turn white—except they were very white already.

Jericho Paich had suffered severe punishment inside the smallest of Ruttenberg's three houses on the estate, after hours when the warehouse workers had gone home. Someone had seen his assaulters load him into their car after the beating, and had let the Federal Bureau of Investigation know about it.

Who ratted Ruttenberg out? There seemed just one answer.

On his cell phone, he dialed a number he used sometimes—that of Skinny, one of the men he'd charged with punishing Jerry Paich. But there was no answer, just a standard message. He cursed aloud and punched out the number of the second man. No one home there, too.

He grew even more angry. Those hit men were not on his regular payroll—they might have other jobs or assignments—but they always seemed easy to locate and quick to obey. And he needed them today, more than ever.

Entering his driveway, Ruttenberg noticed Bria Harstad's car parked where it usually was, next to the second house where she worked every day. His teeth were clamped so tightly together he could barely get them open.

He leaned forward. "Randy!" he said to the chauffeur, "just leave the car in front of the big house—and stick around. I'll need you again later."

Randy's heartburn geared up for a major attack. He'd had plans for himself that evening with a very attractive young Chinese woman he had met when shopping at Whole Foods. But he answered "Very good, sir," and stopped near the huge front door, decoratively wood-carved in Switzerland and shipped on special order to Marshall Ruttenberg.

The drug maven got out, giving a backhanded wave to Randy without looking at him. When inside, he didn't hesitate for a moment, but got to the nearest land line, interconnected to the other two houses, and pushed a button.

When Bria answered, he barked, "Come here immediately. I'll be in my office."

He moved to the hallway beside the kitchen and went into the large room he'd designated as his working room, locked metal file cabinets stretching over one wall, a double-large desk with an executive chair resembling a throne. A relatively well-done copy of a Degas hung where he could see it from every angle. The shades were pulled down, as always, making it dull and dreary inside. He removed his sunglasses and put them in the handkerchief pocket of his suit. He had hidden dark glasses all over the house—office, kitchen, bedroom, three different places in the living room, and in the top drawer of a small table standing right by the front door. He sat behind the desk in the gloom and waited.

It took Bria Harstad ninety seconds to walk between the two buildings and use a side door close to his office before she appeared carrying a stack of papers.

"Well," she said, using her best phony smile, "you're back early. Did you have a nice afternoon?"

"Peachy," he said, the word dripping acid.

She frowned. *Peachy* was a word from the 1920s and rarely

used by anyone in the twenty-first century, and it caught her off balance. She put the papers on his desk. "There's a shipment due from Poland day after tomorrow, if you want to look over the inventory. I contacted the trucking company—they'll pick it up and bring it here."

He nodded. Bria was never comfortable seeing his eyes without the dark glasses, and today the eyes looked furious. "Is something wrong?"

"How was *your* day today, Bria?"

"Usual day," she said, nervous all of a sudden. "I ate lunch at the Legacy Village food court—which is generally awful, by the way. Otherwise, I was here working all day."

"Didn't have lunch with a friend?"

"In a food court? No."

"How about yesterday? Did you have lunch with a friend yesterday?"

"I don't have that many friends, Marshall—and the few I have don't work nearby, so I never have lunch with them during the week."

"I see." He pushed himself up from his chair and walked around the desk so he was standing close to her. "Never have lunch with the FBI either, do you?"

She backed up a step. "What are you talking about?"

"I'm talking about stool pigeons, Bria. Squealers. Or what they call them in the Mafia—canaries." He hitched up his belt, pulling it up over his pot belly—which she'd never seen him do before. "Remember, I asked you to get information on someone named Jericho Paich?"

For a moment the backs of her hands went numb, as though she'd let them fall asleep, and she tried flexing them with her arms down at her sides to wake them up so he wouldn't notice. "Yes," she said, "and I did as you asked. I called County Commissioners, Francis Murgatroyd—a friend of yours, not mine. He gave me what little he could find out—and I passed it along to you."

"Murgatroyd wouldn't report me to the FBI. First of all, he doesn't really know what I do for a living, and secondly, the FBI scares the crap out of him. I take him for big dinners every month or so, either at Johnny's Downtown or at Paladar in Woodmere Village, and set him up with a whore that same night. He'd never do anything to make that stop. No, my dear—it wasn't Francis Murgatroyd. It was *you*."

"I never talked to the FBI. Why would I?"

"Why would you indeed, when I pay you a small fortune just to work here? You think you're so goddamn hot—why do you refuse to fuck me anymore? Why do you peek out windows at things you shouldn't see and then jabber about them to those who would lock me up forever? It was you, Bria. It was you."

Then he swung backhanded, and his knuckles caught her at the side of her jaw, a powerful blow by a strange little man that knocked her head sharply to one side and lifted her off her feet and into a corner. She just lay there, dazed.

He walked to her and stood over her, his mouth a terrifying slash across his chalk-white face. "Traitor!" he practically screamed. "Traitor cunt!"

He grabbed a fistful of her hair, pulled her halfway to her feet, and slapped the other side of her face, the blow sounding like a rifle shot in a quiet, snowy forest in which hunting was against the law. Blood trickled out of the corner of her mouth.

"Don't worry, bitch, I won't mess up your face anymore." Then he let go of her hair and punched her hard in the stomach.

Unless a woman has trained to be a professional boxer, a violent fist to the solar plexus, especially when not expected, does not go well. Almost blacking out from the sudden pain, none of her inner muscles could function, and she couldn't inhale. Bile filled the back of her throat, and her belly felt as if it were on fire.

"The rest of you, though?" Ruttenberg said. "Every inch of you belongs to me." Sucking half the air out of the room and into his lungs, he proceeded to beat and kick her with a savagery rarely seen in a normal human being. Her arms, breasts, chest, ribs, legs, buttocks, and vicious overhand punches in the middle of her back with the albino's hard little fists doing the most amazing damage to her.

She barely could breathe enough to scream.

It took him two minutes of violent attack to so completely exhaust himself he was unable to deliver another punch or kick, his heart hammering against his ribs like a bongo drum. He half-sat and half-leaned against his desk to collect himself, all the while enjoying her agony as she quivered on the floor. Then he went out into the kitchen, filled a drinking glass with cold water, returned to the office and threw it in her face.

Bria was nearly comatose. Her whole body was in so much pain she couldn't even gasp at the cold shock. He had barely touched her face after the first two blows, but she still could barely open her eyes. Agony made everything seem blurred and out of focus.

"Wake up, cunt! Listen to what I'm telling you," Ruttenberg growled as she wheezed for a full breath of air. "Your job here is finished—but you're still working for me, you understand? For the rest of your fucking life, you're working for me. I'm shipping you down to Tijuana as fast as I can to people I know there. You're no spring chicken, so no one will really get rich selling your aging ass—and in Tijuana you'll open your legs for anybody who has five bucks in his pocket. When you get old, they'll make you suck and fuck actual donkeys for the entertainment of drunken Marines from Camp Pendleton up north. And when you're so skaggy and messed up even for that, they'll cut your throat and throw you in the ocean, or leave you rot in the desert as fresh meat for the vultures. Nobody will know the difference."

He moved closer to the door. "Stay right where you are. Move just one muscle, and you get another beating, even worse than the first one." He kicked her in the stomach again, then walked out and locked the door behind him.

Putting his dark glasses back, Ruttenberg found his way outside to where Randy, the chauffeur, waited by the car.

"Go into my office," he ordered, handing Randy two keys and a roll of money, close to three hundred dollars in tens and twenties. "Bria is on the floor. Pick her up—carry her if you have to, but get her out of here. Take her to that apartment in Tremont, just over the river where Jill Taggart used to live. You can remember where that is?"

"Yes, sir."

"Good. Stay there with her, every damn minute, until I manage to get her out of the country—two or three days. Order in food from local restaurants—whatever you want—and enough food just to keep her alive. Make sure she's out of sight when the food deliveries arrive—and warn her if she makes a sound, you'll beat the shit out of her again."

"Again?"

"We had a slight disagreement." He raised a warning finger. "Don't mess up her face, though. Don't hit her where it shows."

"Whatever you say. Do you want me to take her away now, Mr. Ruttenberg?"

"*Right* now!"

"Yes, sir." Randy nodded, his forehead wrinkled in a frown. "Hey, whatever happened to that Jill Taggart, anyway?"

Marshall Ruttenberg paused, considering if he should get furious with Randy for his inquisitiveness. He decided against it. He needed Randy—if only for the present. "Jill is no longer with us. Mind your business, Randy."

Randy almost snapped to attention. "Yes, sir." He started for the door.

Ruttenberg moved slightly so he wouldn't be looking into the bright sky. "Do what you want. Fuck her yourself whenever you feel like it—but my guess is right now she won't appeal to you. She'll have bad bruises all over her body. Besides, at the moment, sex might just kill her. You have your personal cell phone with you?"

"Never go anywhere without it."

"Excellent. I'll be in touch tomorrow night, and probably the following day, someone will come and take her away." He headed for the front door, then stopped and said, "There's a generous bonus waiting for you, Randy—if you do this job well."

He went inside and immediately headed upstairs to his master bedroom, where he stripped off all his clothes and put them in two different piles—one for the laundry and one for the dry-cleaner, as they were all soaked in sweat from his recent barbarous exertion.

Then he stepped into the shower—a huge shower with six nozzles at various heights and angles, just in case five other people might want to join him. So far, none had.

Soaping his chalk-white body with unscented tea tree soap, he took a moment to be annoyed, angry, and disappointed. Bria had worked in his organization for a long time. He was enraged; after all those months, she betrayed him. In the end, he knew they all betray. Everyone—women especially. There is no one he can trust—nobody except himself.

He stepped out of the shower, drying himself with two enormous towels and then throwing them on the bathroom floor for his housekeeper to find in the morning. Feeling somewhat refreshed as he dressed himself in one of his light gray suits, he thought of where he would go for dinner. Shuhei, the famous sushi restaurant in Beachwood? Texas di Brazil for an exotic steak? Paladar, for Latin food? Damn, and Randy left with the car! He'd have to drive himself in one of his other vehicles—perhaps the Alfa Romeo. He didn't feel like driving tonight. The abuse of Bria Harstad had physically exhausted him.

He was sad, too. Where, he wondered, could he find another highly talented office manager?

CHAPTER THIRTY

Unlike the 1960s and 1970s, when winding up in bed with a stranger was considered no more shocking or scandalous than a handshake, nearly two decades into the twenty-first century things were different. Not unheard of, but quite rare anyway. Opening your eyes some morning and discovering someone whom you barely knew next to you on the other pillow becomes a rude awakening.

When Jaimie Peck shook herself from sleep, she was aware who Jerry Paich was. *That* Jerry Paich, Jill Taggart's ex-lover, on the run from people he didn't even know. Why was he sleeping two inches from her face? She could not remember. She'd met him a few times during his Jill years, at a party or in a Happy Hour bar. Jaimie had thought Jerry was on the outskirts of being cute and seemed a decent guy, but hardly a boy toy. Being African American herself, she'd preferred darker males.

But not always.

Jerry Paich had quietly disappeared from her life at the same time Jill Taggart fell off the edge of the earth, too, six months earlier. She'd gone out of her way to track Jill down, to find out why she had faded into the mist, but came up empty each time. After that, both Jill and Jerry were just fading figures in her memory.

When Jerry suddenly appeared at her door, barely able to stand up from a beating he received and not explaining anything more as he begged to sleep on the sofa for a few days so the two men who'd punched him around couldn't find him to do it again—if not worse—she couldn't find it in her heart to turn him out into the street.

A longer conversation revealed Jerry had been selling drugs for Jill while she vacationed in Cincinnati and had been nailed by the number two guy in Cleveland's anti-drug task force and threatened with a choice: heavy-duty prison time, or be a confidential informant continuing to sell dope and then ratting out users to the police. That became a wake-up for Jaimie Peck. She'd never admitted it to anyone she, too, had been corralled and forced into becoming a snitcher by Detective Keenan Mayo.

After mutual confessions and finding themselves in similar situations and embracing, tears dropping freely like summer rain bursts, they got quietly drunk on Sauvignon Blanc, exposing to each other their terrible situations, and found themselves ending up in her bed in what both of them would later recall as a "mercy fuck."

Both suffered white wine hangovers in the morning, but there was hardly any awkward conversation between them until they showered—separately—and dressed. Jaimie made strong coffee. Neither were hungry, but they sat together at the table in the kitchen. Jerry kept shifting positions in his chair; his body still ached from the punishment—and sex had not lessened pain. Embarrassment and humiliation added up to his inability to sit still.

Jaimie glanced out the small kitchen window several times, as the sky was gray, threatening a damp day. It was dangerous driving when the roads were wet rather than when they were snowy or even coated with black ice—the kind you don't see until your tires won't go the way you want them to. At length she said, "I'll have to take an umbrella. Goddamn rain!"

"I'm—sorry," Jerry said eventually.

"The rain isn't your fault, Jerry."

"I mean—about last night. I never meant for that to happen."

"Neither did I." She didn't look at him. "Forget it. It's no big tragedy."

The clock on the kitchen wall ticked loudly, and Jerry felt it was ticking away precious moments. He said, "That's not why I showed up here, Jaimie. I had nowhere else to go. If I had to wander the streets on foot, I'd be dead by now."

"I wouldn't want you to be dead." She sipped her coffee slowly. "We're both exactly in the same kind of trouble, and no way of getting out of it. So we got drunk—to commiserate with each other—and one thing led to another. Now we're both hung over and feeling down."

"I don't think we should be guilty."

"No."

"Shit happens."

"It does."

Jerry was growing more terrified than the night before when he found himself in bed with her. "I mean, we're not going to pick out furniture together or anything."

"I don't need furniture."

He put both hands around his coffee cup as if they were cold, and he was warming them. "I'll—I'll move out while you're at work."

"Where will you go, Jerry? You don't have a car, you can't go back to your own apartment, you can't live with your mother again." Jaimie sighed. "Don't be silly. Just stay here like usual. There's stuff for lunch in the fridge, and I'll buy some dinner before I get home. Spaghetti okay?"

Jerry shrugged.

"Just—sleep on the sofa tonight. Or I will."

"It's your home. You don't have to sleep on the sofa."

"Yeah, but you're the one hurting, not me."

She finished her coffee and put the mug in the sink, then waved at Jerry and left. No kiss goodbye—obviously—and as she walked to her car, she had to think seriously of why she and Jericho Paich had sex in the first place.

She slid in behind the wheel of her car, engaged the engine and pushed the button that blew mist from the inside of her windshield so she could see to drive. Too much Jericho bruises notwithstanding, the sex had been pretty good.

Jerry didn't leave her apartment. He had no place to go, anyway. Discomposed because of the previous night. Frustrated, feeling helpless to aid himself in any way. Terrified the moment he stuck his nose out the door, they would kill him.

He got more coffee and switched on her living room TV. As a working man, he had no idea what daytime television is really like. He'd grown up when texting and Internet and cell phones came far after the days of a solid morning of game shows and a lengthy afternoon of soap operas and re-runs of decades-old shows like "Bonanza" and "Have Gun, Will Travel," the only respite for those who stayed home all day. Using the remote, he hopped around until he found MSNBC, and while their general political outlook matched his, he was too hung up on his own troubles to even think about Ukraine, North Korea, Russia, or *collusion.*

He hit the *off* button, and the screen went dark. He didn't need the world's troubles to make him forget his own.

There were no bookcases in the living room, and when in Jaimie's bedroom, he hadn't taken a furniture inventory. She apparently was not a book reader, as he found none anywhere, though there was a basket of magazines at one end of the sofa— all female-oriented and nothing that interested him.

He spent almost an hour staring out the window at the street; heavy clouds masked the sun hanging over the lake. No cheery sky to make him feel better.

He'd seen many movies in which prisoners are punished by solitary confinement—stuck in a dank, dark cell, never speaking to another human being, day after day and week after week. Now he was in a comfortable apartment with the faint smell of a woman and her cosmetics and cologne and the recollection of surprising but satisfying sex.

He had his cell phone, but the only people he could think of to call were his mother and her live-in boyfriend, Laird Janiver.

Arielle was impossible. She even cried on good days, but hearing her only son hiding for fear of his life would really send her over the edge.

He desperately needed moral support, and Laird was the only one who might supply that for him. He dialed Laird, but the line was busy.

Damn! He drank another cup of coffee—was it his third? His fourth? In any event, he wouldn't get a wink of sleep that night. Then he tried again.

"Where are you, Laird?" he asked after the hellos.

"In the Hilton Garden Hotel, right across the street from Progressive Field. I haven't had time to look for an apartment."

"You and Mom are—?"

"Looks that way. Relationships more often than not run their length, and then it's over." Slight pause. "Who was the guy who had you beat up, Jerry?"

Jericho said, "He didn't do it himself. He had two other guys do it."

Laird Janiver was quiet for a moment. Then he said, "Those two guys won't bother you again."

"How? What did you do?"

A sigh. "Let's just say I learned a lot during basic training at Camp Lejeune."

Jerry felt his heart choking his throat. "You didn't—Jesus, I hope you didn't—"

"The war is over for me, but I won this particular battle. Big victory. Take it from me, and forget them."

Laird had not forgotten them, though, and never would. They wound up weighted down in a rarely visited twist of the Cuyahoga River not too far from Public Square. The chances were excellent they'd be swept out to Lake Erie and never be heard from again. If they washed ashore in the tide at Edgewater Beach, tracing them back to him, or to Jerry, were slim-to-none.

"Oh, by the way," Janiver said, "the door to your apartment

got kicked in. I called someone to drop by and install a new door."

"You kicked in my door?"

"Not me. The big muscular guy did it for me."

Now Jericho Paich was hopeful. "Does this mean no more C.I. business? The cops will leave me alone, too?"

"I haven't worked that part out, Jerry. Tough, mean cops are like pit bulls; once they grab hold of something in their jaws, they don't let go." He filled his lungs with air, then expelled it. "But so do I."

"Shit!"

"I started the ball rolling already—but there's not much I can do to this Keegan Mayo character. You don't know the big drug king's name?"

"He didn't tell me."

Laird nodded thoughtfully. "I think I know anyway—but he's got a big organization behind him. I'm just a weary middle-aged guy with one foot. I can only go so far."

"I'm not worried just for myself," Jericho assured him. "After I got busted, my girlfriend disappeared. I couldn't get her on the phone. There was no one in her apartment. Her best friend doesn't know where she is either. I don't know if she went back to Cincinnati or if something bad happened to her. But it's not like her to fade away."

Laird said, "Someone saw you right after the beating—when the two guys were loading you back into their car. This person—a woman—came to your mother's house because she somehow found out who you were and where you lived. I was the only one there, so she didn't learn anything from me. I went to her home the following day—and she told me as much as she knew. Now this guy who ordered his two goons to hurt you—"

"He said I owed him fifteen thousand bucks plus interest—probably from the stash Jill was selling—and if I don't pay him, he'll kill me."

"Describe him."

"What do you mean?" Jerry asked.

"What does he look like?"

"He looks like a freak. His skin is the color of Tide flakes—very white—and his hair is the same color. I noticed, too, that he has really pink eyes."

"An albino."

"I guess so."

Laird nodded, though no one could see him. "Then I know exactly who he is."

"Tell me."

"No—you'll get yourself killed."

"Then tell this cop Keegan Mayo."

Laird Janiver's short-term memory flashed back to his ugly meeting in Keegan Mayo's office. "I don't think so. It's like talking to a brick wall."

Jericho thought about that, remembering his visit with God-father Don Franco and his son John, who was targeted by Mayo. It would have been a gold star on Mayo's arrest record if he took down the son of the local *capo di tutti capos*, and probably a kick upstairs to a police lieutenancy on which he could retire.

Who knows if the Italian mob handed out gold stars to their hierarchy, but Jerry got the idea the Don was not happy.

"Talking to a brick wall?" Jerry finally said to Laird. "I wish Keegan Mayo could be buried under one."

CHAPTER THIRTY-ONE

After his phone talk with Jericho, Laird Janiver's mind juggled too many ideas and responsibilities. For the first time in being a servant to his country, he was more than a bit confused. He paced his hotel room, frustrations goading him with every step, passing his window dozens of times without even looking out across the street to Progressive Field, where the Guardians played baseball in the warmer months.

Bria Harstad had a life, a job, an entire existence that had not included him until 48 hours earlier. He didn't know where she spent every moment of her time, so it's logical she was not at home nor at her employment. But why didn't she answer her cell phone? Why didn't she reply to his texts? Was she—God forbid—seeing another man?

He had firmly fallen in love with Bria at first sight. Now he worried Ruttenberg had not only fired her, but had ordered her to be killed. An illegal drug company was not run the same way Procter & Gamble or General Motors operated their empires. In any event, he couldn't do a thing about it.

When finally dragging the whole story from Bria, including Jericho Paich's beating and the visit to his work from two hit men again, she'd given Laird much to digest. He had no clue how hideous Ruttenberg really was. Now he thrashed around in his hotel room like a tiger trapped in a too-small zoo cage, running over every single word she'd uttered that evening, hoping for a shred of truth he could get his teeth into. He needed to find her, find something about her. He'd only seen her three times in his life, but had arrived at the decision that he couldn't go on without her.

The trouble was, he had no real power. At the moment, he didn't even have a place to live, other than a rented hotel room. He couldn't sit back and wait for someone else to create a happening. That wasn't how he was made. Retirement and prosthetic foot notwithstanding, he was still a Marine.

What had Bria told Laird about, exactly? She did mention Ruttenberg had no friends, just business associates and most politicians in Cuyahoga County. Ruttenberg also had a young housekeeper who keeps the house clean and neat. He had no live-in cook, but ate at restaurants nightly, alone, tipping big for the protection from strangers who stare at him, wondering if he was a real albino. For his above-board business, he imports valuable historical artifacts from all over the world, especially paintings worth millions of dollars that were stolen by Nazis during World War II, and sells them off to antique dealers, museums or art auction houses.

He makes big money that way.

He lives in an elegant estate in Hunting Valley guarded by armed hoodlums, mostly because he is also a major dispenser of crack cocaine and methamphetamine, delivered from all over the world. His sprawling home had minimal furniture and no artwork whatsoever, with two smaller outbuildings used for preparation and storage. A crew of illegal immigrants who worked with plants and rocks, chopped them up and pack them for distribution. Some local drug mules—pushers—move the final product through streets and college districts, mostly to young people preying on other young people for their sales. They operate out of their own homes, and drop by every few weeks or so with fistfuls of money for him.

No one buys illegal dope on credit cards—and cash, big hunks of cash, never reported to the Internal Revenue Service.

Marshall Ruttenberg, then, was protected. So how in hell could Laird Janiver get to him and force him to say what had become of the woman with whom he had fallen in love?

Drab. Dingy. Somber. It was a tacky apartment on the first floor of a remodeled house, with a second apartment upstairs. Though the furniture was relatively new, it was Value City all the way, not built to withstand more than two years of ordinary living before it began to shred, sag, and droop. Who in their right mind would buy a bright orange sofa in the first place?

To Bria Harstad, it would be solitary confinement for her, even though Randy was there all the time, watching her every move. He spoke little, but she was the office manager, and he was Ruttenberg's chauffeur, who also picked up his dry cleaning and did his grocery shopping for the week, so they had little in common.

Until now. Now, apparently, he was her jailer.

She didn't feel like talking, anyway. Her entire body ached and throbbed, at least from the neck down. The beating had been brutal, lasting far too long, and with broken bones—probably a few ribs and a collarbone, although she couldn't really tell. It was better, she supposed, than if Marshall Ruttenberg had killed her—but not by much. No one ever repeatedly kicked her in the breasts before.

She'd spent the first eighteen hours or so on the bed in the single bedroom, waiting for terrible pain to lessen. Then she managed to stagger to the living room, where Randy spent his time. She tried ginning up a conversation, but they were hardly acquainted. She'd seen him in and around the big house and said little to him. Now, he would not answer questions. Instead, he told her how things would go for a while.

"I'll send out for your meals for as long as you're here, Bria," he said. "You can even order whatever you want—Chinese, Mexican, Italian—whatever. If you need anything from the drug store—your personal needs—I'll phone the nearest one and ask them to deliver what you want, ASAP. Otherwise, I won't bother you."

"That's good to hear," she said with difficulty. "How long are we stuck here together?"

"I—don't know. Mr. Ruttenberg didn't tell me."

"And what happens after that?"

He looked away, not having the balls to meet her glance with his own. "He just told me to watch you and take care of you until—until whatever else he decides."

"Great!" she croaked.

Randy looked pained. "Bria—I don't know you very well, but I think you're a nice person. My job, though, is to make sure you stay here. When anyone knocks on the door to make a delivery, you'll have to go into the other room and keep quiet, okay? So don't make me hurt you. Don't try to scream or to get away, because if you do, I'll have to hurt you. Don't make me. *Please* don't make me."

Her shoulders slumped. "I can hardly move, Randy. I'm so fucked up right now, it'd take fifteen minutes to walk to the corner. So don't get all bent out of shape about it."

"That's—good. Thank you."

"Where is my car, anyway? My purse? My personal cell phone?"

He had no idea, which suggested she count the remaining hours of existence on her fingers.

Had she given up the rest of her life because of Laird Janiver and his live-in's son, Jerry? The big surprise of the past few days had been meeting the first man she thought would be in her future, and now—because of his girlfriend's dorky son—she's going to die? A tiny corner of her mind envisioned Laird riding to her rescue on a white horse—but he had no idea where she was, what had happened to her already, and what lay ahead of her—empty darkness.

Even if he wanted to, Laird Janiver could never get near Ruttenberg even to ask him.

Randy said, "Do you need anything right now, Bria? We have bread—butter and peanut butter, too, if that sounds good to you."

"Peanut butter? Jesus Christ!" With difficulty, she pulled herself to her feet, leaning against the wall because she feared falling. "Randy—I have to lie down."

"That's fine. I'll be here."

She wobbled into the bedroom and collapsed onto her bed. The spread was cheap-looking. smelling of some other woman's perfume. The bathroom looked as if hadn't been cleaned for weeks or more. What kind of place was this? Does Ruttenberg own the apartment? The entire building? What does he do with it when he's not storing women there he'd beaten half to death? Is this a way station to be sent to a foreign country to die like a rabid dog infected with syphilis—or something worse? This was morphing into a nightmare purgatory in which to await an execution.

She closed her eyes and tried drifting off, her only option, but her dreams, or hallucinations, such as they were, made the Spanish Inquisition look like a church picnic in the park.

She thought, as her eyes opened every few minutes before she dropped off again, that everyone is aware they'll die someday—but rarely do they prophesy the death would be horrifying, painful, and fueled by the revenge of a madman?

CHAPTER THIRTY-TWO

Ian Holloway, dressed in his Batman pajamas, crawled into bed and pulled the covers up under his chin. His blanket was from the Cleveland Browns, and over his bed was a very large poster of LeBron James in a Cleveland Cavaliers uniform, who was such a huge icon in Northeast Ohio no one cared he was now on a different team in a different city. Besides his dream of becoming an actor, Ian was a huge sports fan. "Thanks for reading me a bedtime story, Nico," he said to the man perched on the edge of his bed. "You're a pretty good guy."

"You're a pretty good guy yourself, Ian," Nico Brigandi said, closing the book—*Tom Sawyer*, a Mark Twain classic. "That's why I brought ice cream for your dessert tonight."

"Rocky Road," Ian beamed. "That's my fave."

"Mine, too," Nico lied. He actually hated Rocky Road, but one can't always be honest with a nine-year-old, especially when the thought of becoming his stepdad in the near future was beginning to take form. He rumpled Ian's head, messing up his hair a bit. "All right, slugger. Good night. Sleep tonight. Don't let the bedbugs bite."

"Eeeww!" the boy said, and covered his head with the blanket.

Nico flicked out the light and went back out into the living room, where Courtney Holloway waited for him. He shook his head, embarrassed. "I really like that kid."

"He really likes you, too," she said, "a major deal because

now he's a big important superstar."

"Playing Joseph in the Nativity Play?" He laughed. "It's been so long since I read the bible, I don't remember if Joseph has any lines in that particular story. Besides, superstars always get the girl. I don't think Joseph got that lucky."

"Blasphemy!" Giggling, she moved over and patted the sofa so he could sit beside her. "Nico—Ian is nine years old. He doesn't know about getting laid or not." She rolled her eyes. "I hope he doesn't know."

"He's got a few more years, Court. Enjoy it while you can."

She stretched her legs across his lap, and her look became serious and worried. "You want to turn him into a real actor, though—all having to do with the—uh—*group* you work for. Things the Malatesta family gets into can be dangerous. What you're talking about could be dangerous, too—for him, for me, and for you."

"It can't be all that dangerous," Nico said. "One particular cop wants to nail John Malatesta, who hasn't done a damn thing illegal since he boosted a candy bar out of a Walgreens when he was eleven years old—not counting smoking a joint every once in a while. If my father were the Italian Godfather, I'd be toking dope, too. Half the Ohioans get sentenced to a twenty-year stretch for smoking a joint. This Keegan Mayo is a twisted, crooked cop, but a very ambitious one, and he wants to retire with a gold badge, which means a bigger retirement package. He's probably a half-hearted police officer, but his ambition got in the way."

"Detectives," Courtney observed, "carry guns."

"What'll he do? Shoot a child? Shoot all three of us?"

"Cops protect other cops."

"Maybe so," Nico said, "but not when he blows away an entire family in his own home. If the department tries to whitewash him, it'll start a go-to-the-mattresses war with the entire Italian community—here, in Pittsburgh, in Chicago, maybe even in New York—led by Don Franco, naturally." He looped his arm around Courtney Holloway's neck and pulled her close, kissing her on the cheek and the ear. "I won't let Ian get hurt—and not you, either. When it's all over, you're gonna look back on it and laugh your ass off."

"Convince *him* he won't get hurt."

"He's an actor, baby."

"He's an actor playing a thirty-year-old virgin from the Middle East twenty-one centuries ago who pretends he's the real father of a baby that isn't *his* baby."

Nico laughed. "That says how good an actor he really is."

"Teach Ian to be careful, Nico, no matter what." She sounded wound up, tense and frightened to pieces. "Otherwise, we'll all get in trouble."

Nico Brigandi leaned back against the arm of the sofa. "I know all about careful, Court," he said with confidence and a smattering of arrogance. "Just think of what I do for a living."

"I don't want to think about that."

"Then don't. Nothing violent will happen, not to us."

She took a deep breath. "When do you plan on doing this?"

"Tomorrow. Late tomorrow afternoon, like when Mayo gets home for dinner."

"How are you going to practice with Ian?"

"He can stay home tomorrow, and I'll work with him all day." He grinned. "Don't worry, they won't start rehearsals for the Nativity Play for a while. I checked."

She shook her head sadly. "I won't sleep a wink tonight worrying about this, Nico."

He rubbed his face into her soft hair. "Come to bed, Court," he said softly, seductively. "I'll make you forget all about it."

Francis P. Murgatroyd was having a hell of a life. When he ran for city council in the eastern suburb of Garfield Heights a generation earlier, no one had bothered to tell him politics, at best, is a dirty business. He tried to ignore it and kept his head down, took whatever grift or bribe or "favor" found its way to his desk, and bulled his way forward until they elected him one of three Cuyahoga County Commissioners. Fine, as far as it went—and he knew in his heart it was *actually* as far as it would go for him.

He sucked around political big shots for a living, jumped as high and as often as he was ordered, talked one way to the few who gave a damn what he said and ignored everyone else. He voted just as his constituents told him to, and tried hard not to piss off too many people at one time.

Now, for some reason he was unable to decipher, he managed to get sucked into the Ruttenberg-Paich-Mayo mess. He'd never heard of Jerry Paich until Ruttenberg ordered him to dig up as much dirt as he could—and sent his top employee, Bria Harstad, to do it for him. That ticked off Detective Keegan Mayo, who personally insulted and humiliated him, just across the street from the courts in a restaurant where lawyers, judges and cops he associates with daily were having lunch there to witness it.

Murgatroyd wished it would all go away until he got a surprise early morning phone call.

"Franny, how're you doing? Marshall Ruttenberg here." He rushed on, sounding almost jovial. "I want to thank you personally. I'm thinking this Jericho Paich kid will never bother me again. It's all because of the hard work you did for me."

Hard work? Councilman Murgatroyd had only made four personal phone calls to get what minimal information about Jerry Paich was available to him, which kept him from internet porn sites for several minutes—normally a major part of his office day. 'Hard work' didn't begin to cover it. Then why this congratulatory phone call?

For whatever reason, Murgatroyd thought, go for it. "I really appreciate your support of me, Marshall. Ask me for any favor," he said, hoping like hell there would be no more favors.

"You'll be up for re-election pretty soon, aren't you, Franny?"

"Next year," Murgatroyd answered.

"Well, I'll be behind you all the way."

"Marshall—I'm really touched. And flattered."

"I'll write you a check when the time comes," Ruttenberg assured him.

"I'd love that, Marshall. I'm grateful in advance, if you know what I mean." He stopped short, almost afraid to ask his next question, but sitting up a bit straighter, even though no one could see him, he decided to risk it. "Marshall—you never *told* me why you needed background on this Paich guy."

Silence for about ten seconds. Then Ruttenberg said, "If you recall, I never told you anything at all. Your conversations on this deal were between you and Bria Harstad."

"Yes, yes, that's true, Marshall. I just didn't think to ask."

"I understand. I know you've had the hots over Bria for years. You were thinking so hard about what you'd like to do with her you didn't ask any more pertinent questions."

Francis Murgatroyd's cheeks were burning, thankful no one on the other end of a phone call could see him blush. "Well—"

"That's all right. I understand lust. I particularly understand the idea of unrequited lust."

"It happens. I've lived lots of years, Marshall—and there's plenty of women I letched after and never got the chance to do anything about it."

"Even totally gorgeous women like Bria?"

Franny smiled, just thinking about it. "She's Number One— not counting movie stars."

"Movie stars," Ruttenberg almost whispered.

"Emma Stone," Murgatroyd breathed dreamily. He grew more stupid with every comment.

"I don't know Emma Stone personally, Franny. Bria works for me, though now she's in a different—department."

"Oh?"

"Well, before I write you a check next year, I want to do you another favor right now."

"What's that?"

"Franny—how'd you like to fuck Bria Harstad?" Marshall Ruttenberg suggested. "Tonight?"

CHAPTER THIRTY-THREE

After the Hang-Up—Ruttenberg

Marshall's offer left him feeling good about himself. He needed that self-love moment for a change. Despite his wealth and success, despite the fear of other people whom he's has existed under for his entire existence, he never felt comfortable with his own life. His albino condition had caused pain, shame and constant bullying as a child, and even as a top-level drug dealer—among other things even less pleasant—that fear never really went away.

It's all well and good for people to change their minds, he thought, as Bria Harstad obviously had. Most did not appeal making a fortune in the illegal drug trade. But to turn against someone who's trusted you, who paid more goddamn money than you were worth, to contact the Federal Bureau of Investigation and spill her guts about what she'd earned for keeping secret—that, in his mind, was treason of the worst kind.

The worst kind? He shook his head, aggravated with himself. Stupidity made him more furious. Even his thoughtless idea being stupid put him into a funk.

What was the best kind of treason, anyway?

Despite having contractors who hurt his enemies on his demand, he didn't think of himself as violent—but then most violent people perceived themselves as angelic and saintly until brutality became necessary. Looking back, he knew he'd totally lost control with Bria. The first backhand blow was all he'd meant, but somehow it pushed him further, using fists and feet, eventually injuring her very badly. Now he wished he'd finished the job and killed her right then.

However, his mantra had always been: Don't get mad—get even. He knew Bria's bruises would fade—and to Ruttenberg, simple beating did not come close to 'getting even' for what he looked on as betrayal. Further revenge on Bria would take planning—and he'd even make money off the deal.

He was trying to reach men with whom he'd done business on occasion. Smuggling and selling European art works was a big profit-maker, but he rarely needed physical cruelty for that. Several times he'd functioned as middle man in sex trafficking, usually of young girls. He planned to sell Bria Harstad to one of them, and now he thought of two tough guys—Skinny and The Wrestler—who could assist him in making that business deal happen.

Bria was obviously past the age of young teen girls usually enslaved in third world countries, but she was not only beautiful, but had all the classic Nordic features—blue eyes, fair white skin, blond hair she'd been born with. When she wound up where he'd eventually put her—probably somewhere in the Middle East, she could earn three or four times the money for her pimps as those young teens.

No one close to him had ever forsaken their loyalty to him. Therefore, Bria deserved more than a beating, even more than just death. She'd end her days miserably tortured, used, abused, and finally thrown away.

He wanted more personal triumph for himself, though, before he shipped her off. He didn't control prostitutes in Ohio, so he couldn't rent her out before she left. But if he could do something to humiliate her terribly, that would make him feel better about himself and his rage.

What would be more gross for Bria, then, than to be force-fucked by a man she did not like at all—a fat drunken slob who lucked out in local elections because he's a funny guy to have at *a drinking bash, and who did favors for powerful Cleveland mavens and accepted elegant dinners in expensive eateries, plus the gift of a beautiful hooker for an evening, which after all is what kept him going?*

The dumbshit had been ridiculously smitten with Bria for years. Maybe once he gets to realize his "impossible dream" to have sex with her, he'll probably fall in love with her and try to find her again, never knowing she'd be turning tricks somewhere in the Third World at forty bucks a pop.

He called Randy on his cell phone, telling him he wanted Bria to look decent that evening—nice clothes, nice make-up, make sure she shaves her legs. She was going to have company.

Then, smiling all the way, he rang up his favorite Cuyahoga County Commissioner.

"Franny, how're you doing? Marshall Ruttenberg here. I want to thank you personally…"

After the Hang-Up—Francis Murgatroyd

Franny Murgatroyd clicked off the phone and then just stared at it—stunned, barely able to have said "Goodbye and thanks" to Marshall Ruttenberg. From the day he first set eyes on Bria, or even talked to her on the phone, his concupiscence would cross the line into the red danger zone, his mouth would go dry and he had to work hard to lick his lips back into their proper function. Butterflies fluttered in his stomach.

No, not butterflies—they were too gentle, too fragile for his insides. A better thought for him was Peregrine falcons, flapping hard and diving toward its prey faster than the speed of light!

He was not in love with Bria, not in the usual way, though she inspired his heavy lust. His mother, the last in his family actually born in Ireland and reared in a lace curtain Irish family, had it set in her head her first-born son, Francis Padraic, would be a Catholic priest. However, after struggling through a Jesuit high

*school with mediocre report cards and a record-breaking num-
ber of times he was sent to the principal's office, Francis decided
he enjoyed partying, booze and hookers more than wearing a
turned-around collar and jerking off alone in his small cell for
the rest of his life.*

He became an Irish politician instead.

*He knew how to bullshit his constituents, no matter their eth-
nic background. He didn't like Italians having Greater Cleveland
by the short hairs for the past century, had no use for Jews or
Hispanics, and the lately-come criminal Russian mob terrified
the crap out of him. Still, he showed up smiling, hand-shaking
and back-slapping at all local ethnic parties and festivals on
weekends, bringing with him a genius memory for names of
those whose hands he shook, even on those occasions when he
was not completely sober.*

*The thoughts of sex with Bria overwhelmed any other thought.
He asked his hard-working secretary to hold all phone calls unless
they came directly from the governor's office in Columbus.*

*He planned to go home early, shower, shave, and change
clothes before he went to the address Ruttenberg had given him
where Bria Harstad awaited him—hopefully with open arms.*

*How many times over the past two years had he fantasized
what she would look like without her clothes on? Were her nip-
ples large or raisin-small? Red or pink? Presumably not brown,
as she was the quintessential Nordic beauty, pale of skin and
blond of hair.*

*Did she shave her pubic hair? Was that blond, too? For half
an hour Franny cogitated on that subject, finally deciding he
preferred fuzziness there, though he disliked women who did
not dispose of growth on their legs or armpits.*

*No matter—he'd know for sure in approximately seven hours.
What a gracious gift to him from, of all people, Marshall Ruttenberg! Ruttenberg had taken him out to several dinners at Hyde
Park Grill, Johnny's Downtown, or Giovanni's in Beachwood,
and had also sent over a few hookers for him at times when
he'd granted a favor—a good thing. His success with women no*

one paid for was almost non-existent. In our strange, tribal society, one does not have to look like a movie star to get laid— but one should be halfway classy, halfway clean and decent, and relatively sober.

There had been times when Franny's relations with paid prostitutes had ended badly. Often for a man pushing sixty, erectile dysfunction becomes a total block for successful penetration. Daily drinking was a major cause.

Therefore, he swore off his lunch, guzzling on this day of all days, instead ordering a takeout sandwich to be delivered to his office from a nearby restaurant and washing it down instead with plain ginger ale. He felt good about that—deodorized and fragrant. Pure and upstanding—and hopeful when the time came later that evening, his penis would be upstanding, too, the way it used to be when he was twenty. Bria would be glad to see him, he figured, and would do anything he wanted her to.

He began not feeling very good at about three o'clock in the afternoon.

Bria was a college graduate, an efficient office manager and businesswoman. Now, Marshall Ruttenberg said she still works for him but in a different capacity.

A beautiful, successful woman in her mid-thirties suddenly decides to become a prostitute?

Franny recalled what Ruttenberg said on the phone—his chauffeur would make sure Bria did what she was told. That he should enjoy the hell out of himself, all night if he so desired, because Bria would relocate to another city soon—so make the most of it.

Why, he wondered, if Bria Harstad had chosen prostitution over office management, and is Randy, the burly chauffeur, there to enforce her activity?

Is it possible Ruttenberg changed her occupation against her will? Franny knew damn well Bria had never been the slightest bit interested in him. Was spending all night with his dick inside her an agreed-upon hook-up, or was she being forced?

Franny had been a liberal Democrat his entire life, and the circus-like Senate Judiciary Committee meetings on the Brett Kavanaugh Supreme Court nomination gave Murgatroyd a new outlook on women who were sexually abused and then totally ignored by police, government, and white men in general. He didn't like that at all, realizing call girls who visited him at the behest of those richer than he weren't doing what they do because they loved it.

As the thought drilled into his head, his lechery for Bria dissolved into anger and a lightning flash of bravery. Breathing heavily, he picked up the phone again and dialed a number.

After making arrangements, he told his secretary he'd be gone for the day, and made his way to The Little Bar, just off West Sixth Street's Restaurant Row, waved to one of his familiar bartenders, and ordered a double Jack Black, which he put away within two minutes and then ordered another one.

What the hell was the difference now? he thought? Bria wasn't going to see him with his clothes off, either.

CHAPTER THIRTY-FOUR

Missing her like crazy and worrying where she had gone, Laird Janiver drove by the address Bria Harstad had given him, the place where she worked in Hunting Valley. One hell of a sprawling estate, he thought, at least six or seven acres, even though he could only see part of it from the road, the driveway framed by two large brick columns. One quarter of the sweeping lawn, off to one side, was being used as a parking lot. Eight dusty inexpensive cars were parked there, most ten years old or more, along with two yellow school buses no longer used by any education facility—vehicles that bring the workers to and from a pickup and drop-off location. Many of them, dark-haired and swarthy and calling to each other in Spanish were Puerto Rican, who had found their way to Greater Cleveland after Hurricane Maria brought normal living on their island to a complete stand-still in 2017.

The main house, furthest from the road, was not a mansion, exactly, but a very large house—far too big in which just one person should live. Two men in lightweight zippered jackets were hanging around the main door—checking their surroundings, being watchful, suspicious, and very much on duty. Laird noticed the bulges under their left arms, indicating they were former military and had spent much time in places like Damascus and Baghdad and Beirut. He understood that type of attention in a zone could be dangerous. Those who lived in expensive houses like this one did not have 24-hour security at the front door—which made the Ruttenberg estate more interesting.

The second largest building—Bria had told him it was the one she worked in could be a spacious home for a family of four, except what few windows visible to the road were heavily curtained so no one could peer in, no sunlight could penetrate, and none inside could see out. Several husky, muscular men with Latino looks walked in and out of that second building lugging large packages—sturdy cardboard boxes wrapped in heavy-duty brown paper. Laird thought they were loading them on some kind of truck parked out of sight.

The smallest of three structures was just the right size for a parent-in-law's home, refashioned. Bria had explained to him the former living room was an area in which clerical workers or temporary laborers spent their time. In its present use, the larger of two bedrooms were for the business manager's job space, and the smaller one was a supply room—a Xerox printer and shelves stacked with all sorts of office gadgets, staplers, reams of paper and marker pens, and dozens of rolls of Duck Tape.

No way anyone could tell exactly what went on at this estate, but Laird understood his chances of getting in and confronting Marshall Ruttenberg face-to-face were less than nil. Knowing Bria had been unreachable for two days put him on a lonely hunt. Until he found her, he would keep going.

He checked his watch—six thirty in the evening. Bria had explained Ruttenberg, anti-social at best, always went out to dinner alone between seven and seven thirty. That gave Laird a better chance to confront him alone, anyway. He was a tough guy, whether with one foot or two, but he would not go to war with an entire army.

There was no place for him to park on that road to wait for dinnertime, and Laird knew he couldn't drive onto the estate without being noticed—and hassled. This time he didn't give a damn about being messed with, because his Marine DNA had kicked in. His Glock 26 9mm was fully loaded, tucked neatly into his waistband and easy to reach, a second clip in his pants pocket—but blowing anyone away was not what he had in mind. He was after Ruttenberg himself—and he had only one question to ask him.

Unable to park unnoticed so he could watch the compound's entrance, he motored about half a mile down the road, pulled into someone else's driveway, backed up and cruised by again.

He continued this boring back-and-forth drive for about twenty minutes until he spied in his mirror a shiny black Alfa Romeo snaking out of Ruttenberg's estate between the two columns, turning right, and heading south toward Chagrin Boulevard.

Dinnertime! Laird wasn't certain, but thought he saw someone fitting Marshall Ruttenberg's description—a face the color of skim milk behind the wheel, half-covered by oversized sunglasses, wearing a light gray jacket that might match the pants Laird couldn't see, and a broad-brimmed off-white fedora. When was the last time he saw a fedora being worn on the street? Strange, the tie Ruttenberg wore—most people in this part of the twenty-first century rarely donned ties other than for political meetings, business or a funeral—was plain blue.

Ice blue.

Boring blue.

At Chagrin Boulevard and Ohio 91, the Alfa went a quarter of the way around the traffic circle and headed south. Laird wasn't sure what he would do when they both got where they were going, but he played it by ear, the way he had in Afghanistan. In any situation—driving, combat or football—waiting for that nanosecond of space and time, that extra inch of manipulation and then plowing forward and using it to the best advantage. That was how games and deals and wars were won or lost.

The Alfa Romeo pulled into the huge lot and parked as close as possible to the Paladar Latin restaurant. When the driver got out, straightening his hat and checking the tie knot with his fingers and checking his reflection in the closed car window, Laird got his first good look at Marshall Ruttenberg. Ruttenberg's complete lack of coloring was worth only a quick second glance, but the rest of him—the pale gray suit, the 1940s Bogart hat that eighty years later looked ridiculous eighty years later, giant sunglasses covering his face as though a celebrity wouldn't want anyone to recognize him as a movie star. Everyone *would* recognize him behind the shades, and worst of all, the bulging potbelly which made him appear to be a slim man who had just swallowed a soccer ball.

Ruttenberg headed into the Paladar. Janiver knew he couldn't follow that closely, so he sat in his own car, anger growing by the minute. Ignoring that it was Jill Taggart who dragged Jericho Paich kicking and screaming into the dope business, it enraged Janiver Detective Sergeant Keegan Mayo not only locked Jerry into indentured servitude and tossed him out of his office, but sent two cops into another civic venue to arrest *him*. Then this kingpin of sleaze ordered Jerry beaten—and Bria Harstad had witnessed it, or at least the end of it.

Now she had disappeared into the layers of fog that often attack one's mind. Ruttenberg's office said she didn't work there anymore, she didn't answer her land line or her cell phone, and no one could tell him where she was or what happened to her.

He admitted the thought of Bria had brought him to this parking lot with a loaded Glock jammed into his waistband. Was it love, just plain raunchiness, or something else entirely? He neither knew nor cared. She'd become a very important person to him and he felt responsible for taking care of her. If he didn't find her again pretty goddamn soon, then Marshall Ruttenberg was going to get hurt.

After ten minutes, he got out of the car and left it unlocked, then entered Paladar to be welcomed by a pretty hostess, menu in hand. She looked twenty years younger than the youngest of her customers.

"I'm just going to sit at the bar, if that's all right," he said.

He ordered a bourbon straight over ice cubs from another young pretty behind the bar, and tried not looking at the albino occupying the dark corner table as far from the door and window as possible. Ruttenberg hadn't removed his hat until after giving his order, but now he was bareheaded, his lank white hair almost invisible in the low light. His hands were folded across his stomach, not really looking at anyone else or making eye contact. Despite his illegal wealth, Laird thought, he must live a dreary, lonesome life.

Normally, when one eats lunch or dinner in an upscale restaurant, the time to enjoy the meal was never less than an hour and usually longer than that, the time usually shared with someone else. After thirty-five minutes, Ruttenberg called for the bill, paid with an American Express Platinum Card, and headed out the door, once more donning his hat and dark glasses, though eight o'clock on a November evening in suburban Cleveland does not call for Ray-Ban shades. Laird Janiver wondered if he would keep them on to drive home in the dark.

He threw a ten and two singles on the bar and followed his target out the door. He remembered where Ruttenberg had parked, so it was easy to spot the Alfa Romeo, even when the sun and residual light in the sky had disappeared.

As he snaked his way through the parked cars, head down, he slipped on a pair of latex gloves, took the weapon from his waistband, and held it at his side. He wanted Ruttenberg's attention from the start.

Bria's employer was at his car now, fumbling in his pocket for the remote control that would open the driver-side door. Laird moved up behind him.

"Mr. Ruttenberg. Do you have a moment?"

The chalk-white man turned quickly, startled—irritated. "I have no time for you," he said. "Whoever you are, call my office for an appointment."

"You need to make time." Laird brought up his Glock and pointed it at Ruttenberg's midsection.

Ruttenberg's watery pink eyes flared and then flickered with amusement. "I know who you are—the Negro who lives with that Jericho kid's mother."

"Negro?" Laird tried not to laugh.

"I rarely see Negro men, so the guess was easy, especially one pointing a weapon at me. Don't be an ass," he said. "What will you do? Shoot me right here in a busy parking lot?"

"Here? Not exactly." Laird jammed the muzzle of the Glock into Ruttenberg's gut—hard.

The drug maven groaned, bent at the waist and grasped the fender of his Alfa to keep from falling.

"Don't fuck with me, Ruttenberg," Laird said. "Sending you to whatever it is they call Boot Hill these days wouldn't be a big deal at all."

For a second, he thought about that. Many men, women and children lost their lives to his Marine company when he was in the Middle East—but they were strangers. He didn't know who they were, whether they had mothers and fathers, or spouses or sweethearts. He had no idea if they did anything besides being an ISIS soldier. After their death, he didn't bother finding out. They were a job well done; now move on to the next one.

This was no Afghanistan, but Woodmere Village, Ohio—a tiny suburb not much more than six blocks long and famous for busting automobile operators who drive three or four miles over the speed limit. It was a fifteen-minute trip from downtown Cleveland—Public Square, the sports venues, the theater district, the elegant hotels, University Circle with its magnificent museums and concert halls, and even the shores of Lake Erie. It took him a few seconds to wonder what the hell he was doing.

Then it all fell into place again.

He put the side of the gun against Ruttenberg's face and pushed upward so he could run his free hand all over his body to certify he was unarmed. He couldn't remember being anywhere near an albino person, had certainly never touched one before. He avoided contact with Ruttenberg's bare skin, even on his hands or face. The thought made him shudder. "Unlock your car door, Mr. Ruttenberg. You and I are going for a ride."

CHAPTER THIRTY-FIVE

Courtney Holloway was busy in her bathroom, combing her son Ian's hair so he would look nice for what might lie ahead that afternoon, even though she knew Nico Brigandi's idea was unglamorous. Nico stood at the door, watching, smiling, shaking his head—the perfect avatar for a father, even though he was not one. At least not yet.

"Ian's not ready for his close-up yet, Mr. DeMille," he said. "He's a kid who's been playing outside all day, not a Brad Pitt lookalike."

"He's not a homeless immigrant, either!" she snapped back. "I want him looking decent." She sighed, exhaling through closed lips that provided a Bronx cheer. "There's nothing decent about any of this, Nico."

"What's decent is that a corrupt Cleveland cop has painted a target on the totally innocent back of the son of the man I work for and care about—and it's my job to do something about it. You have to live with that, Court—if you care about me."

"I do care about you—but I'm a mother!"

Ian pulled away from Courtney's ministrations to his hair, shaking his head so the front lock fell over his forehead. "Hey, guys, I'm in the room too, okay?"

"Nobody's forgetting you, buddy," Nico said. "You're the centerpiece today." He rumpled the boy's hair, destroying all the work his mother had done brushing it.

"Yeah—but I'm a little scared."

"Well, I guarantee you won't get hurt, get shot, or anything else bad. It's all just pretend."

The child sighed. "You said before you wanted me to cry, but I probably can't. I don't cry much, Nico. Did you ever see me cry before?"

"Never. Well, if you can't cry, at least pretend you're hurt real bad. You're a good actor. You can do that, huh?"

'A good actor' echoed inside the boy's head and made his smile a mile wide. "No prob," he beamed.

Nico snapped his fingers. "Let's go into the kitchen and get some ice cream and cake, and we'll go over this one more time."

"I get dibs on Rocky Road," Ian shouted as he scampered down the hallway toward the refrigerator.

"Rocky Road," Courtney whispered, running her fingers through her own hair. "Tell me again why I'm allowing you to do this, Nico."

"Besides that, you love me clear to the moon and back?"

"Besides that."

Nico threw an arm around her shoulders. "This crooked cop decided to take down John Malatesta, even though John never did anything wrong. He manages his father's restaurant, he dates lots of women, and that's it. His only guilt is being born a Malatesta."

"You're a Malatesta, too."

He shook his head. "Adopted—and accepted. But I'm a Brigandi, remember? Johnny Pockets is pure Malatesta blood."

"His father's not so pure."

"Nobody's completely pure," Nico said, "but as far as I know, Don Franco never ordered a killing—not anyone from a rival mob or of anybody else. That murder shit went out even before the Godfather movie."

She chuckled, which was at the moment her only choice besides screaming. "You wops treat that movie like it was the Bible."

"The bible has lots of murders in it. That's why we go to Sunday mass—to remind us the killing business is just a story."

"Then why is it 'Don Franco?' Why isn't it just 'Frank?' Or 'Mister Malatesta?'"

"He's not just Frank. He's not 'just' anything. He's a godfather, and I work for him because he's good to me. That's why I have to take care of his son." He pulled her closer and kissed her beside her right eye, the only place he could reach. "I'm taking care of *your* son, baby. Trust me."

"You better take good care of me, too, Nico."

After the ice cream and cake—carrot cake, bought at a Market District the previous day and not made from scratch, as Courtney often did—and the final run-through of what their plans were for later. Courtney took Ian in her car, Courtney's expensive camera slung around her neck. Ian wore an autumn jacket and khaki slacks. Nico, in his own car, was aware of the Derringer in his waistband, hoping like hell he wouldn't have to use it.

It took them more than half an hour to reach the rented apartment of Detective Keegan Mayo in the Tremont area just west of the Cuyahoga River downtown—usually not that long a drive, except this was rush hour, or as Clevelanders often refer to it, a rush fifteen minutes. Courtney parked directly in front of Mayo's building, Nico's car behind her. As soon as both engines were off, Ian got out of Courtney's car and headed directly for Nico's, while Courtney got into her own back seat and scrunched low so no one would see her unless they were actually looking.

"You doing okay?" Nico asked.

Ian said, "I'm kinda nervous, I guess. I never did anything like this before."

"First time for everything. You'll get great experience with this, so by the time the Nativity Play comes around and you're playing Joseph, everyone'll think, 'Hey, where did they get the professional actor?'"

"Don't jerk my chain! It's just a grade school play."

"Okay—but don't worry."

"Why not?"

"Because I'm here," Nico said. "You trust me, don't you?"

"Well, yeah, but—"

"No buts. You know I love your mom, don't you?"

"I guess."

"No guessing. I do. And you know damn well I love you too, don't you?"

"Yeah, I figured that out a long time ago. And by the way, you're not supposed to say bad words."

"You know *darn* well—"

"Better."

"So trust me. Just trust me." Nico looked at his watch. "He'll be along any time now, so we'd better get ready." He leaned over, reached into his glove box, and pulled out three small individual packets of ketchup.

"You're gonna ruin these pants," Ian warned.

"I'll buy you another pair. I'll buy you ten more pairs."

The kid shook his head theatrically sad. "This is gonna be yucky. Besides, I hate ketchup."

"You won't have to suck it out of your pants." He carefully tore open all three packets and squeezed the ketchup on Ian's pants, on the outside of his left thigh about three inches below his hipbone. Then he said, "We'd better go sit on the steps, Ian. You ready?"

"I'd rather you taught me how to be a great quarterback."

"If I could," Nico said, "then I'd *be* a great quarterback and too famous to even talk to you. Come on, Ace, let's go."

They got out of the car and walked across the sidewalk to the stairs leading up to Keegan Mayo's porch, then sat down two steps from the top.

"When I tell you go," Nico said, "you start rocking back and forth like you're in big-time pain, okay?"

"Should I start now?"

"No. He might not get here for a while. But when he does, you'll know what to do, right?"

They had to sit another ten minutes until Nico Brigandi saw

Keegan Mayo's car come around the corner and drive partly up the driveway, heading to the garages in the rear of the house—but he actually saw Nico and Ian on the steps. He also saw what he believed was blood on the leg of the kid's pants. He stomped on the brake, jumped out, and moved quickly toward them.

"Jesus, what's going on here?" he said, actually looking concerned.

Ian, already method-acting his role, had twisted his face into a portrait of agony and kept saying, "It hurts! It hurst so bad!"

Nico was deep into the acting bit, too, his hands trembling and his voice raspy and shaky. "He chased a ball out into the street and *bang!* The car that hit him didn't even stop—it just headed down the street and disappeared."

"When did this happen?"

"About two minutes ago."

Ian's howls of pain increased in volume.

"Did you call an ambulance?"

"Yes," Nico lied, "but their line was busy. Listen, can we come in for a few minutes? Please? While I try the EMT again so we don't have to sit out here with him bleeding in the street?"

Mayo hesitated, then shrugged it away. "Well—that'll be okay. Come on." He walked up the steps to the door, Nico and Ian following. Ian was limping badly, like a nameless movie extra who'd just been shot by Liam Neeson in an action film.

Right inside, Mayo turned left toward a door marked "1-B" and opened it with a key. "Come on in," he called over his shoulder. Ian staggered in first and headed for the sofa. Nico hesitated in the doorway—but he discreetly pushed the button just by the latch that would make sure he could still open the door from outside.

"How bad is it?" he asked Mayo. "Can you tell?"

"All I see is blood."

"We ought to take his pants off so we can look."

That made Mayo start. "He's your kid—you do it."

"I'm—I can't." Nico held his quivering hands out so Mayo

could see them. "My hands are shaking so bad. Nothing like this ever happened to me before. Look—let me try the EMT again, okay. Can you just pull his pants down so we can see?"

"Christ, you can't dial a call, either."

"It's just—9-1-1."

Mayo rolled his eyes toward the ceiling. He didn't sign up for this, he thought. He didn't like kids, didn't like being around them. Ever since his rookie days pounding a beat in the Glenville neighborhood morphed into plain clothes and a detective's shield, he made a point of staying as far away from children as possible.

Now here was a kid, hit by a car, bleeding like a stuck pig, and sitting on his sofa. Hell, he had to do something. On the drug detail with nothing to do with traffic accidents—but a cop is a cop. 'Protect and Serve' and all that shit.

"Make your call," Keegan Mayo said to Nico, and moved over to Ian, who was writhing on the sofa.

"Let's have a look," he said gruffly. "We gotta stop the bleeding until the EMT gets here." He bent over, unbuttoned the boy's khaki pants, and took them down around his knees. Ian, still grimacing, wore white Jockey shorts, and it took less than a second for Mayo to see there was no injury.

That's when Nico Brigandi stepped back out of the way— out of the photo shoot—and shouted *"Now!"*

The front door slammed open, Courtney Holloway burst in and took five very quick photographs—with flash.

"Run!" yelled Nico, and Ian jumped up from the sofa like a frightened cat, holding up his unbuttoned pants with one hand, and ran like hell out the front door along with his mother.

Shocked into immobility for a moment, Keegan Mayo wasn't quite sure what happened. By the time he figured it out, the boy and the photographer had gone. The man running the situation was pointing his own weapon directly at the middle of Mayo's chest.

"Who the fuck do you think you are?" The cop sergeant demanded.

"Don't get all excited, Mayo," Nico said quietly.

"Excited my ass! I'll blow your goddamn head off."

"Not if you keep your hands up. Besides," Nico Brigandi said easily, "you don't want to shoot me in your own living room. You really don't. If you do—well, I'd hate it a lot—just not as much as you'll hate those photographs on the local TV news shows tonight and tomorrow morning, and in the *Plain Dealer* and the *Akron Beacon-Journal*. And if the national TV networks get hold of them when they get bored with telling the world everything the president does every day—wow!. Imagine those headlines, Mayo. '*Top Cleveland drug cop sexually attacks child.*' Did you see that little boy's face? Terrified. In pain. And a fat, dumb cop pulling his pants down. Can you guess how they'll think of you in your own precinct? It'll make the whole department look like perverts, so say bye-bye to that promo to lieutenant—with the nice gold badge. So long. See you later. *Adios. Hasta la vista. Au revoir*—and *w*ave goodbye to your current rank, too. Back to rookie again, Mayo—pounding a beat in the Third District, where if the black mobs don't get you, the Russian mobs will if you just look at 'em wrong."

Mayo let loose a stream of obscenities, some Nico had heard before, others brand new to him. He waited until Mayo ran out of them.

"Done, Detective? Good. Just listen up, then, because this is important. John Malatesta. Sound familiar? It should. Your plan was to set him up buying drugs and then put him in prison for twenty years—which will piss off his dad no end. So, here's the thing. Lay off John Malatesta now—and the entire Malatesta family—now and forever. Pretend there's no such thing, and you might retire with a brass band playing. If not, those photographs will be on nation-wide television. You'll be Cleveland's asshole of the year. No, I take that back—asshole of the decade."

At first, Keegan Mayo's anger had made his face turn red. Now it was ash gray. He was breathing heavily as though he'd just run a six-minute mile.

"Go back to the office tonight, Detective. Get those arrest reports you never signed and never turned in, even after six months. One is for Jaimie Peck and the other for Jerome Paich. Don't show them to anyone. Put each in an envelope addressed to the so-called perp. Put stamps on them, and in the morning drop them in the mail.

"I'm leaving now," Nico said, moving toward the opened door. "You can shoot me in the back, if you so choose—that'll turn you into a famous celebrity real quick—and your photos will be the pictures of the decade. Otherwise, I'll just say good-bye—and we both hope I'll never see your face again."

He replaced his weapon. Behind him, the cop cleared the frog from his throat, his voice different. Soft. Low. Frightened half to death. He whispered, "Who the fuck are you, anyway?"

Nico Brigandi stopped, turned around, and gave Detective Keegan Mayo his most pleasant smile.

"During my normal human moments, I'm Clark Kent—the civilian version of Superman. I'm faster than a speeding bullet. I leap over tall buildings in a single bound—and I land hard, right on your fucking neck!"

That evening, less than two hours after they got home, copies of the photographs of Keegan Mayo in his home taking down the pants of a nine-year-old boy were emailed to the main subject, and to Franco and John Malatesta, to Jaimie Peck, to Nico Brigandi's father Joe, whose home was in Hudson, a suburb halfway between Cleveland and Akron, and to the lawyer, the Malatesta family *consigliere* who lived in an elegant suite in the Pointe Towers, an old office building converted into condos in downtown Cleveland.

Another set was emailed to Jericho Paich, who was not at home or in his office, so at that moment could only see it on his iPhone, with a note attached: "See? No worries. Enjoy. Then Delete. Do it!"

CHAPTER THIRTY-SIX

Laird Janiver's weapon pointed at the right ear of Marshall Ruttenberg, who had driven to an obscure thickly forested park virtually no one ever visits after dark. Those living near the county line separating Cuyahoga County from Geauga County understand West Park, as it's called, is less a recreational park than a mini-forest, home to deer, foxes, raccoons, coyotes, owls and falcons that would attack you as soon as look at you, and occasionally a black bear. There was no one around at nine p.m. to notice a sleek Alfa Romeo pull in and drive deep into the brush, where no one could see it from the road.

"Stop here, Mr. Ruttenberg," Laird ordered. "Turn off your engine and hand me the keys."

Ruttenberg reluctantly did as he was told. "Are you stealing my car?"

"Close, but no cigar. Get out."

The animal night sounds were not as loud as each of them believed, but leaves and twigs crackled as the wildlife stalked its evening prey. While he'd never admit it, Ruttenberg was quietly terrified, but Laird was relaxed. There wasn't a thing to fear from a fox unless it was rabies-infected. Coyotes are more frightened of humans than the other way around. Raccoons, as a rule, did not bite people unless they are being kept from their dinners. This was mating season, however, so they all had more on their mind than chewing on visitors. And bears? Black bears do show up in Northeast Ohio every so often, but they are more popular in the southern parts of the state, and wouldn't attack a human being unless their baby cubs were in danger.

Laird took a flashlight from his belt and switched it on. During the day, walking this park would be difficult because there were so many trees Laird couldn't identify if he carried his high school botany book with him—growing so close together it even blocked the bright summer sun. At this time of night, it was the darkest corner of the world.

They both exited the car. The air had grown chilly after the sun had disappeared. Snow was not that far away, perhaps less than a week. Ruttenberg finally removed his dark glasses and put them in his inside jacket, because except for the gibbous moon hovering over this eastern suburb, there were no headlights, nothing that would make him squint. Laird wondered if, like a cat, the albino could see in the dark.

They moved toward the deepest part of the woods, Laird behind Ruttenberg, pushing him forward with the gun poking into his back. Low-hanging boughs whipped at their faces, and the fallen leaves of autumn—yellow, orange and red, snapped and crackled beneath their feet.

"Are you going to shoot me in the back?" Ruttenberg called over his shoulder.

"I'm thinking about it, Mr. Ruttenberg—but I'd prefer shooting you in the front."

They reached a small open space, more of a half-clearing, and Laird ordered, "Stop here! Turn around."

They faced each other. Dark as it was, it was harder for Janiver to see than Ruttenberg, who said, "Exactly what is it you want from me? My car? It's an Alfa Romeo. The cops will spot it in a minute. Money? I have about eight hundred bucks in my pocket, give or take. It's yours if you want it. Drugs? I don't have any crack. I always thought you colored guys were more into crack than marijuana."

"Colored guys?" Janiver said. "Seriously? Colored guys?

Welcome to the 1940s."

"If it were the 1940s," Ruttenberg said, sounding bored with all of it, "I'd be calling you a nigger—but I'm not. Look, I'm not into guessing games. Tell me what you want from me. I'll do it, and we part friends, or you can shoot me dead."

Laird thought it over. "You mentioned drugs—illegal drugs. Is that how you make so much money and live on a huge estate and drive a hundred and fifty grand car?"

"The car didn't cost quite that much. Yes, drugs help pay my mortgage."

"Thought so. Is that why you had Jericho Paich beaten up?"

"Ahh, Jericho Paich," the drug dealer said.

"How did you find out about him?"

"I had my—executive assistant—contact Commissioner Francis Murgatroyd, who found out as much about him as he could. I never laid eyes on him before that day, but he owed me money. A lot of money. The so-called—incident was simply a reminder."

"I get that. But why send the same two guys after him again? Another beating so soon after the first one?"

"I had second thoughts. Mr. Paich could never raise that much money in a few days. I can't have people steal from me. If I let him, then I let the next guy, and the next guy after that, and pretty soon I'm handing out carts at Walmart for eight bucks an hour."

"So you were going to kill him?"

"If one fucks around in a dangerous business, they take their life in their hands every morning."

"Well," Laird said, "you better run out and find two other guys to do it, because your first team is out of business."

"Interesting. Did you kill them?"

"They're—not in town anymore."

"So Paich won't pay what he owes me? I guess I'm fucked, then."

"Something like that." Laird nodded, but he didn't lower his weapon. It still pointed at Ruttenberg's chest.

"You made me drive all the way out here and walk half a mile through the woods just to tell me that?"

"Just partly."

Ruttenberg's eyebrows went up. "What's the other part?"

"Bria Harstad."

"Never heard of her."

"Lie again," Laird warned, "and I'll blow off your kneecap. I know she works for you."

"She doesn't work for me anymore."

"Then where is she?"

"How should I know?"

"She doesn't answer her cell phone, and she's not at her apartment—"

"Maybe she took a long trip to London, Paris, Rome, Barcelona—"

Laird jammed him in the stomach with the barrel of the gun. Hard. Mean. It doubled Ruttenberg over again. Laird gave it almost a minute before he said, "Keep it up, Ruttenberg, I can hurt you all night long and not even break a sweat."

Ruttenberg managed to straighten his body out again, so he was more or less standing up. "She's at an apartment on the near west side," he gasped. "Until tomorrow, or maybe the next day."

"And what happens after that?"

Marshall Ruttenberg licked at his lips, as his whole mouth was going dry. Finally a nasty sneer changed his facial expression to pure evil. "You won't want to hear about it."

The next blow opened a bleeding cut between his left sideburn and the edge of his eyebrow. Staggering backwards, he kept going until his spine hit a tree. Laird Janiver followed, putting his face close against his enemy's. "The next one will make you barf up that yummy dinner you just paid fifty bucks for, because I'll go to work on your testicles."

Ruttenberg's pinkish eyes opened as wide as possible. "I'm

telling you the truth. She'll be leaving the country tomorrow or the next day."

"Leaving for *where?*"

"Someplace in Mexico—or some other Latino country."

"You have businesses in Mexico?"

Ruttenberg wiped away the blood running down his face. "I have businesses all over the world."

"But you say she's not working for you."

"Not anymore."

"She was working for you two days ago," Laird reminded him, "but she doesn't today. Did you fire her, or did she leave of her own accord?"

"Just call it—a difference of opinion."

"I call it an outright lie." He shrugged his shoulders and took another step forward. "Okay, here I come for your balls."

"No, wait! *Wait!*" A scream.

Laird Janiver's shoulders drooped a bit. He actually felt disappointment. "What?"

Ruttenberg was shaking all over. Eventually he said, "I make a lot of money doing shit that's illegal, okay? I sell meth and crack all over Northeast Ohio. People all over the world send me stolen antiquities, and I resell them for a fortune. And yes, I operate on the edges of sex trafficking, too."

"No shit," Laird almost whispered.

"So I admit—I'm not a very nice person."

"Big surprise." Said with no surprise at all.

"Prostitution is a huge money-making business—not just here in the United States, but all over the fucking world—so sure, I make a ton of money—but people work for me and I have to pay them. Pay them goddamn well, too. Then—when one of them accepts my money and good treatment, and they betray me? Fuck me over? Get me in trouble? What do I do then, pat 'em on the back and give 'em a raise? The hell I do! I punish them—bad enough so nobody else will ever try it again."

"Bria Harstad betrayed you?"

Ruttenberg's breaths began coming faster. "Betray? She talked to a county commissioner, and two days later, the fucking FBI is up my ass."

"She talked to a commissioner because of what you'd done to Jericho Paich."

"Another traitor!"

"You had him half-killed because he was misled into owing you a ton of money?"

Ruttenberg nodded.

"Then why send the same two goons back to beat him up again. He wasn't close to recuperating from the first time?"

There was a fifteen-second silence while Ruttenberg tried to figure out the best way he could phrase his answer. Then, nodding to himself, he said, "He's not—one of our people. In the business—the criminal business, I admit—everybody knows to keep his mouth shut. You lean that early—or else you don't make it to middle age. Paich was a scared kid. Kids talk."

"Jerry Paich doesn't talk, Ruttenberg. The reason he got fucked up in the first place is when the cops busted him, he refused to name his girlfriend, the one who dragged him into selling shit in the first place—so they told him he either had to become a Confidential Informant, or spend twenty years in prison. Those were two choices that scared him silly, but not enough to kick his girlfriend under the bus."

"Jill Taggart?"

Laird nodded.

"Another cunt too dumb to live!"

"You killed her?"

"No. She's working overseas too, now—in Southeast Asia."

"She chose to go there?"

"She didn't choose shit! I owned her ass—and I sold her to one of my business partners in Cambodia for fifteen thousand dollars. I could've gotten more, except she's past her prime—as far as hookers go in Cambodia."

Ruttenberg mopped the blood on his forehead again and ran

his hand through his lank white hair. "Look here, my man—we don't have to be enemies. Nobody needs more enemies. We can be friends. Money can buy anything. Even friendship. How about you be my friend and forget this ever happened? Go home, have yourself a beer, relax—with fifteen thousand dollars in your pocket. Cash."

"Fifteen thou?" Laird laughed. "I leave more than that as a tip at Orange Julius. I'm not nearly as rich as you, but I have a nice healthy bank balance, and my banker would never notice fifteen thousand bucks."

"Twenty thousand, then."

"Twenty thousand couldn't light my cigar. And just so you remember—I am not 'your man.'"

Ruttenberg had never felt terror like this before. No one ever pointed a weapon at him—and always, when confronting those with whom he needed to negotiate, he had tough guys at his back—guys like Skinny and The Wrestler, whose real names he knew, of course—and big tough chauffeur/muscle man Randy. "Fifty K, then. Just think of it. Your banker will sure as hell take note of fifty thou."

"Fifty thousand sounds like a pretty fair night on *Wheel of Fortune*. Not interested, Mr. Ruttenberg."

Eyes closing, Ruttenberg's whole body turned chill. He tried not to shiver enough for this gunman to see him. "Seventy-five thousand, then. That's my final offer." He forced a chuckle that didn't come out that way. "And for an extras bonus, I'll let you fuck Bria yourself. No charge."

After a violent twist to his gut and a rage that appeared bright red and bubbling before his eyes, an icy calm overtook the moment for Major Laird Janiver, USMC, Ret. Unlike the grunts, the gunnys, the non-coms, the lifetime Marines who were raised and trained to kill from the moment they took the military oath, field officers did little actual boots-on-the-ground fighting. But there was always some, and each time before he pulled the trigger and blew into hell a complete stranger with brown skin and a rabid love for his religion, Laird Janiver had felt this same quiet calm.

"Where is Bria now?" he said softly. "Right this minute, where is she."

A cocky sneer upturned one corner of Ruttenberg's mouth. He said, "Unless we make a deal—right now—then it's for me to know and you to find out."

"I see." Laird nodded—just before he pulled the trigger and blew off Marshall Ruttenberg's left kneecap.

They were so deep in the forest no one would have heard the shot, or if they had, anyone would assume it was an automotive backfire. As for the scream that followed—one rarely hears a person shrieking in agony if they live in upscale Chagrin Falls, Ohio. It was probably a nighttime animal.

For a few minutes, Laird watched the writhing wounded rolling around in the dirt and bellowing. It was akin to seeing a small animal run over by a car on the highway and taking far too long to mercifully die—but he always had sorrow and sympathy for dying animals. For Marshall Ruttenberg? Not so much.

He finally said. "I warned you I'd shoot you in the balls, but then you'd probably bleed to death before I found out what I wanted. So I shot off your kneecap. I'm going to ask you the same question, Ruttenberg, and hope you realize you have one kneecap still intact—plus your elbows and Christ knows what else. I'm very creative, I've always lived with a weapon in my hand, and I'm just getting started. Here we go, then: where is Bria Harstad right this minute?"

"Please—take me to a hospital," Ruttenberg whimpered. groaned. "I'll tell you anything you want to know. Just get me—to a hospital."

"I'll shoot off your other knee first. Talk!"

"I—own a house in Ohio City."

"So?"

"That's where I—keep the women—before they get shipped off to some foreign country."

"Nice," Laird Janiver said. "That's where you're keeping Bria?"

A positive head nod.

"Address. Now!"

It took the drug king a few seconds to remember before he recited it, the roaring upset in his stomach almost as painful as his forehead or his kneecap. "Now," he said, his voice quivering from the suffering all over his body. "Please. Hospital."

That frigid calm sifted down onto Laird's shoulders, numbed him from nerves, from fear, from conscience, and put him into an almost hallucinatory sense, as one might suffer from as they waver between consciousness and sleep. He watched for a while longer as Ruttenberg thrashed about in the dirt, fallen leaves and twigs, tormented by pain never experienced before. No fan of horror movies, Laird had the sense he was watching a scene from "Saw" come to life.

As for being *in* one of them—well, he didn't like that at all.

"Roll over!" he ordered.

Ruttenberg did as he was told, now lying face down in the dirt and leaves. "Are you going to shoot me in the back?"

"No, I'm not," Laird said. "I'm a big fan of John Wayne. John Wayne never shot anyone in the back."

He moved closer and put one hand behind Ruttenberg's head and, snaking one arm around him, he grasped the opposite edge of Ruttenberg's jaw. It only took one quick jerk of Laird Janiver's powerful Marine hands to break the neck of the albino drug kingpin and end his life.

CHAPTER THIRTY-SEVEN

There were some people whose very appearance fascinate and intimidate those who meet them, Commissioner Francis P. Murgatroyd thought, as he spoke to his part-time bodyguard, Demetri Molik. He'd hired Molik as a bodyguard on several public occasions—not because he needed protection, but because it made him seem more important to those who might vote for him the next time he ran for political office.

"I don't quite understand," Demetri was saying. They were in Murgatroyd's private office in the County Commissioner's headquarters, Demetri in a visitor's chair too small to accommodate him. His parents, who were put together in an arranged marriage by both their families, were from Mumbai, but he was born and raised in Cleveland—ergo, no foreign accent. "We're going to this place where they got this hooker—and you're not gonna fuck her or anything, you're gonna *save* her?"

"*We* are gonna save her—the two of us. She's not a hooker, Demetri. She's a friend. She's caught up in some bad situation. I think they plan to sell her to some big brothel in another obscure country, so she'll turn ten, maybe twenty tricks a day. I can't have that."

"So, why am I coming with you?"

Franny Murgatroyd just shrugged his shoulders. "They must have somebody there making sure she doesn't just walk away. You're gonna take care of him."

"Does he got a gun?"

"How should I know? Do you have one?"

Demetri patted his left breast over the London Fog wind-breaker he wore. "The only time I don't got one is when I take a shower."

"That's good to know—but I don't want anyone killed."

"Killing a guy is my second choice."

Murgatroyd said, "I appreciate you're in with me on this."

"That's what I get paid for."

"Yeah, but those other times, Demetri, I didn't go anywhere somebody'd want to hurt me. Those were fake times, and having a big, tough bodyguard like you was mostly for show. This time—this is real."

"Real, fake, someplace in-between. I don't give a damn, Commissioner." He cracked his knuckles; to Franny, it sounded like a ten-pin strike at a bowling alley. "I'm ready to go."

Franny pulled his tie straight, donned his suit jacket, and the two of them went down to the underground garage where the commissioners park their cars. Franny's named parking spot was nearest to the door. Like most home-based vehicles, there were only two seats in the front. Demetri Malick filled up his own seat and half of Franny's.

"She's a beautiful woman, Bria Halstad," Franny explained as he crossed the Cuyahoga River across the Detroit-Carnegie Bridge—now rechristened the Hope Bridge on which the late Bob Hope's construction-worker father labored mightily when it was being built. "She worked—well, I guess she still works—for a guy out in Hunting Valley, Marshall Ruttenberg. She's the manager of his entire business operations. There's a big rumor about Ruttenberg around town—that he's a drug kingpin, and a sex trafficker on the side."

"Drug kingpin?" Demetri chuckled, sounding more like a cough. "Where the hell did you read that? In some newspaper from the nineteen seventies? Drug kingpin? Holy shit!"

"You weren't even born in the nineteen seventies."

"I wasn't born during the Civil War either—but I still know the South lost." He shifted slightly, squishing Franny even closer to his door. "So, if she works for this guy, why'd he call and say you could fuck her for free?"

Uncomfortable with the question as well as the upcoming situation, Franny mopped at his forehead with his free hand. "That's a problem. I had a thing about her, and Ruttenberg knew it. But she kept turning me down. I mean, look at me, for cry sakes! If I want to be with a hot chick, I gotta pay for it. So every once in a while, Ruttenberg sets me up with one—like I do you a favor, you do me a favor. Today, though, I'm talking to Ruttenberg and he tells he's selling her to some Arab whorehouse and figured he'd give me a free shot at her before he ships her off."

"If he's selling her to some pimp, that sounds like slavery."

"It sounds like that to me, too," Franny said, "which is why I'm paying you to help me set her free—if that's what she wants. It's like you riding to the rescue on a white horse."

Demetri demanded, "Do I look like I'm sitting on a white horse?"

"No, but you get the idea."

They moved westward for a while. Then Demetri said, "I don't mean to butt in, but this sounds pretty personal."

"It is—but I'm too old, fat and scared to do anything about it. That's why you're here."

"Then this is pretty damn weird."

Five minutes later, they pulled up in front of the building. It looked to be a two-flat, recently remodeled and made halfway modern-looking—at first glance, anyway—with a sleek street front tacked on seventy years after the house was built. That had happened a lot, though, in Tremont and Ohio City—regentrified neighborhoods very near downtown.

One apartment was upstairs and one down, and on the porch the security cameras around the front door and the well-curtained windows were fairly obvious, their tiny red lights glowing merrily in the late twilight.

"Step aside," Franny told Demetri Molik, "so you won't show up on the cameras. They're expecting me alone."

The big man moved away from the door, pressing himself against the side of the building, out of camera range. However, in plain sight, anyone would have spotted him from two blocks away, as his breadth filled up half the length of the porch.

Franny pushed the button, and in a moment the speaker clicked on.

"Yes?" came the male voice from inside the apartment.

"I'm County Commissioner Murgatroyd," Franny was aware of being on camera, so he smiled as he spoke into what he thought was a microphone. "Mr. Ruttenberg sent me."

"Oh, yeah. Come on in." The loud, rasping buzz indicating the front door was unlocked, and Franny and Demetri entered quickly.

The apartment door swung open, and Randy, the muscular, bulky chauffeur to Marshall Ruttenberg, came face to face with Demetri Molik. It was akin to two huge sumo wrestlers meeting in the center of the ring.

"Who's this guy?" Randy asked.

Demetri answered him with one roundhouse punch to his left eye that shot him backwards across the living room until he lost his balance and crashed onto the carpet. He just lay there, semi-conscious, not really concussed but simply stunned. Both hands clutched his eye.

Demetri moved over to him and knelt down on his chest. Randy was wearing a black T-shirt, and obviously no weapon beneath it, which left Demetri just checking his pants pockets and ankles. No guns—Randy hadn't expected hostile company.

Murgatroyd said, "Where is Bria Harstad?"

Randy groaned.

Demetri slapped him very hard on the side of his head. "Quit whining! Answer the man!"

Before Randy could open his mouth, he could clearly hear a

pounding. Someone was banging on the inside of what must have been a bedroom. Murgatroyd rushed over and tried opening that door, but it was locked.

"Bria!" he shouted. "Is that you in there?"

He heard Bria's muffled voice say, "Help me! Please help me!"

The Commissioner moved back over to where Randy was still on the floor, Demetri kneeling on his chest. "Where's the key to the bedroom?"

Demetri said, "We won't need a key." He clambered to his feet, heading for the bedroom door. "Step aside, Commissioner."

Franny got out of his way. Demetri took a deep breath and smashed the bottom of his boot into the door, near where the lock was. "Get out of the way, lady," he called loudly, backed up a few steps, and took another huge kick at the door, putting much of his weight behind it. The door cracked at the lock point and flew open.

Bria Harstad was standing as far from the door as she could, almost leaning against the bed. She looked terrified, her hand to her chest as Demetri Molik blasted in, sucking much of the air out of the room. She'd never seen him before; he looked like an attacking demon. But then he said, "Hey, lady—are you okay?"

Then he moved out of the way, and Franny moved into the room. Bria gasped in surprise, and threw herself at him, hugging him tightly and sobbing his name into his neck.

It was now approximately 9:45 in the evening as Laird Janiver made his way carefully through a forest-like park so dark it was dangerous just to walk. What light from the moon through the canopy of leaves overhead was now covered over by low-hanging clouds. There are few sunny days or bright nights in Northeast Ohio in November.

Before leaving Marshall Ruttenberg's body, he'd emptied the pockets—Ruttenberg's wallet, cellphone, car keys, and house keys. They were now in his own pocket.

His left leg—minus the foot—was sore, shooting pains up through his hipbone, and despite the chill, his shirt and jacket were sweat-soaked at the armpits and his lower back. He'd known since first donning a Marine uniform killing is what Marines are trained to do—but Afghans and Iraqis whose deaths he'd ordered were faceless strangers. It was like cutting grass in your front lawn and destroying the dandelions you didn't really give a damn about.

This day had been different.

He'd driven the two hit men he'd murdered that afternoon to a backwater stream of the Cuyahoga River, shot them both through the head, and tossed them into one of the deepest parts of the water. He hoped the current would wash them both out into Lake Erie, but even if they stayed where they'd been put, it would be days before anyone would notice them. Their faces, though—empty, shallow eyes bespeaking hired executions no more difficult than taking the trash out the morning after a party installed them on the edge of anonymity—made the killing of them easy for Laird Janiver. They'd been described to him as Skinny and The Wrestler, but when they were both dead, he'd removed their wallets with driver's licenses and credit cards which bore their real names. The skinny one was Wilbur Owens, and the chunky one was Hans Krautz. Now dead, he didn't care what their names were. Later, he'd set their identification on fire.

Killing Marshall Ruttenberg was different. Laird knew his name well, along with his occupation. Ruttenberg was about to sell Bria Harstad to a pimp to turn high-priced tricks for middle-aged tourists until she got too old and beaten down and left only with fucking donkeys onstage in Tijuana for dollar tips. As an amputee, Laird empathized with those physically handicapped, and he felt a twinge of sorrow at his recent victim's albinism. Still, it amazed him as he felt for the branches, bushes and trees with an outstretched hand, trying to get back to the Alfa Romeo, that shooting this monster didn't ravage his guilt pangs in the slightest.

There are people in this world who die before their time. Whether foreign terrorists, hired hit men, rapists of preteen children, those who tortured animals just to hear them scream, or simply undesirable scum like Ruttenberg, they have to die. That's why Laird joined the Corps—to eliminate those whose earthly presence wastes breathing air that belonged to the vast masses who deserve it.

The killing of the unarmed Ruttenberg shook him up quite a bit, but at least now Laird knew where Bria Harstad was being held—Ruttenberg spilled his guts after being shot in the kneecap hoping there was no more punishment ahead.

As he walked through the blackness, he heard something off to his left, a crunching of leaves and branches covering the ground. It could have been a large animal, a deer, or at least a coyote—but possibly a human being, too.

His weapon appeared in his hand. Damn! He didn't want to kill anymore.

He moved off to his left, again leaving the path he could barely see. He walked about eight steps and then stopped.

Immobile.

Listening.

Listening to breathing.

Someone else's.

"Where are you?" he demanded—softly but firmly. "Show yourself—or die."

"I ain't done nothin'," came the reply from beneath the branches of a tree that swept all the way to the ground. "Don't kill me. Please don't kill me."

"Come out here where I can see you!"

"Yessir. Yessir, comin' out."

More rustling of fallen leaves, more *shushing* of tree limbs being pushed to one side. Laird's flashlight beam revealed a man wearing a heavy parka over another heavy Eisenhower-length wool jacket. He had a ratty scarf wrapped around his throat, and those pile caps from the 1950s Korean war, with furry ear flaps tied atop his head but quick to make warmth if November chill turned into blasting Cleveland winter. He also wore heavy-duty work pants and a pair of old boots that were not tied up or buckled and flapped around his ankles. His hairline, too long in back and grizzled gray, had gone north decades earlier.

The beard on his face, ragged because he hadn't shaved in a long time, was ragged whitish-gray—a medium-skinned black man who looked to be about seventy years old, missing several teeth in his picket-fence mouth. His hands were raised ear-high in surrender on each side of his head in hopes he wouldn't be shot on the spot.

"Don' hurt me, brother," he said in a half-whine. "I didn' see nothin.' Didn' hear nothin.'"

Laird sounded angry. "What are you doing here?"

The old man seemed puzzled, looking all around, basically seeing nothing but the darkness. "I live here."

"You live in the park?"

"Sure do. Right over here. Come on, take a look."

"You live alone?"

He nodded almost happily.

Both of Laird's hands were busy—his cocked weapon in his right and a strong flashlight in his left. "Show me where. Keep your hands raised," he said.

They left the path, heading deeper into the park. The old man halted a bit—his joints hurt, partly from age and mostly from sleeping on the ground. Laird limped, too, his prosthesis less comfortable when not walking on paved surfaces.

They came upon another, much smaller clearing with a. tiny portable tent in the center—the type used in basic training exercises fifty years ago. Inside were several old faded blankets, obviously found in Dumpsters or at a charity thrift store, and a separate pile of clothing. A pair of bedraggled boots were lined up neatly, in case the old loafers the resident now had on his feet wore out. Not far from the tent was a tiny grill stocked with small pieces of wood rather than store-bought charcoal briquets so the man could cook whatever food he could find.

"This is where I live, my brother."

Laird nodded. "What's your name?"

"Rashon," the answer came. "Rashon Washington—like the first president of the USA."

"Homeless?"

"Naw, sir—this here's my home." He puffed his scrawny chest out with pride. "I useta live in Cleveland—worked for the sanitation department. But smack brought me down."

"Are you on smack right now?"

"Naw, naw—I got a li'l bit two nights back. I only got a pinch left." His eyes widened in terror. "Don't take my smack away, man. Please. I gonna die if I got no smack."

"I don't want your smack. I want your silence. You saw what I did, didn't you?"

Rashon Washington shook his head, hard, as if his brain rattling around would help him forget what just happened. "Didn' see nothin'. I swear on Jesus Christ Almighty."

"You saw what I did back there."

"Nuh-uh! Too dark to see *you*, my brother. All I seen was that really, really white man—an' I just seen him cuz a your flashlight."

"But you heard, didn't you, Rashon?"

Rashon's whole face wrinkled up, his eyes tight shut, as he tried remembering. "I's in my tent—thinkin' about goin' to sleep. Then I hear two guys talkin'—so I creeps up closer, just to see what was what. I hear that other guy talkin' a lot. Screamin'. I didn' get most of it—but I think he was a bad man. He *said* he was a bad man—talkin' 'bout two ladies, I think."

Laird studied Rashon Washington. The homeless old man had observed what he had done to Marshall Ruttenberg—the only witness who could talk to a cop and show him the way to Death Row. His weapon, still warm from firing at Ruttenberg, tingled in his hand. He'd also killed the two hit men planning to execute Jericho Paich. Would a homeless heroin junkie be his next victim?

Yet, Rashon hadn't gotten a good look at him. The flashlight made him squint when the light shined in *his* eyes, and his vision probably was iffy at the best of times. Even if Laird were arrested, no jury would believe an old man who lived in a tent, had a Big H monkey on his back, and only a nodding connection to reality.

What the hell! Laird Janiver put the gun in his jacket and dug into his pants pocket, coming out with a wad of money he hadn't even counted.

"Here, Rashon," he said, handing him the cash. "This is for keeping your mouth shut. I hope you'll spend it on food—but I figure you'll buy yourself another fix. Either way—you never saw me. I don't exist—and you found that money in the gutter."

"God bless you, my brother. Thank you a million times."

"Just remember those million thanks the next time you feel like talking to a cop."

The old man's eyes widened in Laird's flashlight beam. "Talk to a cop? You shittin' me? I ain't talked to no cop for the last ten years." Then, stuffing the money into the pocket of his own ratty coat, he chuckled, turned, and walked away.

CHAPTER THIRTY-EIGHT

Laird wore latex gloves to drive Ruttenberg's luxury car from the overgrown rural park back to the Palador restaurant, but he parked as far away from the eatery as he could. There were fewer cars around now than several hours earlier—but still, an Alfa Romeo stood out, no matter where it is.

He took five minutes wiping down every single surface he remembered touching without gloves. No professional cop, he knew all about leaving fingerprints where you shouldn't. He thought about taking the car keys with him and disposing of them somewhere, but came up with a better idea. He left the keys on the dashboard in plain sight, and didn't lock the door. It was almost like hanging a big sign on the windshield reading *STEAL ME*. The cops will catch the kids who decide to take possession—punk car-stealers do not safely drive Alfa Romeos around town. On the off-chance the police already found Marshall Ruttenberg's dead body, they'd figure the thieves had committed murder to get the car. They'd never make it stick, though—little or no evidence—but the bad boys go to court on car theft, and Laird Janiver is in the clear.

He walked at least fifty yards to his own car, then got in and drove only a few blocks to a different parking lot, stopping at another Dumpster and throwing away Ruttenberg's wallet, wiping off fingerprints, removing money, driver's license, and credit cards first. Somewhere else—miles away, across the Cuyahoga

River on the west side—he'd find a trash can and set fire to everything that had Ruttenberg's name on it. Police would eventually figure out who the murdered man was, but if Laird made them slow down a bit, that was a good thing.

Half an hour later, he found himself parked across the street from the building Ruttenberg had confessed he owned and where he kept young women—mostly but not always young teens—before he shipped them off to another country to become a tiny part of a huge sex trafficking business earning billions off the incarceration, punishment and abuse of those whose lives are forever doomed.

Laird hoped beyond hope he'd be able to rescue Bria Harstad, the woman with whom he had just fallen in brand new love. He hoped Jericho Paich would be freed from enforced slavery as a Confidential Informant for the police, as he no longer had a drug distributor who would make it possible.

Laird had killed three people in the past twenty-four hours—all of whom deserved it, at least in his mind. Would he be forced to commit another execution before he can extract Bria out of danger and into his life? He hoped not—but when he was back in his own car, sitting across the street from where he was sure he'd find Bria, he re-loaded his weapon.

Just in case.

He walked up onto the porch. All the blinds covered the windows on the first-floor apartment, but there was light shining through, even at this late hour. That means someone was still awake.

He easily discerned the TV cameras covering the front door, and a bright light shining on him, assuring the people inside could see who was visiting—so he knew they would question him. On the drive over, after leaving West Park just east of Chagrin Falls, he had decided what his approach would be.

He was going to be tough.

"*What?*" The voice was male, low, shaky.

Laird Janiver took out his weapon and waved it in front of

his face to be sure it was seen. "Let me in—or I'll blow this goddamn door off the hinges. And then I'll blow *you* off the hinges, too!"

"Jesus," came an answering buzz, the two s's slurred. Laird went through the front entrance. Then the apartment door opened to reveal a large and very battered man.

"Put your fucking gun up," he said to Laird, "I got nothing you want." Randy turned, walking slowly to the sofa. With a groan, he lowered his bulk onto the cushions.

"Holy shit, what happened to you?"

"Something fell on me the size of the Terminal Tower," he said. "He makes me look like a sixth-grade kid." Apparently he had trouble every time he used a word with an *s* in it. He rubbed his forehead.

"Where's Bria Harstad?"

He shrugged, or as much as he could, since his back and neck were aching. "I dunno. They took her away."

"They?"

"Two guys."

"What two guys?"

"One of 'em—the guy who kicked the crap out of me—I dunno who he is, or what his name is."

"Are you a bodyguard?" Laird demanded.

"Not really. I'm a full-time chauffeur."

"For who?"

"Mr. Marshall Ruttenberg."

Laird couldn't help but gasp. Yet things were slowly falling into place—in his mind, anyway. He said, "Are you working for Ruttenberg here? Kind of guarding Bria Harstad so she wouldn't go away?"

"Something like that." Randy sighed deeply, then coughed. "Shit, Ruttenberg's gonna kill me."

"I wouldn't worry about that. So, this big goon—was he hired muscle?"

"How would I know?"

"Do you think they took her away to hurt her?"

"I don't think so. She was glad to see them—at least the older guy. She even hugged him—cuz I think he was here to rescue her."

Laird Janiver put his weapon back in his pocket. "What older guy?"

Randy was having trouble breathing. He waved a hand, hoping Laird would disappear—but it didn't happen. "Too old to hurt anybody. A politician or something, I think. Local. Or county—a county politician."

"A sheriff?"

"Naw. Too old, too fat for a cop. I think he'd been drinking some, too. Cops don't drink on duty, right?"

"So maybe he was like a county commissioner?"

Randy managed to nod. "Yeah, that's it. That's who he said he was."

"One of the county commissioners is Italian. One is Irish. And one is an African American. So which one?"

"Not black," Randy said. "So the other two...?" He ducked his head.

Janiver turned to leave. Over his shoulder he snarled, "Guess."

CHAPTER THIRTY-NINE

Jericho Paich, the Confidential Informant, was going berserk all by himself. He was in hiding—unusual for most Americans in these chaotic days—because he had approached his mother's live-in boyfriend. Apparently, that relationship no longer existed; Laird Janiver and his mother busted up, mostly because of him. Embarrassed to ask for help, he'd hoped Janiver could extract him from an exhaustive and frightening mess with the police department that wouldn't keep him on the level of stool pigeon, nor send him to hardcore prison for decades. The only person who knew where he was hunkered down so as not to be noticed was Jaimie Peck, once the best gal pal of his own girlfriend, Jill Taggart, now disappeared. Jaimie was a young woman, also in psychological chains to Keegan Mayo as a C.I.—all due to Jerry's cowardice as a squealer.

The one night they wound up having mercy sex neither had lusted after was beside the point.

Jaimie had departed for her job, which left Jerry in her apartment with temporary solitary confinement—a one-bedroom apartment with doors locked and windows heavily curtained, nothing to read and no one to talk to. He couldn't possibly spend another eight hours watching daytime television—even obscure films on Netflix—but he didn't dare use the phone. How could he confess to anyone two men were out to kill him?

He was afraid to call his mother. Arielle Paich spent most of her life, especially since widowhood, becoming upset almost daily—enraged, flustered, and sobbing her heart out. Jerry couldn't take that.

There was no way he'd get in touch with his boss, either. He'd been out of touch for too long. He'd left his own car in the company parking lot for several days, certainly noticed by everyone he worked with. He figured he'd probably been fired.

And no one had the foggiest notion of how to reach *him*.

Pacing back and forth, hands in pockets, shoulders hunched, head lowered, he felt like a full-grown tiger cruelly imprisoned in a twenty-by-twenty cage at a zoo.

Carefully peeking out the window to see whether the two men who had beaten and threatened him were lurking around outside, even though he was certain no one knew where he was.

Eventually he threw himself on the sofa and tried to snooze, though for the past several days he'd spent much time asleep to avoid his gut-busting worry he wouldn't live to see another morning.

Finally, unable to countenance one more moment of hollow silence, he dialed the Hilton Gardens Hotel, just steps from the Lorain-Carnegie Bridge, and from Progressive Field. When he got the operator, he asked her to ring Laird Janiver's room.

"I just wanted to check in with you," Jerry said when Laird answered the call. "I'm all right—but I'm still hiding."

"You won't have to hide now," Laird assured him.

"Why not?"

"Those two guys won't bother you anymore."

"How come?"

"They left town. Permanently."

"How did that happen?"

"Coincidence."

"I don't believe that, Laird. You did something to make them leave."

"I'm—very persuasive."

Jericho sank down on the sofa. "What about the guy who

sent them after me in the first place? The one who ordered them to beat me up?"

"He's out of town, too."

"Where?"

Laird's tone grew harsh. "Walla Walla, Washington! How the hell do I know where he is? He's out of your life and out of the business—let it go at that."

"But—what did you do?"

Laird perched on the edge of his hotel mattress. "Drop it goddammit! You came to me for help. I gave it everything I had. You're okay to move back into your apartment—and your next job is trying to convince your boss into not firing your dumbass. Let. It. GO!"

Jericho was quiet for a moment. Then he said, "I'm sorry, Laird. I don't know how to thank you. I mean—Jesus, you're an incredible person."

"I didn't want to see you get killed—or get hurt again." He waited, thinking of what else to say. "Your mom and I—we're all over with. That's why I'm in a hotel. I'll look for another place to live. I hope that doesn't bother you. Relationships—do that sometimes. They drain themselves out. Sorry."

"I—I'm sorry, too," Jerry said. He took a deep breath. "I hate to ask you, but—how about me still working for Keegan Mayo? I mean, that's where we started, right?"

Laird rubbed his eyes with his fingers. "I hit a brick wall on that one. You can't imagine how many people got involved, but at the moment there's still no deal. Mayo's a cop with a lot of powerful buddies. As far as I can see, he's untouchable."

Untouchable. They used to call Eliot Ness that, too, Jerry recalled—and while the iconic lawman was incredibly effective in Chicago during the "dry days" of the 1920s when he jailed dozens of whiskey runners and major Italian mobsters, when he came to Cleveland and could not catch the elusive Mad Butcher of Kingsbury Run, his fame suffered greatly. Eliot Ness, buried in Lake View Cemetery, wasn't so Untouchable anymore.

So how in hell could Keegan Mayo handle that strangely bestowed honor?

Laird said, "Where's your car?"

"At my job—in the parking lot."

"Can you get someone to drive you there?"

Jerry's inhale was shuddering, as he had no idea, and he let the air from his lungs rush out in a blast. "I suppose so."

"I'd suggest you go back to your apartment. Call your mom and tell her you're okay—but I don't suggest moving in with her, even for a few days. She's in a difficult mood."

"Tell me about it," Jerry said.

Laird checked his wristwatch. It was already past eight o'clock in the morning. Time was flying. "Jerry, I have to go now. Something important to do."

"What is so important?"

"A—friend is in trouble. Or has been—I'm not completely sure. So I have to make sure the trouble has gone away."

"A female friend?" Jerry asked.

There was no sound on the phone for about fifteen seconds. Then Laird said, "It doesn't upset me. You've done so much for me, Laird, so I've got your back—whatever I can do. So tell me what's happening."

Laird shrugged, even though he knew Jericho couldn't see him. "I will," he said. "If it works."

After parking across the street in a tacky public garage, Merrill Braithwaite, Cleveland's FBI Deputy Special Agent in Charge, walked into the downtown police headquarters, showing the cop in charge at the walk-through arch his badge so he could enter without giving up his firearm. He wore his in a shoulder holster, tucked tightly under his armpit, and all his expensive suit jackets were hand-tailored to leave more room so the weapon didn't make a bulge.

He took the elevator to the drug enforcement department,

trying to keep his briefcase from slamming into anyone's knee or goosing whoever stood in front of him. The sullen, broken or shattered people on the elevator were heading up to the floors of the courtroom, unlike those who visited FBI Headquarters a few blocks north. Even the criminals. At least at the FBI they had cleaner clothes.

The desk sergeant barely looked up as Braithwaite got off the elevator and came toward him. "Help you?" he said without lifting his head from whatever he was reading.

Braithwaite raised his badge shoulder high so the sergeant could see it. "I'm Merrill Braithwaite, Deputy SAC, FBI. I'm here to see Detective Mayo."

The meeting of the eyes was painfully brief until the cop looked away and continued studying the papers in front of him. "You have an appointment there, pal?"

Pal? One never referred to FBI Special Agents as "pal," especially when you were the deputy in charge—of anything. Kindly—too kindly, all things considered—Merrill Braithwaite repeated himself, saying aloud "Federal Bureau of Investigation" this time instead of just the letters.

The desk sergeant frowned. Like most local street cops, he was not fond of the FBI. He pointed his chin toward the bench across from him. "Take a seat."

"I'll just stand—if it's all right with you."

"Stand on your fuckin' head if you want," and he gestured again to the bench, "as long as you do it over there." He picked up his phone and pressed buttons, turning away so Braithwaite couldn't read his lips.

The FBI Deputy SAC leaned against the wall and studied the waiting room, vastly different from the FBI headquarters in size, appearance, and mood. Those busted for federal crimes and brought into the FBI offices overlooking Lake Erie were often suit-and-tie wearers, while the bad actors who found themselves in this difficult Cleveland police situation looked more homeless than not. There was a powerful smell on this floor on which felons come to be processed—fear sweat, armpits, frightened farts, and a hanging stench of cigarette smoke that had been sucked into the clothing of perpetrators and police officers alike, even though there was no smoking allowed in the building. It bothered Braithwaite so much he decided to breathe only through his mouth until finally the desk sergeant directed him to Keegan Mayo's office.

Mayo, wearing a plaid shirt and possibly the ugliest tie in the world, was hunkered down behind his desk, his head thrust forward and his jaw aiming at his visitor like an anti-aircraft gun. He made no effort to shake hands, but instead looked angry. Perhaps after so many years of facing criminals across the desk, a furious look had been permanently imprinted on his face.

He was also extremely dismayed over what had happened to him the evening before and worried like hell at what might ensue from the horrific "candid-camera" attack on him in his own living room. Naturally, he was too terrified to share that damaging experience with anyone else, and was terrified his new guest knew about it already.

He chose to ignore it and fight his way through, hoping nothing else its exposed to the fresh air

"So you're the big FBI maven in this town, right?" he said, ignoring both Braithwaite's badge and his outthrust hand of friendship. "Just drop by to throw your weight around a little?"

Merrill Braithwaite's eyes narrowed. "Nice to meet you, too, Detective."

"You know what FBI stands for in this office? Fucking Busybody Idiots. If I had a dollar for every time you Feds march in here and take over one of my busts without asking—because you're all such big hotshots—I'd be retired and living somewhere like Cancun."

Braithwaite shook his head in sorrow. "I'd heard you were an asshole—but I never realized they ought to *frame* you and hang you on the wall." Braithwaite sat down in one of Mayo's visitor's chairs, putting his briefcase on the floor beside him.

Mayo frowned, irritated. "I don't remember inviting you to take a seat."

"I don't remember either. If it's illegal for me to sit down in your office—call a cop." He smiled, in spite of himself—it was a very small smile, but Merrill Braithwaite was not well-known for smiling. "Do you want to keep trading insults, or are you even the teeniest bit interested in why I'm here?"

"The only thing I care about is how fast you can get the hell out of my office," Mayo said. "I got no use for Feds. They don't dig how a real cop puts his pants on. I've got work to do, see? Clean up the streets. That's what we cops do. We catch perps and we lock 'em up so they stop making the streets dirty. I got no time to hear one of those patriotic speeches you guys haul out and wave around when you think you've got the upper hand."

"No patriotic speeches. I'm more of an art lover." Merrill Braithwaite cleared his throat. "Have you ever heard of a man named Ayman Kader?"

"Who?"

"Colonel Ayman Kader, retired from the United States Marines."

"What the hell kinda name is Ayman? Is he some kinda Arab? I don't know no Arabs, and I don't know no colonels. All the Marines I know were grunts—*real* Americans. Tough guys who don't take shit from nobody. They don't wear silver birds like this colonel guy, and they don't sit behind a desk telling other guys to get themselves killed for the glory of their country, making their living crawling on their bellies, and icing lots of other scum so you Feds can strut around and brag about it."

"Well," Braithwaite said. "He is Muslim by birth—and he is a very good friend of mine, but he was born in the USA, and he didn't get that bird colonel collar pin just because he has nice curly hair. He's got another friend, and that friend has friends, and so on."

"So?"

"So, one of his friends of his friends is a guy named Jericho Paich. Ring a bell?"

The room grew eerily quiet, as in his mind, Keegan was looking down a long, dark hallway. He rumbled, "So?" again, this time with a threat behind it.

"Jericho Paich is one of your finks. Right?"

"He's a Confidential Informant."

Braithwaite nodded. "One of your stool pigeons. You pay squealers for whatever they bring in, don't you?"

"Some police officers pay, and some don't. Me, I don't pay Paich shit! What are you, poking around for the IRS? Paich works for me on a—volunteer basis."

"Volunteer," Braithwaite mused. "I see. He works for you as a volunteer, huh? Or else you throw him into prison for the next twenty years for selling crack."

"Listen, Fed—in case you don't know this, considering you guys have your heads up your asses so far you never know whether it's night or day—the police use C.I.'s all the time. Helps us to solve cases. Some of them volunteer like Paich does, because we caught him peddling recreational drugs, which is a criminal case, in case you forgot. So he works off his criminal behavior to repay his city. It helps him, it helps us."

"The drug maven he worked for was found dead last night. You might know the guy? Marshall Ruttenberg? The albino?"

"I've heard about Ruttenberg," Mayo said, "but I never met him. Albinos freak me out anyway."

"Ruttenberg freaked out a lot of people—especially Jericho Paich. Paich has been working for you, squealing on other small-time offenders for six months. Isn't that just about enough?"

"It's enough," Mayo said brusquely, "when I say it's enough. You get my drift—Fed?"

Braithwaite took a twenty-second pause, then bent down for his briefcase, setting it on his lap. Two clicks unlocked it. "You might recall a few minutes ago, Detective Mayo, that I said I was an art lover."

Mayo interrupted him. "Only fags are art lovers."

"I think you're a bit fucked up about that—unless they cover that in your attendance at the police cadet academy," Braithwaite said. "But no, Detective—I want to share something with you. You might call it an artistic moment."

He removed a manila envelope from his case and took out two eight-by-ten photos and tossed them, face up, on Keegan Mayo's desk. "Art is always most important when it moves someone emotionally. Are you moved, Detective?"

Keegan Mayo's face turned pink, then red, finally angry purple. He could not talk at first. Eventually he croaked, "Where did you get these?"

"Oh, there are lots of copies all over the place," FBI Deputy Special Agent in Charge said, "although no one else has them—yet. After that? Hell, maybe on the TV networks. You won't be getting that lieutenant's badge you want to retire with, I'm afraid, because these photos would ruin your reputation. You might not even be able to stay on the force—they'd be too shot in the ass about having a Short Eyes wearing their uniform." He leaned over and picked up one of the photos to study it. "Still, you'll be famous forever, Mayo. Great shots of you while you're pulling down a little boy's pants, and he's looking right up at you, terrified and crying his eyes out. I like this second picture better, don't you? I mean, the look on your face is classic. Total surprise to you, right? When pedophiles sexually attack small children, usually they don't want anyone else around?"

"Who—who took these pictures?"

Braithwaite laughed without any mirth at all. "You want more pictures? Maybe one with your junk hanging out for the world to see? Just ask. I'll give you the number."

Keegan Mayo slumped back in his chair, breathing heavily, his hand to his chest, and for a moment Braithwaite thought he was having a heart attack. But then he managed to say, "You're the FBI, for crysakes! This is blackmail!"

"This is no blackmail, Mayo. I didn't ask you for money. All I want from you is two things, both suggested to me by Colonel Ayman Kader, a retired Marine. Between him and me, we know everybody in town, and we don't take crap from any of them. Make it easy on yourself. Cooperate with me, and these photos will disappear forever, and you'll never hear from me or Kayder or the FBI again."

"Two things?" Mayo sputtered. "What are they?"

Merrill Braithwaite said, "It's easy, Detective Sergeant Mayo. Easy as falling off a log."

CHAPTER FORTY

Laird Janiver drove up to the residence on Clinton Street, ten minutes west of downtown, and eased the car next to the curb. The house was about the same size as the rest of those on the middle-class street, but there had been so much additional work done to it, including a new porch with artistic carvings over the door frame, an elegant archway over a brand new heavy oak doorway, brick facing all over the house, broad windows installed much later than the house had been built, and a locked brick gate heading to the rear of the house. He had no idea about the backyard, but he imagined a swimming pool and a bathhouse for changing, and an enormous barbecue stand and a pit for flaming warmth on cooler evenings. It felt to him like coming upon Buckingham Palace suddenly set in the middle of the East Woodland Avenue District of Cleveland, several miles away and peopled almost entirely by financially challenged families. Laird figured the remods and improvements, less than ten years old by the look of them, had probably cost triple the original price of the house.

The resident was either very greedy or very lucky—perhaps a combination of the two.

Again, Laird had chosen not to wear his Marine uniform, but donned instead a hip-length leather jacket over a medium blue dress shirt. His handgun this time was stuffed into the waistband of his dark blue slacks, mainly because it was a chilly morning and he didn't wish to unzip his jacket to defend himself, should that become necessary.

He rang the doorbell and waited, fists in his pockets, until the door was opened by a solidly-built, dark-skinned man whose body reminded him of a superstar Chicago Bears football player who had played during his childhood, and whose nickname truly fit his appearance: "Refrigerator." This guy, however, looked five times as mean as the now-retired gridiron star.

"Can I help you?" Demetri Molik rumbled.

"I'm Laird Janiver, and I'm here to see Commissioner Murgatroyd. Is this his house?"

"It might be."

Laird tried not to sound desperate. "It's very important."

"Can I ask what it's in regard to?"

"I'd prefer not."

Demetri didn't think it over. "Then call the commissioner's office to make an appointment. He doesn't like unauthorized visitors showing up at his front door."

Laird grew aggressive, mainly because he was in a hurry. "He'd better talk to me."

Demetri's eyebrows raised, and whatever air he inhaled made him look even bigger. "Or what?"

Or, Laird thought quietly, his fingers tingling, keenly aware of the weapon stuffed into his waistband, *I'll shoot off your goddamn dick!* Instead, he said, "Tell Murgatroyd I'm a good friend of Jericho Paich. Let's see if that gets his attention."

Demetri Molik considered whether or not to tear this guy apart with one hand, knowing too well how much intimidation he brought to almost any conversation. He decided against it. He had always lived with discrimination because of his dark Indian skin, so he felt this African American deserved a smidgin of consideration, despite what he considered arrogance. "I'll see. Wait here," he said, and closed the door, leaving Laird Janiver out on the porch.

What would happen, Laird mused, if Murgatroyd refused to

let him into the house? He was fairly certain Bria Harstad was inside—or if not, Murgatroyd alone knew where she was. At least he'd believed that, which had come from the lips of Marshall Ruttenberg—right before he broke his neck. So, by hook or crook, he was about to make the Commissioner see him.

He certainly couldn't fight it out with the large East Indian who could kill him without breaking a sweat. Though his gun felt slightly awkward tucked into his slacks, he sure as hell didn't want to shoot him, or anyone else, either.

All he wanted, he ultimately thought, was Bria. Even at this early stage—they'd only had sex with each other once—he was probably in love with her, or at least well on the way. Love or no love, though. He was going to rescue her from what Ruttenberg had actually foretold—a fate worse than death.

He'd been an atheist since he was a young teenager and challenged his mother's wrath by refusing to attend the Baptist Church, where she prayed several times per week. But he was willing to pray now—to whatever spiritual being was out there listening—he was not too late.

Waiting outside in the chill morning, his stump had begun aching and the steel reaching almost to his knee had grown cold and uncomfortable against his skin. He leaned against the wall and lifted his left leg slightly so it would not bear any more of his weight.

The door opened and Cuyahoga County Commissioner Francis Murgatroyd stood there, dress shirt opened at the neck and gray suit pants held up by a pair of suspenders. Demetri lurked several steps behind him.

"Hey there," Franny bubbled, sticking out a hand for a friendly shake. "I'm Commissioner Murgatroyd. So Demetri says you're some sort of friend of Jerry Paich?"

Some sort of friend? Laird didn't know how to answer that fully, so he just nodded and said "Yes, sir."

"Okay then, come on in," and Franny stepped aside so Laird Janiver could enter. "I'm having my morning coffee, so come on into the kitchen and join me."

"Hold it!" Demetri said. Then, confronting Laird Janiver, he frisked him thoroughly, removing the handgun from his waistband. "You'll get this back when you leave," he said, and put it into his own pocket.

Franny frowned. "I didn't think you'd be carrying," he said. "Are you some sort of criminal? Or a cop? I never did anything to anybody."

"I'll decide whether that's true or not as soon as I try your coffee, Commissioner."

The three of them headed for the kitchen, Laird after the commissioner, with Demetri bringing up the rear. Laird was sure his limp was noticeable and wondered whether that would affect the rest of the morning.

The kitchen had apparently been completely overdone, too. Granite-topped counters, oversized steel refrigerator, dishwasher and oven, and overhead a rack of copper pots and pans dangling from a rack stretched all across the breakfast area and looking as if no one had ever cooked anything in them. There were four stools with leather backs and seats along the counter, one pulled out and a half cup of coffee in front of it. Franny waved at one of the other stools. "Sit, be comfortable."

Laird sat. "Thanks, but this is not a social call."

"I figured that. But we don't have to be best friends forever to drink some coffee." He reached for another mug and filled it, then pushed it toward his uninvited visitor. He somehow knew a man with the aura of toughness and stubbornness would only drink coffee that was black and strong.

"I've been told you knew where Bria Harstad was being held, and you know where she is now. True?"

Franny fingered the handle to his mug but made no effort to drink. "Why do you want to know?"

"Personal reasons."

"I'm a politician. I don't know a damn thing about personal reasons."

"They're none of your business," Laird said.

"Then you shouldn't come to me. You have a water leak in your neighborhood? Fine, I can do something about that—if I want to. Are people driving too fast down your street where children play? I'll have a stop sign erected on your corner. But personal reasons? Go fuck yourself, sir. I'm sure if Demetri here hadn't taken your gun away, you'd be waving it in my face—but otherwise, you'll have to convince me why you want to know where Bria is."

Laird Janiver was certain if he did what he wanted to, first Demetri would physically destroy him. Then he would spend years in prison for reaching out and grabbing Franny Murgatroyd by the throat and choking the truth out of him. A sharp pain shot up his left leg, and he took hold of the granite edge of the counter to keep him from wincing.

Then he said, "It's because I love her."

Franny's face almost collapsed. He had gone out of his way, hiring Demetri Molik to ride shotgun for him, so he could rescue Bria Harstad from what would easily ruin her life and lead her to drugs or suicide. He had maintained an unrequited letch for her since the day he met her, was thrilled to fantasize he could thunder into view on a white horse and spirit her away to a lifetime of love—only to find out some light-skinned black guy wearing a gun had come knocking at his door to spirit away the woman of his daydreams, right out from under his fingers.

He managed to stutter, "You—love her?"

Laird managed to avoid a direct answer. "Nothing bad will happen to her now. I made sure of that. And I busted my ass finding out she was with you—so here I am."

"Here you are," Franny said as quietly as he could. He looked at Demetri, but he did not hire the oversized bodyguard to give advice, just returning an "I-don't-know" shrug. Franny swallowed hard, then sighed, "Go up and get her, Demetri."

"What if she's asleep?"

"Wake her. It's time for her to go home."

Demetri nodded—one quick up-and-down head jerk—and disappeared up the stairs, leaving Laird Janiver and Francis P. Murgatroyd in a very awkward silence.

The Commissioner finally said, "She was injured before I found her. I had the doctor come over yesterday."

Laird felt his stomach clench. He tasted bile—and the pain from his stump went from where his foot used to be clear up into his neck. "What happened to her?"

"I think she got—beat up pretty bad. Not her face—nobody touched her face. But the rest of her was all bad bruises. I think one or more of her ribs are cracked." He shivered.

"How did you find her?"

"Somebody told me where she was. He also told me he was going to—sell her to some Saudi pimp."

"Somebody told you?"

Franny ran a hand over his face as though wiping away cobwebs. "I couldn't let that happen. So, I hired Demetri, and we went to go get her. There was only one guy watching her—a chauffeur, it was. Supposed to be a big tough guy, but next to Demetri, he looked like a skinny old woman." His chuckle was a one note staccato. "He didn't put up a fight."

Laird nodded.

Paced.

Kept glancing up the stairway.

Franny said, "One thing."

"What?"

"She only goes with you if *she* wants to. Otherwise, she stays."

"What if I say no?"

"Then you take it up with Demetri."

"Uh-huh."

"That'll be a short goddamn fight. He's twice your size."

Laird said, "I know, Commissioner. But I was a Marine. I don't fight. I kill." He pushed his hands back in his pockets so

Franny couldn't see his knotted fists. "I'd much rather get what I came for and leave on good terms."

"Let's hope," Francis Murgatroyd said.

Demetri came back down the stairs very slowly, holding up and practically carrying Bria Harstad, who was wearing men's faded pajamas and a terrycloth bathrobe, her eyes half-closed, her face twisted in the pain that had attacked more than half the muscles in her body. Halfway down the stairs she looked up and caught sight of Laird Janiver, and whatever was keeping her body vertical quit working and she slumped weakly between Demetri and the banister railing. He had to hold her up tighter, so she didn't fall.

"Oh my god," she choked. "Oh. My. God."

And the tears began.

CHAPTER FORTY-ONE

The raw wind off the lake apparently was born in Western Canada and headed southeast, snaked through Cleveland's east side streets, kicking up trash, old newspapers and strange things that had been dumped somewhere, like old tennis shoes, or socks with a hole in the toe, moving them around like the start of a moody movie.

Don Franco Malatesta was having his breakfast at the table in the corner of his restaurant where he visited, depending on whichever meal made him the hungriest. Usually conservative in his attire and his friendships, on this particular morning he had worn a flashy black and white ski parka one of his friends had gifted him for the Christmas of the previous year, though he'd never been near a pair of skis and, at his advanced age, highly unlikely to take up the sport. Draping the parka and his pullover ski cap over the back of an extra chair at his table, he kept the extra-long, lush knitted bright purple scarf wrapped around his neck, even as he ate.

The music from the audio system was louder than usual, as whenever the Don arrived for a meal, no matter what time of day, the bartender on duty would play Enrico Caruso or Luciano Pavarotti singing opera by Verdi or Rossini.

"This coffee!" Don Franco complained to his son, John Malatesta, who was sitting next to him—and this was far from the first time he whined about it. "This is shit coffee, Giovanni.

What kinda shit coffee you make in this place? No caffeine in here, right? And no milk, no sugar either? Why don't we get a cat to piss for us in the coffee pot every morning, save some money, eh?" He pushed the cup away.

"The doctor said no more caffeine for you, Papa," Johnny said. "Keeps you awake at night."

"The doctor should die with a hard-on!" the Don snarled. "I don' even know anymore how many years old I am. But I stay awake all night anyway, no matter what I drink! I watch movies all a time. I watch that gangster movie ten, maybe twenty times. That's bullshit! And you're growin' up like that Fredo punk—he just stands there like a dumbo *strunz* when his old man gets shot!" He adjusted the scarf so it wouldn't trail into his breakfast. "Ahh—don' be like Fredo, okay?"

John hung his head. He did that a lot, probably because as the Don's only son, he had been expected since birth to take over the local family organization when his Papa grew too old, or passed away. He was no more adept at being a godfather than becoming the new quarterback for the New England Patriots. He was good at running a restaurant, though, both business-wise and socially, despite his father's bitching on the bad taste of his decaffeinated coffee—but he sure as hell didn't want to be thought of as the inept middle son in *The Godfather* who finally goes out fishing in a small boat and is never heard from again.

Giovanni Malatesta—Johnny—made a decent living, knowing whatever happened, he'd be named in Don Franco's will, and live and die wealthy. In the meantime, many pretty women fascinated with "bad boys" from a notorious family who were as handsome as Johnny Pockets managed to show up at the restaurant almost every night, so he had few complaints.

The front door opened, and Nico Brigandi entered quickly so as not to let the chill wind sneak in and make the Don cold. Don Franco saw him and waved him over.

"Good morning, Don Franco," Nico said, bending to kiss

the old man's hand, but the Don reached up, pulled him down, and kissed him on both cheeks. "You're a hell of a guy, eh, Nico? You saved my son's life. He told me all about it."

Nico blushed. "I didn't exactly save his life, my Don. I—saved his ass."

Johnny blushed deep red, but the Godfather roared with laughter. "Sit, sit, I need to hear all about it."

Nico took off his coat and laid it atop the Don's, then pulled out the chair next to his boss and quietly sat down. "I framed this crooked cop into the most embarrassing position I could. See what you think." He removed a manila envelope from his overcoat, opened it, and put the two photographs down on the table. "This here is Detective Keegan Mayo in his own home, with an anonymous little boy, if you know what I mean. Mayo knows if I published these photos anywhere, he'd be tarred and feathered and run out of town on a rail."

Malatesta frowned. "Tarred and feathered? What's that?"

"That's the old-fashioned punishment of chasing someone away."

"So what is this guy, a fag?"

"No sir," Nico assured him, "but I set up these photos to make him look like one. If anyone gets hold of them—there goes his reputation, there goes his job, there goes his pension, and I'd bet he'd have to leave town and go somewhere far away—like Seattle."

"I don't know any family which is big in Seattle." The Don pushed the photos around on the table and studied them as if he would take a test later. Then he said, "This goddamn cop is pulling the little boy's pants down. Makes me wanna puke!" He looked at the photographs some more. "So who's the kiddo? Yours?"

"No, sir. Not yet, anyway."

"Hmm. Good shots. Who took the pitchers? That pretty girl you used to go with?"

"I still go with her, yes. I love her a lot, Don—and that's her son. They both did me a favor."

Don Franco stopped eating. "That's a goddamn dangerous favor. That cop coulda shot 'em both dead. And you, too."

"He's not so dumb he'd shoot a child."

"Knock wood," the old man said, and did so on the table in front of him. "This chick and her kid—they really stuck their necks out to do this for you?"

Nico nodded. "I never told them why, except I was doing it for you. For something you needed—you and Johnny."

Franco looked up at the ceiling, knowing his own personal god was up there, and he wanted to tell him how grateful he was. "Remind me about this when you get married, Nico."

Nico Brigandi blushed, bowing his head. He knew there will be an envelope stuffed with Malatesta cash for his bride on the day she got married.

Johnny said, "He'll never come after you or anyone else around here, Papa—not ever again."

The old man ignored him, still speaking to Nico. "And this cop? He don't even know your name?"

"No, he doesn't. Just that I'm well known in—this family."

Don Franco took a final bite of his muffin. "Well-known? My *ass* you're 'well-known.' You're *part* of this family now." He leaned over and pinched Nico's cheek the way a grandma would do to a three-year-old. Then he turned around and hollered for any waiter within earshot. "Hey! Another breakfast over here for one a my boys!"

Elizabeth Kennedy Kader finished rinsing the breakfast dishes and stacking them into the dishwasher, and then went back upstairs to put on her make-up and get dressed for lunch with two of her friends to spend the rest of the day browsing—and probably spending money—at the sprawling Crocker Park shopping center on the far west side of the county. Her husband, Ayman Kader, had left a few minutes earlier to meet with city and county officials regarding the shoddy treatment of veterans returned from combat in the Middle East.

She was proud of her husband for that, for his own service; one does not earn a silver eagle on one's shoulder for nothing. She knew vaguely by law, they were pretty damn rich. The high military field officers were much better paid now than in the post-World War II days—but several million dollars in banks and the stock market were not rightfully earned while fighting for the democracy of the United States of America.

She had never asked, though. Ayman Kader was very good-looking, kind, occasionally funny, quite sexual—especially in the earliest days of the marriage—and somehow very wealthy, so her decision to marry him had not been a tough one. He did not totally entrance her at the beginning, but her love grew and flowered as the years went on.

The melodious announcement of the doorbell at eleven o'clock in the morning startled her. Those who live right at the edge of Lake Erie rarely, if ever, had unexpected visitors, unless someone was delivering an Amazon package. Even the Seventh Day Adventists only banged on front doors on Saturdays to ask residents whether they've accepted Jesus Christ as their personal savior, and force their pamphlets on those who could not be less interested.

She stepped out of her bathroom and into the bedroom, where a TV monitor focused on the front door. The man ringing the bell was superbly dressed, somewhere in his early fifties, and she had to squint because she thought she might have seen him sometime before.

She flicked the sound switch and said, "May I help you?"

"Ms. Kader," the man answered, "my name is Merrill Braithwaite—Deputy Special Agent in Charge for the local FBI. I see the colonel frequently—lunch and things. And I believe you and I have already met." He lightly touched his fingers to the elegant knot in his tie. "May I come in for a bit?"

"I'm upstairs. Give me a minute."

She quickly re-checked her make-up. She was happy in her marriage and not looking for outside erotic entertainment, but she liked appearing as beautiful as possible in any situation. She knew damn well she was hot.

Slipping into two-inch heels, she clattered down the stairs and opened the front door.

At the sight of her, Braithwaite had a brief moment of sheer jealousy. Like Beth Kader's husband, he was at least twenty years her senior—but he was a lifelong bachelor, married to The Bureau and incapable of even a thought he'd have to wake up next to the same person for the rest of his life. Instead, he smiled his Special Agent smile and said, "It's nice to see you again, Ms. Kader—Beth, isn't it? I think we first met three Christmases ago at some sort of FBI party at the Renaissance Hotel."

"Oh, yes—I remember," Beth said, not remembering.

"I'm assuming the colonel is not at home."

She shook her head. "He goes out a few times a week—meetings, lunches—and he does play golf in decent weather, too." She tried checking her watch without being noticed—and failed. "Would you like some coffee?"

"No, I don't want to bother you."

"It's no bother, really."

"That's okay. Will Colonel Kader be home this evening?"

"I'm sure he will be. He never goes out in the evening without me hanging onto his arm."

"I'll come back then." Braithwaite started for the door, then stopped and turned around. "May I ask you—are you familiar with another ex-Marine named Laird Janiver?"

"Sure," she said. "They were in the Middle East together during the hottest part of the war about seven or eight years ago. Laird was a major. He served under Ayman—and now they're pretty close friends. Why?"

"Has Janiver met with the colonel recently?"

"He was here just a few days ago."

Braithwaite's heart began pounding. "Do you have any idea what they were talking about?"

"No. They were out in the backyard—it was a warm morning, and they were drinking coffee and playing with the dog."

Playing with the dog, Braithwaite thought. "I'd like to get in touch with him. Do you have his address and phone number around anyplace?"

"I don't think so." Beth ran a few thoughts through her head. "I've never had the need to call him myself. Ayman has that information on his cell phone—and of course he carries it with him, so—" She shrugged.

"Thanks anyway, Beth. I'll find his address on my own."

"It's a big city, Agent Braithwaite. How are you going to do that?"

Because I run the FBI! Why the hell would you even ask? He almost bit his tongue to keep from saying it. Oh, well—all people ask dumb questions some of the time. Instead, he smiled at her, winked, and said, "I can't tell you. It's a secret."

After the goodbyes, he drove his car about two blocks away, then parked and got out his own phone, punching the one button that connected him with the FBI office at which he worked. He asked to speak to the woman who worked directly under him, Leticia Earle.

"Early," he said when she answered her phone, "I need you to look someone up for me. First name Laird, L-A-I-R-D. Last name Janiver, J-A-N-I-V-E-R. He's a retired Marine, and friends with Retired Colonel Ayman Kader, an acquaintance of mine. I want Janiver's address and phone number, I want to know where he eats and drinks and works and what car he drives—year, make, model, color, or whether it's a two-door or a four-door. While you're at it—find out if he's ever been arrested anywhere, anytime, for anything?"

Leticia Earle rubbed her tired eyes with her fingers. She'd had phone calls like this from Braithwaite many times before. It just about defined her job, even though he insisted on calling her "early," which ticked her off at least three times per day. She said, "I assume you want all this within the next fifteen minutes?"

"Sooner than that," Merrill Braithwaite replied. "I won't go into this now—but two hired hoodlums were shot to death and dumped into the Cuyahoga River—and the biggest Ohio drug pusher winds up in an almost secret Emerald Necklace park just outside Chagrin Falls with his kneecap shot off and his neck broken. And according to the spider web that ties up every major crime ever committed, this Janiver guy is either the only fucking angel saint in America—or he goes to the head of our Ten Most Wanted list."

CHAPTER FORTY-TWO

Jerry Paich was gathering the few items of clothing and cleanliness he had at Jaimie Peck's apartment. He'd be happy to get back to his own apartment, his meager library and classical and jazz DVDs he'd collected before everyone decided they could better listen to music on their iPhones, because in Jaimie's residence there is nothing at all to indicate who lived there—not even art posters on the wall, which left him confined for several days without even a glimpse of the sun or a gulp of fresh air, but stuck with watching daytime television.

Also relieved after several days of voluntary quarantine, he wondered if he'd would ever walk outside Jaimie's door again or perhaps carried out in a body bag.

The hell of it all—a savage beating by two thugs hired by some albino drug maven, and again waiting for him outside his office just three days later. Jerry didn't know if they intended to beat him some more, which would probably kill him, or were they sent on a specific mission to end his life more quickly.

Jaimie hadn't been particularly close to him, even after one evening of sympathetic sex. In retrospect, she thought he was pretty good under the covers, although they never made it back to bed for all the remaining time he stayed with her.

She left for work each morning while he remained inside, fretting whether he still had a job, being spooked by every shadow from the sun that crept through the drawn shades or the smallest sound from out on the street or somewhere else in the building. Unmitigated terror had made him invisible to the rest of the world.

Now she was on her second cup of coffee, held in one hand, a half-eaten bagel with cream cheese in her other, and she hadn't yet put on her shoes.

"Are you sure it's safe to go home, Jerry?" Jaimie said. She actually sounded concerned.

"The guy who owns the Italian restaurant—Malatesta's— told me it was okay," he replied. "It's all been taken care of. Plus, I don't have to be a C.I. anymore—and neither do you."

"That's great—but I wonder why."

"He wouldn't tell me. But Mayo actually tweeted me on my iPhone to tell me I'm out of the Confidential Informant business for the immediate future—and both our arrest records will be in the mail by today—tomorrow at the latest. They were never signed or registered, so we're both in the clear."

"I hated doing that, Jerry, hated it worse than anything I ever did. I was worried I'd have to fink for the cops forever, so this takes a ton of bricks off my back," Jaimie Peck said. "But I still don't get it."

"You will when you set fire to your arrest sheet and flush it down the john."

"I'm still worried about you. What about the two guys who beat the crap out of you?"

"Well—there was this man who used to be my mother's boy-friend. I didn't know where to turn, Jaimie—he was the only per-son I knew who was hard enough and tough enough to help me. My mom told me from the beginning he only had one leg. I mean, only one foot, missing just above the ankle—not the entire leg gone."

"Didn't that slow him down?"

Jericho heaved his shoulders. "Probably a little bit."

"So, what did he do about your problem?"

"He wouldn't tell me, either, except it was all taken care of.

Those two guys left town, he said—and the one Jill had worked for was out of business, too. That's all I know about it."

"And Jill? Where did she run off to?"

Jericho Paich hung his head. "Nobody seems to know."

Jaimie's eyes filled with tears, but none escaped to run down her cheeks. "She's my best friend, Jerry."

"I know," he said softly. "Mine, too."

For the next few minutes, they were silent, she finishing her bagel and coffee, he packing the rest of his things and snapping his suitcase shut.

They looked at each other.

"Well," she said.

He lifted his case and moved toward the door, then stopped. "Jaimie, I can't thank you enough for letting me hide out here. You actually saved my life."

She shook her head. "You saved my ass, too, Jerry. I have no idea how you did it, but I'm off Keegan Mayo's hook—same as you are."

"So—"

"So I guess everything's back to normal, huh? Or as close to normal as it's gonna get."

"Yeah. Well—I guess I'll see you around, then."

"Yeah, you too, Jerry. Take care."

He stepped closer to her, and they hugged, co-survivors of what only a strange god understood. Jaimie's body felt good against his.

"Uh—" he said.

She didn't say anything.

"I should call you sometime," he said. "Just to make sure you're okay." Pause. "You know?"

That drove the final nail into the imaginative casket. She'd changed her mind. She wanted to fuck him again—perhaps turn it into a relationship of its own, as she hadn't had a steady boyfriend for almost a year now. She stepped far enough away from him to look him square in the eye. "Yes, Jerry," she said, a smile playing at one corner of her mouth. "I know."

Arielle Paich had decided not to attend her weekly book club meeting. Happy her son Jericho was safe enough to move back into his own apartment and resume his normal life, she still wished he'd come back home and use his old bedroom so she'd have his company all the time. Sad because her live-in lover, Laird Janiver, had left her for another woman, ignoring she was over-emotional, easily upset, and crying copious tears whenever the wind blew or episodes of her favorite TV shows were canceled because of Breaking News stories or evening football.

Jerry had told her Laird Janiver saved his life, freeing him from what might have been a lifelong slave job selling crack and meth to other people and turning them in to the Cleveland cops—but in her melodramatic state she could neither accept it nor process it.

So she sat in her now-empty home all day and all evening, crying, watching non-stop television, and often screaming at the wall nobody loved her and she no longer wanted to live. All the aids to suicide—sharp knives, razor blades, prescription drugs to be swallowed by the handfuls and washed down with strong liquor, keys to a car that could easily be driven off a bridge, even a strong rope were available in her home, but she did not touch any of them, or even thought about using them. The suicide threat had become a habit with her.

When her doorbell rang one afternoon, she was not ready for company, as she was not fashionably attired the way she usually was most other times. She was even more surprised when she opened the door and discovered Ayman Kader on the front step. They'd met several times before, but at parties, and then only spoke briefly. She knew he'd been Laird's field commander during his combat years, and now they were good friends—but she had no idea why he'd knocked on her door.

She stood there with him in the hallway—living room on one

side, dining room on the other, stairway straight ahead, as she was too flustered to invite him to sit down and have a cup of coffee. "Laird no longer lives here," she said, fluffing at her hair, sorely aware she was wearing no makeup at all and believing Kader was comparing her to his beautiful and much younger trophy wife. "He was at a hotel for a while, just across the street from where the Indians play baseball—but he's gone now, and he probably won't ever come back. I think he's moved in with some goddamn woman."

Kader frowned. "What woman is that?"

"How should I know? She was working for some drug dealer out in Hunting Valley, and showed up here unannounced one night while I was someplace else." She shook her head the way a wet dog would. "Christ knows what went on here before I came home. Convenient, huh?"

"I'm sorry to hear that, Arielle."

"You should be!" she shot back quickly. "You've known him for years. You were his boss in Iraq and Afghanistan. Why don't you order him to get his shit together and come back here where he belongs."

Colonel Kader sighed. He'd never been fond of Arielle. Laird had often complained about her, so he was well aware of her violent shifts in mood and temper—and as a bird colonel, he was not used to being snapped at. "First of all," he said, "we are civilians, meaning I can't order him to do anything. And even if we were still in uniform, I wouldn't get involved in his personal life unless it threatened the security and safety of the United States." He moved his head around, as his neck was getting stiff and sore just being in Arielle Paich's home and presence. "As it happens, I have no idea where he is, which is why I'm asking you in the first place."

"He's fucking some bitch!" she screamed, her face growing red as a Granny Smith apple. Then she burst into tears again and hurled herself at Ayman Kader, burying her face in his neck and clawing at his back as if he'd suddenly disappear if she stopped. It was more passion than grief.

No, thought Kader. *No!* Gently he disengaged himself from her, aware her tears had soaked a spot on the collar of his cashmere sweater, and he hoped it would dry without discoloring the fabric so he wouldn't have to explain it to this wife. He backed off a few steps. "Arielle," he said softly, "things happen. Relationships begin and then sometimes they fade away. You can't allow it to destroy you. You have to be strong. You have to dig deep inside yourself and find the strength to move on."

She sniffled, her cheeks wet and her nose running, and she fished in her pocket for a tissue that was already well worn. "Is that what you learned in the Marines?"

A thundercloud enveloped Kader's face. "Let's leave the Marines out of it," he said in a voice sounding fast-frozen. "What about this woman?"

"If I had the guts," she offered, "if I had the *balls,* I'd go find her and scratch her eyes out."

Ayman Kader said seriously, "Whether you like Laird or not anymore, he could be in very serious trouble. If he is with this woman now, she might be the same one who worked for this drug pimp and witnessed your son getting so badly beaten up he could barely walk—and she first approached Laird to tell him about it. I won't go into any more details, but I have to let him know what's going on. Otherwise, he might wind up in prison for the rest of his life."

"Good! I hope he does!"

"No, you don't hope!" Kayder's politeness disappeared into the ether, as he was now truly angry. "Laird spent his entire adult life serving his country, and he lost a foot fighting for America. That's not a guy one puts into solitary confinement. Like it or not, he helped Jericho get free from whatever shit he lived in—making him more important than who he is or is not fucking!"

The redness in her face slowly modified into the color of expensive stationery as Kayder spoke. Her mouth stayed slightly open as if too shocked to close it.

"Arielle, make up your mind he's gone from your life—whether his idea or yours doesn't matter. I'm no psychologist. My best friend—your ex-lover—needs my help—and I need yours. Now one more time, Arielle—and remember, I can get just as tough as Laird can—what is the name of this woman?"

CHAPTER FORTY-THREE

One week later, Bria Harstad was still in pain, but able to get around a bit more, though she hadn't left her apartment since Laird Janiver found her at the home of Franny Murgatroyd and taken her back home to recuperate. He'd had his own doctor—a retired Marine major, too, who had patched up many wounded military warriors in Afghanistan—to make a house call, do a complete physical examination, and to assure her she had just one broken rib, though her back and one hip were so horribly bruised her recuperation was slower than usual. She wore a tight bandage around her abdomen to advance the rib to re-attach itself. Her right wrist was badly sprained, probably from a kick, wrapped tightly, too. Despite the miracles of medicine over the past hundred and fifty years, there wasn't much to do for her besides give her pills to ease the pain. Dangerous to Laird, when opioid addiction was killing many addicts.

She was gratefully aware, when Laird had first seen her wearing Francis P. Murgatroyd's pajamas and bathrobe at his home, he had not asked her why. Her own clothes had been torn during the beating, and naturally there were no women's clothes available at the Murgatroyd house, and she was in too much agony to have tried on anything Franny or Demetri would have bought for her. Besides, until Laird had somehow found her, she spent most of her time resting and trying to lose consciousness so she wouldn't notice the pain. It was no surprise everyone recuperating from a damaging injury sleeps too much. Sleep was respite—the only possible reaction to agony.

Nightmares, however, involving what probably awaited her, were not under her control. The pain, already experienced, was an excruciating nighttime memory, but what had awaited her was far worse.

Laird took charge. He did all the shopping for her, mostly at Giant Eagle in the shopping center on the corner of Cedar and Richmond in the Legacy Village shopping center. He was on the phone with his doctor, who had taken care of her. He offered to hire a housekeeping service, but Bria refused—she didn't want strangers wandering into her bedroom with a duster and vacuum cleaner. So, he did his best at keeping the apartment relatively clean and neat himself. Maybe it was all that Marine training.

She had a TV set in her bedroom, running all day and most of the night, usually on Turner Classic Movies, but she rarely stayed awake long enough to finish watching an entire film.

He'd moved from the hotel when Bria returned to her own apartment, but he slept on the downstairs sofa every night.

He had fallen in love with Bria Harstad at first sight—in erotic love, if he were ready to admit it. But now he was totally involved in her fight for recovery, which had nothing to do with sex. Certainly, in her present condition, Bria had no erotic thoughts whatsoever—certainly not with a man she hardly knew, a man of a different race, a man who spent his entire life in the promotion of armed combat. The other thing both of them had to remember daily, was that due to a wartime explosion, his own body was not *all there*.

At the moment, Laird Janiver had no real home. He had moved from Arielle Paich's house to a hotel room for several days, and was now Bria's visitor—one who'd never really been invited—in someone else's living space.

When Bria eventually recovered, he'd have to find another apartment. In the meantime, he realized she had no income of her own, and he had no idea whether she had a bank account with enough money in it to pay her rent, heat, food, and water. He could handle those payments easily—as he'd paid Arielle's mortgage all the months they'd cohabited. Whether Bria would want him to or not, he didn't yet know.

For the first week, he had fixed all three meals and brought them up to her bedroom on a tray decorated with flowers he'd bought that day, though she'd barely nibbled enough to keep herself alive. Eventually she managed to come downstairs, at least for breakfast each morning, though he always had to help her back to the second floor. Quite a spectacle—a one-footed man aiding a half-dead woman to climb the stairs.

Down in the kitchen—her second day of coming down from her bedroom, Laird set an ice-cold glass of orange juice in front of her, and poured her coffee. "What do you feel like this morning?" he said. "An omelet?"

She made a yakking sound. "I couldn't handle an omelet. Just two pieces of toast, please—no butter."

"I'll toast it light, then." He moved into the kitchen, re-set the toaster and deposited two slices of bread inside. "You have to eat something solid, Bria, or you'll get so skinny you'll blow away in the first good breeze."

"You're not eating very much yourself," she said.

"I sit here chomping a big thick steak while you nibble at mixed vegetables?"

She sipped her juice. "Laird, you can't make a living taking care of a sick woman."

"First of all, you're not sick—you're injured, not sick, and get a little better every day."

She waited a while. "And what's second of all?"

"Second of all, I don't have a job, and I don't need one."

"Rich as all that?"

Laird laughed softly. "I'm not up there with the Amazon guy—but I'm comfortable."

"All right, fine," she said. "But you don't sit around the house all day, either."

"Sometimes I do. I read a lot."

"I don't have many books about the U.S. Marines, though."

"I know where the nearest Barnes and Noble is, Bria—and the library, too."

This time she tried the coffee, and wrinkled up her nose, not enjoying it. She wasn't a coffee nut to begin with, and Laird Janiver didn't make it very well. "You can't be my nursemaid for much longer."

"I'll stay for as long as I'm needed."

"Where will you go eventually, Laird? Back to the hotel?"

"I'll find an apartment somewhere," he said, trying not to sound miserable about it. "Probably here in the Heights, or maybe even downtown."

The toast popped up, and he crossed the kitchen to get it. "No butter at all?" he asked. "No nothing?"

She shook her head. "Maybe just raspberry preserves—or whatever else is in the fridge."

He looked for some, found it. "I never heard of anybody eating toast with just jam and no butter."

"Is this going to be our first fight?" Bria queried.

"Raspberry Jam is too important to fight about." He brought her toast back to the table and sat down opposite her. All he'd had for breakfast so far was coffee. "Enjoy," he said.

She spread the jam on one piece of toast and took a small, gentle bite. Neither spoke for a while, though Janiver was aware of the noise she made chewing on a piece of toast. He'd never heard it before, though now he was sure everyone crunched on toast in the morning.

Bria finally said, "You could stay here, you know."

"I could?"

"You could—but you lived most of your life in officer's quarters, alone. Then you spent a few years cohabiting with someone and it didn't work out, so I imagine you'll want to live by yourself again."

He gave that too long a thought. Finally he said, "Arielle and

I were never joined at the hip. She went places, I went places—many times we never saw each other during the day."

She nodded. "Yes, but at night..."

"Arielle had a hair-trigger temper," Laird told her. "I went to an American Legion meeting twice a month, and she thought I was out chasing women."

"She knew you and I fucked."

"She knew it before we did it."

Bria pushed the plate of toast away from her. "You want to stay here? I mean, to live here permanently?"

That last word kicked up some dangerous white water for Laird. He said, "We hardly know each other—really. What will happen if I snore? If you pick up men in bars whenever the need strikes you? If either of us is a religious fanatic who has to pray at every meal and before bedtime?"

"I snore, too," she told him, "but I don't pick up one-nighters in bars, and I haven't been inside a church in the last fifteen years. How about you?"

"I only pray when I bet on the Super Bowl—and I'm not much on one-nighters with strangers."

"We were strangers."

"That was different."

"How?

Laird looked down at his lap for a long moment. Then he said, "It took me about forty-five seconds to fall in love with you. I don't know if you're in love with me, too. Either way, time will tell. So let's not use the word *permanently*. The whole world is full of divorced people. Let's just play it by ear."

She nodded.

"I can pay your rent—"

"I pay my own rent," she said. "If you want to chip in, buy some groceries."

"Whatever."

"And one more thing," she said. "You'll have to sleep on the sofa for a while longer. I still ache like a sonofabitch!"

Laird reached out and covered her hand with this own—the good one that wasn't bandaged—and squeezed gently. "Like I said, Bria—play it by ear."

After a day of Franco Malatesta raving over his vitality, imagination and talent, Nico Brigandi was driving towards the home of the woman he loved and wanted to marry, and feeling pretty good about himself. He had taken a big risk that paid off handsomely. One wrong move would have been a disaster, and precious lives could have been snuffed out. But his crazy wolf trap had snapped shut on Cleveland drug cop Keegan Mayo, who now must ask Brigandi how high he should jump.

Mayo, who had tried desperately for years to bring down the godfather with nary an arrest because the Mafia boss hadn't ever even spit on the sidewalk, had decided instead to go after the Don's son, John, and frame him. John, like so many other men in their thirties, used more bad drugs than he should have.

But asked by his boss to make Mayo back off, Nico came up with the most bizarre dirty trick that ever flickered across his consciousness, and now Keegan Mayo was *his* bitch, even though he had no idea who Brigandi was.

The Don, pleased with the results, relieved his son wouldn't be going to jail, and impressed with the creativity of one of his underlings, brought Nico Brigandi into that special group of "family members" who can do no wrong, and had written Nico a very generous thank-you check which Nico hoped would help pay for his wedding to Courtney Holloway. The fact Nico adored Courtney's son, Ian, made the whole deal that much sweeter.

But three days after the "dirty trick" Nico, Courtney and Ian had used to more or less destroy Keegan Mayo's career, Nico came from work to Courtney's home and and found her in a strange and distant mood. The first thing he noticed was when he bent down to kiss her hello, she turned her head away so all his lips touched was her hair.

"Hey, babe," Nico said. "Not feeling well?"

Courtney sighed. "I'm fine."

Nico felt his face flushing red. He knew, as most men do, when a woman answered with "I'm fine," it means she isn't fine at all. "Where's Ian?"

"He's having dinner and a sleepover at his best friend's house."

"That means we have the evening entirely to ourselves."

She didn't answer him, but simply shrugged. It took him a minute to figure out something was awry, but finally he took Courtney's elbow and glided her over to the sofa. "Something's amiss tonight, isn't it? Tell me about it? Please?"

She shook her head, not negatively, but to get the hair off her forehead. "The last two nights, Ian woke up screaming."

Something inside Nico's head made the skin on his hands and arms ripple, and his mouth went completely dry.

"This is your fault, Nico," she said.

"I haven't even been here for three days! What did I do?"

"I can't believe you'd ask such a stupid question!" He frowned. "So what's going on? Did that Mayo cop come poking around here? I wouldn't think so—he doesn't even know who we are."

"He might know who you are by now." She set her jaw at an angry angle. "He's no dumb-ass! He's a sergeant, which means he's not stupid. You wanted him to quit harassing Johnny Pockets, so how hard would it be for him to figure out you work for the Malatesta family? He makes one phone call, and he has your name, address, and how you like your eggs in the morning."

He felt himself growing defensive, and he didn't like it—but he couldn't help himself. "I warned Mayo if anything happens to me, the photos will be on every TV station, every newspaper—maybe even all over the country. So why are you bothered?"

"Because Ian could've gotten killed!"

Nico shook his head. "That wouldn't happen, Court—not in a million years."

"How can you be sure?"

"He's a high-ranking cop. There's no way he would shoot a child in his own home."

"In the last several years, law officers have shot and killed unarmed children all the time." Courtney's eyes flashed with anger. "*Black* children!"

"Yeah," Nico said, "but Ian is white!"

That got her onto her feet and halfway across the room. "I can't believe you said that."

"Why? I knew Mayo wouldn't shoot him—or you or me, either. It was a perfect twist for us—and so far, it's worked."

"I can't do this," she said. "I can't live with someone who lets my child risk his life."

"There was no danger, Court."

"There could have been. How could you ask Ian to do something like that?"

"You didn't complain then."

"Because I trusted you!"

"Don't you trust me anymore?"

Courtney took a few moments to consider. Then she said, "No. I don't think I do."

"I didn't lie to you," Nico said. "If I thought there was even a flicker of danger, I wouldn't have done it."

She turned to face him. "And then you'd have been in big trouble with the Malatesta family. The Don was more worried about what might happen to his beloved son—who, as you've told me many times, is a sweet, stupid asshole. That's the most important thing in the world to you, Nico—whether or not you're a—a 'made' guy."

"'Made' guys kill people, Court. I don't do that—never have."

"Nobody ever told you to! If they did, you'd twist yourself into a pretzel to do it in a New York minute—just so the old man is nice to you when you show up for breakfast."

Now he felt himself growing angry, and he hated it. "Why are you pissed off? It's been three days!"

"Three days of my son's screaming nightmares gave me lots of time to think—and now I think you have a shitty job."

"I work for the godfather," he said. "When you have a job, you do what the boss tells you."

"But you aren't *my* boss, Nico," she said. "Not anymore. And I'll never do what you tell me to again." She started out of the room.

"Where're you going?"

She hardly slowed down at the stairway. "Somewhere," she said, "that you are *not*."

He listened to her pound up the stairs, waiting until he heard the bedroom door slam shut, a sound that broke his heart. Then, deflated from his previously great day, he slouched his way out to his car.

Heading to his own home, his gut on fire and his head swimming with confusion, he wondered whether his recent shocker with a very upset Courtney was just a bad evening for him, or loneliness for the rest of his life.

For the past several months, he'd thought soon he would be a husband and an instant father—he was crazy about both Courtney and Ian, even though the kid was just a few years away from becoming a pain-in-the-ass teenager, which he could probably handle. After his success in turning the tables on Police Sergeant Mayo and being warmly welcomed into the personal group of faithfuls who surrounded Don Franco Malatesta—with a promised raise in salary—he assumed he'd have the kind of money he wanted to become head of his own nuclear family. The fact he was not a "made" guy, that he'd never killed anyone but was still accepted by the local Italian "tribe" had made him feel better about himself.

His current relationship had suddenly grown rocky, and he felt completely torn. Does he walk away from Little Italy and the powerful, charismatic man who had grown to care for him, the big boss who called all the shots in Greater Cleveland? Or does he turn his back on the woman and child he loved?

Stopped for a red light, frustrated, he hammered on the steering wheel and bellowed "Shit!" where no one could hear him.

Nico had saved John Malatesta's sorry ass for a reason—that he was basically incompetent. Great at running a restaurant and charming all the customers, Johnny could no more step into Don Franco's shoes and run the quasi-legal organization than he could walk on water.

Nico figured as the Don grew older and hoped to step to the side in the next five years or so, it would be logical for him to take over. That meant the kind of power and privilege he'd hardly dreamed of before.

To clear his head, he rubbed the bridge of his nose with his thumb and forefinger, then sucked in a lungful of air and let it out slowly. He was still mortified—but he hoped Courtney would come around. And if not—well, goddammit, there are lots of beautiful women in the world.

CHAPTER FORTY-FOUR

Laird Janiver huddled on a bench overlooking Lake Erie in Edgewater Park, his jacket collar raised to protect his neck. Ayman Kader called and said they had to meet as soon as possible—privately.

That meant Laird's staying in Bria Harstad's apartment would no longer be private—and while Laird enjoyed visiting Kayder's home and his pretty wife and beautiful dog, that seemed at the moment to be another no-no.

Sitting on a park bench near the lake on a chilly morning made Laird consider himself more than irritated. He preferred talking inside where it was warmer and out of the breezy weather. Ayman Kader, however, was adamant.

The wind, coming from the northwest, cut through Laird's fawn-colored leather jacket, which usually kept him cozy on non-stormy winter days, making him realize it had been many years since sitting out in the cold desert winter in Afghanistan, waiting for a firefight to begin—and just as he was put on edge waiting for his superior officer to pull bothersome rank on him, now on this nippy Cleveland morning, he knew in his heart it wouldn't be good news from Kayder.

Besides, he wanted to be home with Bria. They had spoken last night she might be able to get dressed the next day and go out for a little while, even for coffee and a snack. He never tired of looking at her, even now, with her beautiful face drawn and somewhat twisted by pain, and was sure everyone in a Star-bucks or a Panera would gape at her, too.

A car entered the parking area, Ayman Kader's year-old Buick. The bird colonel carried a McDonald's tray with two large cardboard coffee mugs and came directly to Laird's bench.

"Here," he said, handing Laird one of the mugs, "warm your soul." He sat down and pried the lid off his and took a sip, then fanning his mouth because it was still too hot. "It's a pain in the ass to sit here in the cold, but I have to run a few things by you, and nobody else needs to hear it."

"Nobody hiding in the trees with a rifle-like microphone that can pick up and record every breath we take?"

Kayder chuckled. "Nobody's hiding in the trees, Laird—there are no leaves anymore. Winter is right around the corner."

Laird opened his own coffee and blew on it for a while. "Then let's get to whatever this is before it starts to snow."

Kayder took another sip. "You're something of a problem to me, Laird. You always have been. That's why you interest me."

"Do I have to drop and give you fifty pushups, right here on the cold sidewalk?"

"You remember my ever mentioning a Merrill Braithwaite?" Laird frowned, and Kayder explained, "He's the Deputy Special Agent in Charge at the local FBI office."

"Did he visit you on a park bench, too?"

"No, at my home. We've been friends for many years. I wanted to find out if he knew Marshall Ruttenberg after you asked me if I knew the name."

Laird nodded. "And you didn't know Ruttenberg, I recall."

"Braithwaite knew him," Kayder explained, "or knew about him."

"So?"

"So, he showed up to tell me Ruttenberg was murdered in a quiet little park in Chagrin Falls."

For a moment, Laird feared the homeless old man who lived in a tiny tent in that park had squealed on him, but he shook it off. The drifter didn't even know his name. Why would such an old fart search out a police officer to whom he would tell his story? "Sorry to hear that," he said softly.

"Also, they found two punks—both have jail records a mile long—floating in the river west of the salt flats, heading toward the lake. Both shot in the back of the head—execution-style."

"So you hauled me out here in the cold to recite to me all the people who got killed in the last few days?"

"No. You want to hear a funny coincidence?"

"Should I laugh?"

"Probably not. Ruttenberg died from a broken neck, Laird."

"Eww!"

"But he was shot in the knee first. The coincidence? The bullet in Ruttenberg's knee was identical to the bullets the punks got in their heads. Back of the head—like an execution. I think the guy killed all three."

"Could be it was a girl killed all three, Ayman. You can't be sexist these days."

Kader thought about it. "Did the girl break Ruttenberg's neck, too?"

Laird Janiver shrugged. "Maybe a big, strong girl."

"Maybe." He held the cardboard coffee mug in both hands as if to warm them. "Hey, Laird—you still have your handgun?"

"The one the Marines issued me? I think I lost it. You know, when I moved from my old place to Arielle's a few years ago, I couldn't find it when I unpacked."

"My God, Laird! You're going into the Guinness Book of World Records!"

"Why is that?"

Kader said, "You are the first retired officer in American history who actually *lost* a sidearm issued you by the Marines."

Laird drank more coffee, which was growing cooler by the minute. "I'm wondering why this FBI guy got you involved."

"You asked me about Ruttenberg, so I asked Braithwaite. Don't worry, I never mentioned your name."

Laird sucked in a deep breath, as though taking in air was difficult for him. "Why would you—"

"We fought the same war, remember?"

Laird sighed.

"Here's the thing, though," Kader said. "I'll bust my nuts making sure I'm not a suspect, Laird—and if the FBI gets the idea of you killing the biggest drug lord in Greater Cleveland, they'll do a deep investigation. That means they'll find out if you ever swiped a comic book or a pack of gum from the local drugstore when you were ten or so. They'll learn every chick you boffed in your lifetime, starting with the first one in the back seat of a Dodge Dart, and they'll probably interview all of them. They'll also glom onto your military record, especially the last days few years of the Middle East wars—which means they'll find out about me, too—and how we got black market dirty-rich by breaking international laws."

"I put all my money into a Swiss bank in which no one can touch but me," Laird Janiver said, "so the FBI has no idea I have a small fortune squirreled away."

"Mine is in the Cayman Islands. No one will crawl up my ass about three murders, though. We're good friends, Laird, and I like your company—but I don't want to spend the next thirty years as your cellmate."

Kader finished his coffee, tossing the cardboard container into the trash basket next to the bench, and stood up. "I think we should stay away from each other for the next several months. SAC Braithwaite was suspicious enough to ask me about this Ruttenberg guy—and he wants to know who else I hang out with. So let's give it until spring, okay?"

"No opening Christmas morning presents together in our jammies?"

"Take this serious, Laird."

"We can stay in touch by phone."

"No, we can't," Kayder said. "If the FBI is interested, they'll have both our phones bugged. When I called you to set up this meeting, I used a burner phone I bought at Walmart a few years back, just in case I got famous—or infamous. And don't use Facebook or Twitter or whatever to contact me, either. We can live without each other for a while."

He started to walk back toward his car, then stopped. "They never got your name from me, Laird. You know what that means, don't you?"

"It means I owe you a favor, right?"

"A big-time favor." He grinned into the wind which chugged across the lake, and made a gun out of his thumb and index finger, shooting in Laird's general vicinity, then blowing away the imaginary smoke with a breath. "*Semper Fi,* brother."

Laird nodded, giving him a small wave, and quietly said, "Ooh-rah!" He sat there long after Kader had driven away, the coffee growing cold in his cup.

Finally, he went back to his car, sitting behind the wheel for a few minutes just to get warm again. Then he put it in gear and drove back to Bria Harstad's apartment.

Where he belonged.

CHAPTER FORTY-FIVE

Jericho Paich was in a Panera restaurant, a two-day beard stubble darkening his cheeks. It wasn't he was trying for a more modern look; he'd just been too lazy to shave. For the past few days, he found himself spending most of his time there, since he had nowhere else to be.

He was on his fourth cup of Panera coffee that morning. He'd become addicted to the java for hours at a time. It might have been caffeine, or maybe just nerves, but his hand was shaky for a man in his mid-twenties. Psychopath in the making, he worried he would suffer that unfortunate palsy for the rest of his life. His ordered bear claw was long gone, but there was a limit to how many sugar-laced pastries one could consume before lunchtime.

Jerry was free and clear, as he had not been for months. He'd teetered between sending more innocent druggies into the arms of the Cleveland cops, or a long prison sentence of his own. Now, however, he was grateful and relieved he was no longer a confidential informant—a C.I.

Keegan Mayo, Cleveland's Number One drug cop who had plucked him off the street in the first place, had torn up his arrest report in front of him, terrified at what might happen if candid photos of him taken by someone involved with the Malatesta mob "family" were released.

Jerry hadn't dared even to smoke ganja since Mayo had busted him. He'd never been much of a toker, even in college, and while terror had fueled him daily since his threatened arrest, Mayo's relentless glare on him made weed a thing of his past.

Still, he remained certain a guillotine, which hung over his head for the past year, could fall and decapitate him if the slightest breeze disturbed it. He had little left in his life. His girlfriend Jill Taggart had been out of sight for more than half a year, and his only sexual experience since she left was when he hid out in the apartment of Jill's best friend Jaimie Peck, who, due to him was now also a C.I. The two of them wound up in bed together *once*.

His landlord required him to pay the entire rental each month since Jill went away—and while he'd been in hiding, his front door had been kicked in and not repaired. There must be neighborhood looters, he thought, because many things were missing when he got back, including several expensive sweaters, a vintage Cleveland Browns sweatshirt featuring the legendary Jim Brown, and his MacBook Pro laptop, leaving him only with his Target-sold wristwatch and his Apple iPad, which he carried in his car.

He could return to his mom's house, which she no longer shared with Laird Janiver, but Arielle—emotionally convulsive at the best of times—was jockeying a seemingly unstoppable crying rage that would make her son's life unbearable.

Janiver had emerged from post-combat adventures, putting undue pressure on his artificial foot that caused constant discomfort, and risked his neck trying to help Jericho with his police problems. He deserved all the thanks and gratitude in the world. Still, they had never gotten along before that, and Jerry assumed if either sought to sweeten that awkward history into friendship, eventually it would turn sour again. Besides, if they were anywhere near each other, he'd feel the urgent necessity of saying a thank you every goddamn day! Naturally, the still-smoldering rift between Laird and Arielle required Jericho to choose sides—and although she irritated him all the time, Arielle was his *mother*.

That left him with no choice at all.

He no longer had a job. He had left his car in his office parking lot for several days while he was in hiding and couldn't possibly explain his AWOL days to his company's CEO, so his middle-management position was no longer available to him.

Born and raised in Greater Cleveland, Jerry realized the city had nothing for him anymore. But where could he go to start over?

Most native Clevelanders who decide for reasons beyond control to relocate in the United States, think first of someplace in which the weather is more clement, though, when truth be told, Cleveland winters are not nearly as severe as those in Chicago or New England or the Central Plains. Jericho Paich immediately thought of Florida, Arizona, Southern California, or even Hawaii, though he had no clue what career he could pursue in that Pacific Paradise.

When Panera became crowded at lunch hour, he decided to go home. Irked as he approached his front door, still boarded over by sheets of thick lumber, since the landlord was probably hoping he'd get the hell out of there for good.

Once inside, he checked his closets and dresser drawers to make sure he had enough clothes to wear until he moved out of town, wherever that might be. He had a huge bookcase full of volumes which would cost too much money to have them shipped wherever he was going, so he'd either have to sell or donate them. As for the bookcase itself, he had no clue whether his new apartment would be spacious enough to handle that large piece of furniture.

There were people he could say goodbye to, but most were not real friends but co-workers, college classmates from several years earlier, and neighbors. He needed the sound of another human voice to get his feet back on the ground. He tapped out his mother's cell number, but she wasn't answering calls. She was either at a book club meeting or at the upscale Beachwood Place Mall with her friends, revenge shopping to punish Laird

Janiver before he removed her name from all his credit card accounts.

He mentally chewed on it for a long while, watched a film on Turner Classic Movies he'd never heard of, probably because it wasn't filmed in Technicolor. He tried to recall what other films he'd seen in his life that were black-and-white, but the only one he could remember was *Casablanca.*

Here's looking at *you*, kid.

For his dinner he ate an entire bag of Lay's Potato Chips with Ripples, and a bottle of Great Lakes Brewery's Eliot Ness Amber Lager. Eliot Ness was a famous cop, especially after a hit TV show and a big-budget film about him, and the city buried him in the legendary Lakeview Cemetery along with assassinated president James Garfield and original robber baron John D. Rockefeller. Great Lakes Brewery named a beer after him.

Thinking of nothing better to do, he dialed the number of Jaimie Peck.

"Oh God," she said, worry almost choking her voice, "you're not moving back in again, are you, Jerry?"

"Relax, Jaimie. I'm just calling to tell you you're off the C.I. list," Jerry told her. "Both of us are. And I think our troubles are over."

"I know," Jaimie said. "Sergeant Mayo told me. I even heard him rip my arrest report up over the phone." She sighed. "For all I know, he might have been tearing up an old copy of Playboy and lying to make me feel good, so when he sends me to prison, he can laugh about it. Vicious sonofabtich!"

"Well, he tore mine up right in front of me, Jaimie, so he's probably telling the truth."

"It's good news, then."

"You're doing okay?"

"It's taking time to get over Mayo's foot on my throat for so long. Otherwise—well, one day at a time, right?" Then she was quiet for half a minute before she said, "What about Jill Taggart?"

Jericho was startled tears suddenly filled his eyes. Jill Taggart got him involved in drug-peddling in the first place. "I don't know where she is, Jaimie. She just—disappeared."

"My best gal pal." Jaimie tried to catch her breath. "Let's keep in touch, Jerry. As friends. Just friends."

For the rest of the evening, he stared sadly at the wall, his cellphone in hand, thinking of Chicago, Phoenix, San Francisco. He had no arrest record, so a job anywhere in the country was possible.

Shit! he thought, and scrunched his eyes shut. He'd lived in Greater Cleveland for his entire life, and now realized he had no friends at home, either.

He snoozed on the sofa until six the next morning. Another day, he sighed forlornly—another goddamn day when he was no longer a C.I. for the Cleveland police.

He showered but again did not shave. At a few minutes past seven, he got into his car and drove to the nearest Panera he'd grown accustomed to in the past few weeks. Several older men sat alone at tables, as they seemed to do so daily, looking as lonely and miserable as Jericho Paich felt.

They were there for coffee. Always, every morning.

For coffee.

Four months later, after sending out bona fides to several headhunter outfits, he was finally offered a job similar to the one he'd held ever since he graduated from college and moved into the business world.

Unfortunately, this one would put him in Hong Kong—far from everything he'd ever known—in one of the major banks of the world, the Hong Kong and Shanghai Bank, known all over Asia in the slightly jocular name of Honkers and Shankers.

Jericho Paich worked there for nearly a year, and began dating a co-worker, a Brit. He found many Chinese women to be attractive, but an unwritten law in Hong Kong is when a *gwai lo*—a non-Asian Caucasian male—dates a local Chinese woman, the morning after their first intimate sexual encounter, she appears at your door with at least ten members of her family in tow, asking when they will all go home to America with you.

When heading out from the bank to his tiny apartment, he was caught up in a huge protest movement that choked the streets and sidewalks on the Hong Kong side—locals of all ages, genders and financial positions complaining the tight grip mainland China keeps on the formerly independent Hong Kong protectorate. The crowd surrounding him became violent, surging forward despite nerve gas and rubber bullets fired at them by the Hong Kong police. Jericho felt as if a tsunami of people were going to drown him.

He was shoved, pushed, and buffeted until he fell onto the main street, stepped on by dozens of angry, shouting people who truly didn't give a damn who lay beneath their feet. Late that evening when the loud angry protesters went home, he was found by police and taken to the nearest hospital, at which he died from severe brain trauma the next morning at the nearest hospital.

The American consulate-general went into action, and two weeks later, Jericho Paich's battered body was flown home to his native Cleveland. After a small funeral, he was buried at the famous Lake View cemetery, about half a mile from the magnificent mausoleum in which President James A. Garfield was interred.

At the gravesite for the final words were his mother, along with a few of his friends, and some co-workers from his old company in Solon. Jaimie Peck had the decency to attend, too, though she'd not heard from him since he moved out of her apartment.

Laird Janiver was there, though he'd not spoken to Arielle Paich since he first moved from her home. Naturally he left his love, Bria Harstad, at home, but still, Arielle refused to even look at him.

Laird's friend and black market partner, Ayman Kader, and his wife, Elizabeth, stood sadly with him.

The interment was on a January morning, despite a sometime sun that moved in and out from behind the clouds, warming the usual chill. The cold wind blew down from Canada and whipped across Northeast Ohio. According to the Weather Girl on Channel Twelve, the afternoon would probably bring blowing lake effect snow.

Jericho Paich had always hated winters in Cleveland. At the graveside, his weeping, hysterical mother silently wished if he'd had to die at all, he should have waited until summertime.

LES ROBERTS came to mystery writing by winning the very first "First Private Eye Novel" Contest, which gave him his literary start. Prior to that, he worked in Los Angeles for a quarter of a century, writing and/or producing more than 2500 half hours of network and syndicated television. A Chicago native, he has lived for the past 31 years in Northeast Ohio.

On the following pages are a few
more great titles from the
Down & Out Books publishing family.

For a complete list of books and to
sign up for our newsletter,
go to DownAndOutBooks.com.

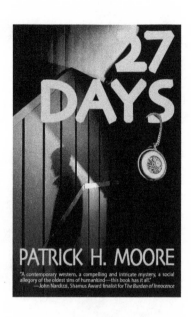

27 Days
A Nick Crane Thriller
Patrick H. Moore

Down & Out Books
February 2023
978-1-64396-298-6

27 Days is a topical political thriller in which veteran Los Angeles PI Nick Crane races against time to save his partner Bobby Moore, who has been abducted by a powerful right wing domestic terrorist named Marguerite Ferguson.

If Nick doesn't surrender to Marguerite within twenty-seven days, Bobby Moore will be sent to Scorpion Prison in Egypt where he will be tortured and killed.

Quietly Into the Night
Vincent Zandri

Down & Out Books
February 2023
978-1-64396-299-3

A bestselling author wakes up on a train and has no idea how he got there. When he finds himself accused of throwing a fellow author off the balcony of a New York City high-rise apartment building, he now must battle not only memory loss, but he must also fight for his very life.

From *New York Times* and *USA Today* bestselling Thriller and Shamus Award-winning author Vincent Zandri comes a novel of deception, murder, and double-crosses that only Alfred Hitchcock could concoct.

Right Between the Eyes
Scott Loring Sanders

Down & Out Books
February 2023
978-1-64396-300-6

When a young girl is abducted in an historic New England town in 1981, a family seeks full and total revenge.

Decades later, when two boys skip school to go fishing at Thoreau's iconic Walden Pond, instead of catching a trophy bass, they reel in a human skull which once again brings to the forefront a litany of wicked lies and murderous betrayal.

Yesterday Rising
Three Crime Novellas
Stephen Burdick

Down & Out Books
February 2023
978-1-64396-301-3

Joe Hampton seems destined to continue living a life of solving crimes—a life from which he officially retired. The old itch won't let him rest, and he can't resist the need to help his friends Detective Carly Truffant and Detective David Sizemore as they go about uncovering the truth surrounding the mysteries that arise.

"An authentic police voice. It's like going on a ride-along."
　　　　　　—Colin Campbell, author of the Jim Grant Thrillers